*Sweet Rogue of Mine*

*The Survivors: Book IX*

*Shana Galen*

SWEET ROGUE OF MINE
Copyright © 2021 by Shana Galen

Cover Design by The Killion Group, Inc.

All rights reserved. Except for use in any review, the reproduction or utilization of this work in whole or in part in any form by any electronic, mechanical or other means, now known or hereafter invented, including xerography, photocopying and recording, or in any information storage or retrieval system, is forbidden without the written permission of the author.

All characters in this book have no existence outside the imagination of the author and have no relation whatsoever to anyone bearing the same name or names. They are not even distantly inspired by any individual known or unknown to the author, and all incidents are pure invention.

## *Also by Shana Galen*

REGENCY SPIES
*While You Were Spying*
*When Dashing Met Danger*
*Pride and Petticoats*

MISADVENTURES IN MATRIMONY
*No Man's Bride*
*Good Groom Hunting*
*Blackthorne's Bride*
*The Pirate Takes a Bride*

SONS OF THE REVOLUTION
*The Making of a Duchess*
*The Making of a Gentleman*
*The Rogue Pirate's Bride*

JEWELS OF THE TON
*If You Give a Duke a Diamond*
*If You Give a Rake a Ruby*
*Sapphires are an Earl's Best Friend*

LORD AND LADY SPY
*Lord and Lady Spy*
*The Spy Wore Blue (novella)*
*True Spies*
*Love and Let Spy*
*All I Want for Christmas is Blue (novella)*
*The Spy Beneath the Mistletoe (novella)*

COVENT GARDEN CUBS
*Viscount of Vice (novella)*
*Earls Just Want to Have Fun*
*The Rogue You Know*
*I Kissed a Rogue*

THE SURVIVORS
*Third Son's a Charm*
*No Earls Allowed*
*An Affair with a Spare*
*Unmask Me if You Can*
*The Claiming of the Shrew*
*A Duke a Dozen*
*How the Lady Was Won*
*Kisses and Scandal (anthology)*
*The Highlander's Excellent Adventure*
*Sweet Rogue of Mine*

THE SCARLET CHRONICLES
*Traitor in Her Arms*
*To Ruin a Gentleman*
*Taken by the Rake*
*To Tempt a Rebel*

STANDALONES AND ANTHOLOGIES
*Bachelors of Bond Street (anthology)*
*Stealing the Duke's Heart (duet)*
*The Summer of Wine and Scandal (novella)*
*A Royal Christmas (duet)*
*A Grosvenor Square Christmas (anthology)*

## *Dedication and Acknowledgments*

This book is dedicated to all teachers, whether they work in elementary, secondary, or at the university level. You are devoted and amazing and make such a difference in the lives of our kids and youth.

Thank you to my awesome team—Abby Saul, Gayle Cochrane, Sarah Rosenbarker, Maddee James, Kim Killion, and the Shananigans!

## *One*

Someone was in the house. Nash Pope might be half asleep and half drunk, but he knew when someone was in his house. He was a trained sharpshooter, and his body was attuned to even the most subtle changes in atmosphere. Just a few minutes before, the air in Wentmore had been stale and still, the only sounds were of mice scampering in the attic and the creak and groan of the ancient timber beams and floorboards settling.

But now the mice had gone silent and the air stirred. The house seemed to straighten and take notice of someone new, someone far more interesting than its current occupant. In the dining room, the curtains closed against the daylight, the lone candle that burned flickered as though the house exhaled softly in anticipation.

Nash raised his head from the sticky table and heard the shuffle of feet and the squeak of a door hinge.

He reached for his pistol. He didn't need to see it. It was an extension of his arm and his favorite pistol by far. He owned at least half a dozen, including a brace of matching dueling pistols made by Manton, a pepperbox pistol made by Twigg, a more decorative pistol he'd purchased from the London gunsmith Hawkins—who liked to advertise that the former American President George Washington owned one of his creations—and this one, made by the Frenchman Gribeauval. Gribeauval had made Napoleon's personal pistol, and though Nash was no admirer of Napoleon, he did admire the French armory of St. Etienne.

Nash's thumb slid over the polished walnut gunstock, over the pewter filigree, until his finger curled into the trigger guard as though it were a well-worn glove. He lifted the pistol, not feeling its weight, though it was heavier than some, and then waited. It would do him no good to seek out the intruder. The world, what he could see of it, was gray and full of shadows. Better to let the interloper come to him. He could still shoot straight if he was still.

All had gone silent. Perhaps the uninvited guest had paused to listen as Nash did.

If the game was patience, Nash would win. As a sharpshooter, he had waited more than he had ever fired at the enemy. He often stood in one spot, unmoving, for four or five hours. He stood in the heat or the cold or, if he was fortunate, in the cool, scented breeze of a spring day. The weather might change, but his rifle at his side never had.

The rifle had been put away. He couldn't sight in the rifle anymore, and it was basically useless to him now, but hitting his target with his pistol and one poorly working eye was possible.

"Nash!" a voice called out. If he hadn't been trained as well, he might have jumped. But Nash's jaw only ticked at his name shattering the silence.

The floorboard creaked again. The intruder was in the foyer. He was not directly outside the dining room. The voice was still too distant.

"Put your pistol down, Nash. I came to talk to you."

Nash did not lower the pistol, though the voice sounded familiar now. Stratford? No, this voice wasn't refined enough. Stratford had been here a few months before. Apparently, he'd sought out Nash's father, the Earl of Beaufort, in London and told him Nash needed him. Stratford obviously didn't know that the earl didn't give a damn about Nash. He'd sent his solicitor, and Nash had fired the pistol he held now over the bald man's head and sent him running back to Town.

A door opened and the man said, "Nash?"

It was the door to the parlor.

"Nash, if you shoot me, I'll kick your pathetic arse all the way to Spain and back."

Nash felt his lips quirk in an unwelcome half-smile, as he finally recognized the voice. "And if I kill you?" Nash asked.

"Then I'll come back and haunt you." Rowden was just outside the dining room now, standing at the door. Nash and Rowden had met in Spain, both serving in His Majesty's army. They'd become close friends, even if their skill sets were quite different.

"If I open this door, will you shoot me?" Rowden asked.

"It depends," Nash said, still holding his pistol at the ready. "Did my father send you?"

A pause. "Of course, he sent me." Rowden spoke like he fought—directly and plainly. He did not pull punches.

"Then don't open the door."

"Shoot me and the next to arrive will be men from an asylum. Beaufort is ready to send you to an institution right now. Mayne and Fortescue managed to talk him out of it and arranged to have me sent instead."

Nash considered. The Duke of Mayne would have done the talking as he was the negotiator of the group. Stratford

Fortescue would have decided to send Rowden. Fortescue was always the strategist.

"Why you?" Nash asked. Seeing that Mayne was the negotiator, it would have made more sense for him to come.

"I needed the blunt."

Nash winced and set the pistol down. That hurt. His father was paying Nash's friends to intervene. He expected as much from his father, who had given up on Nash a long time ago. But his friends...still, what could he expect when he had shot Duncan Murray this past summer? That misstep was bound to have repercussions.

"I'm coming in," Rowden said, his tone one of warning. The latch lifted and the door opened. In the flickering candlelight, Nash made out a dark form. Of course, he remembered what Rowden looked like. He was broad and stocky with short brown hair and coal-black eyes. He had a pretty face, or he would have if his nose hadn't been broken so many times. Nash remembered what every man he had ever served with looked like. His memory was more of a curse than a blessing, though, as he remembered every woman and, yes, child he had ever shot too.

"You look like hell," Rowden said, still standing in the doorway.

"I wish I could tell you the same, but I can't see worth a damn."

"Still feeling sorry for yourself, I see."

Nash's hand itched to lift the pistol again, but he was not hot-tempered. He would not have lasted a week as a sharpshooter if he had been. "What do you want, Payne? To what do I owe the pleasure of a visit from one of Draven's Dozen?"

Rowden pulled out the chair at the opposite end of the table and sat. Nash saw only a gray, amorphous shape but his other senses filled in the missing information. "Considering you're one of us, I'm not sure why you're surprised. We Survivors take care of our own."

It was a lie, but Nash decided not to point that out. Not yet. The Survivors were a troop of thirty highly skilled military men who had been recruited as something of a suicide band to kill Napoleon or die trying. Eighteen had died trying. Twelve had come home. They had been brothers-in-arms, but Nash did not feel any fraternal affection now. The others were moving on with their lives, while he would be forever alone, locked in a world of darkness.

"You're thin," Rowden observed. To a stocky fighter like Rowden Payne, thinness was a liability. "Don't you eat?"

"You must need my father's money badly if you're playing nursemaid now," Nash said.

Shot fired.

"I want to keep you alive, and no one has to pay me for that."

Missed target.

"I'm alive." But Nash knew that wouldn't be enough. Not after the accident with Murray a few months before. Nash had known some intervention was coming. He supposed he should be glad the Survivors had convinced his father to send Rowden before the men from the asylum. Very little frightened Nash anymore, but the prospect of the next fifty years locked in an asylum drove a spike of fear into his heart. He would put the pistol in his mouth and pull the trigger first. "What do I have to do to keep the asylum at bay?"

"So you haven't completely pickled your brain yet."

"What do I have to do?" Nash repeated. He would do what was required and then, hopefully, the world would leave him alone. After all, he'd given his sight for King and Country. Why couldn't they leave him in peace?

"I don't have a comprehensive list," Rowden said after a pause, during which, Nash assumed, he was looking about the dining room. "Off the top of my head, I would say this old pile needs some repair. It looks like there was a fire at some point."

Nash did not comment.

"And clearly you need to ingest something other than gin."

Nash lifted his empty glass. "This was whiskey." At least he thought it had been whiskey. Maybe it had been brandy.

"You need staff."

"No staff," Nash said.

Rowden let out a quiet grunt. "We'll discuss it. But suffice it to say, I can smell you all the way over here. When was the last time you put on a clean set of clothes or took a bath?"

"Will you scrub my back?" Nash sneered and then was sorry for it. None of this was Rowden's fault. None of this was anyone's fault. Nash had known the risks when he went to war. He just hadn't thought anything would happen to him. He'd been so young. Like most young men, he'd thought he was invincible.

Rowden rose. "I'll make you some coffee. We can start there."

Two hours later, Nash was willing to concede life might be easier if he had a few staff members. Not that he needed them to tend to him personally. He could damn well take care of himself. But he did grow tired of Rowden's muttering as he crashed about in the kitchen making awful-tasting coffee, hauled water up to the tub in Nash's bed chamber, and even laid out Nash's clothing. The muttering had ceased once Mrs. Brown made an appearance. Nash didn't know why she still came every few days. She hadn't been paid for months, and Nash wasn't exactly welcoming toward her. Half the time he didn't even eat the food she set in front of him. But he supposed he owed it to her that he had clean clothes and a bar of soap and something edible in the larder.

Nash wanted to be left alone, and she did her best to leave him alone. That was why he hadn't run her off completely.

Now, dressed in clean, uncomfortable clothing with his too-long hair still damp on his neck and forehead, Nash made his way gingerly across the foyer. His belly rumbled. He'd had a bit of bread with the coffee and now his body seemed to want more. Nash thought he might see if any more food had been left in the dining room, but then he heard voices. Rowden and Mrs. Brown were in there. Nash turned his head to catch their words.

"—so glad you have come, Mr. Payne. I've been so worried."

"You're a good woman to have endured all of this."

"Pshaw. My family has worked for the Earls of Beaufort for generations, and I remember Mr. Pope when he was just a baby. I couldn't leave him. He was always such a good lad. Not a bit of temper in him. Always smiling and laughing. Always with a kind word. It was the war what did this to him."

Nash didn't know if Rowden answered. He couldn't stand the pity he heard in Mrs. Brown's voice, and he knew he would either explode in rage or get away. He chose the latter, and before he knew what had happened, he was outside, squinting in the sudden brightness. He could see even less in the sunlight than in the shadows. The light seemed to wash away what little vision he had left in his right eye, making everything into a white blob. Nash closed his eyes and used his walking stick to feel for any obstacles before him. He remembered walking the streets of London with this same stick. He'd swing it about or twirl it, trying to appear dashing to the young ladies. Now he needed it to keep from falling on his face.

How pathetic.

He moved toward the back of Wentmore, where there had once been an informal garden of tall flowering trees, vines, paths, and foot bridges over babbling brooks. It was certainly overgrown now, but at one time he had known that garden so well, he could have walked it blindfolded. Ironic that now that was, in essence, what he would need to do. The informal garden was one of the reasons his father had given Nash the care of Wentmore. The estate was not his, of course. All of the Beaufort properties would go to Nash's eldest brother when he inherited the title. But no one in the family had wanted Nash at the estate in Richmond. It was too close to London. Too close to Society, where everyone might see the horror of his injury.

So they'd sent him north, to Wentmore, which was buried in the countryside and close to nothing but a tiny village named Milcroft. The family had come here when the children were young as Lady Beaufort thought it was quaint and had wanted to expose the children to "simple people." And indeed, the area surrounding Milcroft was inhabited by dairy maids, blacksmiths, bakers, a country doctor, a vicar, and many crofters—some of them Beaufort's tenants. The people had been kind and welcoming, and Nash had spent a few weeks each year running about barefoot along Wentmore's extensive grounds.

How he had dreaded returning to the formalness of the estate in Richmond and, when he grew older, the schoolroom. Although he had patience and focus, Nash had never been a good student. His mind worked quickly, solving problems and working out rationales. But his professors seemed to drone on and on about the same material until Nash was bored senseless and stopped listening. He had done well enough as most of his studies required rote memorization and he could memorize easily, but he had never truly excelled.

Nash paused now, having lost himself in his thoughts and remembrances and tread deep enough into the garden that the sunlight had been somewhat obscured, and he could make out shapes here and there. He hadn't been outside in weeks, but from the crisp feel of the breeze, he knew it must be autumn, late September or early October. He could imagine the colors--quite a bit of green and patches of yellow and red and brown as well. In the distance, he heard the burble of the brook. He would walk toward it and sit for a while on the footbridge, listening to the water rush by. It seemed no matter how much his life changed or how many years passed, that water was always traveling under that bridge, undeterred.

Using his stick, Nash moved toward the sound of the water. He had a good idea where he was now, could picture the path in his mind. Of course, it was more overgrown than it had been before he'd left for the war and the brambles caught on his trousers, forcing him to pause every few minutes to free himself. He wasn't even sure if he was still on the path—or if there was a path—but the sound of the brook grew clearer.

Nash lifted his walking stick to feel for the wood of the bridge and hit what felt like a tree trunk. He moved around it, to the left, thinking maybe he was too far south of the bridge. But then the ground began to slope downward, and he realized that he had misjudged. The bridge was on higher ground and he was now on the banks of the brook. He swung his stick again and, moving forward a bit, he finally found the gentle rise that led to the bridge. He turned that way, but his foot was mired in the soft earth of the bank. He pulled it free, but he'd had to lean on his stick to do so, and then that had become stuck. Nash had to yank it out, which threw him off balance and his foot sank back into the mud.

So much for his clean clothing. His trouser legs must now be muddy almost to the calf. He vaguely remembered hearing thunder a couple of nights ago and the crash of heavy rain on the roof. If he'd remembered before he would not have headed for the brook. Without his sight, everything was so goddamn difficult. Before he would have walked directly to the bridge, dangled his feet over, and sat for as long as he liked. Now he couldn't even manage that because he couldn't navigate well enough to stay out of the mud and muck.

He pulled his foot free again, and struggled to take a step, but he only sank into more mud. Was he moving toward the brook or away from it? He'd become disoriented and made himself pause to listen. He needed to pinpoint the location of the brook and move away from it.

Nash went still, cocking his head to listen. He heard the rush of the breeze through the tree limbs, the chirp of birds high ahead, the singing of a woman, and the burble of the water.

The water was to his...

Nash frowned. Singing?

*"I met a young girl there with her face as a rose*
*And her skin was as fair as the lily that grows*
*I says, My fair maid, why ramble you so*
*Can you tell me where the bonny black hare do go"*

Her voice was clear and sweet, but Nash knew this song and it was anything but sweet. He tried again to wrest his foot from the mud, but he all but lost his balance and only righted himself at the last moment from falling backward and landing arse-first in the mud.

*"The answer she gave me, O, the answer was no*
*But under me apron they say it do go*

*And if you'll not deceive me, I vow and declare
We'll both go together to hunt the bonny black hare"*

The voice was closer now, the song sung lustily and without any self-consciousness. She obviously did not realize she was not alone. Nash tried to clear his throat as her voice came closer, but she was singing too loudly to hear.

*"I laid this girl down with her face to the sky
I took out me ramrod, me bullets likewise
Saying, Wrap your legs round me, dig in with your heels
For the closer we get, O, the better it feels"*

Nash was still now, wanting to hear the rest of the song. He'd heard the bawdy song many times in one tavern or another, but never sung with such abandon or enthusiasm. Indeed, on that last line, she had belted out, "For the closer we get, O, the better it feels."

*"The birds, they were singing in the bushes and trees
And the song that they sang was"*

"Oh!"

Her singing had ended abruptly, and Nash realized she'd seen him.

"What are you doing here?" she asked. Nay, it was more of a demand. As though she owned this garden, and he were the one encroaching. Nash tried to stand up straight and turn his face toward the sound of her voice. She was on the other side of the brook, as near he could calculate, possibly on the other side of the footbridge.

"I think the better question, miss, is what *you* are doing on my land and how quickly you can leave. Unless you fancy a charge of trespassing, that is."

## Two

Prudence Howard stared at the man standing by the side of the brook, sunk to the ankles in thick mud. He had wild black hair that swept over his forehead and covered one eye. The visible eye was a lovely blue. If she had been feeling poetic—and she was almost always feeling poetic—she would have called it the blue of the sky before a storm. Or perhaps she thought of storms because his handsome face held a rather stormy expression at the moment.

"Good afternoon," she called, hoping to see him smile. He was obviously a gentleman. His clothing was of fine quality, though somewhat ill-fitting, as if he had lost weight recently. Her eyes traveled over the rest of him, noting that he was pale as well as thin. Perhaps he had recently been ill.

"Good afternoon?" He scowled, obviously not appreciating her perusal of him. Admittedly, her behavior was rude. Mr. Higginbotham was always chastising her to be less forward and more demure.

Her eyes landed on his mud-covered ankles again and his ebony walking stick, also mired in mud. "Do you need some assistance?" she asked.

"Assistance?" he all but exploded. "I do not need assistance. What I need is for you to get off my land. I will have you charged with trespassing and fined accordingly."

*Oh, my.* What a temper! Pru started across the footbridge, wondering how she could assist him and manage not to get stuck herself. "Don't be silly," she said as she walked.

He jolted as though something had bit him. Were there snakes in the mud? She dearly hoped not. She had an affinity for all of God's creatures, but she did wish God had been less creative when it came to snakes and spiders.

"Silly?" he asked, sounding as though he were in pain now.

"Yes. How can anyone trespass here?" She laughed. "It's nature and beauty, and no one can own nature or beauty."

He was tracking her movements, though not really looking at her directly. She imagined she looked quite a fright. She was one to speak of beauty when she had always been as plain as the day was long.

"I have news for you, miss. Someone can and does own this part of nature and beauty. And that someone is me."

She reached the other end of the footbridge and looked down at the slippery bank beneath. "Oh, you must be the Earl of…" She couldn't remember which earl it was. "The earl who owns that lovely but dilapidated old house."

"Wentmore."

"Yes. It's simply criminal how you have allowed it to languish in such a decrepit state. But also romantic." She sighed. "On a moonlit night, the place looks almost haunted but also lonely and forlorn. Was that how you wanted it to appear? Are you a reader of gothic novels? Mr. Higginbotham disapproves mightily of gothic novels, but I confess I cannot read enough of them."

He stared at her with that one stormy blue eye. "Who are you?" he demanded.

She gave a sweeping curtsy. "Miss Prudence Howard, at your service. And you are the Earl of…Butter?"

"My father is the Earl of Beaufort."

"A pleasure to meet you, my lord." She gave another sweeping curtsy, but he still did not smile.

"I am not a lord. I'm a younger brother, simply Mister Pope."

"I see. And you live at Wentmore?"

"I do, and this is my garden."

"Well, I must commend you on it, sir. I have never seen such a wild and unruly place. I quite adore it. I can see we must be kindred spirits as Mr. Higginbotham often says disruption and disorder follow me wherever I go. But I do so enjoy a mess and a jumble. It makes life more adventurous; don't you think?"

"No."

"But it does! Because when everything is a jumble you never know what you will find. Perhaps you will lift a pot and find a hat you haven't worn in a week or move a stack of books and discover your favorite brooch had been hiding just there. Oh, but I see you scowling and imagine you must envision this mess is one of filth. Not at all. I am very clean. I daresay I dust and sweep as much as the next person, but I have never subscribed to the notion that everything has a place and a place for everything. Why must everything—"

"Miss Howard, was it?" he interrupted.

"Yes. Have I gone on too long?"

"Yes. Is there any chance you might go on about your way at some point before dark?"

She looked up at the sky. Through the canopy of multi-colored leaves, she could still see patches of blue. She judged it not even half past two. Plenty of time before dark. She elected not to point this out, though, as she did not think he would appreciate the observation. Mr. Higginbotham often told her that she should control her tongue and not chatter so much.

"I will, of course, be happy to go on about my way as I have wandered quite a distance from Milcroft." This was not intentional, of course. She had only intended to take a brief stroll and enjoy the mild weather and sunshine. But as usual, her intentions somehow went awry and she'd ended up miles from home, conversing with the son of an earl. "But I cannot leave you stranded here."

"I am not stranded."

She glanced down at the mud. "Are you certain?"

There was that scowl again. She wondered if he had practiced it in the mirror. It was quite effective. "Of course, I am certain."

"From where I stand, you seem rather stuck. I could—"

"I said I do not need assistance."

She crossed her arms. "All right then."

"Good. Then go on your way."

"Not just yet," she said. "I want to see how you go about extricating yourself. Purely for educational purposes," she added quickly when she saw the storm clouds forming on his face again. "I myself have been stuck any number of times after a heavy rain, and I freely admit I could use an effective method of escape."

The earl's son pressed two fingers to the bridge of his nose as though it pained him. "Miss Howard, I would rather not do this in front of an audience."

He wouldn't say such a thing if he was confident in his ability to navigate the muck without falling face first. Men were so confounding. Why would he not just allow her to help him? She supposed it was an issue of pride, in which case, she had to turn the tables so he could protect that pride.

"Sir, I have a confession to make," she said, trying to sound as helpless as possible. His brow lowered, and she realized she might have overdone it just a tad. "I cannot find my way out of your garden. I am quite lost and need you to help guide me." She managed to keep from laughing as she spoke and hoped he did not see the way her lips curved. The idea of being lost in this place was ludicrous. She had only arrived in Milcroft two months ago, but she had been here half a dozen times. Even if she had been lost, she would not have minded. She would have enjoyed the adventure of finding her way out.

The earl's son stood still for a long moment, obviously thinking about what she'd said. "Fine. I'll help you. Just give me a moment." He looked toward the brook and then away, twisting his body and seeming to gauge his footing. Pru had an idea of how he might extract himself, but how to offer it?

"Sir, I would feel so much better if you were here beside me," she said. "Could you hold out your walking stick? I can grasp one end and pull you this way."

His lips thinned. He was clearly suspicious of her suggestion. But she was glad to see he was no fool. He lifted the walking stick and turned it, so the muddy end was in his hands. So he hadn't just been born a gentleman, but he had a sense of chivalry as well. He held the top of the stick—the end with the pewter handle—out to her. It was just to the right of where she stood, and she had to adjust her location to grasp it. "I have you," she said. "Now I shall pull."

She did just that, pulling him toward her as he lifted his feet and moved through the muck to the firmer ground. At one point her hands slid and she thought she might lose her grip, thus causing her to go flying into the mud beside him. Fortunately enough she managed to hold on as he reached the slight slope at the edge of the bank. He'd have to pull harder to make it up the slope and she compensated by digging her heels in and leaning back.

Too late, she realized the man had anticipated having to exert more effort to climb up the slope, and being a gentleman, had not wanted to disturb her footing. He had actually lessened his pull on the stick. Which meant when she pulled harder, he came tumbling forward and crashed into her, sending them both sprawling on the leaf-strewn ground.

For just a moment Pru lay still, the breath knocked out of her and her head ringing a bit from being jounced on the ground. Then she realized her breath hadn't been knocked out at all, but the earl's son was lying on top of her and squishing the air out of her lungs. He swore, and she had a sudden image of what the two of them must look like. She probably had leaves in her hair and dirt on her nose, and he was covered to the knee in mud and trying to find a way to push off her. Oh, dear. If Mr. Higginbotham were to see her now, he would deliver a fiery sermon, indeed.

The whole situation struck her as amusing, and she giggled.

"You find this humorous?" the earl's son said in that gruff tone of his.

For some reason the fact that he took it all so seriously only made everything seem even funnier, and she started laughing.

"Stop that at once!" Mr. Pope ordered, finally managing to wriggle off her.

Well, Pru never could obey an order. She had an allergy to authority, her father always said, and she only laughed harder. Try as she might to quell her guffaws, they only grew. "I'm sorry," she said between laughs. "I don't know why I should find this so amusing."

"Neither do I." He struggled to his feet and then reached down, feeling for his walking stick. It was on the other side of her, so she handed it to him. He held out a hand, and she quelled her chuckles long enough to take it and allow him to assist her to her feet. He looked quite disreputable now. His black hair had leaves in it and fell so that it almost obscured both of his blue eyes. His clothing was rumpled and dirty, and what must have been once-lovely boots were ruined by the mud.

"I should see you home," he began, but Pru interrupted.

"No, that's not necessary." And then she wished she had not spoken because she sensed he had been about to give an excuse as to why he couldn't see her home, and she was curious to hear it.

He grunted and looked about. "I find I am all turned around. If you could point me in the direction of Wentmore, I should be obliged."

He was rattled, and she understood completely. She was a bit churned up inside herself after that unexpected tumble. Still, that didn't explain what she did next. Perhaps it was his stiff demeanor, so out of place in a garden while covered with dirt. She grasped his shoulders and bodily turned him to face the path leading back to the estate. He stiffened at her touch and seemed happy to step away when she said, "This way."

"You'll be able to find your own way home?"

"Oh, quite," she said, waving her hand. She knew a shortcut through the brush to the village road. She only took it when she had stayed later than she should as the thick underbrush snagged her skirts, but that wouldn't matter today. Her skirts were already a lost cause. She watched Mr. Pope start away and then turned and scampered back the way she had come. A glance over her shoulder showed her he was intent on his path and not watching her. A little while later, she was well on her way and safely out of his hearing. With a deep breath, she returned to her song.

*"The birds they were singing in the bushes and trees.*
*The song that they sang was, O she's easy to please.*
*I felt her heart quiver and I knew what I'd done.*
*Says I, Have you had enough of my old sporting gun?"*

"But of course she hasn't had enough of his sporting gun," Pru said to herself. Then hummed a bit as she couldn't remember the way the next verse began. So she sang again, *"I felt her heart quiver and I knew what I'd done."*

Her own heart had quivered when Mr. Pope had landed on top of her. Perhaps that was why she'd been unable to stop laughing. He'd smelled clean, and the weight of him, when he'd stopped crushing her, was pleasant enough. She supposed it was a good thing she was plain and all but invisible to most men, else she might be as much a wanton as the wench in the song.

Ah, and that reminded her of the next verse.

*"Oh, the answer she gave me, her answer was, Nay.*
*It's not often, young sportsman, that you come this way.*
*But if your powder is good and your bullets play fair,*
*Why don't you keeping firing at the bonny black hare?"*

Pru emerged from the garden by degrees. First the trees thinned, then the flowering bushes receded, and finally the green graduated to yellow and brown as she started toward the road leading to Milcroft. She didn't know why the garden should hold on to the green of summer when the rest of the world had succumbed to the colors of autumn. Perhaps it was some sort of enchantment.

Oh, but she could weave a vastly entertaining story about fairy queens and enchantments, but then she would grow lost in her thoughts and be late for supper. She might be late anyway. And so she lifted her skirts and ran most of the way back to the village.

When she reached the vicarage, she slowed, and tucked the loose pieces of her hair behind her ears. She could hear Mrs. Blimkin at work by the clank of pots and pans. Pru glanced at the sky and figured supper was still being prepared and not being put away. With Mrs. Blimkin busy in the kitchen, it would be better to enter through the main door, though that meant Pru risked being spotted by the vicar. But perhaps he was in his small library, hard at work on the sermon he was to give tomorrow. Or he might be dozing by the fire. If she was quiet, she might be able to sneak upstairs, wash and change, and no one would be the wiser.

Pru was quiet. She was exceedingly quiet, but Mr. Higginbotham had been waiting for her, and was ready with a lecture and a preview of the sermon he would give the next morning.

\*\*\*

She recognized the sermon Sunday when she sat in the first pew, her head facing forward, her gaze never wavering from her guardian as he preached about the Fires of Hell and Eternal Damnation. Pru did not think God would damn her for enjoying a garden he himself had created, and she did wonder if God really valued cleanliness as much as the vicar seemed to believe. She hadn't argued these points, of course. Her own parents were also deeply religious. In fact, they had left several months ago on a mission trip to the Far East. Having grown up with parents who had given her a similar version of Mr. Higginbotham's sermon many times, Pru had learned not to argue.

Her questions and comments would only be deemed heretical, and then she would be given an even longer lecture. By the age of eight, Pru had realized there was no common sense to be had in religion. She might try to look at the whole thing logically and reasonably, but this only seemed the path to more trouble. Better for everyone if she thought of religion as little as possible.

And so she gave every appearance of listening to Mr. Higginbotham intently, but in reality she was hoping he would shut up so that the congregation could sing the next song and she could look about again. She had never before seen Mr. Pope in church, but that did not mean he would not attend this morning.

She had given surreptitious glances to her right during an earlier hymn, and during the next hymn she intended to give surreptitious glances to her left. Finally, the signing commenced, and Pru stood, her muscles cramped from being forced to remain so still for so long. She looked about under the guise of being moved by the song, but she saw no one new or interesting.

At the end of the service, she was eager to return to the vicarage and change out of her itchy Sunday dress and into one of her more comfortable day dresses, but the vicar informed her they were to dine with Mr. and Mrs. Dawson and would need to walk there directly.

The Dawsons were one of the wealthier families in Milcroft. Pru hadn't been in the village long, but there were some things one learned right away. They had no children, but they did have three small dogs, and Pru enjoyed throwing a ball for the pups and feeding them scraps she sneaked under the table. The Dawsons were tedious but could be borne except on Sundays when she was forced to wear the stiff white dress with the high, itchy collar.

Pru did not complain, though. Firstly, it would be of no use. Secondly, the vicar would only tell her she was an ungrateful child, and she already knew that. She held her tongue and walked with the vicar until they reached the manicured lawns of the Dawsons' home. The Dawsons had a small garden with pruned roses and perfectly even hedges. Pru found it utterly lacking in imagination. No fairy queens had cast any enchantments here, but to her surprise and delight, once they entered the house, she discovered they were to be joined at dinner by Mr. Langford, who was the village surgeon.

Mr. Langford was not as ancient as the Dawsons and the vicar, being only about forty, and he always had interesting and bloody tales to tell about accidents involving sharp farm implements and butcher knives. More importantly, Mr. Langford did not treat every question she asked as an opportunity to lecture her. She might ask him about the Earl of Beaufort and his son and receive more than a lesson on gossip.

Of course, the vicar and Mrs. Dawson might still consider the conversation gossip, but they would never dream of chastising Mr. Langford.

Pru waited through the chatter about the weather and the meal and the lovely sermon and was rewarded by Mr. Langford recalling how he had been called to the home of the Finker family because one of their children—who could say which one—had got his head stuck between the railings on the stair.

"Oh, but I hardly see as they would need a surgeon for that," Mrs. Dawson said. "I would imagine some goose grease or butter would do the trick."

"And that is what I prescribed, Mrs. Dawson," Langford said with a smile. "But I'm afraid Mrs. Finker had not thought of that and had come to the conclusion that the little one would have to lose an ear in order to be set free. She had a knife waiting and handed it to me quite solemnly when I arrived. *Do it quicky, Mr. Langford*, she told me. *Don't let him suffer*.

"At least I think that is what she said. It was difficult to hear over the child's wailing."

Pru could picture the scene and smiled at the poor child's distress, thinking his ear was about to be severed from his head. Was it horrible of her to think if she were the surgeon that it would have been amusing to pretend—just for a moment—that she would actually sever the ear?

"But I soon calmed the child and assured him I would not need the knife. I greased him up like a Christmas goose and pulled him free easily enough."

"Ridiculous waste of your time," Mr. Higginbotham said. "You must have more important matters to tend to."

"I did not mind," Langford said, smiling at Pru across the table. She took that as her opportunity.

"I wonder, Mr. Langford, if you have ever been to Wentmore to treat the occupants there. I saw the earl's son yesterday, and he looked quite thin and pale."

Silence fell and the other diners looked so shocked one would have thought a massive boulder had crashed down from the sky and flattened the dining table.

"You saw Mr. Pope yesterday?" her guardian asked.

"Yes," she said carefully, now aware she had made a misstep somewhere. Pru was not unfamiliar with the tightening in her belly that seemed to squeeze all the food she had eaten into an oily blob. Her mother always said trouble followed her like a hungry puppy. Pru often wondered if that puppy's belly would ever fill.

"Did you speak to him?" Mrs. Dawson asked, her voice rising.

"Yes." Pru looked around the table. Everyone was staring at her, wide-eyed, even Mr. Dawson who had been half-asleep in his chair a few moments before. "Is that unusual?" Pru asked finally because she hated silence and hated being stared at, and both had become the preferred activities at the dining table.

"I forget you arrived only two months ago," Mrs. Dawson said.

"No one has seen Mr. Pope in over a year," the vicar said. "The earl gave him use of Wentmore when he returned from the war, and he's not stepped foot outside in all that time. The last time anyone saw him was about three months after he took up residence. A fire began in the kitchen and a few of the village men rushed to help put it out."

"My nephew was one of those who rendered assistance," Mrs. Dawson added, "and he said Mr. Pope ran everyone off with a pistol."

"How was the fire contained?" Pru asked.

"Mrs. Brown probably put it out," Mr. Langford said. "She is the housekeeper there and the only servant Pope will keep. I doubt she's been paid in a year, but she has been with the family since she was old enough to mop and dust, and she stays out of loyalty."

"That seems quite noble," Pru said.

"It's dangerous," Langford said. "Pope is dangerous. If you see him again, go the other way. I was at Wentmore this summer because Mr. Pope shot a man."

Pru inhaled sharply.

"Oh, Mr. Langford, please do not tell that gruesome tale again," Mrs. Dawson said in a tone that all but begged the surgeon to tell the tale and with as much detail as he could muster.

"I am afraid I must, Mrs. Dawson," Mr. Langford said. "Miss Howard needs to know the danger she was in."

"Oh, dear." Mrs. Dawson produced a fan and began to wave it in front of her face.

"I do not think Mr. Pope would have shot me," Pru said. "I was not a threat to him."

"Neither was the man he shot," Langford said. "In fact, the man was a friend of his. Pope served under Lieutenant-Colonel Draven in the war." He paused as though this name should mean something to Pru. "You've not heard of Draven?"

"Should I have?"

"He commanded one of the most skilled troops ever assembled. Along with Wellington, Draven is credited as one of the men most responsible for the defeat of Napoleon. His troop was comprised of highly skilled gentlemen. Not heirs to any titles, but third and fourth sons for the most part. None of the men were expected to come home again. Twelve of the thirty did, and they are hailed as heroes."

It did not seem to Pru as though Mr. Pope was being hailed as any sort of hero. "What was Mr. Pope's skill?" she asked.

"Sharpshooting," Mr. Dawson said, speaking for the first time since they'd sat down at the table. "One of the best in England. I saw him shoot when he was younger, before he went off to war," Dawson said. "He never missed, and his aim was always perfect."

"I rather think the Scotsman he shot would have preferred his aim less perfect. Apparently, two of his former brothers-in-arms came to visit him and instead of greeting them warmly, Pope opened fire," Langford said. "I was called to treat the Scotsman. He was a big man and I expected him to make a full recovery. He left before I could do much more than remove the pistol ball and stitch him up. Apparently, Pope threatened to shoot him again if he stayed."

Mrs. Dawson fanned her face violently, her eyes bright with interest.

"I don't think it's a breach of confidence to say that the house was a shambles," Langford said. "I've no doubt Mrs. Brown does her best, but the place was dusty and in extreme disorder—chairs turned over, candle wax on the floor, rugs with holes in them."

"I don't understand why Lord Beaufort has not come and taken his son in hand," Mr. Higginbotham said.

"I heard that the earl sent his son here to die. He told him to leave the family home in Richmond and that he never wanted to see him again."

Pru gasped. "Oh, but that's horrible. Surely no father would ever disown his own child." Even as the words left her lips, Pru knew she was wrong. Hadn't her own father all but disowned her? She still remembered the day they told her they had accepted a post in the Far East to serve as missionaries. Pru had asked, "Where will we live?" and her parents had said, not unkindly but firmly, "You will not be coming with us."

"The point is," the vicar said, "Mr. Pope is dangerous, and I do not want you near him, Prudence."

"Yes, sir."

"To think you might have been shot and killed!" Mrs. Dawson said.

"I really do not think I was in any danger of that," Pru said. After all, Mr. Pope had been stuck in mud, and the only weapon he had with him had been that fierce scowl.

"Oh, you might think his injury prevents him from aiming true, but I saw the Scotsman," Langford said. "Mr. Pope is still a good shot."

"What injury?" Pru asked, trying to remember if she'd seen Mr. Pope walk with a limp or show any sign he favored one arm. He had looked thin and a bit wan but not injured.

"You did not notice?" Langford asked.

Pru shook her head.

"Mr. Pope is blind."

## Three

Nash sat in his dining room nursing a headache. Rowden certainly wasted no time in clearing the house of anything decent to drink. He'd put cup after cup of coffee and tea before Nash but nothing stronger. He'd also managed to have three meals served on Sunday. Nash hadn't been able to eat much as his belly was used to a liquid diet, but he'd eaten enough that Rowden stopped badgering him.

Rowden was somewhere in the house right now, crashing about, making notes of what needed to be done or undone. Nash just wanted a whiskey or a brandy. Hell, he would have settled for cooking wine, but he'd already searched the kitchen in vain.

He took another sip of his weak tea and closed his eyes. A few moments later Rowden entered and tore open the curtains. "Must you do that?" Nash asked, turning his face from the light.

"You look like a ghost," Rowden said. "You need fresh air and sunlight."

Nash scowled. "Since when did you ever care about either? You've spent most of your life sleeping all day and battering men for money in the back of a tavern at night."

"Ah, the good old days," Rowden said fondly. "But now I spend a number of days giving nobs like you lessons in pugilism at Mostyn's studio. The sunlight does wonders for my disposition."

"My disposition is just fine," Nash said.

"You do seem in a cheery mood. What was that tune you were humming?"

Nash started. "Humming?"

"When I came in, you were humming."

"You must be hearing things." But Nash suspected he *had* been humming. Ever since meeting Miss Howard in the informal gardens, he hadn't been able to extricate "Bonny Black Hare" from his head. The song went around and around, and the worst part was he heard it sung in her clear, high voice.

"Well?" Rowden said and Nash realized he must have been speaking while Nash wasn't attending.

"Well, what?"

"Will you come outside and hear my plans?"

"You have plans?"

"Clearly, someone needs a plan. Unless you would prefer to be shut away in an asylum for the rest of your miserable life."

Nash did not answer.

"Come on. Up you go," Rowden said.

"Bloody damn hell, but I hate this cheerful side of you," Nash said, rising to his feet.

"I hate it too. I much prefer knocking men down to pulling them up, but then I owe you at least this much."

Nash looked at Rowden, trying to see him with his one good eye, but it was too bright with the curtains open. "You don't owe me anything."

Rowden didn't say anything until they were outside. Nash would never admit it, but the crisp autumn air did seem to infuse him with energy. His headache subsided slightly, and he lifted his head so the breeze might catch his hair.

"You saved my life at least three times," Rowden said, pausing at the bottom of the steps leading to the front door. Nash was carefully navigating them, knowing depth perception was all but impossible with only one half-blind eye.

"I was doing my job," Nash said once he reached the solid ground. He followed Rowden into a patch of sunlight and was relieved when the other man sank onto a square of brown grass. At least he wouldn't be made to walk about. Although a small part of him wondered if he would encounter the unpredictable Miss Howard again.

"You were damn good at your job," Rowden said. "Two of the times you saved my life, I didn't even see the men coming."

"I had a good vantage point."

"You were also good at what you did."

Nash didn't answer. *Good at what you did.* Of course, Rowden wouldn't say it outright. Nash was good at killing men. Sometimes he had killed them when they threatened his friends. But sometimes he had killed them simply because they might be a threat. And sometimes he'd made mistakes...

"We all came back with scars," Rowden said quietly after they'd been sitting in the sun long enough for Nash's cheeks to feel warm. "Some of us have visible scars, like you. But we all have to come to terms with what we did and who we are now. The war changed us."

Nash lifted a hand and slashed the air angrily, cutting Rowden off. "That's easy for you to say. You still have your sight. I'll never see again." He was surprised at how bitter his voice sounded. He hadn't said the words out loud very often, but in his mind, they hadn't sounded quite so petulant.

"You will never see again," Rowden said, and the words were like the final nail in Nash's coffin. "But you are alive and the rest of you is in good working order. You can marry, have children—"

"What woman would want me?"

"Hell, what woman would want any of us? Yet, I keep receiving marriage announcements. Mostyn is going to be a father."

Nash had been lounging on his elbows but now he sat up. Ewan Mostyn had been the Protector of the group, a big man with little to say and no charm to speak of. Nash had watched him toss men as though they were mere ragdolls. He could not imagine the large brute as a father.

"That was my response too," Rowden said, obviously observing Nash's shock. "But his wife told me herself."

"The child would be two before Ewan said anything to you," Nash observed.

Rowden laughed, and Nash smiled. It did feel good to smile. It had been a long time.

"Now that I have improved your mood, let's discuss how we might keep you out of Bedlam," Rowden said.

It was all very well to make plans and talk about the future on a sunny, cool autumn day when Nash had slept the night before and his mind was clear. Nash had made many such plans on days like this. Today was a good day.

But he knew better than to assume the good days would continue. He might have a stretch of three or four before The Cloud descended and he had a dozen bad days. Those days were so dark, so bleak, so devastating, it could take weeks to climb out.

When he was caught in The Cloud, Nash couldn't stop his mind from going over and over the mistakes he'd made in his life. In particular, the mistakes he'd made in Draven's troop. The innocents he'd killed. The men who hadn't died right away after he'd shot them. Men who he'd watched writhe on the ground, crying, begging for help as their blood and their life seeped slowly away and they died a slow, agonizing death.

When he was caught in The Cloud, even the act of breathing seemed to take too much effort.

"Maybe I should go to an asylum," Nash said after a long moment of silence.

"If that was your attitude, you could have saved me a trip here," Rowden said, his voice filled with annoyance.

"I didn't ask you to come."

"But I came anyway." Rowden's voice was steely.

"For the money."

*Sweet Rogue of Mine* | 51

"For friendship and brotherhood. Because I'm your friend. Mayne and Fortescue are your friends. We're trying to help you."

Nash stood. "I don't want your help."

"Clearly. The last time Fortescue was here, you shot at him. You wounded Duncan Murray."

Nash raked a hand through his hair. "I didn't know it was Murray."

"Who did you think it was?"

Nash didn't answer. It sounded too mad, too unreasonable.

"You thought it was the French. You thought you were under attack," Rowden said calmly.

Nash sank back to the ground. "I told you I belong in an asylum."

"You think I don't wake up sweating some nights, about to piss myself from fear over some imagined threat? You think Neil and Jasper and Colin don't remember the faces of the men they killed, the screams of horses, and the cries of widows and orphans?"

"When did you become such a poet?"

"Just because I can break your nose doesn't mean I don't have a brain. Some would say I'm good at breaking noses because I use my brain. But you're changing the subject.

Why do you think we founded The Draven Club? Not because we all needed one more place to drink or eat beefsteak."

The Draven Club was located on King Street in London. Membership included a dining room, reading room, card room, and billiards. The members numbered only thirteen—the twelve survivors from Draven's troop and the colonel himself. Nash had been there once or twice, but with his limited vision, he found he didn't like being in unfamiliar places or around too many people who might be staring at him.

He wasn't certain what he looked like now, but he could feel the scar over his left eye and thought it must be hideous enough that he'd grown his hair to cover it.

"It helps to talk about it with people who understand," Rowden said.

"And what if I don't want to talk about it?"

There was a lengthy pause. "Then I suppose you end up here. Or in the asylum." Nash heard Rowden rise. "If you've given up then I'm wasting my time. I'll go back to London, and your father can cart you away." The grass crunched under his feet as he walked away. Then silence. Nash supposed he had stopped and possibly turned back. "But if you want to fight…well, that's something I know a bit about."

His footsteps faded, and after a moment, Nash heard the door open and close.

Nash sighed and fell back into the grass, the blades scratchy against his back and neck. Sometimes he thought he did want to fight, but most of the time fighting was such hard work. And Nash was tired. He wanted to sleep and never wake up. Even now he felt the weight of his Gribeauval pistol in his pocket. Rowden hadn't managed to take that away. If Nash had the stones, he would prime it, cock the hammer, stick it in his mouth, and fire.

That would end his pain and make life easier for everyone. He wouldn't be a burden to his parents. Colonel Draven wouldn't need to worry about him. Rowden could go home. It was the easy way out, and Nash was not too proud to admit he was tempted to take the easy way. The last two years had been nothing but uphill and the summit was still not within reach.

He felt inside his pocket, rubbing his thumb over the filigree on the gunstock. He wondered if it needed polishing.

The grass crunched again, and Nash froze. Was Rowden coming back or—no. The grass was crunching from before him, not behind. Slowly he withdrew his pistol from his pocket then sat and aimed it in the direction of the sound. He was at a distinct disadvantage as he couldn't really even see shapes in the sunlight. But he could sense a presence, and he trained the pistol toward it.

"Would you mind not pointing that at me?" said a female voice. It took him only an instant to place it as Miss Howard's. Had he fallen asleep? Was he dreaming that she was here?

"I don't approve of weapons," Miss Howard went on in a cheerful, mildly lecturing tone. "Diplomacy is far more effective than warfare."

Nash lowered the pistol and slid it into his pocket. "Words are powerful weapons. I daresay more than one war has begun because of injudicious rhetoric."

"I can't argue, but I don't use words as weapons. You have nothing to fear from me, Mr. Pope." She moved closer, and he thought she must be standing in front of him now. "Might I sit beside you?"

"You'll soil your dress," he said. He wanted her to sit beside him for some reason. And the fact that he wanted it made it dangerous and something to reject.

"It's an old dress. Quite ugly," she said and promptly sat beside him. He scooted away from her, needing some distance between them. But it was too late. He caught the scent of pine and smoke and cinnamon and knew they were part of her unique fragrance.

"Why do you wear it then?" he asked. Stupid question. Why was he talking about clothing? He had no idea what he wore himself. He'd pulled clothing at random from the clothespress and did his best to dress himself. He'd gotten pretty good at it, but he doubted he looked presentable.

"I'm poor and don't have many others."

Her response made him forget whatever retort he had planned. No one discussed how poor they were. It wasn't done.

"I..."

"You needn't feel sorry for me," she said, placing her hand on his arm. Nash jumped at the contact. It had been a long time since anyone had touched him casually or without violence. Her hand was small and light, but he pulled his arm away as though she'd burned him.

"My parents are missionaries and they gave all they had to the parish church," she went on, not sounding offended by his rejection of her touch. In the meantime, Nash wished she would touch him again. If she did it again, he wouldn't pull away.

"There were four of us children, and we never had enough to eat or new clothing to wear, but my parents took care of the church before their own."

Nash would have expected some bitterness in her voice, but she spoke matter-of-factly and without rancor. In fact, she sounded almost bemused. As though growing up in poverty was entertaining and watching her parents give away all their worldly goods a diversion.

"Is your family living in Milcroft?" he asked, thinking he would need to have a word with the vicar. This family was obviously being taken advantage of. It did cross his mind that there was no reason he should care as this was not his concern or his problem, but it bothered him, nonetheless.

"Oh no." He could picture her waving her hand to dismiss the very notion. "This was in London. And Marrakesh. Constantinople and Rome and Cairo."

"You've traveled the world."

"You could put it that way. My parents went wherever the heathens might be."

"Are there many heathens in Rome?"

"The Catholics," she whispered conspiratorially then laughed. She had a laugh like a bell. Not one of those small dainty bells at the end of a pull that summoned servants, but a large booming church bell that rang out in a large city.

He almost smiled in response. Instead, he waited until her laughter died down. "But you've come to Milcroft to reform the heathens here. Presumably, you mean to start with me."

"Is that what you think?" she asked, still sounding amused. "That someone would travel all the way from Cairo to Milcroft because Mr. Pope needed to find religion?"

When she put it that way, it did sound rather self-absorbed. "Then why *are* you here?" he asked, losing patience.

"Here in Milcroft or here in front of your house?"

"Both. Either." He shook his head. "Yes."

"I am in Milcroft because my parents left me behind while they travel to the Far East to join another missionary group. I have been entrusted to the care of Mr. Higginbotham while they are away, though at three and twenty I hardly think I need a guardian. Still, after the incident in Cairo I suppose they don't trust me."

This was a lot to take in, and Nash was trying to sort his questions. Unfortunately, the first that came to mind was the least important. "Who is Mr. Higginbotham?"

She laughed then went quiet. "Oh, but you really do not know. My goodness! You *are* a heathen. Mr. Higginbotham is the vicar of Milcroft. Don't you ever attend church?"

"No. You mustn't have been here long if you don't know that."

"Only about six weeks. Or perhaps eight weeks. Time seems particularly slow in this part of the world."

Nash could not argue with that. There were times he thought a week had passed and it would only have been two days.

"And why are you in front of my house?" he asked, this being the question he'd wanted to ask before. She was not, apparently, wrong about him being self-centered.

"I wanted to apologize."

"For?" He could think of any number of things she might apologize for, but he wondered what she thought worthy of regret. She had been trespassing on his land. She had been singing a bawdy tune. She had pulled him down on top of her. Though he hadn't minded that last part so much.

"For offering you assistance."

Nash waited for her to go on as that statement made no sense whatsoever.

"And so I apologize, but you see, I didn't realize."

"You didn't realize."

"Yes. I saw you were stuck in the mud and offered you assistance, but I didn't realize you were blind."

The word *blind* shot through him like a lance. He hated it. Hated to be reminded of his defect. But the blow was tempered by his genuine confusion. "Wouldn't you be more likely to offer a blind man assistance?"

"*Me*? Oh, no. Definitely not. I never offer to help the blind."

Nash wasn't certain he had heard her correctly. "You *don't* offer to help the blind?"

"Never. I don't help the lame either. Or the deaf and dumb. I simply won't do it."

He must have stared at her with open-mouthed bewilderment because she spoke again. "You seem confused."

"You are a confusing person."

"Because I don't help the crippled?"

"Yes."

"But surely *you* understand why I won't lend assistance."

"I can't claim to understand, no. It seems exactly the sort of thing the child of missionaries would do."

"Oh, it is, but I hope you don't consider me a typical child of missionaries."

He did not consider her a typical human being. She was odd. Very odd, but in an almost endearing way. "I will not make that mistake again."

"And I will not make the mistake of offering you assistance again."

He supposed that was what he wanted. He hadn't asked for her assistance in the garden and had even rejected it. "Are you saying that you did not realize I was partly blind the other day?"

"Have you not been paying attention? That is my whole point."

"I have been paying attention," he said. He had the low throb in his brain to prove it. "But you might explain it again."

"Of course." She sounded as though she were speaking to a small child. As though what she said made perfect sense rather than being absolutely backward and inside-out. "It's very simple, really. Those who are blind or deaf or crippled want to be treated with the same dignity as everyone else. You told me in the garden that you did not need assistance. You wanted to extricate yourself from that mud alone. Had I known you were blind, I would have left you to it."

"You offered assistance because you thought I had perfect vision."

"Exactly. I thought you were just being a typical man and refusing help out of stupidity."

Nash all but choked at that statement.

"But it turns out you were just being determined. I have been scolded by enough one-legged beggars to know that they would rather do it on their own. It's a point of pride. To offer assistance would be to imply I thought you were not competent. I did not mean to make you feel so."

"That's certainly an...interesting way of thinking about the world."

"I shall take that as a compliment." She sounded satisfied with herself, and Nash felt even more confused by her. Why was she sitting here speaking to him? He'd threatened to have her arrested for trespassing. He'd pointed a pistol at her. And yet she sat beside him chattering as though these were the most normal things in the world.

"I suppose you have not wanted to ask anyone for help with your house," she said after a moment. He could imagine she was looking at Wentmore. He did not know what she looked like and even the brief feel of her beneath him in the informal garden hadn't given him much more than a vague impression of woman.

"No," he said. He hadn't expected the vehemence in his voice.

She laid a hand on his arm again. "I was not about to offer assistance. I told you, I will not do that again."

He did not pull his arm away from her touch this time. He was too busy thinking that perhaps there had been something to her earlier gibberish about never helping the blind or crippled. He was easily offended at even the idea that someone might think he could not take care of his own affairs.

"I imagine it was once an enchanting home. Not too manicured but just wild enough to provide fodder for the imagination. Do you have brothers and sisters?" she asked.

"Of course." Why was he answering her? Why did he not tell her to go away?

Why was her hand still on his coat sleeve?

"Did you run about playing at being Guinevere, Launcelot, and Merlin? When my sister and I had to stir a large pot at the hearth, we would always pretend we were Merlin and that was our cauldron. We'd toss in a spice and say a spell."

Nash couldn't ever remember playing any games like that. He vaguely remembered a set of toy soldiers. "I think we played War. Since I am the youngest of my brothers, I always had to be the French."

She patted his arm and removed her hand. Immediately, he wanted to tug it back again. "That is too bad. But then I suppose you could enact a dramatic death scene on the field

*Sweet Rogue of Mine* | 63

at Agincourt. Lots of moaning and groaning and spilling a bladder of sheep's blood at just the right moment."

Who the devil was this woman? What sort of children carried around sheep's blood to enact death scenes?

"Quite."

"Well," she said, and he could hear in her voice she was preparing to leave. "I suppose I should return to the vicarage before Mr. Higginbotham notices I've gone. There is probably some chore or other I was tasked with this morning which I've clearly forgotten and which he will waste no time in asking if I've completed."

Nash wondered what sort of chores she was required to complete. He wondered if she resented her parents leaving her with Higginbotham, and if he was a relative or a complete stranger. But she was leaving, and Nash would not ask her to stay. And he certainly would not ask when she would come back again.

He started to rise to his feet. "Good—"

"Shh!" Stiffening suddenly, she clutched his arm and squeezed it tightly. "Do not move," she whispered. "Do not speak."

## *Four*

Pru thought she must have allowed her imagination to run wild again. When she'd been a child, her parents had chastised her for that more times than she could count. But then she had never seen things that were not there before. She had imagined a bump in the night was a spirit or sparks from a fire were fairies dancing, but she had never imagined a peacock.

She closed her eyes and opened them again. The bird was still there. Its majestic tail feathers were lying flat and out of sight in the hedgerows from whence it had emerged, but she would have recognized that bright blue breast anywhere. She had seen peacocks in Constantinople and Cairo. Never had she expected to see one in Milcroft.

"What is it?" Mr. Pope asked, not even bothering to lower his voice.

The peacock jumped at the sudden sound and then turned and melted back into the overgrown shrubbery. She turned to scold Pope and noticed he had drawn his pistol again. Really, the man was impossible.

"I told you not to move or make a sound. And then you made a sound and moved." She pushed at the pistol. "You can put that away. He's gone."

Mr. Pope lowered the pistol but seemed to hesitate before putting it back into his coat pocket. "What was the danger?" he asked.

"No danger," she said. "Unless I am going mad." She said that last bit under her breath, but not quietly enough.

"There was nothing there." He turned to look at her directly, and for what must have been the dozenth time today, she found it difficult to catch her breath. She knew he could not really see her. Langford had said Pope had some vision left in his right eye, so perhaps he could see something of her, but she still felt as though Mr. Pope saw her much more clearly than other people. For one, he looked at her. Most people looked past her. She was not pretty or even interesting to look at, and most people's eyes skimmed right over her. A man like Pope would not usually even give her a moment's attention. It was a bit dizzying to be so close to a man with his looks. He was still pale and thin, but he looked slightly better than he had on Saturday. And even pale and thin, that black hair falling over his forehead and one eye and that

*Sweet Rogue of Mine* | 67

beautiful blue eye she could see were arresting. He had thick black eyebrows as well and short black stubble on his jaw. He might be thin, but he was powerful. She had felt the strength of his forearm even under the layers of his coat and shirt.

It would take little more than a few weeks of hearty meals and exercise before he was quite the prime specimen of maleness. She sighed, just imagining it.

"Miss Howard, I do not appreciate your games."

She frowned. What was he going on about? Oh, yes. The peacock. "I was not playing a game, Mr. Pope. I saw him, but for a moment I doubted what I saw. It's so rare and unusual. But I closed my eyes and then opened them again, and he was still there."

"Who?"

"The peacock."

"The what?"

"The peacock. I saw a peacock standing amongst the shrubberies. His tail feathers were lying down, but he had the blue breast and crown and those long stick legs. And now you must think me completely mad."

"You're not mad. I thought all the peacocks were gone."

"*All* the peacocks?" she said, jumping to her feet. "There are more?"

He rose to his feet as well. "No. Don't go traipsing about looking for peacocks. No wonder you forget your chores. I said I thought they were all gone."

"But why were they here? Where did they go? Oh, damn it!" He blinked, and she realized she shouldn't have cursed. "I mean, drat it. I must take my leave. Now I shall never know about the peacocks." She would think about that peacock for days. Perhaps someone in Milcroft knew why peacocks were at Wentmore. But then she'd have to explain why she'd gone to Wentmore—again—when she'd been told to stay away.

"You could come back," Mr. Pope said, seeming almost surprised at his own words.

"I could?"

He shrugged. "If you want." Clearly, he did not care if he ever met her again.

"If I come back, you will tell me about the peacock?" She was not too proud to admit she wanted the story of the peacock and a chance at another sighting. She wouldn't mind seeing Mr. Pope again either. He was a strange and all but intoxicating mixture of gruff and genteel. She liked the contrast.

"I might," he said.

Pru rolled her eyes. Men were so difficult. But two could play at this game. "Then I *might* come back. Good afternoon,

Mr. Pope." She started away, waving. Of course, he didn't wave back. *He can't see you, numbskull*, she told herself. Still, she walked until she was out of sight of the house then she picked up her skirts and ran.

When she reached the wooden bridge leading into the village, she slowed, stuck her bonnet back onto her head and tied the ribbons under her chin. She pressed a hand to her belly, trying to slow her breathing then made her way toward the vicarage, smiling at the people she saw and trying to look as though she had all the time in the world.

"Oh, there you are!" Mrs. Blimkin said when Pru slid into the kitchen. Mrs. Blinkin stood at a table in the center of the kitchen, copper pots and pans and herbs dangling above her head. She was carefully placing dough into a pie pan. "The vicar was looking for you."

"Oh?" Pru tried to sound innocent. "Why?"

"Something about sweeping the front room."

*A-ha!* That was what he'd asked her to do.

"I told him I swept it this morning as I always do." Mrs. Blimkin pressed the edges of the dough, creating scalloped edges. "But he obviously thinks I can't do even the simplest tasks anymore."

"I'm sure it's not that, Mrs. Blimkin. No doubt Mr. Higginbotham feels I need some responsibility."

Mrs. Blimkin gave her a sideways look that implied she thought the same. Pru sighed and made her way to the front room with the broom. The door to Mr. Higginbotham's library was closed, which meant he was either sleeping or working. Pru would have wagered he was asleep in his chair with a volume of sermons resting on his chest.

Pru began to sweep the already clean floor. She liked the vicar well enough. He was a kind man, although old-fashioned. This was to be expected, considering he was old enough to be her grandfather. He had ideas about what young ladies should read and what dinner topics were acceptable conversation. He thought Pru should make an effort to call on the families in the village—in particular those who gave generously to the church—and have tea with their daughters. Pru had tried to make friends when she'd first arrived, but her overtures had not been welcomed or returned.

Still, she couldn't spend the next few years sweeping a clean floor. She had to find something to do. And it was probably best if that something was not calling on the dashing Mr. Pope. She was already planning when she could sneak away and return to Wentmore. She wanted to hear about those peacocks, but more than that she enjoyed spending time with Mr. Pope. He was so serious and rather dangerous, and she had a bad habit of showing too much interest in dangerous men. But Mr. Pope wasn't a crime lord or a stolen antiquities dealer. He was a former soldier trying to adjust to a new life without his sight. He was scared and uncertain, though he tried valiantly to hide it.

Pru leaned on her broom and sighed. Perhaps this time it was the man's vulnerabilities that drew her more than the danger he posed. He wouldn't really hurt her. Not intentionally, at any rate. She could be mistaken, but she thought he enjoyed their conversations as much as she. Mr. Pope could certainly use more of her visits. The poor man was all alone in that tragic, moldering house. But the vicar was unlikely to countenance her spending any time with Mr. Pope, and so she needed to find a more acceptable pastime.

She enjoyed visiting the tenant farmers in the area. The vicar visited on a monthly rotation. He had consented to take Pru with him when she'd first arrived, but lately he said her incessant chatter made it hard for him to think and insisted she stay at the vicarage.

Her parents had given the vicar a bit of money for Pru's upkeep, and she had asked him for enough to buy material for a new dress. He had initially refused, saying it was vanity, but after a week, he had seen all of her dresses and handed over the money without her even having to ask again.

Pru looked down at the dress she currently wore. It was the color of smashed peas after they had stewed in the pot for a few days and had to be scraped off the sides. Pru would have never chosen it for herself, but her parents rarely ever bought their children or themselves anything new, and this had been in the donation box at the church. Pru would have left it there, but her mother had taken it home, made Pru try it on, and since it fit, she had been made to wear it.

Having swept the floor, Pru put the broom away and went to a chair in the corner where she sometimes liked to sit and read sermons after supper. Which meant, she tucked a novel between the pages of a book of sermons and pretended to read sermons.

But she also had a book of patterns Mrs. Dawson had lent her, and she took it up now to see if she might be able to choose one and begin making herself a new dress. The problem was that though she liked many of the patterns, she had never made a dress by herself. She had helped her mother, especially after her sister, Anne, had become sick with fever, but completing tasks another assigned was quite different than beginning the project oneself. Not to mention,

*Sweet Rogue of Mine* | 73

she had bought only as much fabric as necessary. There was no room for mistakes.

She studied the book, lifted the material, examined her current dress, and then set it all down again.

"You look like you just received news the church's autumn festival was canceled," Mrs. Blimkin said from the doorway. Pru jumped, not knowing how long the housekeeper had been standing there.

"It's not that." Then she brightened. "*Has* the festival been canceled?"

"No."

Pru deflated again. Mrs. Blimkin gestured to the pattern book. "Looking to start on your new dress, are you?"

"I've been wanting to start on it for a week."

"I know." Mrs. Blimkin entered, passing a cloth over tabletops and lamps. "But all you do is pick it up and put it down again."

Pru had thought of asking Mrs. Blimkin to help, but she was aware the other woman was a servant and Pru was, while not exactly her employer, a pseudo-employer. She couldn't pay Mrs. Blimkin, and surely dressmaking was not one of the tasks Mr. Higginbotham expected of her.

"Why don't you ask Mrs. Northgate to help you?"

Pru made a face. She had met the Northgate girls and their mother. All three of them had turned their noses up at her. She heard them whispering at church each Sunday, and she just knew they were whispering about her.

"Not the wife," Mrs. Blimkin said. "Mr. Northgate's mother."

Pru tried to think back to the Northgate pew at church. There were only the five of them—the husband and wife, the son, and the two girls. "I don't think I know her."

"Probably not." Mrs. Blimkin was close enough to whisper now. "She's a heathen."

"A heathen?"

"That's right. She never attends church, and when the vicar called on her to invite her, not long after he arrived at Milcroft, she told him she didn't believe in God."

"But that must have been thirty years ago," Pru said. "She's never attended church in all that time?"

"No." Mrs. Blimkin was not even pretending to dust at this point. She looked over her shoulder to make certain Mr. Higginbotham's door was still closed. "Not a once. And do you know what else?"

Pru knew she should not gossip, but she was absolutely fascinated. She had never considered *not* attending church. She had gone every Sunday and more for as long as she'd been alive. She hadn't realized until she'd been fifteen or sixteen that some people did not attend church.

"What else?" Pre asked.

"I have heard—I haven't seen it with my own eyes, mind you—but I have heard that she does housework on Sundays."

Pru sat back. "She cooks and cleans on Sunday?"

"She must! The servants have the day off—as they should—and when they return on Monday morning, let's just say that the kitchen is cleaner than they left it and there's often a pie or a newly baked half loaf of bread that wasn't there when they left Saturday evening."

This was indeed shocking, and also rather exhilarating. Pru liked people who broke the rules. Perhaps because she broke them so often herself—not intentionally, of course. She had been known to forget it was Sunday some weeks as well and accidentally pick up a broom or duster. She always repented of her sin right away, of course. And unlike when she repented for reading novels or uttering a curse, Pru was genuinely sorry for breaking the commandment to honor the Sabbath. She did not want to clean any day, and it was only habit that caused her to lift the broom in the first place.

"How can Mrs. Northgate help me with the dress?" Pru asked. Mrs. Blimkin seemed to have forgotten all about that suggestion and stared at Pru blankly for a moment before nodding.

"She was quite the fashionable lady in her day. Made all her own clothes and makes many of the dresses her granddaughters wear. Not that Miss Northgate or Miss Mary appreciate it.

Pru doubted the Northgate girls appreciated much, but they were always well-dressed. "And you think she would help me?"

"I think she'd be happy for the company. You're an odd one, but you're pleasant enough."

"Thank you." Pru added, "I think," under her breath. "Do you think the vicar will mind?" Pru glanced at the closed door again.

"Not if you drop a Bible verse or two into your conversation. He can't get near her. If you can, he'll see it as an opportunity."

Pru nodded. "Might I go now?"

"You don't need my permission."

Pru gathered the material then put it back down. It might be too forward to bring the dress material with her, as though she expected Mrs. Northgate to agree. Instead she took up the pattern book, donned her coat and bonnet, pulled on her gloves, and set off down Milcroft's main street.

The vicarage was at the far end of Milcroft, as though the church had been built as an afterthought. The shops were closer to the river and the mill so they might easily cater to farmers who brought their wares to sell or their grain to be milled every week. The wealthier families had homes just outside the town. The Earl of Beaufort's estate was about three miles outside of town. The Northgate house was only a quarter of a mile. The Northgates had an orchard and exported the apples, pears, cherries, and plums they did not sell locally. Pru had recently learned that Mr. Northgate also sold apple cider during the harvest season, and the congregation of the church was atwitter about Northgate's promise to bring a cask of it to the autumn festival for all to enjoy.

It wasn't until Pru drew close to the Northgate house that she felt the flutter in her belly. She hadn't felt nervous when she'd gone to see Mr. Pope, even though he might have shot her. She supposed she truly was a vain creature as she was more worried about the Northgate girls laughing at her ugly dress than being shot through the head. It did not hurt that Mr. Pope was so handsome. In addition to her weakness for dangerous men, she had a weakness for dark-haired men. It had gotten her into trouble in Cairo and was the main reason she was here now and not on a ship bound for a port in the Far East with her parents and brothers. Or perhaps they had arrived by now. She couldn't expect a letter for at least another month unless her mother had mailed one at a port of call. Speaking of letters, she should write to Anne…

But she was straying from her current task, which was not writing to her sister but knocking on the Northgates' door. Pru squared her shoulders, took a breath, and made her way up the gravel walk and to the door. She tapped lightly on the door, and it was opened immediately by Mary Northgate. Mary was the younger of the two daughters. She was probably thirteen, but unlike Pru, who had been gangly and awkward looking at thirteen, Mary looked poised and elegant. She had blond hair that cascaded down her back in perfect curls, secured away from her face by a blue ribbon that matched her eyes. She stared at Pru and did not speak.

"Good afternoon," Pru said. "Is Mrs. Northgate at home? Your grandmother, that is."

Mary closed the door in Pru's face, but Pru heard her yell, "Grandmama, the vicar's ward is here to see you."

Pru opened her mouth to tell the girl that she was not the vicar's ward. She was three and twenty and too old to be anyone's ward. But what was the point? The door was closed, and Miss Mary Northgate was already gone.

*Sweet Rogue of Mine* | 79

Pru stood and waited for what seemed a long time. She wondered if she should knock again or just give up and go home. Finally, just as she was about to turn around and return to the vicarage, the door opened and a tall woman in a dove gray dress stood before her. Pru was tall herself, but she looked up at the woman, who must have been close to six feet. She looked even taller because of the coil of silver hair piled high on her head. It was quite an impressive coiffure, and Pru imagined the woman's hair must reach all the way to the floor when unbound.

"Who are you?" the woman asked.

Pru curtseyed then wondered why she had done such a thing. She didn't think she'd ever curtseyed before in her life. "I am Prudence Howard, ma'am. Mr. Higginbotham is my guardian while my parents are away on a missionary trip."

The woman looked Pru up and down. "You look too old to need a guardian. Haven't you a husband?"

"No, ma'am."

"And not likely to marry with a face like that and wearing a dress a color and style that does you no favors."

Pru began to wonder if she had made a mistake in listening to Mrs. Blimkin. "The dress is actually what I came to talk to you about, ma'am. Mr. Higginbotham's housekeeper, Mrs. Blimkin, said you might be able to help me make a new one."

Mrs. Northgate put her hands on her hips. "Oh, so I am the local seamstress, now am I?"

"I don't think she meant to imply that at all. I believe she took pity on me after seeing me staring forlornly at this pattern book yet again."

Mrs. Northgate glanced down at the pattern book Pru held out in supplication. She harrumphed. Pru thought she would close the door and that would be the end of it, but she stood in the doorway. "Are you the sort of girl who can take instructions or do you insist on having your own way?" Mrs. Northgate asked.

Pru considered. "I fear I do tend to go my own way, ma'am."

"Good. Come back tomorrow after noon—not before. Bring your dress material."

Pru blinked. "Thank you!"

"Do not thank me yet, young lady. I can see we have a lot of work to do."

"Yes, ma'am. Should I bring the pattern book?"

Mrs. Northgate looked at it again. "Goodness, no. Nothing in there will suit you."

"Oh."

"Tomorrow. Not before noon. You can tell time, can you not?"

"Yes, ma'am."

"Good. Then between noon and one, I should think." And she closed the door. Pru stood on the steps a moment longer, wondering if she should go or if the woman would open the door again and bid her a proper good-bye. After a moment, she backed away and, when she was a sufficient distance, turned and ran back to the vicarage.

## *Five*

Pru wore her second-best dress to call upon Mrs. Northgate the next day. She trudged through the light drizzle that had been falling all morning and knocked on the door at exactly five past twelve, and this time a servant opened the door and led her to an upper floor to what she called Mrs. Northgate's boudoir.

Mrs. Northgate was waiting for her, seated at a table that had been positioned in the middle of the room and obviously brought in for the purpose of making a dress. The table was sturdy and plain, the sort of table Pru's family would have owned in their room in London.

The rest of the chamber was far more opulent. Pru looked about at the dark woods and plush fabrics on the chairs and the reclining couches. The drapes were heavy velvet, open to the day and would, on a sunny day, allow a great deal of light into the room. A closed door on the far side of the room most likely led to the bed chamber. This chamber must have acted more as a receiving room.

"Your eyes look as though they might pop out at any moment," Mrs. Northgate said. "Have you never seen a lady's boudoir?"

"I confess, I have not, ma'am."

"Sit down." She indicated the sturdy chair across from her. "I asked about you," she said as Pru took a seat. Pru's hands froze in the act of placing her dress fabric, wrapped in paper to keep it clean, on the table.

"Oh, yes, that's right. I wanted to know something about the young lady in whose company I would be spending several days. I understand you are recently from London, and that your parents are missionaries."

"Yes, ma'am."

"And where are they now? These parents of yours?"

"Bound for the Far East, ma'am."

"Do they never take you with them on their pilgrimages?" She gestured for Pru to hand over the dress fabric and Pru did so.

"They have in the past."

"Ah, so you have seen something of the world then." She unwrapped the paper on the dress and winced. "Oh, dear."

"What is it?" Pru peered at the bright yellow fabric, hoping it had not been damaged or soiled. She saw no imperfections, though. She had been inordinately careful with the material.

Mrs. Northgate looked at Pru then looked at the fabric. "Go stand by the window, girl."

Pru did not particularly like being called *girl*, but she did as she was told. Mrs. Northgate brought the material over and held it up to Pru's face in the gray light. "Ghastly," she said.

Pru stared at her. "I know I am plain but—"

"Come here." Mrs. Northgate took Pru's wrist between her bony fingers and tugged her to the cheval mirror in one corner. Pru immediately adjusted the dress she wore. It had been white at one time but was now a faded ivory with a pattern of tiny roses sprinkled throughout. The neckline was modest but not buttoned all the way to her neck. A smattering of freckles was visible on Pru's collarbone. "Look at your face, Miss Howard."

Pru looked. It was odd to look at her face with someone like Mrs. Northgate observing. When Pru had been younger she had looked in the mirror quite a lot. She'd hoped her freckles would fade or her brown eyes would lighten or darken or her thin lips would grow plump. But she looked as she always did—a thin, long face, a sharp chin, and wide brown eyes that were almost too big. It was a very ordinary face which might have been acceptable had she not had so many freckles. It was her own fault, really. They would not have been so pronounced had she worn a hat in the sun as she ought.

Pru's mother had always scolded Pru for those long gazes in the mirror. She did not hold with vanity. Pru looked a good deal like her, except her mother had deep red hair and always wore a bonnet to shield her skin from the sun. Her freckles were quite pale. Pru had hair the brown of tree bark which she wore in a simple topknot as she had no skill in hair dressing.

"Now look at your face again," Mrs. Northgate said as she draped the new dress material over Pru's chest so it was beside her face. Pru saw the difference immediately. She had looked plain and unremarkable in her dull white dress, but when the yellow fabric was placed beside her skin, she took on a sallow, sickly color. Her freckles looked almost nauseatingly green and the skin under her eyes seemed to sag and darken.

"Do you see the difference?" Mrs. Northgate removed the dress fabric then put it back again. "This is not the color for you, Miss Howard. You will have to return it."

"It's already been cut. Mr. Clark will not take it back."

Mrs. Northgate raised a brow. "We shall see about that. Sterns!" The door opened and the maid who had shown Pru inside appeared.

"Yes, Mrs. Northgate?"

"I am going out. I want my coat and my walking stick."

"Yes, Mrs. Northgate." She held the door open and Mrs. Northgate started out, still holding the yellow fabric. "Come along, Miss Howard."

Pru moved to follow then dashed back to collect the paper for the fabric. By then Mrs. Northgate was in the vestibule and Sterns was assisting the older lady in donning her coat and hat.

"Where are you going?" Pru asked, feeling as though she had opened a book to the middle instead of the first chapter.

"*We* are going," Mrs. Northgate said. "Put on your hat and coat and come along."

Pru looked at the maid, hoping for some assistance or explanation, but Sterns merely stared back at her. Pru shoved her arms into her coat, hastily buttoned it up and grabbed her hat just as Mrs. Northgate was gesturing for the maid to open the door.

88 | *Shana Galen*

"Grandmama," said a high voice. "Where are you going?"

Pru looked back to see Miss Eliza Northgate standing in the doorway of what was most likely the family drawing room. Like her sister, she had blond hair, though hers was pinned up. She wore a pink dress that was somehow feminine but not too frilly and which showed off her figure to perfection. Pru glanced at her face, judging that the color of the dress suited Miss Northgate's complexion quite well. Perhaps Mrs. Northgate knew what she was about.

"I will be back before dinner," Mrs. Northgate said, not looking at her granddaughter. "Your mother needn't worry."

Miss Northgate's blue eyes landed on Pru. "What are *you* doing here?"

Pru opened her mouth to answer but then was struck with self-consciousness. She did not want to tell this stylish creature that Mrs. Northgate was helping her with her dress. It was too embarrassing. But the girl was looking at her and even Mrs. Northgate had paused, waiting. Pru took a breath. "Mrs. Northgate has graciously agreed to help me make a new dress."

Miss Northgate's pale brows went up. "How *kind* of you, Grandmama," she said, making it sound as though Pru was a charity case, which Pru supposed she was. "I daresay we have all been wondering when someone would help poor Miss Howard. I just did not think it would be you, Grandmama."

Mrs. Northgate turned steely gray eyes on her granddaughter. "Are you quite done?"

Miss Northgate curtseyed in response, directing a small sneer at Pru.

"Good." Mrs. Northgate took her walking stick in one hand. "Then we shall be off. Come along, Miss Howard."

Pru followed, tying the ribbons of her sagging bonnet under her chin as she followed. She wished she could return to the vicarage. She didn't know what had possessed her to listen to Mrs. Blimkin and go to Mrs. Northgate in the first place. She did not want anyone's charity or pity.

"You needn't go out of your way or to any trouble on my account," Pru said, as she followed Mrs. Northgate toward town. The older woman walked quite briskly for her age, and Pru had to increase her own pace to keep up. Mrs. Northgate made no indication she had heard Pru, so Pru felt compelled to go on. She often felt so whenever there was a silence. She did not like silences. "I do not want your charity or your pity. I had only thought to ask for your advice."

"And I am giving you my advice," Mrs. Northgate said. "I call that neither charity nor pity, though I cannot entirely rule out pity for I did pity that awful dress you wore yesterday. It should be burned. Why on earth would you or your mother purchase material in that shade of..." Words seemed to desert her. She made a gesture with her hand and finally said, "In that color?"

Pru explained that the dress had come from the bin for the poor and that since it had fit her, she had been given it to wear. "My parents give almost all of their money to the church, and there was seldom ever any left for frivolities."

"I hardly think a decent dress a frivolity. How many dresses do you have? Four?"

"Three," Pru said.

"The third is your Sunday dress," Mrs. Northgate stated. "Is it any better than the two I have seen?"

"It is a great deal itchier."

"Ah, here we are," Mrs. Northgate said as the road widened, and the buildings came into view. "I am an old woman, Miss Howard." Mrs. Northgate slowed her pace to a dignified stroll.

"I would not say that, ma'am."

"Oh, yes, you would. And what you will learn, should you live as long as I, is that with age comes liberty. I spend my days as I like."

"Mrs. Blimkin said you do not go to church."

Mrs. Northgate cackled. "Are you worried for my soul, girl?"

"Are you not worried?" Pru was always worried for her soul. She was always forgetting to say her prayers and was forever committing some sin or other. Even when she repented of singing inappropriate songs or reading novels, she knew she did not really mean it and would do it again the next day. "I, myself, find it very hard to be good," Pru admitted.

"So do I," Mrs. Northgate said as they entered the village and received waves and curious looks from the people out and about. "And to tell you the truth, I have quite given up trying to be good. I do not believe in charity and good deeds."

Pru's eyes widened. "You don't?"

"No." She gestured ahead. "There is Clark's, just there. So you see, you need not worry I consider you a charity case. You are something else entirely."

A few men were gathered to one side of the general store, and Pru glanced at them briefly. They seemed quite intent on their conversation, though, and took no notice of her. She recognized one or two of the group of six or seven from church, but the man in the center, who seemed to be doing most of the talking, was quite unfamiliar.

"Something else entirely," Pru repeated. "What is that?"

Mrs. Northgate turned to Pru, pausing before the door to Clark's. "You, Miss Howard, are a project."

Pru was not quite certain what to make of this description, but she had no time to question it as they were soon inside the store and Mrs. Northgate was demanding attention. Pru wanted to stand back and hide, but Mrs. Northgate insisted on pushing the fabric beside her face in order to show Mr. Clark and his wife what a bad choice it had been and to question their judgment in allowing Miss Howard to buy the fabric in the first place.

She caused quite the commotion, and Pru could only watch in awe as she not only harangued the shopkeepers into taking the material back but also into bringing out their best fabric so she might hold it beside Pru's face and determine which colors might suit her.

Finally, after what seemed hours but was most likely only a quarter hour at most, Mrs. Northgate decided on a thick russet-colored fabric which would be warm enough to see her through the winter and which, she claimed, brightened Pru's complexion so it was almost pretty. Then came the haggling. This material was slightly more expensive than the material Pru was returning, and Pru was worried she would have to explain that she did not have money to pay for the difference, but Mrs. Northgate told her to leave the negotiations to her and shooed her out of the shop.

Pru stepped outside, pleasantly surprised that the drizzle had abated—though the sky was still gray and colorless, at least she would not have to hunch under Clark's awning to stay dry. She strolled to the window and peered inside, watching as Mrs. Northgate gestured grandly and pointed her finger at Mr. Clark.

"I'll pay you at the end of the week," a man's voice was saying. "Work sunup to sundown, rain or shine, and you'll receive a fair wage."

Pru glanced down the walk and noticed the group of men who had been clustered in front of Clark's had shifted one or two shops over. It might have been a different group of men now, but the man speaking was the same stranger she had spotted earlier. Of course, many people in Milcroft were still strangers to her. She hadn't lived here long enough to know everyone, but he was the sort of man she would have remembered if she'd seen him before.

He was big and brawny. His chest was wide and his shoulders broad. He dressed in a way that was better than some but not so well that he would stand out among the townspeople. He stood out anyway because of his size and his short dark hair. He wore a hat low over his forehead, and she could not make out his eye color. He sounded like a Londoner, though. She had lived there long enough to recognize the accent.

"What's a fair wage when you've a hole through the head?" one of the men from the village asked. The other men grumbled their agreement.

"I personally guarantee your safety," the big man said.

That silenced the grumbling. The big man looked toward Pru, and she turned her head back to the window and the continuing scene inside Clark's. Mrs. Northgate was no longer gesturing widely. Now she was watching Mr. Clark measure the russet fabric.

"It's harvest time," one of the men said. "I can't afford to be away from my land."

"Then don't come," the Londoner said, sounding unconcerned. "But if you could do with an extra few coins in your pocket, then we'd be happy to have you." He tipped his hat and the men dispersed slowly, speaking amongst themselves in low voices.

Pru thought how unfair it was that she was not a man. She had time and would like a few coins in her pocket instead of having to ask Mr. Higginbotham any time she needed funds. Yes, he'd given her the money for a new dress, but how was she to ask him for a few coins for a new chemise? The one she had was frayed and patched. Her shoes were another issue. Like her pea-green dress, they had been rescued from the donation bin. They had been serviceable when she'd first received them two years ago, but now the sole was coming apart and her stocking had gotten wet when walking in the rain this morning.

Even if she asked Mr. Higginbotham for the money, she did not know how much her parents had left for her. For all she knew, the money he'd given her for the dress fabric was all they'd left. Pru hated being a charity case, but that's exactly what she was. It was what she'd always be since she didn't have the education, references, or skills to be anything else.

"Do I have a wart on my nose?" the Londoner asked, moving toward her. Pru jumped, realizing he was speaking to her.

"I don't think so," she said. "Why do you ask?"

"You were staring at me."

She waved a hand, feeling her cheeks heat. "I was thinking and have a bad habit of staring off into space when I think. I wasn't looking at you so much as *through* you."

"That's a disappointment." He moved close enough that they could converse without raising their voices but with plenty of space between them.

She tilted her head. "Why?"

"A man never likes for any young lady to look *through* him."

Pru rolled her eyes. "So it's like that."

He raised his brows in question.

"You are a charmer."

"I do try." He took off his hat and she saw his eyes were green. Quite a pretty green too. "Allow me to introduce myself, Rowden Payne."

"It's nice to meet you, Mr. Payne. I am Prudence Howard."

"And what were you thinking so hard about, Miss Howard?"

"Money," she said with a sigh.

"Not romance?" He smiled.

"Gads, no. Romance won't buy me a new pair of boots."

He gestured to the store window. "Were you thinking of going inside and inquiring about a position?"

"No. I'm waiting for…a friend of mine to come out. She's purchasing fabric."

"Ah."

"Are you here from London?" she asked.

"Yes." He brightened. "You've heard of me?"

She narrowed her eyes.

"Rowden Payne? The Royal Payne?" he asked hopefully.

"No."

He laughed, seemingly in spite of himself. "You are most direct, Miss Howard. I am staying at Wentmore, helping Mr. Pope to repair the old pile."

Pru straightened. "Then you are friends with Mr. Pope?"

"You know him?" His brow furrowed in surprise.

"I've met him. Is that why you are hiring laborers? To repair his house? I am ever so glad to hear that. I think it must have been a beautiful house in its time."

"It will be again, I'm sure."

There was a pause in the conversation, and Pru glanced through the window again. Mr. Clark was wrapping the fabric in paper. She turned back to Mr. Payne. "How will you guarantee their safety?"

"Whose? The laborers?"

"Yes. You know Mr. Pope shot a Scotsman just a few months ago."

He smiled. "I had heard that, yes. But he won't be shooting anyone while I am here."

"How can you be sure?"

"You ask a lot of questions, Miss Howard."

She shrugged. "Everyone says that. Oh, here comes Mrs. Northgate. Step over there or I shall have to explain why I am speaking to a man I don't know."

"But I introduced myself."

"Over there!" she hissed. Obligingly, he stepped aside, and Pru went to the shop door, opening it for Mrs. Northgate. She handed Pru the fabric.

"Now that's done. Shall we go home and begin?"

"If you're not too tired," Pru said, watching Mr. Payne out of the corner of her eye. He was paying them no attention, which was a relief.

"Tired? My girl, I have enthusiasm to spare! Come along now."

Still carrying the bundle, Pru hurried after her.

\*\*\*

"I have a letter from your father," Rowden said that evening at dinner.

Nash set down his fork. Up until that point, he'd actually been enjoying the meal. Rowden had purchased bread, soup, and pies in Milcroft and Mrs. Brown had managed to warm them up and present a decent dinner. But now Nash's stomach tightened. He peered at Rowden with his right eye but could not see the paper Rowden held. He could hear the man rattling it, though. "What does it say?"

"He's not sending the men from the asylum. Yet," Rowden said. "So you needn't look like you've been summoned to a funeral."

"Easy for you to say. You aren't threatened with spending the next twenty years in a strait-waistcoat."

"He does say," Rowden went on, "that he is coming for a visit."

"My *father* is coming for a visit?" Nash asked. This was difficult to believe. At the end of their last meeting, the earl had said he never wanted to see Nash again. The earl never said anything he did not mean.

"A representative is coming," Rowden said.

Nash relaxed slightly. He would not have to face his father again. Not yet. Perhaps not ever.

"I thought I had better mention this before the men arrived in the morning and began pounding and hammering. It will be a bad start if you shoot one of them before they've made any real progress."

Nash's hand went immediately to his pocket where his pistol lay comfortable against his hip. "Absolutely not. I will not have strangers traipsing about Wentmore."

"I've already made the decision. The men arrive tomorrow. They're not strangers. I've hired most of them from Milcroft."

"I said no."

"Nash, be reasonable. For once."

"Now you think I have gone mad too?" Nash asked, even as his hand curved around the butt of the pistol. He could hardly blame Rowden if he did think Nash daft. What other man walked around with a loaded pistol in his pocket and felt the need to touch it whenever distraught?

"I don't think you have gone mad, but you cannot see what I see."

"So you throw that in my face." Nash stood. "You think I am weak? I might be blind, but I'm not helpless." He lunged toward the form of Rowden, crashing into him and sending both of them tumbling to the floor. There was the sound of splintering wood—most likely the chair Rowden had been sitting in—and then the feel of Rowden's large hands pushing Nash off him. Nash rolled away and came up swinging. He missed with his first punch but landed the second. If the blow made any impact on Rowden, the man gave no sign. There was no exhalation of sound or an attempt to move away.

Nash struck again, but his fist sailed through empty space as Rowden ducked far more quickly than Nash could react. Nash climbed to his feet and Rowden was up too, moving backward and out of Nash's range.

"Stand still," Nash panted.

"You're behaving like an arse," Rowden said. "Hitting me won't solve anything."

"We'll see about that."

Nash lunged for Rowden, missed, tripped over a chair and cursed as pain shot through his knee.

"Are you finished?" Rowden asked.

"Come and fight me," Nash said. "Or are you afraid of being beaten by a cripple?"

"You're not a cripple, and you're not weak. But you can't see the state of this house and your father's representative—whoever that may be—can and will see it."

Nash was following the sound of Rowden's voice and the shadowy form of his large frame. He swung again, missed, and fell forward. Rowden moved out of the way, and Nash crashed into a wall.

"He will report back that not only do you carry a pistol in your pocket and brandish it at anyone who comes close, you live in a house damaged by fire and falling into ruin."

Nash struck again, and Rowden caught his fist in one hand, closed around it and yanked Nash close. So close Nash could feel his wine-scented breath on his face. He was almost ashamed that his first thought was to wonder where the wine was.

"The kitchen is scorched by fire and so is the back of the house."

Nash knew this. He could smell the charred wood when he passed that way. He made a point never to pass that way.

"The roof leaks in a dozen places. Furniture is broken and overturned. The paint is peeling, and I've seen more cobwebs than in a crypt in Paris."

"Let me go." Nash struggled against Rowden's hold.

"I haven't seen any rats, but that's probably because there's no food to be had. How Mrs. Brown even warmed this meal in that wreck of a kitchen is beyond me." He shoved Nash back, releasing him. "Any sane person who comes here will consider it uninhabitable. They will consider you mad, and that is *your* funeral."

Nash stood still, heaving with rage, his hand in his pocket on the pistol.

"So if you want to hit me for hiring laborers to make repairs to, in effect, save you from yourself, then go ahead.

Hit me." He moved closer, close enough that Nash could not miss if he struck.

Nash pulled the pistol free and pointed it at Rowden. "I could kill you."

"No doubt." Rowden did not sound frightened, only tired. "No doubt you want to kill me right now, but I am not your enemy, Nash. I've never been your enemy. If you want me to go, you don't have to shoot me. Say the word, and I'll leave. I'll go back to London, tell Draven I did my best, but that you were determined to ruin yourself. And you can start packing tonight because you'll be gone by the end of the week."

Nash held the pistol steady, the barrel aimed directly at Rowden's heart. It would take just a flick of his finger, a small muscle jerk, to fire the pistol and end Rowden's haranguing. The pistol might misfire, of course. It rarely did, but there was always that possibility. Rowden didn't move, though. He wasn't even breathing heavily. "You don't think I'll do it," Nash said. "You aren't even frightened."

Rowden made a dismissive sound. "You were beside me in the war, Nash. You've seen what I've seen, done what I've done. You think my own death scares me?" The question hung in the air like the smoke of a cigar. "Death doesn't scare me, and it doesn't scare you. It's life that scares you. Dying is easy. We can both die tonight. Pull that trigger, and I fall. Turn the pistol on yourself, and we're both gone."

The words had appeal. No more pain. No more regret. No more lying in bed, unable to sleep because he couldn't stop thinking of the way a soldier or a woman or a little boy had jerked and fallen to the ground when he'd pulled that trigger. "I don't want to see them anymore," Nash said. "I don't want to hear their cries, see the blood."

Rowden sighed. "I know. But there's no way around it. You live with what you've done, we all do. You want to die? I don't think you're a coward. None of us will blame you for it. We've all thought about ending it. Well, maybe not Rafe. He thinks far too highly of himself."

Nash smiled despite himself. He lowered the pistol. Rowden clapped him on the shoulder. "The men arrive at first light in the morning. Don't shoot them."

Nash put the pistol in his pocket. He was making no promises.

"And Nash?" Rowden said.

"What?"

"Point that pistol at me again, and I'll break your nose. Consider this a warning." Pain slammed into Nash's cheek as Rowden's fist connected with his face. Nash went down, his hand going to his face. He swore but Rowden was already walking away. Nash lay on the floor, knowing his cheek would be tender and probably bruised in the morning. Rowden could have knocked him unconscious, and he would have deserved that and worse. But Rowden wouldn't do him any favors, that was clear as the day Nash couldn't see any longer.

There was only a dark future stretching like an empty maw ahead of him, and he had to decide, every day, if he wanted to fight his way through it.

## *Six*

Pru was sorry she had ever asked Mrs. Northgate for assistance. The woman had very firm ideas about what a dress should look like—in particular, what a dress Pru wore should look like—and she was relentless in her vision. Pru had never had a dress with ribbons or flounces or any of the other fripperies other girls had. She always wore plain, serviceable dresses. That was what she had planned to make this time.

"That sort of pattern does not suit you at all," Mrs. Northgate said when Pru described her vision.

"But that's the sort of dress I am wearing right now," Pru pointed out.

"I know, and I think we should burn it."

"I can't burn all my dresses," Pru said, reasonably. "I won't have anything to wear."

"You will have this one to wear." Mrs. Northgate held up the fabric. "Now, that vicar of yours will probably not like this, but we need a lower neckline."

"A low neckline?" Pru's eyes widened.

"Not low. *Lower*. And ruffles and a ribbon at the bodice. Your bosom is small, but we can make it look more substantial with some additions and padding."

"But won't that mean people are looking at my bosom?"

"That's the point, my girl. Pay attention."

She went on to describe a narrow skirt and tight sleeves. Apparently, these features would show off her trim waist and give the illusion of lush hips. After an hour or so, Pru stopped arguing and simply did as Mrs. Northgate told her. By the third afternoon, when she arrived, Miss Northgate and Miss Mary simply called, "Grandmama, that girl is here again!" and told her to go up to the boudoir.

They'd reached the part of the process where Pru was sewing the pieces of the gown together. Mrs. Northgate said her eyes were too poor to do much sewing these days, but she saw every misplaced stitch Pru made. She also insisted on showing Pru how to sew ruffles and flounces, and Pru heartily wished she had never been shown as they were time consuming and detailed. She could hardly complain, though. Not only was Mrs. Northgate gracious—if that was a word that could ever be applied to Mrs. Northgate—enough to direct Pru's efforts, she had also given her a bit of ribbon and lace to add to the dress.

Not to mention, she liked coming to the Northgate house much more than sweeping clean floors at the vicarage or being shooed out of the kitchen by Mrs. Blimkin. The sewing was really not so bad once she found a rhythm. Mrs. Northgate often did not mind if Pru chattered on, but on this day Pru had been there several hours and had run out of things to say. She was sewing quietly, allowing her mind to run where it might. Often it went back to that day in the informal gardens at Wentmore when she had met Mr. Pope. She wondered how he was faring. The Northgates' son, George Northgate, had reported to his grandmother that the work on the house was coming along fairly well. George had been sent to offer the laborers cider and apples at a price during the midday break and at the end of the workday. He did not report having seen Mr. Pope, but he had told his grandmother everyone kept a watchful eye out as they expected he might emerge from the house at any moment and shoot them all dead.

Pru thought perhaps George Northgate feared that, but she imagined the laborers were too busy to think much about anything other than their work. She should know after all these days of laboring at sewing. But it did rankle that even the son of the well-to-do Northgate family had found a means to earn extra coin, while she still wore boots with holes.

If only she knew how to hammer or patch roofs. Perhaps she could help the housekeeper—was there a housekeeper?—put the inside of the house to rights. But then she would be taking work away from the daughter of a family who probably needed it. She would have done the chore for free if it meant she could see the inside of Wentmore or have another chance at a peek at the peacock. But traipsing through gardens and singing songs and sewing ruffles would be of no use to Mr. Pope.

And then Pru knew what would. She stabbed her finger with her needle and yelped in pain.

"I told you to be more careful!" Mrs. Northgate had a handkerchief at the ready, handing it to Pru before a drop of the blood welling on her finger could fall on the fabric.

Pru wrapped her finger. "Thank you. I wasn't paying attention."

"I should say not."

"It's just that I had the most wonderful idea. I don't know why I didn't think of it earlier."

"Fewer ideas and more concentrating on the task at hand, Miss Howard."

Pru stood and began to pace the room. Her thoughts were coming fast now, and she felt the need to move in order to keep up with them.

"Do sit down, Miss Howard. All this activity makes me dizzy."

"I apologize, ma'am. I am simply too excited to sew at the moment."

Mrs. Northgate watched Pru walk across the carpet and back again before she finally sighed and gave in. "What is this about? What notion has entered your head now?"

Pru paused right in front of Mrs. Northgate and leaned down, which caused the older woman to rear back slightly. "I know how to help Mr. Pope!"

"Do remember yourself, Miss Howard!"

Pru stepped back, choosing to clasp her hands together rather than jump up and down as she wanted. "Yes, Mrs. Northgate."

The older woman removed the spectacles she wore to criticize—er, *correct*—Pru and cleaned them on a small cloth. "Mr. Pope?" She held up a hand before Pru could explain. "Do not tell me. I know the name." There was a long pause. "Are you speaking of the Earl of Beaufort's son?"

"Yes!"

"The youngest? The one who lives at Wentmore?"

"The sharpshooter, yes." Pru sat on the edge of her chair. "He was blinded in the war."

Mrs. Northgate harrumphed. "From what I hear, his aim is still better than most who have perfect vision. You had better stay away from him. Now, pick up your sewing and finish that ruffle."

"But I can't stay away from him," Pru objected. "I want to help him."

Mrs. Northgate perched her spectacles on the tip of her nose. "Why?"

"Why? Why does anyone help anyone else?" The words were out before Pru realized who she had directed them to.

But Mrs. Northgate did not hesitate. "To feel better about themselves, I should imagine. Either that or because they feel sorry for the person in need. Mr. Pope will appreciate neither sentiment, I assure you."

"Is that why you are helping me?" Pru asked, gesturing to the sewing laid out on the table between them. "You feel sorry for me?"

"Feel sorry for you? Ha!" Mrs. Northgate laughed, and Pru thought it might have been the first time she had ever seen the other woman laugh. Her usually serious expression seemed to crack as her smile widened. Then her mouth opened, the lines at her eyes crinkled, and she gave another full-throated laugh. "I should think not. If there is anyone to pity, it would be me. You are a trial, Miss Howard."

"So you often tell me. Does this mean," she asked in a small voice, "you want everyone to pity you?" That possibility was even worse than the first option in Pru's opinion.

"Not at all. You amuse me, Miss Howard. That is the first reason." Mrs. Northgate leaned over the table conspiratorially. "And the second is that it annoys my daughter-in-law and grandchildren." She laughed again, and Pru just shook her head. Mrs. Northgate seemed to like nothing better than provoking others. It was a trait Pru had to admit, reluctantly, she admired.

"But I rather doubt you are helping Mr. Pope to annoy anyone. Neither can he be very amusing," Mrs. Northgate observed.

"Oh, but he can be amusing," Pru objected. Mrs. Northgate's brows shot up. "Not amusing in the traditional sense, but he is interesting to talk to. And then there is the peacock."

"The peacock!"

"Yes. The last time I was at Wentmore I spotted a peacock. Mr. Pope said there used to be several peacocks and peahens too."

Mrs. Northgate nodded. "I remember those birds. The earl was a fool for bringing them here."

"You saw them? How many were there? What did the house used to look like?"

"Too many questions! How is it you intend to help Mr. Pope? Why do you even think he needs your help? Did he ask for it?"

"No, but he doesn't know he needs my help. He probably doesn't even realize I *can* be of help. He may not even know *Ecriture Nocturne* exists."

*"Ecriture Nocturne?"*

"It means—"

"I speak French. It means night writing."

"Yes. I learned it in France. We were in Paris for some months just after the war. My parents had gone to the countryside for their missionary work but found the populace less than receptive to the idea of Protestant conversion from the English."

"I can imagine."

"While we were in Paris, we heard of a man named Charles Barbier. He developed a system of symbols that he thought might be used by the military for nighttime communication. But he had taught several blind people the system as well, and it allowed them to write and even read."

"How?"

"I'll show you. Do you have a sheet of parchment?"

Mrs. Northgate pointed to the small desk on the other side of the room. Pru rose and gathered parchment, pen, and ink. She drew a six by five matrix and labeled it with numbers along the top and side and then characters in the middle. "Do you see how the letter *N* is located at the number 5 on this axis and the letter 3 on this axis?"

"Yes." Mrs. Northgate peered over the table at the diagram.

"We would represent it with five dots in this column and three in this column. If the person reading the dots has memorized the location of the letters and sounds on the diagram, then he would know five dots and three dots is the letter *N*."

"I don't understand."

Pru was not deterred. She had plenty of experience teaching this. "Let's say we want to write the word *not*. We would write five dots then three dots for *N*, one dot then two dots for *O* and four dots then two dots for *T*." She turned the paper over and pressed gently on the opposite side, pushing the paper up slightly in the pattern of the dots. "A blind person would read this with their fingers." She turned the paper and ran her fingers lightly over the raised bumps. "They would read 5-2, 1-2, 4-2 and know the word was *not*."

Mrs. Northgate blew out a breath, seeming to consider the paper and the raised bumps. "This is for French," she said, pointing to the characters of è and é.

"I modified it for English."

"You modified it! Why on earth would you do that?"

"To teach my sister."

"You have a blind sister?" Before Pru could answer Mrs. Northgate waved a hand. "Never mind, I do not want to know. I do not want to encourage you in this, Miss Howard. This is all very strange and…unique, but Mr. Pope is quite mad and trying to teach him all of these letters and numbers will simply result in you ruining perfectly good paper." She crumpled the parchment and tossed it into the fire.

Pru frowned as her work began to smoke and blacken. Mrs. Northgate pushed the sewing across the table. "That ruffle will not finish itself, young lady."

But Pru ignored the material. "He is not mad. I spoke to him myself on two occasions. He is quite sane."

"He points a pistol at anyone who comes near and lives in utter squalor."

"It's not quite that bad." She did not mention he had pointed that pistol at her.

"He shot a man!"

"I am certain it was an accident."

"His father does not take your view of the matter. He is already making arrangements to have Mr. Nash Pope sent away."

Sent away? But where? Her own parents had considered sending her sister to a home for the blind, but Pru had talked them out of it. One heard stories of abuse in these so-called charitable homes. She had cared for her sister until Anne had learned to be independent.

"His own father would do that to him?" Pru rose, too upset to listen any longer.

"It is for his own good, not to mention the safety of those around him. Where are you going, Miss Howard? I have not given you leave."

"I have to go, ma'am. I am sorry. I will be back tomorrow."

Pru ran to the door, opened it, and rushed out.

"You had better not be planning to visit Wentmore!" Mrs. Northgate called after her. Pru ignored her and ran down the steps. At the bottom, Miss Northgate and Miss Mary were coming out of a small parlor, their mouths agape. Their mother, Mrs. Northgate, was right behind them.

"I will thank you not to charge down my steps like a stampede of horses," she said. Pru didn't dare slow down, though. She raced past them with a hasty apology, grabbed her coat from the rack, opened the door, and dashed out into the late afternoon.

She had no time to waste.

\*\*\*

Nash had not come out of his room since the pounding had begun. He found it all but unbearable. Even when he expected the next blow of hammer striking nail, he flinched. The cacophony reminded him too much of the noise of war, the sound of rifles firing. The dull thud when the ball hit its mark.

Nash closed his eyes and covered his ears. He didn't know how long he'd been in his room. Rowden would bring him food, force him to eat, then take the empty plate away again. This morning—or was it yesterday?—he had threatened to plunge Nash in a tub of water himself if Nash did not bathe. So Nash had done as he was told and sat with wet hair and a clean but damp shirt while the incessant hammering continued.

And then it stopped. Nash raised his head. He thought it might have stopped some time ago, only the ringing of it sounded in his ears for so long that he was only just noticing it. The quiet was such a welcome respite that he actually rose and stretched. His muscles ached from holding the same position for so long and from the tight way he'd curled himself. This chamber had been his haven for days, but now he wanted out. Surprisingly, he was hungry. He'd come to rely on Rowden bringing him meals. Nash didn't know what time it was, but it seemed past the time Rowden usually brought him a tray.

Nash didn't bother with a coat, but he pulled on his boots and left his room in shirt sleeves, his waistcoat open. He'd intended to call out for Rowden, but he heard voices after taking only a few steps. As he neared the staircase that led down to the first floor and the foyer, he recognized the voices—it was Rowden and Miss Howard.

Nash halted, feeling an unexpected surge of jealousy that Rowden should be speaking to his Miss Howard. The idea was unreasonable. She was not *his* Miss Howard. She was not his anything. He barely knew her. And yet, it annoyed him that Rowden also knew her. He stood at the top of the stairs, trying to decide whether he should go down or not, when their words began to penetrate.

"If you don't wish to pay me, I will do it for free," Miss Howard said.

*What the devil?*

"It's not that I mind paying you, Miss Howard. I think your efforts will be wasted."

Precisely what efforts was she wasting on Rowden?

"They are my efforts, Mr. Payne, and I believe Mr. Pope would benefit from them."

Nash simply could not keep quiet a moment longer. "How exactly would I benefit?" he asked, starting down the stairs. "And what are you offering?" He held the banister tightly as depth perception was not his strong suit these days.

"There you are, Mr. Pope!" she said, sounding genuinely happy to see him. Nash halted in the middle of the staircase. He could not remember the last time anyone had been happy to see him. No, he probably could remember. It had been during the war, and his fellow soldiers had been happy to see him. But this was the first time in years anyone had been happy to see him and not because he would kill someone for them. "Mr. Payne said you were indisposed, but I knew you would see me."

"It seems I have little choice, being that you are in my house."

"It's a beautiful house," she said as he reached the foyer and solid ground. "Or at least it was. I heard you were doing repairs, and I was so glad. I wanted to help in some way, but I couldn't think how I might help. I can't hammer or plaster or anything like that. And then I thought I might be able to help with the interior—"

"Miss Howard, get to the point," Mr. Payne said.

Nash was actually annoyed she had been cut off. He rather liked listening to her speak.

"The point? Oh, my proposal! Yes, then I remembered that I know *Ecriture Nocturne*. I met Monsieur Barbier in Paris, and I learned it from him. When I came home, I modified it and taught it to my sister. And now she is able to read and write a little."

Nash heard the rustling of paper, and then the scent and warmth of Miss Howard as she came near. She took his hand and placed a paper in it. "This is a letter my sister wrote to me."

He tried to hand the paper back. "I cannot see it."

"But you don't read it with your eyes," she said, pushing the paper back toward him. "You read it with your hands—well, your fingertips."

Nash stared at her, seeing only an amorphous form. She was slim and tall. That was about all he could determine with his one good eye.

"Miss Howard," Rowden said, "It's been a long day. Perhaps you could come back another time."

"Oh, of course. If you think that best." She sounded so disappointed, as though her whole world had crumbled.

"Wait," Nash said.

Miss Howard gasped. She actually gasped in excitement.

"Explain how I read this"—he shook the paper—"with my fingertips."

"Come here, and I will show you." She took his free hand in one of hers, her hand warm and slim and strong in his, and tugged him in the direction of the parlor. He did not like the parlor. It held unpleasant memories, but he went anyway because, well—how could he refuse? She led him so confidently.

"Here we are." She had guided him to a chair, and he felt for the arms then sat. She took his hand and placed it on top of the paper. He thought she would release him, but instead, she stood close beside him and took one of his fingers and tried to drag it across the paper. "Mr. Pope, you have to relax your hand and allow me to guide you," she said. He did as she said, if only because she stood so close to him. He could feel the heat of her body, and he caught the scent of her as she leaned close. She still smelled of pine and cinnamon as well as fresh air. He leaned closer to her, trying to catch more of her scent.

"Do you feel that?" she asked.

Unfortunately, he didn't feel anything. But he thought he could reach out and wrap a hand about her waist, pull her to his lap, and then he might feel something of interest. And then he realized she was speaking of his fingers. She was dragging his pointer finger over the rough edges of a piece of paper.

"It's the paper," he said.

"It's writing," she said.

Confused, he tried to concentrate on what his finger was touching. It was difficult with her hand on his, but focus was a discipline he had mastered, and gradually he was aware that his finger was touching a pattern of bumps in the paper.

"Is it a code?" he asked after a moment.

"In a way, yes. Monsieur Barbier created a type of writing where each set of dots on the paper corresponds to a letter. So this one"—she dragged his hand over a pattern—"is for *D* and this for *E* and this for *A* and this for *R*." Methodically, she placed his hand on each pattern and allowed him to feel it before moving to the next.

"This is a letter?" he asked.

"Yes. This is the salutation. You just read *Dear*." She sounded so very excited that it was difficult not to allow himself to become excited as well. But he'd also had years of training to tamp down any sort of emotion—excitement chief among them. He remained impassive.

"Who is the letter to?"

"Ah! Let's keep reading. This is a *P* and this is…" She trailed off.

"*E*?" he asked. "No, *R*."

"Yes! That is amazing. You learn very quickly."

"What's this?" he asked impatiently.

"That's a *U*."

"Pru? *Dear Pru*?" Could that be right?

"It's addressed to me," she said. "My Christian name is Prudence, but my family call me Pru."

Prudence. Nash felt like laughing at the irony. This woman was anything but prudent. "Then this is a letter from your family?"

"It's from my sister, yes." She was still holding his hand in hers, and she seemed to be absently stroking his fingers as she spoke. He did not pull away. In fact, he held very still, hoping she would not notice and cease. How long had it been since someone had held his hand? How long since he had been touched or caressed like this? Her hand on his was like a drink of cold water to a man who has been wandering in the desert.

"She is blind?" he asked, his voice a bit hoarse.

"Yes. She became sick with fever about ten years ago in Constantinople. She was burning hot for days, and it seemed nothing we could do would cool her down. We would put a cool cloth on her forehead, and a minute later it would be hot to the touch. She finally recovered, but the doctor said the high fever damaged her eyes."

"Where is she now?" he asked. His heart had started to pound. He was afraid he knew the answer. She was in an asylum. Miss Howard had said her parents were missionaries. Certainly, they would not take a blind girl to the Far East if they would not take their daughter who could see. And what else was there to do with a someone who could not see? They were useless.

"She is married and lives in London," Miss Howard said, shocking Nash to the core. "In fact, in this letter she says she has been approached by a wealthy family to teach their young son *Ecriture Nocturne*."

"*Ecriture Nocturne*? Night writing?"

"Yes. Oh, you speak French?"

"Among other languages, yes. This is something being taught?"

"Well, Monsieur Barbier did not specifically intend it to be used by the blind. He was hoping the military or diplomatic corps might find it of use. I believe he has petitioned them repeatedly, but he does realize the usefulness it might have for the blind. He was happy to meet with me and my parents and show it to us when we were in Paris a few years ago. And then I came home and taught Anne. It took her about six months to learn it, but I can see you would learn much more quickly. Now she writes to me, and I write to her using this method. It takes longer than it might to write in the usual way, but with practice it becomes quite second nature. Are you interested in learning?" She paused but not quite long enough for him to answer.

"Oh, say you are. Mr. Payne said it would be a waste of time, but I think it will be useful for you. As I said, I wanted to find a way to help here at Wentmore, and I'm not very good with a hammer and I did not want to take cleaning work away from someone who needs the money desperately. But then my own boots do have holes and I could use a new pair. But that's neither here nor there." She went on, and Nash almost forgot to listen to her actual words. The sound of her voice was pleasant enough. It was low and soothing and comforting. She had a pleasant, happy tone that made him feel all was right with the world, even when he knew that was far from true.

"And then I was sewing in Mrs. Northgate's boudoir and I had the most wonderful idea. Of course, I wish I had not had it with a needle in my hand as I stabbed my finger, and it still hurts."

Nash heard a frustrated sigh from behind and realized Rowden must be standing in the doorway, listening impatiently to her chatter on.

"But Mrs. Northgate had a cloth at the ready, and I did not spill any blood on the ruffles I was sewing, which is fortunate because it took me almost a full day to learn how to sew them to her satisfaction." She squeezed his hand to emphasize her struggle. "What was I saying? Oh, yes! My idea. I was still thinking about you and how I might help, and I realized I could teach you *Ecriture Nocturne*. And that's when I left my sewing and came straight here. Well, not straight here. I stopped at the vicarage to fetch Anne's letter because I thought it might be easier to show you what night writing is as opposed to trying to tell you."

"You were thinking about me?" Nash asked.

"The mind does wander when one is sewing. I was thinking about Wentmore and new boots and you and the peacock. Have you seen him again? Well, you can't see him, but has anyone reported seeing him? I looked for him on my way here but didn't spot him. I suppose it has been too busy and loud. But I can already see the progress. Oh, I should put your hand down now," she said, and placed it on the paper.

Nash wished she would pick it up again. Instead, he traced his fingers over the raised points. He could not find the place where the letter began, where her name was written, but he liked to think his finger traced it.

"Rowden," Nash said, "have you been listening?"

"Unfortunately."

"I think you should hire Miss Howard."

"*He* hire me?" Miss Howard squeaked. "But I thought I would teach you."

"I can't be your employer and your pupil," Nash said. There was no reason he could not pay her himself, but he would rather she not be beholden to him for a salary.

"You're sure about this?" Rowden asked.

"Absolutely. Miss Howard needs new boots, and I would like to learn this night writing."

Rowden muttered something that sounded like a curse. "Very well, Miss Howard, shall you and I adjourn to the library and discuss terms?"

"She starts tomorrow," Nash said. "She can come at the same time as she did today. Does that suit, Miss Howard?"

"Yes! I could come earlier, if you would rather."

"No." Nash and Rowden said it at the same time. There was no point in having her here when the workmen were about, making him jumpy and nervous.

"I see. I will just wait in the library then."

Nash heard her footsteps retreat. He turned and saw the shape of Rowden still in the doorway. "You're sure about this?" Rowden asked.

"Pay her whatever she asks."

"I'll pay her what's fair. Don't expect me to play chaperone."

"I don't need a chaperone."

Rowden made a dismissive sound. "Just remember she is under the vicar's care. If you cause trouble, the whole village will be at your door. I'm trying to keep you out of the asylum, not hasten your departure."

"There's no need for the warning."

"There's every need," Rowden said. "But I doubt you will heed it."

## *Seven*

"It's a very bad idea," Mrs. Northgate said as she pinned the fabric of Pru's dress at the waist. "Hold still."

"Yes, ma'am." Holding still was difficult today. Pru was impatient to be done with her sewing and off to Wentmore. Of course, Mr. Payne had told her not to come until afternoon, when the workers were done, so she really need not be in a hurry. She had two hours at least before she would be expected at the great house.

"I never thought Higginbotham had any sense," Mrs. Northgate was saying. "I am not pleased to have been correct." She gave Pru a narrow look, all the pricklier for the pins sticking out of her mouth. "You told the vicar you would be at Wentmore?"

"Yes."

"With that madman?"

"He is not a madman, but yes, I told Mr. Higginbotham I would be tutoring Mr. Pope."

Mrs. Northgate stepped back. "You mentioned you would be there alone?"

"I won't be alone," Pru said. "Mr. Payne is there"—Mrs. Northgate waved her arms dismissively at the mention of Mr. Pope's friend—"as is Mrs. Brown, the housekeeper. In fact, I met her yesterday and she was very kind."

"Oh, Mrs. Brown is a saint, to be sure. Step down and take it off."

Pru moved behind a privacy screen and struggled out of the dress.

"Be careful!" Mrs. Northgate warned. Pru rolled her eyes. She was being careful. If not, she would have been out of the infernal dress already. When Pru emerged, back in her ugly pea-green dress, Mrs. Northgate dramatically raised a hand to her eyes. "I beg you not to wear that...*thing* in my presence again."

"Yes, ma'am."

Pru sat again, glancing surreptitiously at the clock on the mantel. She wondered if the hands were stuck. They had not moved.

"Mrs. Brown will not help you if that madman decides to shoot you. She could not do anything but bandage the Scot after he'd been injured." Mrs. Northgate laid the dress on the table, adjusting it and eyeing the pins critically. "And there were two ladies with him as well. They were fortunate Pope did not shoot them."

Pru cocked her head. This was the first she had heard of any ladies at Wentmore. "Who were the ladies? Were they also Scottish?"

"I couldn't say, but one came into the village and she had a monstrous dog with her, and he terrorized the farmers for weeks."

"The ladies visited at Wentmore for weeks?"

"Of course not! They left as soon as they saw the state of the great house. Poor Lord Beaufort."

"But you said the dog—"

"The point is, Miss Howard, that Wentmore is not safe for a young lady such as yourself."

"It cannot be any more dangerous than Constantinople or Rome." She would not mention Cairo as that had not ended well.

"Your parents should have never taken you to such places."

"They were doing the Lord's work," Pru said. She sounded so much like her mother in that moment that she almost winced. "And that's what Mr. Higginbotham said. I will be doing the Lord's work at Wentmore."

Mrs. Northgate blew out a breath. "Do not say I did not warn you." She peered at Pru. "I can see asking you to do any more sewing today is futile. Your mind is elsewhere."

"I was thinking about the peacocks," Pru said, relieved Mrs. Northgate would not ask her to pick up the needle and thread. Though she enjoyed Mrs. Northgate's company, Pru did not enjoy sewing. She should be in a hurry to finish her dress so she could wear it. Even though it was not done, Pru could tell it would be the most beautiful dress she had ever owned. Not because it was made of silk or covered with embroidery, because it was not. But because Mrs. Northgate had been right about the ruffles and flounces. Pru had worried those embellishments would make her look silly, but they really did flatter her. The ruffles at her bosom gave it more fullness and the flounces on the hem balanced out her height and long legs. She looked a bit less like a…well, she looked down at her green dress. She looked less like a string bean.

And Mrs. Northgate had been correct about the color as well. Pru could see the warm reddish brown made her skin look pinker and brought out the color of her eyes and hair. She didn't look quite so drab and brown as usual, and though she would never be a beauty, she knew she would look well in the dress.

"Peacocks?" Mrs. Northgate said. "Whyever would you think of peacocks?"

"I suppose I hope to spot the one at Wentmore again. You said before you remember when the earl brought them to the great house. Tell me about it."

"I hardly think what you saw was one of the original peacocks. The earl must have brought them to the house twenty years ago."

"Oh, but it could be," Pru said. "One of the missionaries we stayed with in Constantinople told me he had known one of the peacocks there for twenty-five years."

"He had *known* the peacock?"

"Yes. The bird was quite tame, though not friendly. The man used to bring the bird a few pieces of bread, and the peacock would take the bread from the man's hand. I even fed him myself, though the missionary did caution me not to try and touch the bird. They will peck if threatened. And they can fly. The peacock would roost in a tree near the house where we stayed, and its call was quite awful. The sound was like a baby crying or a cat yowling. Still, I miss that cry some mornings. It was so much more intriguing than a rooster's crow. Do you know I named the peacock? I called him Ahmet."

"You are a strange girl," Mrs. Northgate said, but her tone was one of fondness.

"Won't you tell me about the peacocks the earl brought?" Pru asked. "You said you remembered when they arrived."

Mrs. Northgate sat back in her chair, which caught Pru's attention. The woman usually sat straight as an arrow. "I do remember it," she said, her eyes fixed on the window just over Pru's shoulder. Pru almost looked to see what was on the window ledge that had caught Mrs. Northgate's attention. "He unveiled them at a garden party. Most of the village was invited, and we all attended. The earl and his family were at Wentmore for several months of each year. We saw the children in the village. They were polite, though the boys were a bit wild, I must say."

"How many children were there?"

Mrs. Northgate's gaze snapped back to Pru. "I thought you wanted to hear about the peacocks?"

"I want to hear about everything."

"You are too curious by far," Mrs. Northgate chided before tapping a finger to her chin. "How many children? Let me see. There were the three boys, and goodness, how many girls? The eldest was a girl and there was another in there and then a little one as well. How many is that?"

*Sweet Rogue of Mine* | 137

"Six children. Three boys and three girls."

"The girls were very pretty and well-behaved. At that garden party they all wore white dresses with blue sashes. Very pretty."

Before Mrs. Northgate could give more particulars about dresses worn twenty years ago, Pru thought it wise to turn the conversation. "Did they seem to be a happy family?"

"Happy enough, I suppose. I don't see how anyone could be happy with those two wild boys. The youngest—your pupil—was the best behaved of the lot. Who would have thought he would have turned out as he has? Though none of us were surprised he went into the army."

"Why is that?"

"Oh, he had a gift. He gave a demonstration that day. It was a shooting competition."

Pru gasped. "Not the peacocks!"

"Oh, you and your peacocks! No peacocks were harmed. The men were shooting at clay pots on a fence." Her gaze strayed to the window again and she smiled faintly. "The earl had the men stand quite a distance away, and the men complained that no one could hit the targets from that distance. Oh, but they tried. A few hit one or two pots, as I recall. But as more and more of the men failed, they began to complain.

"And then Master Nash walks up with his rifle—"

"Master Nash? Is that Mr. Pope?"

Mrs. Northgate pursed her lips, obviously annoyed at the interruption. "He was Master Nash then. He walked to the line and shouldered his rifle. Well, the other men began to chuckle. How was this boy—he couldn't have been more than ten—to hit those clay pots?" She chuckled to herself and shook her head.

"And what happened?" Pru asked, impatience getting the best of her.

"Well, the earl told his son to wait just a moment. We all thought he would save the boy the pain of embarrassment, but he told the lad to take ten steps back."

"Back?"

"Yes, *farther* from the pots. Well, everyone was murmuring, and even the women who cared little for such displays had come to watch now. The noise and mutterings did not seem to penetrate that head of Master Nash. He was as cool as could be. He lifted the rifle, sighted the pots, and fired. One by one, he hit every single pot—ten in a row—and knocked them off the fence.

"You could have heard a pin drop," Mrs. Northgate said, her gaze finding Pru's. "We were all so shocked. The boy had focus and steadiness and an eye like we'd never seen. I imagine it was harder on him than it would be for most when he lost his vision. Drove him mad, it seems."

Pru sat back now too. "I don't think he's mad. I think he's just sad."

"Well, we all feel sad from time to time, but not all of us go about brandishing pistols and shooting Scotsmen!"

That was true. There was the sound of voices from below, and Pru recognized the low tenor of George Northgate. When she looked back at Mrs. Northgate, the older woman was watching her. "It seems my grandson has finished for the day."

Pru straightened. "Do you think I might go to Wentmore now?" Her gaze strayed to the clock. It was still more than ninety minutes before she had planned to depart.

"I am not the person to answer that question."

"Oh." Pru sat still, but her body vibrated.

"Go ahead and ask my grandson. I can see we will accomplish nothing else here today."

"Thank you, ma'am!" Pru jumped up and ran to the door. Then, impulsively, she ran back and kissed Mrs. Northgate on the cheek.

"Oh, do control yourself, girl!" Mrs. Northgate said, but she was smiling when she said it.

Pru made herself walk down the stairs. Halfway down, Mr. George Northgate looked up at her. He was speaking with his mother. The younger Mrs. Northgate glanced at Pru then pointedly ignored her. But her son nodded his head to her. "Good afternoon, Miss Howard."

"Mr. Northgate." She reached the bottom of the stairs.

"And how is my grandmama? It is so good of you to sit with her. She has been in need of a companion for some time."

Pru had not been hired as a lady's companion, which she thought Mr. Northgate knew well enough, but she ignored the statement for the moment. "Have you been at Wentmore, sir?"

"I have, but"—and he looked at his mother as though to explain to her as well—"the workers were dismissed early."

"Why?" Mrs. Northgate asked, still ignoring Pru.

"No reason was given. The man who is paying them came out and told them they could go home. He handed out wages, and I sold what cider and apples I could and came home myself." He looked at Pru again. "Are you done for the day? Is your dress finished?"

At this, Mrs. Northgate actually looked at Pru, as though she was wondering when this person would be out of her house for good.

"Not yet, but I have another errand."

"I won't keep you then," George said. Pru nodded and gave a smile to him and Mrs. Northgate. Mrs. Northgate looked away, and Pru gathered her coat and set off for Wentmore. The day was damp and overcast, and Pru imagined the men who had been let go for the day were glad to be home and before a warm fire. She rather hoped Mr. Pope had a warm fire waiting.

She hoped he remembered she was coming.

Mostly, she hoped he didn't shoot her.

\*\*\*

Nash could not have said why he was nervous. It wasn't as though it mattered to him whether or not he learned night writing. Even if he knew it, the only person he would be able to correspond with was Miss Howard. She probably wrote long, rambling letters that went on for pages.

The door of the dining room opened, and Nash forgot his pacing. But it wasn't Miss Howard. He recognized the large shape of Rowden.

"Is she here?" Nash asked.

"Who? Mrs. Brown?"

"Miss Howard."

"Ah! I forgot she was to come today. I have to go out."

"Where?" Nash asked, suddenly not wishing to be alone should Miss Howard not make an appearance.

"I'm going to Blunley to eat dinner and perhaps raise a glass." Blunley was the closest village to the east. It was a bit larger than Milcroft and boasted an inn and posting house.

"Mrs. Brown is making dinner."

"Forgive me, Nash, but while your Mrs. Brown makes do with what she has, cooking is not her strong suit. I want music, people, edible fare. You can come with me if you like."

"No," Nash said suddenly. He could not imagine the confusion and disorientation of being in a place like that without his ability to see.

"Come on," Rowden said. "Aren't you tired of this place? Let's get out. We'll find some pretty girls, perhaps find some trouble."

"You will find trouble and end up in a fight."

"Nothing wrong with a good fight. It cleanses the palate."

"Miss Howard is coming."

"Right." There was a long pause. "Well, then I'll see you in the morning. Don't wait up for me."

He closed the door, and Nash reached into his pocket for the pistol. It was still there. He touched it for reassurance, then stiffened as he heard a voice in the foyer. *Her* voice. She must have been at the door when Rowden opened it. Before he was ready for her, the door opened and she walked into the dining room, crossing directly to him. He almost took a step back, but she grasped his hand and shook it.

"Mr. Pope, how are you?" Her hand was cold, and she smelled of the wind and the damp fields she must have crossed walking there. "Did I interrupt dinner?" Pause. "Oh, but there's no food on the table. Why are you in here?"

"I like it in here," he said. He was aware he should release her hand, but he liked the feel of it. He wanted to warm it.

"Perhaps we should sit in a room with a fire," she said, not trying to pull her hand away. In fact, she squeezed his hand as though she understood his need for contact. Abruptly, Nash released her.

"You're cold. I should have thought of that."

"I am a bit chilled, but if you prefer this room—"

"We'll go to the library." He didn't know why he suggested the library. His only association with the library had been his father. But she would think him strange if he changed his mind now. She did not move, and he realized she was waiting for him to lead the way. *Idiot*! It was as though he had forgotten how to behave when he had lost his sight. "This way," he finally said, moving around her.

Of course, as soon as he began to walk, he realized he did not want her following him, watching him. He navigated the house by touch. He could see the outlines of shapes, but he couldn't always trust his limited vision. Sometimes the shapes were shadows and not objects at all. More than once he had walked into a chair or avoided nothing but a shadow. He debated walking without touching chairs and walls as he went, but then he decided that he would look more a fool if he tripped over something than if he moved carefully.

"How are the repairs coming?" she asked from behind him.

"How should I know?" He realized immediately he had answered too sharply, but it was a ridiculous question. "In case my stumbling about hasn't made it clear enough, I cannot see."

"Oh." The tone of her voice was that of one who has come to understand more than what the speaker has imparted.

Nash turned to face her. "What does that mean?"

"Oh? It's a common acknowledgement used in speech."

"That's not how you said it. You said, *oh*. Like, *oh, now I see*."

"I suppose you are right," she said. It surprised him that she did not argue or try to deny it. "I suppose I should have known you would be angry, but I thought you might have moved past that."

"What are you talking about?"

"When my sister became blind, she went through a similar phase. At first, she was in denial. Even when the doctor told her she would never see again, she didn't believe him. She would insist she saw some light or the shape of something."

Nash could remember these same feelings when he had been in recovery in France. The doctor had told him he would not see, but he hadn't wanted to believe. He thought if he just rested his eye longer or tried a salve or prayed hard enough, his sight would come back.

"When she realized her sight wasn't coming back, she became angry. She would throw things and scream and...well, she generally made it hard for anyone to be around her."

She didn't go on, but Nash knew she was implying he was similar—difficult to be around. Nash remembered feeling the rage Miss Howard's sister had exhibited as well. That was when his father had sent him to Wentmore. Nash had gone willingly because he'd been so angry that he wanted to be alone. He wanted to curse and scream and destroy. But he wasn't about to discuss this with Miss Howard, though it interested him that her sister had a similar experience. He'd thought he was alone in how he'd felt.

"The library is this way," he said, feeling his way again.

"I didn't mean to suggest you could *see* the progress of the repairs," Miss Howard said. Why the devil was she bringing it up again? "There are other ways to evaluate it."

"Don't you think it's wise to change the topic?" he asked as he finally reached the door to the library. He opened it, and she walked past him to enter.

"Oh, no. If I show you any sense of fear or weakness, you will exploit it. I can't back down."

Nash stood quite still. She spoke as though she were in the boxing ring, facing off against Rowden. "You are a tutor, not my opponent."

"I am probably a bit of both," she said, sounding good-natured about it. "Do you mind if I put another piece of kindling on the fire?"

Nash realized Rowden or Mrs. Brown had probably banked the fire, and the room was growing cold. "I should do that," he said.

"Oh, I am quite capable. Would you find a few sheets of parchment we might use? I want to teach you the first few letters and corresponding places on the chart."

Nash made his way to the desk, managed not to hurt himself going around the sharp corners, and sat in the seat his father had sat in for so many years. He could remember sitting in this chair when he'd been so small his feet did not even touch the ground. He could remember swinging them and playing at being the earl, though even then he had known he would never inherit the title. His father had laughed and tousled his hair.

Nash pushed the memory away and opened the drawer, feeling for paper. He pulled out several sheets.

"Do you mind if I light the lamp?" Miss Howard asked.

"Go ahead." He refrained from pointing out that it did not aid him one way or the other. She bustled around, seeming more comfortable in the library than he had ever been. Finally, she sat across from him and went to work writing something. At least that's what he assumed from the sounds of pen nib tinkling as it met the edge of the ink well and then scratching on paper. Nash was content to sit quietly, listening to her write and the crackle of fire.

He had missed the company of others. Nash didn't care to admit it even to himself, but he had been relieved when Rowden arrived. The silence and darkness had seemed to be closing in on him, and it was not difficult to imagine he was indeed going mad. But Rowden was a fighter. He lived to rankle and challenge and stir up discord. He clearly saw that as his task with Nash. And while Nash could admit he had needed a kick in the arse, he didn't like it any more than the next man.

"Come sit beside me," Miss Howard said.

"I thought we would sit across from each other," Nash said. He didn't know why he was arguing. He didn't mind sitting beside her. In fact, he rather liked the idea. But arguing had become second nature, he supposed.

"No," she said simply. Her voice was not stern or angry. It was just a statement of fact: *No, they would not sit across from each other.*

And Nash, even as he wanted to kick himself, felt compelled to argue. "I would prefer to sit here."

"No," she said again, just pleasant as you please.

Now, even if he wanted to sit beside her, he could not. Nash did not lose in battle. His aim was always true, and he always brought his opponent down. Even on that day when—no, he would not think of *that* day.

"You come sit beside me," he said.

"There are two chairs here and room for our legs. Come, Mr. Pope, stop stalling. There is nothing to fear. I can already tell you will catch on quickly."

*Was* he stalling? *Was* he afraid? He had never been afraid in his life. Not until he had opened his eyes and seen only blackness.

"Need I remind you, Miss Howard, we have no chaperone. Perhaps it would be safer for you if I remained over here."

There was a long pause. "Really?" she said, sounding, not afraid, but amused. "You would behave like a scoundrel?"

Hold a moment. Now she sounded almost excited.

"What are you planning? Improper advances or will you go so far as to ravish me?"

Nash stood. "You think because I am blind I cannot overpower you and have my way with you?"

"Have your way with me? Oh, my!"

"Are you laughing at me, Miss Howard?"

"No! I'm simply amazed, Mr. Pope. Few men have ever deigned to look askance at me, and now one can hardly restrain himself in my presence."

"I wouldn't put it that way."

"Then you *can* restrain yourself?" She sounded almost disappointed.

Nash placed both hands on the desk. "Should you not be afraid I might carry through on one of these warnings?"

"I can defend myself," she said. "I have had to navigate the streets of Cairo and Paris and London. I'm not one of your ladies who has a footman trotting behind her, so I know the value of a well-aimed kick. Still, I cannot promise to defend myself. Perhaps I might enjoy your improper advances."

Nash had to sit again. He had forgotten that he had met her singing "Bonny Black Hare."

"I've shocked you," she said.

"I have not shocked you," he retorted.

"I don't shock easily."

Was that a challenge? Nash accepted.

"If you prefer to sit there, you may, but then perhaps we can chat until you are ready to move and begin the lesson."

"You want to chat?"

"I have been wondering about the peacock we saw a couple of weeks ago. Has he been spotted again?"

"I have no idea."

"I suppose all the workmen frightened him away. Do you think he is one of the original peacocks your father brought here? I was asking Mrs. Northgate about it, and she said there was a huge garden party and a shooting exhibition. Apparently, you amazed everyone with your skills."

"I don't want to talk about that." He hadn't thought of that day in years. He did not want to think of it now.

"She did not say whether the party was to celebrate the arrival of the peacocks, but that was what I assumed."

"Who is Mrs. Northgate?"

Silence. "You do not know Mrs. Northgate? She's lived in Milcroft for—well, probably all of her life. Which is a long time. She came to the garden party. She would have been younger then."

"Obviously." They had all been younger then. He had been nine? Ten? "What is this Mrs. Northgate to you?"

"She is helping me sew a dress. Most of mine are quite ugly and Mrs. Blimkin said that Mrs. Northgate has a better sense of fashion than almost anyone else in Milcroft. And of course, if anyone were to look at Miss Northgate or Miss Mary, it's obviously true."

Nash couldn't keep up with all the names or connections, but he thought he was beginning to understand that Miss Howard was not like other women he had known. Nash had never met a woman who would admit her dresses were ugly or that men did not fall fawning at her feet. Nash would admit he was no judge of fashion, but he found it difficult to believe men did not fall at Miss Howard's feet. She seemed refreshingly forthright and plainspoken. Against his better judgment, he could feel himself being charmed by her. He wondered what she looked like. He could make out the general shape of her. Compared to Rowden's hulking form, she was slim but not short. She was tall and at times seemed more like a wisp of something than an actual form.

"What color is your dress today?" he asked.

"This one?" She sounded almost embarrassed. "I must confess, it's quite the ugliest dress I have ever seen. It's the color of old mashed peas. It makes me despondent every time I look down at it. That's all the more reason I should have stayed at Mrs. Northgate's and worked on my new dress, but when young Mr. Northgate came home and said you had sent all the workers home for the day, I could not wait to come here and see you."

She could not wait to see him?

"Why did you send the workers home early?"

"I was tired of the infernal pounding."

"I see we have something in common."

He could not see that at all. They seemed to have nothing in common. "What's that?"

"We were both looking for an escape today."

Nash found it difficult to believe she would see Wentmore as an escape. It felt more like a prison to him most days.

"If you do not wish to study *Ecriture Nocturne* today, would you like to do something else?"

She really did not seem to realize he was blind and could do nothing.

"We could play chess," she suggested.

Nash snorted. "How am I to play chess?"

"Have you played before?"

"Of course."

"I will simply tell you what move I make, and you keep the image of the board in your head. Or, if you prefer, I could read to you. Or I imagine you have a pianoforte in the drawing room. I play terribly, but I can sing loudly enough to hide my mistakes."

"Yes, I am familiar with your singing." And he rather wondered what she would sing and play on the piano, should he agree to listen. But that he would save for another time. He found he really did want to learn this *Ecriture Nocturne*. If only because he could sit beside her, and perhaps she would take his hand again. Pathetic that he was reduced to hoping a woman in a self-described ugly dress would touch his hand, but he was just desperate enough to forgo his pride.

"Show me this night writing," he said, rising and moving carefully around the desk. He felt for the chair, and she took his hand and guided him to the back of the empty one beside her.

He sat, half hoping she would continue to hold his hand, but she released it. "Are you ready?" she asked.

"For what?"

"To close your eyes and imagine."

## *Eight*

Pru was almost glad Mr. Pope could not see her. The looks he gave her were really quite amusing. It seemed almost everything she said puzzled him. His brow would furrow and his lips quirk and he would shake his head slightly as though he had not heard correctly. How she wished she could move the lock of hair that fell over one side of his face. She wanted to see his entire expression. She imagined his left eye must be damaged in some way, else he would not want to hide it.

She liked that he had moved to sit beside her. He smelled so lovely, like soap and starch and just a hint of tobacco. Or perhaps the tobacco smell came from the room. She could certainly picture men smoking and clinking glasses of brandy in this space. A large desk all but squatted in the center of the room. Behind it were shelves of books that reached all the way to the ceiling. Pru itched to run her hand along the spines of those books and read the titles. She had read a few already. Those closest to her seemed to be histories of wars she had either never learned about or forgotten. Still, they had to be more interesting than the books of sermons in the vicar's library.

More shelves of books lined part of the wall behind her, broken by a large hearth where she had built up the fire. An arrangement of chairs upholstered in cranberry and blue had been placed there, and she'd seen the chess set on a table between two of the chairs. She wondered how long it had been since anyone had played with that set and felt sorry for the pieces who had been so long neglected.

The curtains had been closed tight at the window, and Pru also had the urge to open them and peer at the view. It was probably nothing extraordinary—the overgrown lawn and hedgerows. But she could not help being curious.

"Why do I have to close my eyes?" Mr. Pope asked. Oh, but he was stubborn and determined to be difficult. She hadn't expected this to be easy. In fact, she had not really thought he would allow her to teach him anything today. So he was not quite as difficult as she'd supposed.

"Because I want you to imagine."

"I don't need to close my eyes to imagine."

"I do, and we will do this activity together." She turned toward him and took his hands in hers. "Now close your eyes. Close them. There you go. No, keep them closed." She squeezed his hands in reassurance when he did as she asked.

Then she closed her own eyes. "Now I want you to imagine a square, Mr. Pope. Do you have the image of a square in your mind?"

"Yes." He was very still, but she felt the slight tremor of his hands on hers.

"Good. Imagine it drawn on a sheet of parchment. It fills the parchment and is outlined in black ink."

"Fine." His hands tightened and then released in hers.

"Now we will fill in the details about this square. It is full of smaller squares. Thirty-six, to be precise. In your mind, divide the square into thirty-six smaller squares. Across the top, number the first row of squares one to six. Then do the same along the side."

"Go on," he said when she did not speak for a moment.

"I am writing the numbers in the squares," she said. "You cannot possibly be done. It takes a moment to write each."

"I can write very quickly in my imagination."

She huffed, determined not to lose her patience. "It is important that you remember this square, so you must take your time."

"Fine."

They sat there, hands clasped, eyes closed.

"Am I interrupting?"

Pru jumped and released Mr. Pope's hands as though she had been caught doing something she should not. Mr. Pope did not seem surprised at the intruder. He had probably heard her coming. "What is it, Mrs. Brown?" he asked calmly.

"I have your dinner, sir. If you want it, that is."

Mr. Pope had not turned toward Mrs. Brown, and now he tilted his head up toward Pru, who had risen to her feet. A woman in a white cap, plain dark blue dress, and a clean apron stood in the doorway. She was plump with graying hair and a kind smile.

"Have you eaten yet, Miss Howard?" Mr. Pope asked.

"Me?" she asked.

He raised his brows as though to ask who else he might be speaking to.

"No, but Mrs. Blimkin will set something aside for me."

"Mrs. Blimkin?" Mrs. Brown asked. "You must be the vicar's charge then. I didn't realize that when we met yesterday."

"I am, Mrs. Brown. Do you know the vicar?"

"Oh, I know everyone. I am sure you will want to wait and save your appetite for Mrs. Blimkin's fare. She is certainly a better cook than I."

"Oh." Pru did not want to hurt Mrs. Brown's feelings. "I doubt that is true."

"I don't," Pope said.

"Mr. Pope!"

"It's true," Mrs. Brown said. "I was a maid, not a cook, and well, Mr. Payne has replenished the larders to some degree, but he is a man and doesn't know what we need and—"

"Say no more, Mrs. Brown. I understand completely. But I do not mind simple fare. I am quite used to it."

"You'll join me then?" Mr. Pope asked.

"I would be happy to eat Mrs. Brown's dinner," Pru said.

"Bring it in here, Mrs. Brown," Mr. Pope directed. "We're in the middle of a lesson, and I don't want to keep Miss Howard too late. We will eat and…study."

"Yes, sir." She hurried away, and Pru sat in her seat and smacked Mr. Pope lightly on the arm.

"What was that for?"

"How could you criticize her cooking? I'm certain she is doing her best."

"I should hope not," he said.

"Mr. Pope!"

"Don't chastise me until you taste it."

"I am certain it will be delicious. I should speak to Mrs. Blimkin and have her intercede. The farmers and merchants in Milcroft do not know Mr. Payne, and he would not know where to go to get the best flour or produce. I can have Mrs. Blimkin choose some items for the larder and have them sent."

"Why would you do that?"

Pru was at a loss for words for a moment. The answer seemed obvious. "To be helpful."

"Why do you want to help me?" He seemed genuinely not to understand.

"I like you," Pru said.

His head jerked up as though he'd been surprised by a loud noise. Was he stunned that she enjoyed his company? Why was that difficult to believe?

"Shall we continue with our exercise?" she asked. "We were imagining our six-by-six square." She took her seat beside him again. "And we had added the numbers one through six along the top. These are the columns. And the rows along the side are numbered as well."

Pope shook his head. "I'm having trouble imagining it."

"Just close your eyes," Pru said, doing that herself. "When you have the picture in your mind, then think about the square that would be in column one and row one. In square one-one, we have the letter *A*."

"This isn't working," he said. Pru opened her eyes. Pope was slumped in his chair, looking despondent.

"You mustn't give up, Mr. Pope. You had the square in your mind before."

"I did, but now..." He shrugged. "Perhaps if you held my hands again."

Pru narrowed her eyes. She was not so innocent or inexperienced as to not see what he was doing. "If you wanted to hold my hands, you might simply ask," she said.

"It's all in the name of education, Miss Howard."

"Of course." She placed her hands in his again. "Now, close your eyes and picture the square."

"Ah, now I have it. Yes, that's quite clear."

His hands were warm and heavy as they lay over hers. She had begun to feel warmer now that the fire was built up and she was out of the cold, but the heat of his hands seemed to speed up the process until she was almost too warm. "You can picture the *A* in the square at one by one?"

"I do."

"Good. Now picture the square in column two, row one. That letter is an *I*. In another lesson, I will show you how to *read* those letters with the corresponding dots, but for now you just need to remember that *A* is one-one and *I* is located at one-two."

One of his fingers moved against her wrist, tickling her slightly. "And what is the letter in the square one-three?"

That one finger, moving against the skin of her wrist, distracted her. It tickled, and yet it did not tickle. "I'm sorry, what did you say?"

"The square at position one-three. What letter is that?" he asked, his voice calm. He sounded completely unaffected.

"One-three is the letter *O*. So we have *A*, *I*, and *O*."

His finger slid down from her wrist, slowly making its way to her palm. His touch was light and yet she found it oddly erotic. This was why her mother had told her to always wear her gloves.

"Go on," he said as though he was not making her skin prickle deliciously with his slow strokes.

"Very well." She sounded slightly breathless. What was wrong with her? He was only touching her hand. "What square have we come to?"

"One-four."

"Of course. Ah..." She could not seem to remember the letter in position one-four. She could not seem to think of anything but the way his finger slid across her tender flesh and how their legs touched. This seemed to be far more touching than was appropriate. And, sinner that she was, she wouldn't have moved away for the world.

"Is it another vowel?" he asked. "*E*, perhaps, or *U*?"

"It's *U*," she said, glad for the prompt. "And *E* is in the one-five spot." She would simply keep speaking. That would keep her mind focused. "As you probably know, in French an *E* has an accent."

"Yes, *l'accent aigu.*"

Pru's heart almost stopped at the sound of his French accent. She had a weakness for French accents. She had a weakness for a man with any sort of accent, really, and Pope was obviously a proficient French speaker. His accent was flawless.

"And then there is *l'accent grave.*"

"Yes," she breathed.

"Are you feeling well, Miss Howard? You sound rather breathless."

"I've just never found the discussion of accents quite so…stimulating." She swallowed. "But we should continue with the lesson." She sat straighter and forced herself to concentrate. "Since English does not have accents, I have modified Monsieur Barbier's chart. The one-five spot is still *E*, but I put…Mr. Pope?"

"Yes?"

"You are holding my hand." Pru looked down to be certain. And yes, he had threaded his fingers through hers. Their hands were locked together in the most intimate of ways.

"Am I?"

"You know you are."

"Should I release you?"

Pru hesitated. The correct answer was *Release me immediately*. But she did not want him to release her. She wanted him to continue holding her hand. She wanted him to lean closer and kiss her. She looked up and studied his lips. They were pale pink, thin but not too thin, and relaxed. She wondered if Mr. Pope was good at kissing. Pru rather thought she was good at kissing. But if Mr. Pope could make her feel like this just by touching her hand, what could he do with his lips?"

"No," she said.

"Don't release you?" he asked.

She had been speaking to herself, telling herself not to imagine what he could do with his lips. "Yes, you should release me."

His grip loosened.

"In just a moment," she added quickly. "You could hold my hand just a moment longer."

His lips quirked in what she thought must be a smile. His hands closed on hers again and he lifted one of her hands slowly to his lips. She watched, unable to tear her gaze away, as he brushed his pink lips over the pale skin of her knuckles.

"My hands aren't soft," she whispered, afraid her voice would fail her if she tried to speak.

"They're exactly as I imagined," he said. "You're no spoiled miss who is afraid to get her hands dirty." His breath tickled her skin, and she shivered.

"I don't wear my gloves enough," she admitted. "I have freckles."

"Do you?" He sounded intrigued. "Tell me where, and I will kiss each one."

"You can't. There are hundreds."

"Oh, I think I can manage." And he pressed his lips to the back of her hand several times before turning her hand over so her palm was open to him. "What about here? Do you have freckles here?"

"No." She shook her head. "Just calluses."

"Then I shall explore until I find them." He pressed his lips to the center of her palm, and she caught her breath. His tongue darted out to taste her and she exhaled loudly. When he kissed her again, she could not stop a moan. "Oh!"

"That's location one-three," he said. "You see? I am learning."

"Mr. Pope—"

Abruptly he released her hand and a moment later the door opened. Pru blinked in confusion as Mrs. Brown bustled in, carrying a tray laden with dishes covered with cloth. "Here we are then," she said. Pru scooted back in her chair, further away from Mr. Pope. As Mrs. Brown placed the dishes on the desk, she wondered what she had been about to say to him. Had she been about to ask him to stop or to go further?

She should be ashamed of herself, but the truth was, she had hoped something like this would happen. The possibility was the reason she could hardly concentrate on sewing today. Yes, she had been eager at the prospect of teaching Mr. Pope and even more excited at the chance to spend more time with him. But really, she had wanted to touch him again. She had wanted him to touch her. Ever since the first time she had seen him in the informal garden near Wentmore, she had felt drawn to him. She had just never imagined he would feel the same pull.

"Anything else you need?" Mrs. Brown asked, whisking off the cloths to reveal the dishes. She looked at Pru, seeming quite pleased with this flourish.

"I think that is all, Mrs. Brown," Pru said.

"Then I'll be off. Just leave the dishes here, Mr. Pope. I'll wash up in the morning."

"Thank you, Mrs. Brown," he said.

Pru waited until the housekeeper had closed the door behind her. "Where is she going?"

"Home, I imagine," he answered.

"She doesn't sleep here?"

"No. We're all alone."

Pru glanced at his face. His expression was like his tone—challenging. Was she afraid to be alone with him? Oh, yes, she was. But not for the reason he thought. He thought she was afraid he might attempt to kiss her or worse. But the truth was, she was more likely to throw herself at him.

And that would simply not do. She could not carry on a liaison with Mr. Pope. Milcroft was a small village and there were no secrets. She was under the vicar's protection. If he turned her out, she had nowhere to go.

Her parents had made her promise to be a paragon of virtue, and she had agreed. Now was the time to remember her promise and behave herself.

Pru rose and lifted a cup of steaming tea. She could have used a glass of wine, which was more customary during dinner, but she would take what she could find. She drank the tea down, practically scalding her throat, and then lifted a bowl of…

"What is this?" she asked.

Mr. Pope leaned closer to the food on the desk and sniffed. "It smells like some sort of soup."

"Yes."

"Does it look as bad as it tastes?" he asked.

"I haven't tasted it yet, but I would not call the appearance pleasant." She squared her shoulders. She would eat, and that would take her mind off those wicked lips of his. "Still, I am certain it tastes divine." She dipped her spoon into the yellow-ish green broth, put it to her lips, and winced.

"I can't even see you, but I can tell it's disgusting."

"Not disgusting," she said, wiping her mouth with the napkin to remove any trace of the liquid from her lips. "It's not what I am used to."

"That's why Payne went to Blunley. He wanted decent food."

"I suppose I cannot blame him." She reached for a piece of bread and took a tentative bite. "The bread is not too bad. A bit lumpy."

Taking her suggestion, he reached for it as well.

"Will Mr. Payne be back tonight?"

"Not if he finds a woman willing to let him share her bed."

Pru blinked, and the bread she had been swallowing seemed to lodge in her throat. She began to cough and was forced to drink Mr. Pope's tea to dislodge the bread.

"Are you well?" he asked when she had stopped hacking.

"Yes, quite well."

"I've forgotten some of my manners," he said. "I shouldn't have said that in your company."

"It's quite alright. I have traveled the world. I know something of…these sorts of matters. Why…I mean, do you mind if I ask you a question?"

He gave her a wary look. "Go ahead."

"Why didn't you go with him?"

"I had a prior commitment." He made a gesture to indicate the two of them and the room.

"You could have postponed it. You must be hungry," she said, eyeing the food suspiciously. "And perhaps you are hungry for more than food," she said in the most judicious way she could think of.

He smiled. "You mean, why don't I go bed a woman?"

"You seem to be interested in such things," she said, thinking of the way he'd touched her hand and tasted her with his tongue.

"I think the answer is obvious," he said. "No woman would have me."

Pru stared at him—his rumpled clothing, his tousled black hair, a face that had once been handsome but now looked thin and weary. "I'm a woman," she said.

Mr. Pope seemed to go completely still. His visible eye, which had been looking away, now fastened on her and she felt as though he was seeing right through her. She did not know how much, if anything, he could see from that eye, but however much it was, it felt like *too* much in that moment.

"I should go," she said abruptly.

"Wait."

"I forget how early night falls this time of year. If I stay, I will have to walk home in darkness. I'll come again tomorrow."

She moved toward the door.

"Miss Howard. Wait."

"We've made a good start. Remember your squares, and we can continue tomorrow." She opened the door and was through it as quickly as possible. "Good night," she said.

And then for some reason she could not fathom, she ran through the vestibule, out the door, and all the way back to the vicarage.

## *Nine*

Nash lay in bed that night, Miss Howard's words echoing in his mind over and over. *I'm a woman.*

Did she want him? Was that what she was saying?

She had not resisted his flirting, but he had not taken that as a sign of real interest. He'd begun stroking her hand to rattle her more than anything else. He did not need to imagine boxes and numbers. He'd always been able to learn and remember quickly. He hadn't been bored, precisely, but he had thought it might be amusing to make her squirm.

But instead of jerking her hands out of his or telling him to stop, she had seemed to grow breathless at his touch. So much so that he began to think she grew breathless not from discomfort but from arousal.

He shouldn't have kissed her hand or licked her palm, but by that point he was not only curious at her reaction, he wanted to taste her. It seemed every time he encountered her, her scent was slightly different. Today it was faintly of rose water and bergamot tea. But underneath those familiar scents was the underlying mysterious and heady scent that he had come to associate with her alone.

He probably shouldn't have been close enough to her to even know the scent of her, but now that he did, he would not soon forget it.

He was hungry for physical touch. He did miss the smiles and laughter and whispers of women. He was not the kind of man who took random women to bed or sought out a different woman every night of the week. But he'd had his share of liaisons, and the last of those had been a long, long time ago.

He had thought he would never meet a willing woman again. He would not pay for a woman and so, at one and thirty, that part of his life was over.

*I'm a woman.*

Why had she said that? She couldn't possibly want him. He lifted his hand from the sheets where it rested and brought it to his face. Pushing his hair off his forehead, he touched the brow of his left eye. Slowly, he slid his hand down and along the knotted scar that snaked over his eyelid. The doctor had said he was fortunate not to lose his eye. Nash didn't know what difference it made if he could not see out of it.

Unfortunately, he could still remember the moments before the attack. He could remember the yellow of the sun on the stone of the building where he had been hiding, the dark brown of his rifle butt, the familiar weight of it against his shoulder. In his periphery, there had been the blue of the sky and the white of fast-moving clouds. His hair had ruffled in the breeze. He wished he had known these would be his last images. He wished he had looked about and noticed a tree or a flower or something beautiful. But the last thing he remembered was staring down the length of his rifle. And then an explosion.

The troop's leader, Neil Wraxall, had told Nash that a French sniper had fired at him. He'd told Nash he was fortunate because the shot had missed Nash and hit the stone of the building he was leaning against instead. Still, Nash had been unlucky in that the pieces of the stone had flown against his left eye, damaging it so badly that he'd lost his sight.

Ironically, his right eye had not been damaged. The doctors couldn't really explain why Nash couldn't see out of that eye. Something about an injury to the brain that damaged the part of the brain responsible for vision. Over time, a bit of sight had come back to his right eye. Nash had hoped the shadowy shapes would lighten and become clearer. He had hoped he might see color again. But as the days and weeks and months and years wore on, it became obvious that he would be forever relegated to this shadow world. Some days it seemed pointless to even use his vision. It was like looking down into a murky pond and trying to see the bottom. There were only vague outlines of things dark and indistinct.

The doctors had told him his other senses would sharpen to compensate. Nash couldn't say whether they had or not. He'd wanted his vision back, goddamn it. At times he wondered if his limited vision in his right eye had improved as he could recognize differences in size and shape now. But then he thought he had simply become more used to the shadow world. And, of course, a hulking figure like Rowden was easily distinguished from a thin one like Miss Howard or a squat one like Mrs. Brown.

The despair that dragged at him constantly, trying to pull him into the shadow world and under the murky water permanently, tugged hard now. As The Cloud descended, Nash reached for his pistol reflexively. He stroked the filigree and took slow breaths. He realized now that he hadn't thought about the pistol once when Miss Howard had been at Wentmore. Surely it had been in his pocket, as it always was, but he hadn't reached for it, hadn't remembered it was even there.

Was that why he wanted it to be afternoon again? Why he couldn't seem to wait for her to return? Because she kept The Cloud from swallowing him whole? She'd said he was still angry, and he hadn't corrected her. He would rather she think he was angry than know the truth—he was standing on the edge of a black, cavernous hole and very little kept him from tumbling down, down, down.

\*\*\*

"Good morning, sir," said a man's voice. Nash rolled over and ignored it. Just one of his father's servants...

*Bloody damn hell!*

Nash bolted upright and felt for his pistol.

"I set the pistol on the nightstand, sir," came the voice again. What the devil? He was not at his father's town house. He was at Wentmore, and there was a strange man in his bedchamber.

"Who the hell are you?"

"Clopdon, sir. Would you like your dressing gown? I can lay it at the foot of your bed or assist you with it."

He had a dressing gown? Nash scooted to the edge of the bed, reached for the nightstand, and grasped the pistol. He didn't point it at the stranger. A man with a dressing gown was not too much of a threat, but Nash felt better having the weapon in his hands.

"What are you doing in my bedchamber? Did my father send you? Are you from the asylum?"

"I am from Bath, sir. Mr. Payne hired me." He made a *tsk*ing sound. "And not a moment too soon."

Nash tried to imagine the state of his room. Clothes were probably strewn about, left wherever he had dropped them. Mrs. Brown made certain his sheets were clean, but he chased her out of his chamber if she tried to dust or do much more than gather his clothing for the laundry.

"Why would Mr. Payne hire you?"

"Mr. Payne was detained in Blunley. He hired me to serve as your valet."

"Well, you can go back to Bath. I don't need a valet."

"I beg to differ, sir. I will leave the dressing gown on the foot of the bed. I asked a woman I found bustling about to heat water for your bath. I suppose there are no other servants in residence." The valet sounded rather put out by this fact.

"I don't need any servants. Tell Mr. Payne I sent you on your way."

"I will not be leaving, sir, though I must admit it is beneath my station to carry water, but I will make the sacrifice today. I can see this is an emergency."

"Get out."

"Yes, sir."

Nash let out a breath.

"I will be back with tea and your bath, sir."

"No, you won't." Bloody, bloody damn hell! "If you come back, I'll shoot you."

"Yes, sir."

"Did you hear me, Clapton—"

"It's Clopdon, sir."

"I don't care what your name is. You'll be dead."

"Of course, sir. Do you take sugar in your tea?

"No!" Why the hell would this man not leave?

"Very good, sir. I never take sugar either—slave labor, you know. I can see I will have to find soap and towels and the bathing tub. I may not return as quickly as I would hope."

"Do you know who I am, Clopdon? Do you know I shot a man—a friend of mine—only a few months ago?"

"I did not know that, sir. If you give me his name, I will be sure he is not admitted again."

This was ridiculous. "I want you to leave, Mr. Clopdon."

"It's just Clopdon, sir, and no."

Nash raised the pistol. "Then I have no choice but to shoot you."

Clopdon sighed. "Very well then."

"You don't care if I shoot you?"

"Of course, I care, sir. But you won't shoot me." His voice grew fainter as, presumably, he began to move toward the door.

"And how do you know that?"

"I took your pistol balls and gunpowder, sir."

"The hell you did!" But a quick check of his weapon showed this to be true. His balls and powder were missing. Clopdon must have come in while he was sleeping, taken the pistol, disarmed it, and set it on the nightstand.

Nash would kill the valet. Then he would kill Rowden.

Nash jumped out of bed, realized he was naked, and reached for the damn dressing robe. It was easily within reach. Damn Clopdon. Nash pulled the garment on and realized it was clean and starched. Clopdon, again. Damn him!

Nash would throw him out of the house. He would shove his boot—if he could find his boots—up Clopdon's arse.

That's when the hammering started.

Nash knew it was hammering. He knew the workmen were back, but he couldn't stop his body's response. He fell to the floor and took cover. And even though he told himself no one was firing upon him, no cannon balls or pistol balls were incoming, he could not seem to stop cowering at the edge of the bed.

He did not know how long he lay there, rigid with fear, but at some point Clopdon returned, and from the sound of it, he was hauling something heavy. It thudded on the floor, and Nash realized it must be the tub.

"Sir," Clopdon said between ragged breaths. "If you must lie on the floor, I would prefer you not do so until I have it mopped and cleaned. I shall have to wash that dressing gown again."

Nash let out an involuntary laugh that was somewhere between a chuckle and a sob. In that moment, it was clear Clopdon was not leaving.

\*\*\*

"Prudence."

Pru stopped. She had been making her way silently down the stairs, avoiding all the steps that creaked. She was usually the last to rise, so she knew Mrs. Blimpkin and the vicar would already be up and about, but she hoped she'd tarried long enough that the vicar would be in his library hard at work at…whatever he did in there.

But the deep voice that spoke her name was unmistakably Mr. Higginbotham's.

Pru let out the breath she'd been holding and straightened her shoulders. "Good morning, sir," she said in her cheeriest voice. Not bothering to be quiet now, she scampered down the remaining steps and saw the vicar sitting at the breakfast table.

"Morning?" He took out his pocket watch and glanced at it. "Barely."

"Yes, sir. I will start on my chores straightaway." She started for the kitchen where the broom was kept.

"Wait a moment, young lady."

Pru closed her eyes then pasted a smile on her face and turned back to the vicar. "Yes, sir?"

"Sit down and break your fast first."

"I really should start sweeping. I—"

"Sit down."

Pru had rarely heard this tone from the vicar, and she took a seat without arguing further. The teapot was beside the vicar, but he did not offer her any. She hadn't expected she would actually eat anything at any rate.

"You were not here for dinner last night."

Pru blinked. The vicar was often visiting parishioners or took dinner in his library, and she had not thought he would notice her absence.

"I was not, no."

"And you did not return until after dark."

Another surprise as the vicar went to bed with the sun, and she could often hear him snoring while it was still dusk outside.

"I was tutoring Mr. Pope at Wentmore, sir. You gave your permission."

"I did not give you permission to stay out until all hours of the night."

She had been in bed by nine, which was hardly all hours of the night.

"Yes, sir. The problem is I cannot begin the tutoring until after the workmen have stopped for the day, and that is not until four or five. I do not think it's possible for me to return home before dark, especially with winter coming and the days growing shorter." Pru took a breath, but she saw the look on the vicar's face and decided it might be better to keep speaking before he had a chance to say something she would rather he did not. "I know returning so late is not ideal, but I can't help but think of your sermon two weeks ago on the importance of Christian charity. You said, and I believe this is a quote, 'It is our solemn duty as followers of Christ to be of service to those less fortunate than we.'"

"Mr. Pope is the son of an earl. He is not one of the less fortunate."

"But he has lost his sight, Mr. Higginbotham, and I have my sight."

"And that has made him dangerous. I am coming to regret my decision to allow you to tutor him. The loss of sight has made him a danger to himself and others."

"I completely agree," Pru said.

Mr. Higginbotham's mouth snapped shut. He had been prepared to counter her argument, so she did the only thing she could—she did not argue.

"You agree?" he asked, his eyes narrowing.

"Yes. Mr. Pope is dangerous because he is suffering from melancholia."

"Melancholia?"

"At first, I thought he was angry, but now I think he is grieving the loss of his sight. It seems more important than ever that I show him all is not lost. *Ecriture Nocturne* may just be the cure that he needs." Pru didn't believe this at all. She thought Mr. Pope probably needed someone to kick him in the seat of his trousers, but as Mr. Payne seemed to have that task well in hand, Pru would do what she could on other fronts.

"And why are you the one who needs to teach him? I do not like the idea of a young girl like you alone with a man like Pope."

"We are hardly alone, sir." This was true, technically. "As to why I am the one to teach him, well, it reminds me of your sermon of the gifts of the spirit. Isn't it incumbent upon me to use my gifts to bless Mr. Pope? I cannot help but think I was put in the path of Monsieur Barbier for just that reason. And I never would have realized this if not for your sermon on the matter." Pru worried with this last statement she had gone too far, but Mr. Higginbotham looked thoughtful.

"Yes, other members of the congregation have told me how much that sermon impacted them as well."

"It was a very good sermon, sir. Truly the inspired word of God. I do hope if I continue to work with Mr. Pope, I might encourage him to attend services on Sunday."

Mr. Higginbotham frowned. Pru realized her mistake, but it was too late to backtrack. "I cannot help but think how grateful Lord Beaufort will be at the change in his son. Mr. Payne says the earl is a generous man," she said, wincing a bit at her own boldness.

Mr. Higginbotham stared at her for a long moment. At first Pru thought he might be assessing the veracity of her words, but then she realized he was probably listing all of the repairs to the church and vicarage he might undertake if the earl decided to repay the vicar for his kindness in allowing Pru to help his son. The vicar was silent for so long that Pru was about to suggest she retreat to the kitchen for the broom, but then the vicar's eyes sharpened.

"This is all very well, but it does not address the problem of you being at Wentmore with two gentlemen and no one but Mrs. Brown to chaperone. I have known Mrs. Brown for two decades or more, and she is a fine, upstanding woman, but she is not a suitable chaperone. She is all by herself there and can hardly manage the house, much less keep an eye on you and those gentlemen."

"But—"

"Your parents were quite clear when they gave you into my care that you do not have the best judgment in matters pertaining to men."

Pru felt her cheeks heat. She was embarrassed that her parents should share such information with the vicar but not surprised. The heat in her cheeks was more likely due to anger that even at the age of three and twenty she was being treated like a child. It occurred to her that this would be her fate for the next fifteen or so years unless she married, which was unlikely, but even then she would be placed under the care and supervision of her husband.

It was times like this that she had the urge to run away and live free. She dreamed of a cottage in the clearing of a woods where she might sleep as late as she liked, read all day if she wished, and sing all the bawdy songs she knew at the top of her lungs.

But because she was three and twenty, she realized one could not live on books and songs alone. One needed coin to eat and keep cottage roofs from leaking, and so running away was not a very practical solution.

Better to fight for what little freedom she had here.

Pru thought of poor Mrs. Brown and the awful fare she served Mr. Pope. She had wanted to speak to Mrs. Blimkin this morning about recommending merchants to stock the kitchens at Wentmore. But what if Mrs. Blimkin were able to oversee the task herself? "What about Mrs. Blimkin as a chaperone?" Pru asked.

The door to the kitchen swung open. "Me? I am a housekeeper, not a chaperone," Mrs. Blimkin said from the doorway where she had obviously been standing on the other side listening.

"You are also an excellent cook, Mrs. Blimkin. I had the opportunity to sample some of Mrs. Brown's cooking last night, and it is barely edible. She could use your assistance."

"No doubt she could, but Matilda Brown has never been one to take any sort of charity."

"But your charity would be all for Mr. Pope. You would be chaperoning me so we could help him." Pru looked at the vicar. "Think how pleased the earl will be."

"He might be grateful," the vicar said rubbing his chin, which Pru had learned meant he was considering something carefully. "What do you think, Mrs. Blimkin?"

"I think this one"—she pointed at Pru—"talks fast and says what she thinks we want to hear."

Pru's eyes widened in what she hoped was a look of innocence. "Mrs. Blimkin, I have not said anything untrue. Mrs. Brown is an awful cook, and Mr. Pope does need help. And you would be a suitable chaperone." This was not as true as the other two statements. Mrs. Blimkin had never married or had children and probably did not know the first thing about chaperoning young ladies. But then Pru was not really a lady and did not need a formal chaperone.

Mrs. Blimkin looked at the vicar, who looked at Pru and then back at Mrs. Blimkin. He might be an old bachelor, but he knew enough not to involve himself in household matters. "I leave the decision to you, Mrs. Blimkin," he said, rising. "I have work to attend to. Miss Howard, if Mrs. Blimkin cannot accompany you then I will expect you to come straight home after your visit with Mrs. Northgate."

"Yes, sir."

He rose and retreated to his library, closing the door. Pru looked at Mrs. Blimkin, who looked back at her.

"Now you're trying to get me shot as well?"

Pru rolled her eyes. "He won't shoot you."

She sniffed. "He shot that Scotsman, and he liked that man, by all accounts."

"If he so much as looks in your direction, Mrs. Blimkin, I will jump in front of you."

"Why?"

"To save you, of course."

The housekeeper waved her hand. "No, I mean, why do you want to go to Wentmore so much? Do you see Mr. Pope as some sort of romantic hero? One of those brooding lords from those gothic novels you read?"

Pru started to deny it, but there was a grain of truth in Mrs. Blimkin's supposition.

"Just as I thought. I want no part of it."

Pru jumped to her feet and caught Mrs. Blimkin's arm before she could return to the kitchen. "That's not all there is, Mrs. Blimkin. Mr. Pope needs us."

"Us?"

She made a circling motion. "All of us—the town, the people. I know I can help him."

"From what I hear, he is beyond help."

"Oh, Mrs. Blimkin. *Please.* I want to help and what else is there for me? Sitting in the vicarage every night reading sermons?"

"*Pretending* to read sermons."

Pru *pretended* she hadn't heard that. "Sweeping clean floors? Writing letters to my parents when it's unlikely they will ever write me back?"

Mrs. Blimkin sighed. "I told him not to take you in." Her gaze flicked to the closed library door where the vicar had secluded himself, as usual. Pru was startled at this admission.

"You told Mr. Higginbotham not to take me?"

"Young girl like her, I said, girl who has seen the world, I said. She will wither and die in a place like Milcroft. It might be different if you had people here, but you have no place."

Pru raised her head. "I like to think I am making my own place, carving it out for myself."

Mrs. Blinkin raised her brows. "So then who am I really helping? Have you thought about that? Perhaps it's not Mr. Pope who needs help. Perhaps it's you."

And with that, she passed into the kitchen, leaving the door swinging in her wake.

## Ten

Due largely to what he considered harassment on Clopdon's part, Nash found himself washed, dressed, fed, and upright before the noon meal. Nash tried to eat the food Mrs. Brown put before him. It was not too vile if he doused it liberally with salt. The pounding coming from the workmen still made him flinch, but he was determined not to hide under his bed or in his dressing room.

Instead, he wandered the house. Upon hearing voices from below stairs, he went to investigate and learned Clopdon was interviewing footmen. Nash rather wished he would interview cooks, but he thought it unwise to give the valet any more ideas. Instead, Nash left Clopdon to his interviews—there seemed little other choice—and made his way back upstairs. He could hear Mrs. Brown speaking to someone at the door. His heart sped up even though he knew it was far too early in the day for Miss Howard to call.

"I understand that, Mr. Forester, but you will have to call another time."

Forester. Why did that name sound familiar? Forester…

"You'll have to allow me to speak with him sometime, Mrs. Brown. I get no reply from the earl and something must be done before winter or Mr. and Mrs. Smith will starve."

"What is the problem?" Nash asked, moving into the vestibule so he could be seen.

"Mr. Pope!" Mrs. Brown said. "I thought you would be…" She didn't finish, but he knew what she thought. He would be cowering from the noise. Indeed, it was all he could do not to flinch visibly at the hammering.

"I am feeling better today, Mrs. Brown. Mr. Forester, I believe?" He nodded at the shape in the door. "You are my father's land steward, is that right?"

"Yes, sir. If I might come in, I wanted to discuss one of the farmers with you. He has been ill and has fallen behind in rents."

The hammering from the workmen seemed never-ending, and Nash had an idea. "Shall we step outside and walk a bit?" he asked.

Silence. Finally, Forester said, "If you prefer, sir."

Nash would have done anything to escape the noise of the workmen. He took his overcoat and stepped into the cool air, happy to move as far away from the house as Mr. Forester and he could walk. When he returned, he knew all about the harvest, the crops that had done well, those that had failed, the farmers who were lazy, and those who were ill. The Smiths seemed to fall into this last category. The husband had been bed-ridden with an illness for much of the summer and had not been able to work the land. The family was now behind in rent and had little food stored for the winter. Forester realized he was expected to evict the Smiths, but he had written to the earl to plead for forbearance and had yet to receive a response.

Nash hardly thought his opinion merited any weight. He was about to be evicted himself—in a manner of speaking. But he told the steward to hold off and to do what he could for the family in the time being. He hadn't promised to write to his father, but the act had been implied. Nash wondered how he was supposed to advocate for the Smiths when he couldn't even advocate for himself.

It seemed hours passed before the clock chimed five and the hammering ceased. And then it seemed more hours passed without Miss Howard arriving. Mrs. Brown served some sort of meat for dinner, but whatever it was had been charred past all recognition, and Nash did not eat it.

Where the devil was Miss Howard? Was she not coming? Had he scared her off with his behavior the evening before? If that was the case, why had she implied that she found his attentions pleasing? Perhaps she'd changed her mind. Perhaps…

He thought he heard the sound of a horse's hooves. But Miss Howard came on foot, did she not? Nash went to the foyer and tried to appear as though he was not waiting for a knock on the door. But he was waiting, and none came. Finally, he heaved a sigh and started for the stairs and his room. Miss Howard was clearly not coming today.

And then, halfway up the stairs, he smelled something that made his mouth water. He turned his head and made his way slowly back down, following the scent to the dining room. "There you are," came Miss Howard's voice. "I am sorry we are late," she said, sounding breathless. Nash moved through the door and inhaled deeply. He smelled potatoes and fresh baked bread and spices.

"Mrs. Blimkin insisted on baking a tart. I don't know why when she had already prepared enough for an army. We had to borrow Mr. Langford's dog cart to carry it all and ourselves. But we are here now. Have you already eaten? If so, I can have Mrs. Brown put this away—"

"No!" Nash would have snatched the dish out of her hands if he'd been able to see it.

"Are you feeling quite well, Mr. Pope? You look…" She paused. "Quite presentable." But he heard the warmth in her voice. She might not have intended it, but she sounded as though she approved of how he looked. Perhaps Clopdon was not so bad.

No, Clopdon was a nuisance, but he could be born. Especially if his ministrations made Miss Howard's voice lower in that fashion.

"I have not eaten," he said. "What did you bring?"

"Shepherd's pie. I thought I told you that. Would you like a piece?"

He wanted the entire pie. "Yes. Do you mind serving?" If the pie was put in front of him, he would likely eat it right from the plate.

"Of course. Please sit."

He did and heard her rattling about until she located a plate. She set it before him and then placed a fork, knife, and spoon where he could easily find them.

"I hope you will join me."

"Oh! I…yes, thank you." More rattling and more flatware set on the table. He could see the shape of her, and he thought she moved with efficiency. The food was soon before him, and Nash almost groaned at the smell. For months, the alcohol he'd consumed had dulled his appetite. Mrs. Brown's cooking had not helped. But he felt like a starving man who could not wait another moment to taste something edible. He lifted his fork—or it might have been a spoon—and began to eat.

"You have a much better appetite than you did yesterday," she remarked.

"My compliments to Mrs. Blimkin," he said between spoonfuls of creamy mashed potatoes, savory carrots, and delicious crust.

"The vicar has decided I need a more suitable chaperone. Mrs. Blimkin has agreed to come with me and oversee the kitchen while we work. I promised him our lessons would only take a few days more. If you don't mind, we might come earlier tomorrow."

Nash was simply surprised that he only had a few days with Miss Howard. For some reason, he had assumed she might come every day for…well, until he did not want her to come. But he supposed once he mastered the night writing, there would be no more need for her to come.

He set his spoon down, his appetite diminishing somewhat at the prospect of not seeing Miss Howard. "You can come as early as you like. Payne hired a valet and the man will probably wake me up at the crack of dawn."

"I think Mrs. Northgate will be offended if I do not visit with her and at least attempt to work on my dress."

"Ah, yes. The dress." He lifted his spoon to eat more of the pie. "How long does it take to make a dress?"

"A few days, I imagine, but I have never made one and Mrs. Northgate makes me take out half the stitches I sew, so it could be years at this rate." She sounded more amused than frustrated, so he smiled.

"Wait a moment," she said, sounding concerned. Nash reached for his pistol. He'd ordered Clopdon to return the ammunition, but he had not loaded it. Now he wished he had.

"I could be mistaken," she went on, sounding calmer. "But was that a smile?"

Nash let out the breath he'd been holding. There was no crisis, no danger. He'd been overreacting. Again.

"You've seen me smile before," he said, eating another bite of the pie. He would have eaten more, but he feared he would be ill. Instead, he pushed the plate away.

"It's a rare occurrence," she said. "But if my poor sewing is the thing to make you smile, I shall recount my failures more often. I like seeing you smile."

Nash wasn't certain what to say in response. He would have liked to make a flirtatious remark. The old Nash, the Nash before the injury, would have done so, but he didn't feel like that Nash any longer. He cleared his throat. "Are you finished? Should we begin the lesson?"

"We should. Do you want to retreat to the library again?"

"No," he said quickly. Too quickly. He did not want to be reminded of his youth and his father again tonight. "Here is fine."

"Very well. Let's see if you remember the chart. Can you tell me what letter is in position one-four?"

She went on this way for some time, making certain he knew the letters and positions of the first row thoroughly. Then she moved on to the second row. Memorizing that row was simple enough. Nash realized at this rate he would be done with the lessons in no time. Then Miss Howard would no longer need to come.

"You're not holding my hands tonight," he said, interrupting her.

"You seemed to be doing well enough without me holding your hands," she said.

"Perhaps I could do even better."

"Mr. Pope, do you *want* me to hold your hands?"

He shifted. He'd never had such awkwardness with a woman before. He wasn't certain how to behave or what to say or do. "Not if you should object," he said, finally.

Her warm hands covered his and clasped him tightly. "Why should I object?" she said, squeezing his hands. "Now, shall we imagine that third row of the chart or is that too much for one evening?"

It was not too much. Nash would have done anything to keep her there beside him and touching him. "I could learn another row," he said, but he didn't want to talk about night writing anymore. Not now that she was holding his hands.

"Are you such a poor seamstress?" he asked before she could bring up the letters of the third row of Barbier's chart.

He felt her hands tense slightly as though in surprise. "Why should you ask that?"

"I just wondered why the good Mrs. Northgate would make you take out so many stitches. I find it hard to believe there's something you aren't competent in."

"Ah, that." He could all but hear her smiling. He wondered what she looked like when she smiled. He wondered what she looked like period. Was she as pretty as she seemed to him? He didn't think he'd ever met anyone as surprising and patient and calm as Miss Prudence Howard. He was certain it would not be long before he said or did something that drove her away.

"I am not a bad seamstress, but Mrs. Northgate is quite particular, and she insists on adding ruffles and bows and flounces. I've never sewed anything so fancy and delicate, but she says they are necessary to set off the flaws in my...er—to make the dress look as well as can be."

"You don't need ruffles and bows to look beautiful," he said. Even as the words left his mouth, he was surprised by them. He was not the sort of man given to complimenting women. He was not the sort of man to compliment anyone. Not now. Perhaps he had been once. Once he had been the picture of the perfect gentleman. But it had been merely a picture. He was a killer and he supposed now he looked like one.

To his greater surprise, Miss Howard laughed. He pulled his hands away. "I've amused you?"

"Yes. I'm sorry, but I am not beautiful. No one has ever called me beautiful in my life."

Nash was familiar with most ladies' habit of pretend modesty.

"Oh, but I see by your expression—what I can see of it since you have half your face covered—that you think I am being modest. I assure you I am not. I am very plain, Mr. Pope. I have mousy brown hair and unremarkable brown eyes, and I'm too tall and too thin. And since you are not able to see them, I will say I am covered with freckles. I don't stay out of the sun as I should, but even if I did, I would still have thousands. So if you are imagining me to be beautiful, you can stop now. I understand if you no longer wish to hold my hands."

Nash sat very still for a long moment. Miss Howard's words were spoken in a light tone, but he imagined what she'd just revealed was not as amusing to her as she feigned. He heard her chair move against the floor as she pushed back and caught her hand before she could back away.

"I don't need to see you to know you're beautiful," he said, holding her still.

"But I told you—"

"And I want to do much more than simply hold your hand." Nash rose, slowly, still clasping her hand but doing so loosely in case she wanted to escape. When she didn't flee and didn't pull away, he tugged her forward until her body was almost touching his. Only then did he release her hands and hold up one of his own. "Let me see you," he said. "The only way I can."

For a long moment, she didn't speak, and then she took his hand and pressed it to her cheek. Her skin was smooth and warm and impossibly soft. He'd forgotten how soft women's skin could be, but even whatever memories he could muster did not do the softness of her skin justice. She was no fine lady. He had felt the calluses on her hands and the roughness that came from labor. He had his own calluses, and once his hands had been far rougher than hers would ever be. But the skin of her cheek was like the most exquisite silk. He tried to imagine it covered with freckles, tried to trace where those freckles might be with one finger. She wiggled. "That tickles."

"I was tracing a line of freckles," he said. "Right over here." He touched her nose and felt the shape of it. To her credit, she was quite patient with the exploration, though she must have felt strange having a man trace the contours of her nose. It seemed an average nose—not too big or too small. Straight and somewhat narrow.

"Watch your eyes," he said as he moved to the bridge of her nose and slid his fingers carefully over her brow and then over her closed eyelid. Her lashes were delicate against his fingertip. He moved to her forehead, felt how her brow was furrowed, skated high enough to feel the softness of her hair. She'd called it mousy brown. "Is your hair long?" he asked. "And pinned up?"

"Yes, though I must admit I have no skill with hairdressing. It's a very simple knot."

He would have liked to let her hair down, feel it cascade over his skin. Regardless of the color, it was soft and smelled faintly of cinnamon.

He'd saved the best for last because he'd needed to gather his fortitude. His fingers moved back down her face, over her temple and her cheek to her jaw. It was a well-defined jaw and, he soon discovered, a fairly pointy chin. Then his hand moved up to touch her lips.

She inhaled slightly when she realized his intent. He heard her catch her breath and he hoped the sound was more from desire than discomfort. His index finger moved higher until he touched skin so tender it must be her lips. Like the rest of her skin, they were soft and pliant. He tried to learn their shape, finding them not too thin and not too plump, but a shape he could well imagine kissing. "I want to do more than hold your hands," he said again, brushing his thumb over her lips to make the point clearer.

"Mrs. Blimkin," she murmured.

"Is obviously a very poor chaperone."

"She doesn't have much experience."

He leaned closer, so close he could feel her warm breath against his own lips. "How fortunate for us." He slid his hand to the back of her neck, his fingers grazing the small tendrils of hair too fine and short to be caught in her updo. And then he leaned down to press his mouth to hers. He could not see details and fully expected to miss her mouth or catch only the side of it, but she adjusted her position and met him halfway, so their lips brushed together.

A flicker of heat coiled in his belly and spread through his torso and out to his limbs. It had been so long since he'd felt anything other than numbness that the sensation was odd and unfamiliar at first. But as her lips touched his, he realized what it was. Desire. The feeling was faint. It was like a vine pushing out of a seed and through the darkness of the soil above it. But he knew it was there. He knew he was capable of the feeling. Somewhere, under the pain and sadness and hopelessness, were the beginnings of life.

She pressed her lips against his, turning the brush of skin against skin into a real kiss. Contrary to his concerns that he'd scare her away, she was taking the lead. Miss Howard had been kissed before. Her lips parted slightly, just enough that he might taste her, and it was clear she hadn't just been kissed. She knew how to kiss.

His heart began to pound and needs he had not acknowledged, had not known he still had, began to claw their way from the depths of the dark place he'd pushed them. Her arms went around him, and her body met his. He could feel her small, firm breasts against his chest. His hand on the nape of her neck tightened as he struggled to control the emotions swirling inside him. He hardly knew how to feel. He felt too much, and it threatened to overwhelm him.

Nash pulled back, breathing hard, grasping the table with both hands to keep from tumbling backward. He was dizzy and perspiring. His heart hammered as though he were being fired upon by the French. He closed his eyes and forced himself to breathe deeply, to feel his feet planted firmly on the floor, to slow his heartbeat. After a moment, he realized Miss Howard was speaking.

"—shouldn't have done that. I am so sorry, Mr. Pope. I don't know what came over me. Are you well? Do you need some wine or a cold compress?"

He reached out and felt for her hand. She took his, holding it firmly. Her touch anchored him, calmed him.

"Don't apologize," he said, his voice coming out gruffer than he'd intended. "I mean, there's no need for apology."

She was silent, and he could all but feel her grasping for words. Of course, she felt she needed to apologize. He was practically in a full-blown panic. How could he explain?

"I didn't expect to…" he began. Then he cleared his throat, felt for the chair behind him, and sat.

"Here." She placed a glass in his hands, and he drank the water like a man who has just finished a long run.

"Thank you. Miss Howard?" He tried to focus on her, but it was pointless. All she would ever be to him was a nebulous form—except when he'd kissed her. Then she'd been very real, very solid and warm.

"I'm here." She took his hand.

"It has been a long time since I have kissed anyone. That's all. I haven't allowed myself to feel..." He did not want to explain. He did not want to think about his feelings himself, much less explain them.

"I understand," she said. But how could she? How could anyone understand when he was still trying to figure it out?

"We moved too fast," she said. "Next time, we'll take things slowly."

"Next time?" His voice was raspy, but he heard the hope in it.

"If you want there to be a next time. I...oh, I should not have said that. I should not want there to be a next time. I am supposed to be teaching you, not kissing you, but I have to make a confession, Mr. Pope."

He shouldn't allow her to confess anything. They'd already gone too far.

"Go on," he said, uncharacteristically reckless.

"I find you difficult to resist. There's something about you that draws me to you. It's not just that you're so handsome, though no man as handsome as you has ever so much as looked at me twice."

Nash let out a startled breath. "Handsome?" His hand itched to go to his wounded eye. "I'm disfigured."

"Oh, no! You're quite handsome."

He shook his head. Was she mocking him? Or was it possible he looked much as he always had except for the eye, which he was sure to cover with his hair? "You wouldn't think that if you saw my eye," he said, gesturing toward it.

"Yes, I would."

"Miss Howard—"

"Would you call me Pru? I feel awkward enough after kissing you without you calling me *Miss Howard*. And I don't care what your eye looks like. It won't make you less handsome."

"I should show you and send you running and screaming."

"Go ahead." Her voice held a note of challenge. "It won't change my opinion."

There was a long pause. She'd called his bluff, and now he'd been caught with his proverbial trousers down.

"I think I've had enough of lessons for tonight," he said.

"Oh." She sounded disappointed. "I should collect Mrs. Blimkin and go. I'm sure it's quite late."

She moved away from him, and he almost reached out to catch her. Instead, he stayed where he was and said, "Miss—I mean, Pru?"

Her footsteps halted. "Yes?"

"You will come tomorrow, won't you?"

"I will, and I will come earlier. I think it might do you some good to get out of doors and away from the workmen."

"Will your Mrs. Northgate allow that?"

"She will if I can finish the ruffles on the dress's bodice. Wish me good luck. I need it." She muttered the last words.

And then she was gone, and he was alone. For a moment, he thought that the underwater feeling would return. He would feel trapped in murky water, unable to rise to the surface. But he was still warm from her touch, and that flicker of desire was still there. It was faint, but he could still feel it.

# *Eleven*

Pru all but floated down the stairs to the kitchens. She was in a warm, hazy daze of happiness.

Mr. Pope had kissed her. Mr. Pope had touched her. He'd pulled her close and gently cradled the back of her head, and she had never felt more cherished.

The actual kitchen was under repair, and the servants' dining room had been turned into a makeshift kitchen with the dining table used for preparation and the hearth for cooking. Pru was already in the servants' dining room before she realized she had walked into a battle.

"—and I will thank you kindly to keep your opinions to yourself," Mrs. Blimkin said, hands on her generous hips and face red with anger.

Pru froze. Oh, no. If Mrs. Blimkin and Mrs. Brown did not get on then she would not be able to return. There would be no more kisses. But a quick glance at Mrs. Brown showed she looked as concerned as Pru—ostensibly for different reasons.

"There is no reason to take offense, Mrs. Blimkin," said a well-dressed man Pru had not seen before. "Mr. Pope is recovering from a long illness, and simple, bland fare is best until he regains his strength and appetite." The man spoke with authority and, in Pru's mind, bravery. Either he was very brave or very foolish to challenge Mrs. Blimkin's cooking.

He was a few inches taller than Pru, probably right at six feet, and he had dark hair that he wore combed back from his forehead and tied into a queue at the nape of his neck. It was so neat it could have been a wig. Indeed, he need only powder it, and it might pass for a wig. He was impeccably dressed in a dark coat and breeches, his hose perfectly white and his pumps shiny black. His cravat was simple but definitely starched. His light-colored eyes met hers and he furrowed his brow delicately as he took her in. His thin lips pursed, and the nostrils of his aquiline nose flared as though he were a large predator who had just scented prey.

"Precisely how many meals have you prepared, Mr. Clopdon?" Mrs. Blimkin demanded.

The man seemed to reluctantly look away from Pru. "It is simply Clopdon, Mrs. Blimkin. And I have prepared my fair share."

"Well, then. I have prepared more than my fair share and then some, and what that man needs is food to tempt his palate. His body doesn't know how hungry it is, and we need to wake it up."

Mrs. Brown looked from one to the other then cast a pleading look at Pru. She cleared her throat. Pru nodded. "I'm sorry to interrupt—"

"Rich foods will make him ill," Clopdon said, ignoring Pru's interjection. "I have been put in charge of his care, and I will not have it."

"Well!" Mrs. Blimkin was holding a large spoon, and Pru was half-afraid she would throw it. "You have been put in charge of his *clothing*, Mr. Clopdon. *I* have taken charge of his diet, and I will not be told how to cook after forty years of experience. Stick to waistcoats and get out of *my* kitchen."

"How can I stick to waistcoats if you make the man ill? You need—"

"Clopdon, is it?" Pru said loudly enough to ensure all eyes turned to her. She crossed the servants' dining room to stand before him, which had the added effect of putting her between Mrs. Blimkin and the man. "I assume you are the man responsible for how well Mr. Pope is dressed this evening. I am Miss Prudence Howard."

Clopdon raised his head. "I am the man charged with the care of Mr. Pope. Mr. Payne found himself detained and has hired me as the valet. I am also empowered to hire other staff." He pointed at Mrs. Blimkin. "I did not hire *her*."

"You couldn't afford me!" Mrs. Blimkin said.

"Of course, Mrs. Blimkin is not for hire," Pru said loudly. "She is housekeeper for Mr. Higginbotham, who is the vicar of Milcroft. She only came today as a favor to me. I have been engaged as a reading and writing tutor for Mr. Pope, and Mrs. Blimkin agreed to chaperone me. Out of the kindness of her heart and as a favor to Mrs. Brown, who has taken on far too much, she prepared some delicious meals. In fact"—Pru looked over her shoulder at Mrs. Blimkin—"Mr. Pope sent his compliments on the shepherd's pie. He ate almost all of it." She hastily turned back to Clopdon. "But not so much as to make him ill, sir. I do think if you taste Mrs. Blimkin's cooking you will see she seasons it well but not heavily."

"Miss Howard, your loyalty toward this woman does you credit, but—"

"Oh, dear, Mrs. Blimkin," Pru said, sensing that things were about to take another contentious return. "It does grow late, and we should start back if we're to return Mr. Langford's dog cart and get ourselves to bed at a decent hour."

Mrs. Blimkin eyed Clopdon one last time then nodded stiffly. "I know when I am not wanted." With a swish of her skirts she crossed the dining room and went out the door to the yard where they had left the dog cart and horse.

"I do hope she will come back," Mrs. Brown said quietly.

"You do not need her, Mrs. Brown," Clopdon said. "We will get on well enough without a person like *that*." And then he too stormed out, marching up the stairs with a huff. *Clearly*, Pru thought, *Clopdon has not tasted Mrs. Brown's cooking yet.*

"We will return tomorrow," Pru said quietly to Mrs. Brown. "We'll come earlier, and I will take Mr. Pope outside and away from the hammering, which I know grates on his nerves. Mrs. Blimkin will prepare dinner. Did she leave something for breakfast?"

"She did, Miss Howard."

"Good. That means you should be able to rest. You have been working yourself to the bone."

She nodded and Pru noticed that the woman's eyes were moist. She crossed the room and took her hands. "What is it, Mrs. Brown? Did their arguing upset you?"

"No, it's not that," the older woman sniffed. "I am just so happy things are finally taking a turn. I have been so worried for Mr. Pope."

"I do not think he would have survived this long without your care, Mrs. Brown. But now you can stop worrying. I will make sure Mr. Pope is cared for. Mrs. Blimkin will come and this Clopdon seems capable."

Mrs. Brown nodded and dabbed at her eyes. "Yes, all of this is good. I just hope it will be enough."

Pru frowned. "Enough?"

"Yes, Miss Howard. Enough to convince the earl. You see, he plans to send Mr. Pope to an asylum. And if he's sent there, I fear he will never come out again."

\*\*\*

Pru could not get the word *asylum* out of her mind. Mr. Pope in an *asylum*. She couldn't allow that. He did not belong in an asylum any more than she did. He had been through a traumatic experience. He needed comfort and understanding, not to be locked away for the rest of his life. Now she understood why Mr. Payne had moved forward with the repairs to the house, even though Mr. Pope was clearly not ready for that step. And Mr. Pope's friend had hired a valet as well—not because Mr. Pope needed one but because the earl would see such an addition as a sign that his son was doing well.

"Why do you even bother to come if this is the work you do?" Mrs. Northgate said, startling Pru. She'd been preoccupied with the problem of the asylum all morning. Not only had her stitches been uneven, she realized just now she was sitting and staring at the dress and not even sewing.

"I apologize, Mrs. Northgate," she said quickly. She lifted the dress and stabbed the needle into it.

"Cease!" Mrs. Northgate said.

Pru froze.

"Put the dress aside. I won't have you ruin it because your mind is elsewhere. What is troubling you, girl?"

"It's Mr. Pope," Pru said, setting the dress material on the table between them. Mrs. Northgate picked the dress up and frowned down at the work Pru had *not* done. "Mrs. Brown told me the earl plans to send him to an asylum."

Mrs. Northgate looked up. "Really?"

"Yes. How could he do that to his own son?"

Mrs. Northgate picked up the threaded needle and began to work, almost as though it was second nature. "I am sure the earl would never send his son to a place like Bedlam. He will choose a highly regarded institution."

"But Mrs. Northgate! It's an institution nonetheless, and you know once he is taken away, he will never be free again. He will be alone, among strangers. We cannot allow it to happen."

Mrs. Northgate looked up at her, brows raised in surprise. "How can we prevent it? Mr. Pope's family surely knows better than either you or I."

Pru stood. Her indignation was too strong to allow her to remain seated. "If he wants to send Mr. Pope to an asylum, he knows nothing."

"Is that so?" Mrs. Northgate went back to her work, her mouth curved up in a slight smile. "I must say I am surprised that the earl would send his son away. It seems to me that Mr. Nash Pope was always the earl's favorite. Or perhaps his second favorite, after his heir."

"Why do you say that?"

"Haven't you asked about the peacocks yet? I thought you would inquire about those right away."

The peacocks? Pru stopped her pacing and studied Mrs. Northgate. "I did ask about the peacocks, but Mr. Pope said he would tell me at another time. All I know is they were unveiled at the garden party and Mr. Pope won the shooting contest at the same party."

"Is that all?" Mrs. Northgate continued to sew.

Pru took her seat again. "What else is there to know?"

"You are asking the wrong person. But I suspect once you find out the story of those peacocks, you will understand the earl far better. He is a man of vanity, a man who cares a great deal for appearances."

"I don't want to understand him," Pru said. "I want to throttle him."

Mrs. Northgate sighed. "The passions of youth," she murmured. "I am too old for this. Be off. Come back when you can think straight and sew straighter."

"Yes, ma'am." Pru jumped up and started for the door. "I'll be back tomorrow."

"Only if your head is clear!"

Pru all but ran down the stairs, eliciting a contemptuous look from Miss Northgate and Miss Mary, who just happened to be in the vestibule. "Look at that," Miss Northgate said under her breath, but loudly enough to be heard perfectly. "Not only does she look like a horse, she sounds like one too."

The girls giggled and Mrs. Northgate, their mother, stepped out of the parlor and into the foyer. She gave Pru a passing glance and then turned up her nose. "Into the parlor, girls. No need to waste your time out here."

Pru understood the inference. She was a waste of time. She shouldn't allow it to hurt her. They had said and done worse things in the few months she'd been here, but she was already upset about the asylum threat and feeling particularly vulnerable. She told herself to keep quiet and ignore the barbs, but she'd had all she could stomach of misery for a day.

"By all means," Pru said, startling all three ladies. They turned to look at her. "Go waste your time in the parlor. I am sure you need to practice sneering and sniping until you have it just right."

Mrs. Northgate's face went red. "*You*," she said, pointing a long finger at Pru. "I would ask you to leave my home immediately."

"Gladly," Pru said. "I have never felt so unwelcome." Head high, she walked to the door, took her shabby coat from the servant standing there, and marched out the door. Just as she stepped outside, the younger Mrs. Northgate said, "And don't think the vicar will not hear of this."

Pru stumbled. She turned back to say—she knew not what—and the door closed in her face. Pru sighed. She feared she was in for another lecture. Fortunately, even if the younger Mrs. Northgate marched to the vicarage right that moment, she would not be able to speak with Mr.

Higginbotham. He was visiting a sick parishioner. Pru went home anyway to collect Mrs. Blimkin. The housekeeper insisted on dusting shelves she had dusted just yesterday before they could leave, but then they were in Mr. Langford's dog cart and soon on the drive to Wentmore.

Most of the workmen were in the rear of the house, completing repairs to the kitchens, but she spotted one or two on ladders patching the roof. Stationed at the side of the house, Mr. George Northgate waved at her. He was standing beside his cart, which was full of apples and cider. Any other time, Pru would have found all of the activity fascinating and would have wanted to take a closer look at what was being done. She had always been interested in building things. In Rome she had marveled at the Coliseum, trying to imagine it filled with people and the ancient Romans as they built it. In Cairo, she had gone with her parents to see the pyramids. She had asked far too many questions about how they were built. Finally, her mother had told her to try and act like a young lady.

Today Pru couldn't have cared less about the scaffolding around Wentmore. She only cared about its occupant. Was Mr. Pope inside, waiting for her? Was he planning to kiss her again?

She should not allow him to kiss her. She should not want him to kiss her. She should not kiss him back. Her parents and the vicar would have told her all of these things. But Pru failed to see the harm in it. And perhaps a few more kisses, more human interaction, would do Mr. Pope good. He had been secluded for so long, and if his father had his way, Mr. Pope would be secluded in an asylum forever.

They waved at the workmen as they went to the back of the house and left the horse and cart with a groom. Pru wondered where the groom had come from as she did not remember there being a groom yesterday.

Inside the house, the echoes of the work being done reverberated. Mrs. Brown was not in the servants' dining room, and Mrs. Blimkin shooed Pru out so she could begin what she called "dinner preparations."

Pru went upstairs and found Mrs. Brown directing two young men to move furniture in the parlor. Pru blinked in surprise when she saw the room. The curtains were open and the yellow light of the autumn day streamed in. The furniture's style was outdated, but except for a few broken pieces, it was in good condition. Mrs. Brown was directing the men to move those pieces out.

"Mrs. Brown!" Pru greeted her with a wave.

Mrs. Brown beamed. "What do you think?" She waved at the room.

"It looks so much lighter and airier. Is that a word? Airier? I had no idea it could look like this here."

Mrs. Brown's chest all but puffed up. "This was how it looked when I was about your age. Lady Beaufort always kept the house in perfect order. Now that Clopdon has hired these two footmen, we can restore it to some semblance of what it was."

"Footmen?" One of the knots of concern in Pru's belly loosened. Mr. Pope now had a valet, a groom, and footmen. Surely that was a good sign. Would it be enough to persuade his father that he did not belong in an asylum?

Pru would make sure of it.

She pointed to a couch the two footmen were lifting and carrying out. "What is wrong with that couch? It looks in good condition."

"Blood stains," Mrs. Brown whispered.

"I suppose the blood wouldn't come out," came a voice from behind her. Pru and Mrs. Brown turned around. Pru jumped at the sight of Mr. Pope. She had not even heard him approach, not surprising considering the pounding.

"Good day, sir," Mrs. Brown said.

"Mr. Pope," Pru said, not able to keep a smile from her face. "You look well."

And he did. He was dressed in a dark coat and trousers with a deep green waistcoat and a simple neckcloth. His hair, as usual, fell over his forehead and covered his damaged eye. But he had more color in his face and it looked fuller. Gone was the gaunt man she had first met in the informal gardens. This man was still thin, but he was beginning to look healthy and well.

"My head is pounding along with the hammering," he said. "I believe you promised me a walk out of doors today, and if that glare from across the room is any indication, the weather is fine."

"It is indeed," she said. "Mrs. Brown, would you tell Mrs. Blimkin Mr. Pope and I will have our lesson out of doors today? We shall return in about an hour."

"Of course, Miss Howard."

She put her arm through Mr. Pope's, guiding him into the foyer and through the front door. "Why is there blood on the couch?" she asked.

"Slight error in judgment," he replied. She saw his hand go to his pocket, the same pocket where he kept his pistol.

"Do you always carry your pistol with you?" she asked as they stepped onto the lawn. She paused, not certain which way he would want to go. She knew where she would like to walk—the informal gardens. She had missed them these past days.

"Yes," he said simply.

"Why?"

"It's a comfort."

"Not to anyone you point it at, but at least you are doing that less often. Do you have a preference for where we walk?"

"You choose," he said.

"The informal gardens?"

"Lead the way. I can see even less than usual in the sunlight."

She did lead the way, and when they were far enough away from the house that the hammering faded and the sunlight was muted by the damp cool of the shadows under the trees, Pru paused and looked at Mr. Pope. "Why didn't you tell me?"

"You'll have to be more specific, Miss Howard."

"Pru, remember? And why didn't you tell me about the asylum?"

His face, which she had noted he was already quite good at keeping expressionless, went quite blank. "I don't know what you mean."

"It's no use lying," Pru said. She tugged at his arm, leading him to a large log where they could sit. It had obviously been placed in just this spot for just this reason. It was set firmly in the earth and overlooked a small ravine that led down to the brook. If they kept along the path, they would descend gradually, but at this spot, the drop was steeper. "Mrs. Brown told me."

"Mrs. Brown should keep her mouth shut."

Pru sat and pulled him down beside her. "She only wants to help you. All of us want to help you. I don't understand why you won't take help when it's offered."

"Because I'm not helpless!" he roared, jumping to his feet. Pru grabbed his wrist, afraid he might step too close to the edge of the ravine. He shook her off. "I'm not a child who needs his hand held and his face wiped after eating. I'm a grown man."

"And an independent one. You would hate it in an asylum."

He went still and his body became rigid. "I won't be going to any asylum," he said, voice low.

"Of course not," she agreed. "We'll make sure everything is perfect for your father's visit. When is he to arrive?"

"I've no idea. I doubt he'll send word, and it won't matter anyway. I won't go to the asylum. I'll die first." His hand strayed to his coat pocket, and she could see him handling the pistol inside.

"Mr. Pope, no."

"I probably should have done it a long time ago," he said quietly, sinking to the place on the log beside her. "What do I have to live for anyway?"

"What do you have to live for? *Everything!* Why, you have cool autumn days to live for and the sun on your face in the morning, the chirping of insects in the cool of the evening, and the feel of rain wetting your hair. You have plum puddings and apple tarts and mulled wine at Christmas. You have music and poetry and, one day I am sure, a wife and children."

Though he didn't look right at her, his expression was one of disbelief. "None of that seems to matter when I can't see the colors of the leaves or the first rays of dawn."

"Now you are merely feeling sorry for yourself." She gave him a light punch.

"I think I am allowed to feel sorry for myself," he said.

"Yes, you were. I would have allowed you probably two weeks to feel sorry for yourself after your injury."

"Two weeks!"

"Perhaps three," she admitted. "But this injury is two years old at least. It's well past time you stopped feeling sorry for yourself and appreciated what you do have. No, you do not have your sight, but look at everything else you do have. The rest of you seems in fine working order, and you have a country house and an informal garden and a peacock." She grasped his arm tightly.

"Not the peacock again," he muttered.

"Be very quiet and still," she whispered, still clutching his arm. "I see him."

"Who?"

"The peacock."

"Where?"

"He is at the bottom of the ravine, near the brook. He's probably getting some water or perhaps looking for insects to eat. Shall I describe him to you?"

"If you like."

"I can see now that he is an old fellow. The bright blue of his face and neck is turning white. His feathers are not as grand as they once were. Some of his feathers are broken and drooping. Even laying across his back, I can see they are not as fine as they once were. He's lost some of his former grandeur but none of his pride. He still moves as delicately and haughtily as he probably did in his youth."

"I can relate," Mr. Pope said under his breath.

Pru released his arm. "No, you can't. You are still in the prime of your life, and if you don't mind me saying so, your feathers are not broken or drooping."

He laughed, the sound quiet but unmistakable. "Is *feathers* supposed to symbolize a part of male anatomy?"

"No. That was not at all what I meant." Pru could feel her face heating. How did she manage to find herself in these situations? "I only meant you are still a handsome man. But I told you that last night." She cleared her throat. "Speaking of which, we should begin where we left off, don't you think?"

"I do," he said.

"Good. Then we were discussing the third line of Monsieur Barbier's chart, were we not?"

"Actually," he said, turning toward her. "We were doing this." He reached for her, his hand finding her waist, and pulled her close.

## Twelve

He thought she might hesitate or argue when he touched her, but she went willingly, almost—if he was not mistaken—eagerly into his embrace. He'd been wanting to do this since the moment they'd been parted the night before. She felt so good pressed against him. Her body might be reed slim, but it held an unmistakable strength. She would not buckle or bend easily. She could withstand storms.

The flare of her hip, just below her waist, where his hand strayed was not generous. There was no question she was a woman, with a woman's curves, but her charms were not easily apparent. She was like a treasure to be explored and discovered.

He'd begun that journey with a kiss the night before, and the lure of her now was too much to resist. He wanted to taste her again, feel the way her body melted into his.

Her mouth brushed against his, and he couldn't stop the smile.

"You're smiling again," she murmured. "It makes me nervous."

He leaned close until he inhaled her scent. The smells of pine and oak, moss, and late-blooming flowers permeated the air, but underneath all of them was Pru Howard. He would know that scent anywhere. "You think I have a diabolical plan?"

"I wouldn't put it past you."

"I smiled because you seemed impatient for me to kiss you." He found the curve of her neck and nuzzled it lightly. Her hands, which he'd barely felt under the wool of his coat, gripped his shoulders tightly.

"A lady would never admit to being impatient for such a thing," she said, shivering when he pressed a light kiss to a spot just below her ear.

"No, she would not," he murmured against her skin.

"Thank God I am not a lady." She turned her head, and his lips met hers. The kiss was hot and deep and not at all what he'd been expecting. His body reacted immediately to the heat that flared between them as their lips tangled, their mouths seeking and finding and seeking again.

She was the first to flick a tongue out and taste him, but he was the one who cupped the nape of her neck and twined his tongue with hers. She stepped back and then back again.

He followed, and a moment later, he felt her bump up against a tree. He put his hands out, the rough bark behind her anchoring him. He needed the stability as his head spun and his entire body was screaming for release.

They broke apart, and she leaned forward and kissed the spot just above his cravat and to the left of his jaw. She was tall enough that she had easy access, and he allowed the exploration, even as his body burned hotter. When she reached his ear, she took his lobe in her mouth and bit him lightly. A flash of savage desire ripped through him, and his hands fisted on the tree bark as he fought to gain control.

"Where the hell did you learn that?" he asked, gritting his teeth to maintain composure.

"You didn't like it?" she asked, but her voice was not full of concern. She knew he'd liked it. In fact, she leaned forward and swirled her tongue over the spot aching from her love bite.

"I thought you were the daughter of missionaries," he said, sliding his hands over her hips and then up her ribs, pausing just below her breasts.

She sighed. "I'm afraid I'm something of a disappointment to them. There's a reason they left me behind in Milcroft."

"Thank God they did," he said, finding her lips again with his own and kissing her until they were both breathless. "I want you," he said when they parted.

"I can feel that." She shifted her hips slightly, and he knew she felt his erection against her belly. "But you sound surprised."

"Because I didn't think I could feel like this," he admitted. "I hadn't felt anything but numbness in so very long."

"You just needed a good shake," she said. "That and people around who care about you."

She was right. He'd thought secluding himself while he licked his wounds would give him time to recover and heal, but it had only made him feel more isolated and alone. He'd withdrawn further, his injuries multiplying. It was only now, when he'd been forced out into the world and forced to confront the things he disliked—loud noises and people about him he could not see or predict—that he was beginning to reclaim parts of the man he'd been.

"Do you intend to move your hands higher?" she asked. "Or are you just teasing me?"

He realized his hands were still paused just beneath her breasts, his fingers resting on the fabric covering her delicate rib cage. He could feel the light stays she wore, feel the way her breaths came in and out at a rapid pace. "May I?" he asked.

She shook her head and he felt her blow out a breath. "Such a gentleman," she said in a tone that indicated it was not a compliment. "In all the ways *I* don't want you to be. You ask permission to touch me, and yet you have no qualms about pointing a pistol at someone."

"Clearly, I have forgotten my manners."

Her lips traced the curve of his jaw, making his breathing increase. "You should forget them again."

That was all the permission he needed. His hands slid up to cup her small but firm breasts. He would have liked to pull her bodice down and touch her flesh, but he couldn't see the dress she wore and felt no openings in the front.

But he knew where he could find exposed flesh. Both hands slid back down her hips and began to gather the material of her skirts.

"Mr. Pope?" she said, a warning in her voice. "I hope you don't think to—er, have your way with me up against this tree."

"I think you had better start calling me Nash," he said as his hands grazed the bare skin of her thigh. "And, no. I'm not so coarse as to roger you against a tree." Not that the idea didn't appeal, but their first time—if they had a first time—

would not be out here with his trousers about his ankles and her back rubbed raw against a tree trunk. "But I do want to touch you."

She moaned a response as his hand slid higher up her thigh, her skin hot and soft under his fingertips.

"Do you object?" he asked, his mouth on her throat. Her pulse beat madly under his lips.

"Not yet," she said.

He chuckled. Her skin felt so alive, so warm under his touch. He felt so alive when he touched her. He felt alive when he was with her. He hadn't wanted to feel. He hadn't wanted to remember what his life had been like before, but when he was with her, he could handle the pangs of nostalgia and feelings of loss. He would have given anything to see her face right now, as his hand skirted higher, but he could hear how her breath caught and feel how her body trembled in anticipation.

And then his hand grazed something unexpected. He pulled back. "Drawers?"

"Hmm?" And then she hissed. "Oh, yes. I forgot about those. Don't look so shocked," she said, and he tried to school his face into a more neutral expression. "I don't see why only men should wear them. You try wearing a skirt out and about this time of year and see if you appreciate a frigid breeze in your nether regions."

Nash was surprised to find he was scandalized. The only women he had ever heard of wearing drawers were prostitutes or courtesans. They were considered a masculine garment, and it was quite taboo for a genteel lady to wear them. He'd never reached under a lady's skirt and found a pair of drawers. But he was not put off now that he had. In fact, he was rather intrigued. These drawers, in particular, were quite short, not even reaching mid-thigh. From what he had felt, they were made of a soft linen material.

"I can imagine you wouldn't want cold air…there," he said, his hand fingering the edge of the drawers as he tried to picture them in his mind. "What color are they?" he asked.

"White. I sewed them from an old petticoat. They aren't fancy."

"You continue to surprise me, Pru." His hand slid inside the drawers and she shivered.

"Is that a good thing?" she asked, her voice low and husky as his hand brushed against the curls at the juncture of her thighs.

"It's a very good thing. God, but you're warm."

"So are you," she said, breathless. "You're like an inferno."

"I promise I won't burn you."

"Somehow I doubt that. Nash?"

His head jerked up at the use of his Christian name.

"You did say to call you that?" she asked, voice tentative.

"I did. Call me that whenever you please."

"Good. Then Nash?"

"Yes?"

"Do you plan to keep teasing me or do something with those fingers?"

He almost laughed out loud. She was wonderfully audacious. "Shall I do this?" he asked, stroking a finger along her seam.

"Oh, yes." She moaned and pulled him closer. "How about this?" He slid the finger back, pausing at the place where that small nub of pleasure was hiding. Gently, he parted the flesh and brushed over it.

"*Nash.*"

"You asked me to stop teasing you," he said, siding his finger into her wetness. She was tight and hot, and he regretted having begun this because the need to be inside her was all but overwhelming. He withdrew his finger, slaking it over that tight bud again and she tensed in his arms. As he brushed over the sensitive spot, his touch feather light, her hips bucked, and her hands clawed at his shoulders.

"Still no objections?" he murmured into her neck.

"If you stop, I will strangle you," she said, trying to sound threatening but failing miserably as she moaned in ecstasy on the last words.

"I wish I could see you," he said. But he didn't need to see her to know she was close to climax. Her body tightened and her cries grew louder and more frantic. He had a moment to worry someone might hear them, but the informal garden was safer than anywhere else they might go. They were far from the house and the road, and the sound of the brook below would carry over her voice.

That was until she cried out and her body convulsed. She pressed hard against him, and he could feel her throb and pulse. Had he ever felt a woman find her pleasure like that? Had he ever paid such close attention to her ragged breaths and the scent of her arousal? He couldn't see her, but he had discovered other ways to enjoy pleasuring her.

He withdrew his hand, and she slumped against the tree. He pulled her close, burying his face in her hair, soft and fragrant. He took deep breaths, trying to calm his racing blood. It felt so good to touch her, so good to feel her release against his hand. So good to feel his own hunger for the touch and taste and feel of her growing.

"That was not the first time a man has touched you," he said. It wasn't an accusation. Rather, it was a late attempt to be certain he hadn't just given a virgin her first *petite mort* against a tree.

"You're not the first," she said, sounding unapologetic. "If that bothers you—"

He held her close when she tried to struggle away. "Not in the least. I'm no priest myself." He leaned away, cupped her face, and kissed her again to prove the revelation had changed nothing. After a moment, she kissed him back, leaning into him again as though she could not get enough. He knew the feeling. He wanted to keep talking. If he started kissing her again, she might end up under him on a bed of pine needles.

"Is that why your parents left you behind and in the care of our vicar?" he asked.

She sighed. "I'm afraid I disappointed them greatly in Cairo."

"Cairo?" His brows shot up. "Will you tell me?"

"Will you tell me about your first time?" Her voice held a hint of challenge.

"A quid pro quo? Very well, though it's not anything as exotic as Cairo."

"Shall we sit down? I find my legs are a bit wobbly."

He nodded and they returned to the log, Pru leading him. Somehow she managed it without making him feel as though he needed the assistance. They sat together for a few moments in companionable silence. Nash listened to the burbling water of the brook below and the breeze rustling through the leaves. It had been a long time since he had just let the garden envelop him, not cocked an ear for the sound of danger. "Is the peacock still below?" he asked.

"No. We scared him off. You will have to tell me how peacocks came to be at Wentmore," she said. "I know there is a story."

"Are you trying to wriggle out of telling me about Cairo?"

"No. Let's see, where to begin. Have you been to Cairo?"

"No." He'd been back and forth across Europe more times than he could count, but he'd never been sent to Africa. He would never see it now. Not with his own eyes, but perhaps there was another way. "Tell me about it."

"We arrived when I was sixteen. It was the first trip without Anne. She had married that summer and gone for holiday to Brighton with her husband."

"This is your sister who is blind?"

"I only have one sister, yes. She has a little girl, my niece, Rose. Rose is three, and I am hoping the vicar will allow me to visit my sister and little Rose at Christmas."

"Is her husband blind?"

"No. He is a printer. In fact, that is how the two of them met. I had taught Anne night writing—as I *should* be teaching you"—her voice was tinged with censure—"And we had been searching for a printer who might print some pamphlets or poems—something short to begin with—in night writing so Anne could practice reading something other than my drivel.

"Mr. Thomson agreed to try, and he and Anne fell in love."

"What about the pamphlets or poems?"

"He did print a few, but Monsieur Barbier's method seems rather inefficient and lengthy. I don't see how we could ever print books without using so much paper it would cost a fortune to produce and purchase. But *if* you learn night writing and *if* the vicar allows me to visit my sister at

Christmas, I will bring you the pamphlets and poetry back to read."

Nash nodded, but he was still amazed that her blind sister had married a man with sight. Although, he supposed he would not be put off by a woman without sight, but a man without sight was helpless and useless. No woman would want him as a husband. "You were telling me about Cairo," he said. He hadn't meant to divert her from the subject, but it was easy enough. She loved to talk, and Nash found he liked listening to her.

"Yes, it was our first mission trip without my sister, and so I was trapped all day with my brothers who were five and seven. They were little terrors and constantly hitting each other or biting or wrestling on the floor."

Nash laughed. Having two older brothers himself, he understood exactly what she must have witnessed.

"I took every opportunity to escape them, and I would put on a dress called a *sebleh*. I had a very pretty one in black with red and gold embroidery around the neck and along the front. Women in Egypt wear trousers under their skirts. They're called *tshalvar*."

"Ah, so this is where the idea of trousers took root?"

"Believe it or not, in Egypt it is considered scandalous for women to *not* wear trousers. They protect modesty much better than simply hoping a strong wind doesn't kick up one's skirts.

"And then because I wanted to remain anonymous and keep my parents from knowing I was out and about, I wore a head covering called a *burqa* that concealed my head except for my eyes. I could explore the markets and the city that way. Cairo is not so different from London. There are beggars everywhere and vendors with their stalls, calling out their wares. The smells are different. In London you might catch the scent of potatoes, leeks, or onions. In Egypt, I would smell spices like cumin, aniseed, and bay leaves."

As she went on, Nash closed his eyes, finding he could picture all she described. The sounds, the sights, the smells, even the feel of the hot, dry desert air sucking the moisture from his skin.

"And then I met Abubakar. He was the son of a powerful and wealthy government official. I don't know much about Abubakar's father. I just know my parents had to have his blessing to have their church services and continue their preaching. We had met formally several times when my parents came to his father with some grievance or other, and then once we met in the market. He took me to places in the city I would never have found on my own and introduced me to many of his friends. This would never have been allowed if I was an Egyptian girl, but I was given some allowance since I was from the West. Still, it was not proper for the two of us to be seen out on the street very often, so we would go to his rooms to enjoy a light meal and then one thing led to another…"

"He seduced you."

"I think the seduction was mutual, but yes."

Nash heard the tone of wistfulness in her voice and found himself unreasonably jealous. And yet, why should he care about a man she had known years ago in a country far away? But he could picture her on a bed of silk, a man feeding her dates, then leaning down to kiss her as boats floated down the Nile outside the window behind them.

Nash shook his head. He wanted to be that man. He was here now, and for the moment, at least, he was the only man with her.

"And then my parents found out what was happening," she said with a sigh. "You can't ever keep anything a secret in Egypt. Perhaps not in London, either. Too many servants wanting to gossip. I don't know what happened to Abubakar, probably nothing, but I was sent home immediately to stay with Anne and Mr. Thomson. My parents returned some months later, and we lived in less than perfect harmony until I was sent here."

She took a deep breath. "Now they are off on another adventure, and I am here on my own adventure." Her hand covered his, and she squeezed lightly. Nash could not help but smile. He did not imagine spending time with him was anything like an adventure in the Far East or Cairo would have been, but he appreciated her attempt to make her time in Milcroft seem special.

"And now your turn."

He laughed. "Would you believe a hay loft and a dairy maid?"

"Really?" she asked, her hand tightening on his.

"No. It was my first year in the army. My regiment was quartered in the north of England, near Lincoln. The family I stayed with had a young cook, who was always making me a special tart or giving me an extra helping of dinner. One night she slipped into my bed after the family was asleep. A few months later, I was sent to France to fight the French."

"Mr. Langford said you served under Lieutenant-Colonel Draven in a special troop."

"I did, but I was asked to join Draven's troop after I'd already been fighting for a couple of years and had distinguished myself as a marksman. The Colonel was famous for asking the men he invited to join him if we were afraid to die. His orders amounted to nothing less than suicide. We were sent to get as close to Bonaparte as we could and destroy his top men, if not the general himself. We started with thirty and came home with twelve. It's only because of men like Rowden Payne and a few others that even a dozen of us came home."

"I'm sure your skill with a rifle had something to do with it as well."

"I was injured a couple of months before the war ended, and I wasn't there for the end of it."

She leaned against him, resting her head on his shoulder. "That doesn't mean you weren't an integral part of it."

Nash didn't answer. It felt so normal to sit here with her. He could pretend his eyes were closed and he was like any other man, not a damaged man who could not even see the face of the woman he'd touched so intimately just a half hour before.

"What did you say?" she asked a little while later. "When the colonel asked if you were afraid to die?"

"I said, hell yes. Anyone not afraid to die was a fool."

She laughed. "I would have said the same thing."

"Apparently, I'm the only one in the troop who answered that way."

"Really? None of the other men were afraid to die? I can't say I think them very stable after a revelation like that."

"I think any man who joins a suicide troop is at the very best reckless and at the worst completely mad. We were all a bit of both at one point or other."

The brook burbled in the long silence as she digested this. "So the correct answer was that you were not afraid to die. Why did the colonel choose you then?"

"I suppose because I was the best," he said without any pride. He had been the best and being the best at shooting people was not something he would ever boast about. "He needed me. When I told him I was afraid to die, he said, *Then you'd better shoot straight and keep your head down. We'll protect you.*"

Nash thought about Rowden and the other members of the troop who had come to visit him in the past few months, men he had chased away or, accidentally, though no one believed it, shot at. The troop was still protecting him, even if it was from himself.

## *Thirteen*

No one answered the door when Pru knocked the next day at noon. The morning had been cold and rainy, and she was glad she had spent so much time outdoors the day before. Today all anyone wanted to do was stay inside and huddle by the hearth. The weather was damp and gray, and Pru had considered staying at the vicarage, but Mrs. Blimkin had arrived late because of the foul weather and was in a foul mood whenever Pru managed to get underfoot. The vicar was home as well, and the house seemed too small for the three of them.

The rain had slackened by eleven, and Pru had hoped it would stop altogether so she and Nash might walk in the informal gardens again. Perhaps walking wasn't exactly what she had in mind. She had in mind more of what he'd done to her yesterday—the kissing and touching and *more touching.* Her mother would have told her she was an unrepentant sinner. She'd known her parents would think what she'd done was wrong, but being with Nash didn't feel wrong. Being with him felt right.

She was a woman of three and twenty. She was plain and poor and had no prospects or connections. She would never marry. Was she supposed to forgo all carnal pleasures for the next fifty or sixty years? Why had God given her these needs and the ability to feel as she did if he did not want her to enjoy these feelings?

And she did not think anyone would dispute the changes in Nash the past few days. He'd lost that hunted look. He was doing better, and if kissing him was what it took to keep him from the asylum, then kiss him she would.

Pru was about to knock again, when the Northgate door finally opened, and young Mr. George Northgate stood there. He gave her a long look. "If it isn't Miss Howard. Come in." He moved aside, and Pru hesitated before stepping into the house. It was cold and dark and unusually quiet. No servant came to take her coat.

Northgate closed the door and leaned on it. "Not going to Wentmore today?" he asked. Pru did not like the way he leaned on the door, and she suddenly wished she hadn't come at all. But Mrs. Northgate was expecting her.

"I could ask you the same question," she said, avoiding his query.

"You are a forward girl, aren't you?" he said. "The workmen aren't there because of the rain. Mr. Payne sent them home."

"Mr. Payne is back?" Pru asked.

"He returned last night. I'm surprised you didn't know. You seem well acquainted with all that happens in that house."

Pru glanced at the stairs. The sconces were not lit, even though the day was dreary and the house dark. "If you'll excuse me, I will go see Mrs. Northgate. I'm sure she is wondering where I am." Pru started for the stairs.

"Not likely," Northgate said.

Pru reached the stairs and started up.

"She's not here," he said.

Pru paused and looked back. "Where is she?" She had the ridiculous idea that Northgate had done something to his grandmother.

"She's gone to Blunley town with the rest of the family. You and I are alone," he said. Pru shivered slightly. She had not liked the tone of his voice. It had sounded...*ominous*.

"I wonder why she didn't tell me." Pru made her voice light and unconcerned as she slowly made her way back down the stairs. Northgate was still blocking the door. He'd said they were alone, but that couldn't be right. There were always servants in residence, especially in a big house like this one. Except Northgate had answered the door himself, and no one had come to take her coat.

"Why would she?"

Why would she indeed? It was not as though Pru had any standing in this village, and Mrs. Northgate did not owe her any explanations. But the woman had been kind to Pru, in her way. Mrs. Northgate didn't make Pru feel less than as her grandson now did.

"I should return to the vicarage," Pru said. "You should have told me earlier. I wouldn't have taken up your time."

"I saw you yesterday," Northgate said, not moving away from the door or acknowledging her obvious wish to leave.

"Oh, where was that?" Pru asked, wondering if she could leave through a back door. Were the servants downstairs? Could she get out that way?

"Wentmore. You walked into the wood with that invalid."

Pru refrained from pointing out it was an informal garden, not a wood. "Mr. Pope is not an invalid. He has lost most of his sight, but he is still quite capable."

"Oh, really? And what exactly was he capable of in the woods?"

For a moment Pru couldn't breathe. Had Northgate followed them? Had he seen them together?

"I see something must have happened in the wood," Northgate said, stepping away from the door and toward her. "Your face just flushed red. What did you let him do to you?"

So he hadn't followed them. And he was moving closer, trying to intimidate her. He obviously didn't know that she had walked the streets of Rome and Paris and London. She could defend herself. She lifted her umbrella, readying it in case she needed to swing it at him. She knew not to swing out. He would just grab the end and yank it away. She had to wait for him to come close enough and then bring it up unexpectedly, hitting him between the legs.

"I fail to see how what I do is any of your concern, Mr. Northgate. I came to call on your grandmother. If she was not here, you should have informed me of that when I first arrived. Good day." She gave him a long look, waiting for him to move. He looked back at her. Pru's hand tightened on the handle of the umbrella. "Good day, Mr. Northgate," she repeated.

Finally, he stepped aside. She waited, and he stepped aside again, not enough to make her comfortable, but she thought she could get by. Holding her umbrella tightly and her head high, she walked past him. Her skin crawled, and she feared he would grab her as she passed him, but he didn't move. Pru grasped the latch on the door, opened it, and stepped outside.

She closed the door behind her and forced herself to open her umbrella and not to run. She wanted to run. The skin on the back of her neck crawled as she felt his eyes on her. She wouldn't turn back to look, but she just knew he was watching her through the curtains. She didn't particularly want to go back to the vicarage, but at least she was safe there. And so she hurried back, her hem covered in mud by the time she returned.

She spent the early afternoon helping Mrs. Blimkin with the cooking and the mending, and when Mr. Langford's dog cart arrived in the late afternoon, she was actually surprised. "Is that for us?" she asked Mrs. Blimkin.

"Who else?" Mrs. Blimkin said, when she came in from giving Langford's apprentice a small tart for his trouble in bringing the cart.

"I hadn't thought we would go to Wentmore," Pru said. "What with the rain and all."

"Rain?" Mrs. Blimkin gestured to the window. "It hasn't rained for hours."

Pru hadn't even noticed the rain had stopped. A look out the window confirmed that the puddles in the yard had shrunk. Still, a look at the sky did not reassure her. The clouds still hung heavy and low.

"We won't stay long," Mrs. Blimkin said, handing Pru one of two baskets laden with the fruits of their afternoon labors. "I just want to deliver this to Mrs. Brown. Mr. Payne returned last night, and she'll have her hands full feeding two men and that other."

"Other?" Pru asked, putting the basket in the cart and then taking the second from Mrs. Blimkin and stowing it too. "Do you mean Clopdon?"

"I'd rather you not speak his name to me, Miss Howard. He is a trial, that one."

Pru looked back at the house. "What about the vicar? It's almost dinner."

Mrs. Blimkin nodded. "I'll leave him a plate if you write him a note. We should be back before too long." She pointed at Pru. "No walks in the gardens today. You have time for a quick lesson while I tell Mrs. Brown what to do with these provisions. Understood?"

Pru nodded. When she'd seen the weather this morning, she had not thought she would see Nash at all today. She was pleasantly surprised that they would have a brief visit. And this time she was determined to make sure he knew the rest of Monsieur Barbier's chart. They really should begin to practice writing and reading the code.

The vicar's dinner set out, Pru and Mrs. Blimkin made their way to Wentmore. The roads were wet and muddy, and it took a bit longer than usual. A few times Pru worried one of the wheels would become mired in the muck, and she wondered if it wouldn't have been more judicious to walk. But then they would not have been able to manage the heavy baskets of food.

And then finally they spotted the lights of the big house ahead. Pru was surprised at how bright it was, having been there in the late afternoon before and seeing it bathed in foreboding shadows. Now it looked almost welcoming.

Mrs. Blimkin drove to the back of the house, where a groom came out and took the horse. Mrs. Brown met them a moment later, helping to carry the baskets inside.

She greeted Pru quickly, and then she and Mrs. Blimkin were speaking about pies and crusts and fillings. Pru waited to see if she was needed and then wandered to the stairs and started up.

At the top, she went into the dining room, hoping to find Nash, but it was empty. She made her way into the parlor and found Mr. Payne, reading a newspaper. He stood as soon as she entered. "Miss Howard."

"Mr. Payne!" She gasped at the sight of his swollen lip and black eye. There was a cut across his nose and bruising on his jaw. "What happened?"

"Occupational hazard," he said.

She stared at him, and he waved a hand. "I'm fine. In fact, I'm flush in the pocket. Have you come about your wages?"

Pru had forgotten that she'd initially come to Wentmore in search of pay so she might be able to buy a few necessities. Now it seemed wrong to take money when she and Nash had been doing much more than lessons. "No. I can't stay long. Mrs. Blimkin wanted to leave provisions with Mrs. Brown, and I thought I would review what we have learned with Mr. Pope. But if he has retired, I can return tomorrow."

"Clopdon!" Mr. Payne roared, and Pru jumped. He was a big man and his voice probably echoed throughout the house. "My apologies. The bell pulls don't work. Clopdon will know where Nash is lurking."

A rumble of thunder sounded in the distance, and Pru thought about those storm clouds again.

"How are the lessons progressing?" Mr. Payne asked, gesturing to a chair across from him. The fire in the parlor was cozy, but she sat on the edge of her seat as she heard rain begin to patter on the roof and windows. She and Mrs. Blimkin would have a wet ride back.

"Mr. Pope is very quick and clever. I suspect he will be reading and writing using Monsieur Barbier's method very soon."

The door opened and Clopdon stood in the rectangle, a much put-upon expression on his face. "You called, sir?"

"Where's Pope?"

"I was assisting him as he dressed for dinner."

"We are dressing for dinner now?"

"Yes," Clopdon said, drawing the word out.

"I suppose you had better have Mrs. Brown set another place. Miss Howard is here."

"Oh, but I won't be staying," she said, rising.

"You can't leave while it's raining like this." Mr. Payne looked at the window, and Pru realized it was pouring. "You and Mrs. Blimkin can go as soon as it lets up. We can send a lantern to light your way."

Pru looked down at her drab dress. At least it wasn't the pea-green gown. "I'm afraid I won't be able to dress for dinner."

"Then I will join you in solidarity," Mr. Payne said. He looked at Clopdon. "The extra place setting, Clopdon?"

The man gave a heavy sigh and withdrew.

*Sweet Rogue of Mine* | 257

"I don't think he likes having to relay instructions."

"I know," Mr. Payne said, smiling.

"He hired several footmen," Pru said. "I don't have much experience with servants, but I assume that is more in line with their duties."

Mr. Payne shrugged. "What's the fun in that?"

Pru gave him a narrow look. "I no longer wonder at why you have a black eye, Mr. Payne."

He laughed just as Mrs. Blimkin came into the room. "Oh, Miss Howard. I should have listened to you. The rain is coming down in droves." She bobbed a curtsy to Mr. Payne. Then, getting a good look at him, took a mincing step back. "Sir, I am so sorry to have to impose on you a bit longer."

"It's no imposition. I was just telling Clopdon to set another place for Miss Howard at dinner. Why don't you join Mrs. Brown, and I'm sure the rain will slacken this evening and you can be on your way. I'll send my groom with you to light the way."

"That would be much appreciated, sir. Of course, Miss Howard can eat with Mrs. Brown and me."

"No."

Pru turned at the voice and saw Nash had come downstairs at some point. He'd been standing quietly, listening to the conversation. Mrs. Blimkin jumped and whirled around. "Oh, you scared me to death!" She moved aside, probably looking for the best place to hide should Nash produce his pistol.

Pru could understand why Mrs. Blimkin would suggest she eat downstairs. Pru was of a lower class than either of the men, and she was an employee—a servant of sorts. Her employment was more akin to that of a governess, though, which meant it would not be improper to allow her to eat at the table with Mr. Pope, although it was somewhat unusual.

"How nice of you to join us," Mr. Payne drawled. "I already told Clopdon to set another place for Miss Howard."

"Good. She won't be going anywhere tonight, so we might as well prepare a chamber for her." He glanced in the direction of the vicar's housekeeper. "And Mrs. Blimkin."

"Oh, I don't think that will be necessary," Pru said. Her heart had been pounding in her chest since she had heard his voice. Then she turned to look at him, and it had taken this long for her to find her own voice. He looked so incredibly handsome. Clopdon obviously knew what he was about because not only was Nash dressed as a gentleman, he looked better than she had ever seen him. He wore a dark blue coat that contrasted with the stark white of his shirt and neckcloth. His cranberry waistcoat was embellished with gold thread in the shape of vines. She'd never seen him in breeches, and she almost wished she hadn't seen him in them now. They were fawn colored and molded to his body, emphasizing his lean, muscled legs. She couldn't help but glance down at his calves, nicely rounded in the stockings he wore.

But perhaps the biggest change was in his face. He'd always been clean-shaven, but she could tell he'd been recently shaven. His hair had been trimmed. It was still long on one side, worn to cover his injured eye, but it was otherwise neat and styled fashionably. His face had lost even more of the gauntness, and she could see in the time since she'd first met him that he'd gained weight and his features were returning to what they had once been.

He'd been an attractive man before, but now he took her breath away.

And she'd never felt so impossibly unworthy. She wore her dress with the faded tiny rose pattern, which had been mended more times than she could count and probably cost less than one sleeve of the superfine coat Nash wore. Her undergarments, though thankfully no one could see them, were tattered and stained. Her boots had holes, and her hair—well, she didn't know when she had last smoothed it. It was probably a complete mess, lying flat on her head like a straw broom.

"Miss Howard." Nash gave her a courtly bow. She knew he was showing off for his friend and Mrs. Blimkin. She heartily approved. Mrs. Blimkin would go back to Milcroft and tell everyone that the earl's son was as sane as the next man and a perfect gentleman. It could only help his cause, especially if word reached his father's ear.

She glanced at Mr. Payne and he gave her a small nod, indicating he was thinking exactly what she was.

"I understand and appreciate your desire to return to the vicarage. I am certain Mr. Higginbotham will worry about you"—Nash inclined his head toward Mrs. Blimkin—"and you, Mrs. Blimkin. However, unless the rain stops or slows in the next hour, the road back will be impassable. It's raining quite hard, and the first quarter mile leading out of Wentmore has not been as well-maintained as it should have been. I'm afraid the wheels of even a dog cart will sink in mud and you will be stranded. Mr. Forester, my land steward, and I have already discussed improvements, but we have not begun them yet."

"I can attest to that," Mr. Payne added. "I've surveyed the road myself and spoke with Mr. Forester this morning. He told me he had discussed it with you. As soon as the kitchens are finished, we can direct the workmen to repair and shore up the road."

"But, begging your pardon, sirs, I don't think it would be fitting for Miss Howard and myself to stay here overnight," Mrs. Blimkin said. What she didn't say, but what Pru heard, was *I'm afraid you'll murder us in our beds.*

"I think it less fitting that you catch your death of cold in a storm such as this." As if to punctuate Nash's words, lightning flashed, and a moment later, thunder boomed.

"You and I can share a chamber," Pru said to Mrs. Blimkin. "That is, if the rain continues. That should end any talk of impropriety." And perhaps make Mrs. Blimkin less concerned about being shot in her sleep.

"I'll go tell Mrs. Brown." Mrs. Blimkin started away, giving Nash a wide berth. "I suppose I had better help her with dinner as well. Give us a half hour to ready it. I've been up here for ten minutes at least and God knows what havoc she has wreaked below."

Pru covered her mouth to hide a smile. Mrs. Blimkin left, and then it was the three of them. Pru was not certain whether to hope the rain stopped or continued. Of course, she hoped it continued, but she realized she was *supposed* to want it to stop.

"How was your visit to Blunley?" Pru asked Mr. Payne, before remembering he'd gone in search of a bedmate.

"Most productive." He touched his eye gingerly. "And profitable."

"Do you mind if I ask how you make your living, Mr. Payne?" Pru said. "I know it's a bit gauche, but I can't help but wonder if you are a gentleman or—"

"Probably best not to ask," Nash said.

Pru raised her brows. "I see." She tried not to keep staring at Nash, but it was difficult. It was more than just his handsome features that drew her attention. There was something else different. He was behaving differently.

Quite suddenly, she realized what it was. He hadn't put his hand into the pocket where he kept his pistol once. She glanced at that pocket and took in a breath. It was flat and tight against his body. The pistol was not in the pocket, which meant he had either forgotten it or felt comfortable enough to be without it for the time being.

"Well," Mr. Payne said, breaking the silence. Pru realized she hadn't spoken for a moment and it must have been awkward to watch her watching Nash. "I should go dress for dinner."

"You said you would not," Pru reminded him. "In solidarity."

"So I did. Then I won't dress. In which case, pretend I gave some other acceptable reason for excusing myself right now. I can see you two would prefer to be alone."

"Not at all," Pru said at the same time Nash said, "Yes, we would."

"Right then." Mr. Payne walked through the parlor door, leaving it open in what was perhaps a not-so-subtle gesture for them to mind their manners.

As soon as he was out of earshot, Pru said, "Did you tell him?"

"Tell him?" Nash asked.

"About *us*!" she hissed. "About what happened in the informal garden."

Nash made a face. "Give me some credit. I don't kiss and tell."

"Then why is he leaving us alone?"

"I may not be able to see," Nash said, moving forward and reaching out to grasp the back of a chair. "But I can feel the way you were looking at me."

"How was I looking at you?" Pru asked.

Nash moved to the front of the chair and paused. "Like you were hungry for more than Mrs. Blimkin's cooking."

She was glad he could not see because she could feel her cheeks flaming, and she rarely blushed.

"Are you seated?" he asked. "I can't sit unless you do."

Pru sat in the chair across from him. "I am now."

Nash took his own seat, angling himself toward her. "Are you worried it will stop raining or worried it won't?"

"What a question!"

"You're quite safe from me," he said. "Mr. Payne and I have rooms in the west wing. My room is all the way at the end of the corridor. The last door on the left with the tarnished handle."

Pru narrowed her eyes. He was giving her a very specific description. "How do you know it's tarnished?"

"Clopdon has remarked on it a half dozen times. I'm sure Mrs. Brown will put you in the east wing," he said. "You and Mrs. Blimkin."

"That would be wise, considering you gentlemen are in the west wing."

"And it was wise to offer to allow Mrs. Blimkin to sleep with you. I can't slip in bed beside you in the middle of the night."

Pru shivered. Was this hypothetical or was he giving her instructions?

"No doubt she sleeps like a log," he said. "Probably snores too. I hope she doesn't keep you awake past midnight."

Oh, he was definitely giving her instructions. The question was whether Pru would follow them.

"I needn't worry about that if the rain stops," she said. "I think it is already slowing." This was not at all true. In fact, the thunder was so loud the moment after she spoke that the entire house seemed to rattle. She had to raise her voice to be heard over the roar of the rain on the roof. She hoped enough progress had been made on the kitchens that Mrs. Brown and Mrs. Blimkin were not getting wet.

"If it doesn't," Nash said. "You know you will be safe with me."

## *Fourteen*

Dinner was the best thing Nash had ever eaten. The food was simple and there were only two courses, but it was expertly prepared and flavored, and he was so happy to have something edible to eat that he had three helpings of both dishes.

The food had improved markedly since Mrs. Blimkin had stepped in to help, but she had outdone herself this evening. He sent his compliments via one of the footmen after the meal. The vicar's housekeeper was still in residence. Pru was as well because the rain had not let up. Clopdon had reported the front lawn looked rather like a pond. Mr. Forester, the land steward, had sent word that the last of the fields had been harvested a couple of days ago and the barns were all on higher ground. He did not expect there to be a problem as the river that ran through Milcroft was low and could easily absorb the excess water now pouring into it.

Nash was also happy to hear that Forester had called on the Smiths this afternoon and assured them they would not be required to pay their rents that quarter. Mr. Smith was out of bed and doing better, and with Mrs. Brown's help, the family now had provisions enough to see them through the winter. Nash had asked for a list of any other tenants struggling, and Forester was to deliver that by the end of the week.

The rain did slacken after dinner, but not enough to allow travel, and Nash was assured Pru would be under his roof tonight. He liked the idea of her under his roof. A few weeks ago, he hadn't wanted anyone near him. He hadn't trusted anyone. But she had given him hope for the future. That hope had given him permission to trust again.

It wasn't all Pru, of course. Rowden had scared the hell out of him when he'd shown up and told Nash his father intended to send him to an asylum. Nash was still under threat. But at least now he had hope.

As he listened to Pru and Rowden chat about the upcoming autumn festival, he realized that he felt content. He had to think back long and hard to remember when he had last felt content.

A chair scraped back, and Nash saw Rowden's form rise. Nash rose as well.

"Thank you for a lovely dinner," Pru said. "I know Mrs. Blimkin will want to leave early tomorrow so I had better go to bed. Good night, Mr. Payne."

"Good night, Miss Howard."

"Good night, Mr. Pope," she said.

"Good night, Pru."

No one spoke for a moment, and then she cleared her throat. But Nash didn't correct his error. He hadn't said her name in error.

"Good night then," she said and was gone.

Nash's arse had barely touched the seat again when Rowden said, "I hope neither of you has plans to ever tread the boards. You're both terrible actors. She's even worse than you. Do you really think this is a good idea?"

Nash didn't pretend he didn't know what Rowden was talking about. "I want her."

"That's not the point. A couple weeks ago I arrived to find you drunk, contemplating putting a pistol in your mouth, and living in squalor. Your father is still threatening to have you committed. You think a scandal involving a woman from the village—a woman living under the vicar's roof—is wise?"

"There's no guarantee she'll come to me tonight."

"You didn't see the way she looked at you. She'd be in your bed now if she could manage it."

"And I should send her away?"

"You should have a care for your own self-preservation."

Nash nodded. "For the first time in years, I do actually have a care about myself. And that's in large part due to Miss Howard."

"This is the part where you thank me."

"I would, but you foisted Clopdon on me, and I cannot thank you for that."

"Point taken," Rowden said with a laugh. "Now heed my advice. Give her a kiss and send her back to her own chamber. In a few weeks your father will have visited, and we will have convinced him of your sanity and respectability. Once the threat of a lifetime of confinement isn't hanging over your head, you can do what you like. Agreed?"

"Agreed."

"Bloody hell, Nash. At least try to make me believe you're listening to me."

***

Nash tried to drag out the hours until midnight as best he could. He'd prepared for bed and sent Clopdon away then sat down by the fire, listening to its hiss and crackle as well as the steady patter of rain outside. He couldn't read, but he could write a bit now, thanks to Pru. Nash went to his desk, a piece of furniture he barely remembered he owned, and drew out a slip of paper. With effort and patience, he pressed the nib of a pen into the paper until he could feel the message he wanted to create. Pru hadn't told him exactly the process for writing using *Ecriture Nocturne*, but he could improvise until she finished her lessons.

Though, in truth, he rather hoped she never finished her lessons.

Somewhere in the house a clock chimed the hour, and Nash counted the light bells as they sounded ten, eleven, then twelve.

He'd lain awake, pistol clenched in his sweaty hands, many nights listening to that chime, wondering if he would ever have the courage to just end it. He would have broken the damn clock if he knew where it was. He couldn't remember, and he'd tried to follow the sound but couldn't quite pinpoint the location.

A soft tapping drew his attention to the door. "It's open," he said. He looked toward the door as it opened, and a slight figure stepped hesitantly through. He stood. "Lock it," he said. "You can hold on to the key."

He wasn't interested in keeping her here if she didn't want to be. He heard the lock click and then her intake of breath as she drew closer. He realized he was wearing only his dressing gown, and it was open at the chest, revealing the bare skin beneath. He didn't draw it closed.

"You came," he said. "Did Mrs. Blimkin say anything when you left?"

"She was snoring as loudly as a coach and four," Pru said. "She didn't notice my absence." She moved closer to him again, obviously not put off by his state of undress. "What are you doing? Are you writing?"

He shrugged. "I'm trying. What do you think?" He held the paper out to her.

"But we haven't even finished learning all of the rows of Monsieur Barbier's matrix."

Nash smiled. "*You* haven't finished drilling me on them. You told me where every letter was located, and I don't need to be told more than once."

"You don't?"

"No."

"Then why didn't you say something?"

"And end our lessons early? I don't think so." He gestured toward where he thought the paper would be. "You haven't shown me exactly how to write yet, but I tried it on my own."

"May I use your desk?" she asked.

"Of course." She moved past him, the fragrance of her floating on the air and teasing him. He didn't move back, and she didn't avoid his touch. Their bodies brushed against one another, and he felt a powerful wave of desire. He assumed she had placed the paper on the desk and was running her finger along the dots he had made in order to read the message. He knew when she had finished because she made a soft sound.

"Did you read it?" he asked.

She turned toward him. "Yes. It says, *Kiss me*."

He felt a surge of triumph that he had written it correctly. And then she took hold of his hand and moved closer to him. And he felt a surge of a different sort. She placed her other hand on the back of his neck and drew his mouth down slightly to her own. Her lips brushed against his, and he did not hold back. He pulled her hard against him, rewarded by the feel of her body under the thin shift she wore. Of course, she had no wrapper or dressing gown. She'd come in what she'd worn to bed, and he could feel that she wore nothing underneath the light garment.

He ran his hand up from her waist, the softness of her hair tickling his skin as his mouth teased hers until she was kissing him back as fervently as he was kissing her. And then he swept her up into his arms. She made a sound of protest, but he knew his chamber well enough to feel secure. He carried her to his bed and set her down before coming down beside her and kissing her again.

His hands moved over the thin linen of her shift, feeling the curves of her breasts and the delicate indent of her waist. Then his hand dipped lower until he felt the bare skin of her knee. Her legs were long, the skin soft, and he wanted to kiss every inch of them.

"Wait," she said.

Nash stilled, removing his hand and drawing back. "I apologize. I thought—"

She wrapped her arms about him, keeping him from pulling away. "You weren't mistaken. I want you, Nash, but if we're to do this, I want more from you."

His brows rose. "I've only just begun. If you give me a moment, I can give you more."

She laughed quietly. "That's not what I mean. Do you know," she said, smoothing her hands over the silk of his dressing robe, "I have never seen your face?"

"Then we're even."

"I care about you, Nash."

He felt his heart tightening with discomfort. It had been a long time since anyone had said something like that to him. His throat felt like he had swallowed a pound of sand. "I care about you."

"I know." She stroked his back. "I want to be with you. *All* of you. I want to see your face. I want to see the man I'm giving myself to."

He shook his head. "You see me better than most people already. I'd rather not disgust you with the ruin of my left eye."

"Nothing about you can disgust me," she said. "Here." She took his hand and then lay back. Gently, she placed his hand on her cheek. "You want to see my face? See it with your hands."

He hesitated, knowing if he did this, she would want to see him as well. But he couldn't resist touching her. He wanted to *really* see her. He dragged his fingers lightly over her cheeks, feeling the fine bones underneath. "Delicate," he murmured. He traced her sharp little chin. "Stubborn," he pointed out. His fingertip moved to her soft, perfectly shaped lips. "Lush," he said.

He felt her mouth curve in a smile. He moved up, lightly tweaking her straight nose and then stroking the soft lashes of her eyes and the slight arch of her brows. "So beautiful."

"I think your fingers deceive you," she said.

"Never."

She had a smooth high, forehead, and her hair was incredibly soft when he delved into it. Soft and straight, like a waterfall as it cascaded over his hands.

"Your hair is down."

"I'd wear it down all the time if I could. I hate putting it up."

"Why doesn't that surprise me?" he teased.

"I'm not a proper lady," she said, her voice holding a hint of a warning.

"I had no idea." He grinned, thinking back to the first time he'd met her, when she'd been singing "Bonny Black Hare" at the top of her lungs. "Proper ladies have never interested me. I can only sip tea and talk about the weather for so long before I fall asleep."

"And what sort of lady manages to keep you awake?"

"The sort who sings bawdy songs and asks too many questions and kisses me until my toes curl."

"I made your toes curl?" she asked.

"I can't remember." He dipped to kiss her again. "Let me refresh my memory." He kissed her slowly and deeply, and she returned the kiss for a long, blissful moment. His entire body tingled, and his toes curled as he settled his weight against her.

Pru ended the kiss and pulled away. "Nash, if you're not ready for this, I can go back to my room. I don't want to push you"

Bloody hell. This was the sort of thing *he* should be saying to her. He should tell her to go back to her chamber. Rowden was right. This was dangerous, and he did not need any more trouble in his life.

But he needed Pru, and she needed this to mean more than a quick tumble in the dark. Being with her meant more to him than a perfunctory release, but he didn't know how to give her what she wanted. "Don't leave," he said. "I'm trying."

"You're not ready," she said. "I understand."

"I'm ready." He unclenched his jaw and tried to say it again without sounding like he was in pain. "I am ready." Hell, was he ever ready. "I'm not good at this sort of thing. At being vulnerable. I've spent most of my life hiding behind walls and columns, only stepping out to take a shot. I try to avoid exposure, not embrace it."

"I'm not the enemy," she said.

No, the enemy was inside him. It was a voice in his head, telling him he would never be good enough. That no one would ever want him. "The whole world is the enemy," he said, his voice low.

"Then we stand together against it," she answered, her voice also low. "If anyone wants to hurt you, I'll fight for you. They will have to drag me away in chains before I watch you go to an asylum."

He couldn't help but smile at the ferocity in her voice. No one would ever accuse her of disloyalty. He swallowed and sat back on the bed. "Go ahead and light the lamp," he said.

She didn't speak for a moment, and then he heard her soft intake of breath. "I can look at you?" she asked. "*Really* look at you?"

"You'd better hurry before I change my mind."

The bed shifted, and he could just make out her form as she moved about the room, searching for the tinder box and the lamp in the low firelight. Finally, the lamp flared, but she turned the flame down enough that the light didn't bother him too much. And then the bed dipped again, and she took his hands.

"Are you certain?"

"I'm not certain about anything. Make it quick."

"I don't think so," she murmured, and her hands slid up his arms. The dressing robe was silk, and he could feel the warmth of her through the material. When her hands reached his face, he closed his eyes. It was more reflex than anything else. He certainly couldn't see her face as she studied him. Her fingers drifted over his features as his own had done hers just a few moments before. She slid a finger along his jaw and made a sound of approval. He rather liked that sound, and it stirred his hunger for her again.

Then her fingers slid over his lips, just a light brush. He opened his mouth to kiss her fingers, and she clucked and made a sound of admonishment. "How long will this take?" he asked, growing impatient to have her in his arms again.

"As long as I want it to," she answered. Her fingers danced over his nose and then skipped his eyes and slid over his forehead. He knew she was deliberately giving him time to ready himself. Finally, she touched his right eyebrow, and then lightly caressed his lashes.

He knew what came next. But she took her time. She slid her hands into his hair, slowly pushing it back and off his forehead. He could feel the light on the damaged left side of his face as she moved the lock of hair he wore to cover it.

He gritted his teeth and clenched his hands, waiting for the harsh intake of her breath indicating surprise or disgust or shock. Either that or she would make a sound of pity. But as he waited, exposed and naked to her scrutiny, she said nothing and did nothing. Had the horror of his injury rendered her speechless? Was she even now trying not to retch?

He jumped when he felt her fingertips on the brow of his left eye. The brow was divided, a scar running through it. He had felt the knotted skin there but never seen it.

"Shh," she whispered as though soothing a small child. Her fingertips were light as a feather as they brushed over his brow. They didn't skip the scar that marred his brow but traced it as lovingly as she had traced the rest of him. Then she slid her fingers lower, over his damaged eye, barely touching the closed lid until she could also brush her fingers along the lashes of the blind eye.

To his surprise, she leaned forward and kissed his left cheek. "You are a beautiful man," she said. "I can hardly believe I am in bed with you right now."

He could hardly believe what she was saying. *She* was surprised *he* wanted her? Even as she looked upon the horror of his injury, she was still attracted to him. "You cannot be serious," he said.

"I am. If you could see my face, we would not be here. I've told you that I'm not pretty."

"And I am not beautiful, but you don't know me if you think I'm the sort of man who would reject you because you have freckles or an unfashionable dress. I can see *you*," he said. "And I don't need my sight for that."

"Then why can't you believe the same of me? I see you, and you are much more than an injury to your left eye, Nash Pope."

He reached for her hands, which were still holding his hair back. His hands closed on her wrists and he brought one palm to his mouth and kissed it. "Do you still want to lie with me?" he asked. Even after all she'd said and done, a small part of him held his breath, afraid she would reject him.

"More than anything," she whispered.

He released her hand and reached for her waist, sliding his hands down until he grasped the hem of her short shift. He drew it over her head, his fingers trailing her silky skin, left bare as he drew the garment away. He tipped her back then and moved his hands over her naked body, taking his time. Her skin was soft and hot. Her belly was flat and the curve from her waist to her hips slight. Her breasts were small but plump, the nipples hard and sensitive. She moaned when he brushed a hand over them. He could all but feel her ribs as he slid his hand over them, and he vowed to feed her more. Knowing her, she was always too distracted or daydreaming to remember to eat. Then he slid his hand down to the soft thatch of hair at the juncture of her thighs. "What color is this?" he asked as she shifted under his touch.

"Brown," she said. "I told you I have brown hair."

"As do I," he said, moving over her so he could kiss the path he had just traced from her breasts to her belly.

"No," she said, voice breathless. "Your hair is almost black. It's very dark, while mine is a drab brown, not even a deep chestnut."

He'd forgotten his hair was a dark brown, almost black. He hadn't thought about it in a long time, so focused was he on his sight. "I couldn't care less what your hair looks like," he said. "I like the feel of it." He stroked a hand over the pillow, feeling her soft hair there. "I like how smooth and straight it feels."

"It is that," she agreed. "It won't hold a curl and comes right out of almost any style I put it into."

"Sounds like the perfect hair for you. Stubborn and willful."

She might have argued with him. He thought he heard the protest on her lips, but he dipped his mouth to her neck and then her breast, taking one of those small, hard nipples in his mouth. He had always enjoyed the sight of a woman's breast. He liked touching them as well, but he'd never paid as much attention to the feel of a woman's breast as he did now that he could not see Pru's. Her nipple was not smooth but lightly textured. As he circled it with his tongue, it seemed to swell slightly, becoming thicker and plumper. The skin of her breast was incredibly soft, and he could feel how it tilted slightly upward, making his cock harden as he imagined how she must look with her body bared on his bed. She was moving beneath his touch, her body restless for more of him.

He slid down that body, kissing her belly with his lips then moving over to her hips, which were narrow and angular. He kissed down to her thigh and then over to the nest of curls. Gently, he parted her legs and moved to kiss her there.

"What are you doing?" she asked, her voice ragged with desire.

He paused. He knew she wasn't a virgin, but it hadn't crossed his mind that she might not have been introduced to all the pleasures he had in mind. "You haven't done this before?" he asked.

"Done what?"

"No man has kissed you here?" He ran a hand over her sex, and she gasped in pleasure.

"No. There's only been one man, and he never...did that."

The idea that he would show her something new pleased him. She had shown him so many new things over the past weeks. "Then I had better show you."

"But—"

His fingers slid over the slick folds between her legs, and she moaned again. He settled himself comfortably and parted her inner lips. Then, using his tongue he learned the shape of her, teasing and tasting her until he found the places that made her moan the loudest. He was dizzy from the heady taste of her and the scent of her arousal.

Her breathing had grown more rapid and her breaths came short and ragged as he teased at the nub hidden among her folds. She moaned, and that just encouraged him. His hands were on her inner thighs, and he could feel the way her entire body trembled with anticipation and need. He wanted this to be good for her, to be the best she'd ever had. He slowed his caresses, spreading her wider, exploring her thoroughly before returning to that lightly pulsing nub.

"Please," she moaned.

Begging? He liked the rasp of her voice and the blatant carnality he heard in it.

"*Nash.*"

"Hmm-mmm." He flicked at her and she cried out. She was so close to the edge. He could feel her balancing on the precipice, ready to tumble over as soon as he gave her what she craved.

He licked her again and then again and then harder. He felt her tumble, felt her body convulse and her hips buck. As she began her ascent, he slipped one finger inside her, felt her body clench hard around it. She was tight and wet and ready for him. She cried out and he pressed deeper into her, her body so warm and alive against his.

And then, almost as suddenly as it had begun, she slumped and went limp as a ragdoll.

"Pru?" he said with some concern.

She made a sound, which might have been a word, but was completely unintelligible.

"Are you well?" he asked after waiting another moment for her to speak.

She made a moan of contentment, unwilling or still unable to speak. He smiled and was about to lay beside her when her foot—he thought it must be her foot, pushed his chest back.

"Take off your robe," she said, her voice low and husky. "I want to feel your skin against mine."

Well. She obviously was still capable of speech. He slipped the robe off, less self-conscious about nudity than he had been when she'd revealed his damaged eye. He heard her take a long, slow breath in, and then her foot slid to the side and he felt her knees close around his hips as she wrapped her legs about him.

"Come here."

## *Fifteen*

Pru could tell by Nash's expression that he hadn't expected this. Perhaps he'd expected to be left unsatisfied as he had yesterday in the informal garden. Perhaps he'd thought to give her time to rest.

But she wanted him now. He'd just made her feel better than she ever had in her entire life, and she wanted more of him.

How could she not? He looked just as good without clothing as he did with it. He was still a bit thinner and paler than he probably should have been, but underneath the slimness he was strong and sinewy. His arms and shoulders, in particular, were tightly muscled. She imagined that was from years of holding heavy rifles for hours at a time.

His chest had a light smattering of hair, dark like that on his head and arms. Under his navel, a dark path of hair led to his jutting erection. Men called it a cock, she knew. It was proud and most definitely at attention.

It had been years since she had done this, and she was more than a little nervous now, but she was also powerfully aroused. She wanted him inside her, wanted him to fill her, make her feel as good as he had a few moments ago with his mouth.

He came down on top of her, balancing his weight on his elbows on either side of her, their bodies pressed together. Oh, she liked the feel of him against her, liked the sensuous slide of their flesh as he kissed her and moved over her. She wrapped her legs around his waist, bringing their bodies closer until his cock was right at her entrance.

He kissed her again, and she lost herself in the pleasure of his mouth. He had the most persuasive lips, playful and insistent. He must be impatient to find his own pleasure, but the way he kissed her was so slow moving, she felt as though a drug languidly spread through her body, heating her and stoking the flame of her desire all over again. She dug her hands in his hair, enjoying the thickness of it and the way her roughness seemed to unsettle him for a moment before he kissed her into senselessness again.

All the while his cock was warm and hard at her entrance. Finally, she reached between them to stroke it, to guide him inside her. He tensed and she looked up at him.

She knew he couldn't see her, but it seemed as though he was looking right at her. "You're sure?" he said.

"I'm practically begging you," she whispered. She wasn't sure if the rain had picked up again or if it was the rushing of the blood in her ears, but she could hardly hear her own voice. Thunder rumbled in the distance, and it seemed to echo the fast, hard beating of her heart.

She guided him to her entrance then sighed in pleasure as he pushed slowly inside. She slid her hands over his bare back, pausing on his buttocks, then stroked the muscles of his lower back as he slid deeper.

"*Yes*," she said, her head tilting back at the pleasure filling her as he moved deeper. "Nash, *yes.*"

"You feel so good. I didn't know how much I wanted this."

She had known. She had known since the first time she saw him in the informal garden that she wanted him. She had imagined his body between her legs and his cock pushing into her just like this. But in her imaginings, it hadn't felt this good. She could never have imagined anything that felt this good.

He slid even deeper, filling her completely as he sheathed himself to the hilt. His body was pressed intimately against hers as he began to move. She moved with him, his rhythm seeming second nature to her and the push and slide of their bodies causing delicious friction that caused her to gasp and sigh and, when he drove deeper, to moan.

His lips met hers on one of those moans, swallowing it as his tongue delved into her mouth. Her hands clawed at him, wanting more of him, wanting him closer. He broke the kiss, and his mouth moved to her jaw, his teeth scraping against her skin gently. He moved lower, still inside her, kissing her nipples and teasing them with his teeth and mouth. She arched her back, offering herself in a way she had never given herself.

She had thought this would be quick, a few thrusts and he would lie spent in her arms, but Nash showed no signs of flagging. He seemed to have all the time in the world to stroke and kiss, changing the rhythm of his movements inside her slightly even as he did so. As much as she liked his mouth on hers, she wanted the closeness now. She pulled him back until their bodies touched in every place possible.

"I won't last much longer this way," he said.

"Neither will I. I want to feel your heart pounding against mine. I want us so close our spirits can touch."

He gave her a startled look, and she knew she had probably said something odd. She was always saying odd things before she could think better of them. But Nash nodded slowly. "I like that," he said. "I want to know your spirit," he murmured. "Intimately." He thrust deep inside her, and she gasped and raked her hands down his back.

"Yes?" he asked as he withdrew then dove deep again, burying himself inside her.

"Yes. *Oh, yes.*"

He moved slowly as the pleasure built inside her and became something more, something out of her control. Her body arched, pressing tighter against his as she sought the heat of him.

"Oh, God," he said as her climax rushed over them both.

He withdrew only to thrust into her again. She was beyond comprehension now, her body soaring on acute pleasure, but she heard a voice that sounded like her own cry, "Again. Harder."

He thrust again, deep and hard, and she came apart. She bit her lip to keep from crying out too loudly as her body seemed to splinter into tiny points of ecstasy. And then, almost too soon, he was gone, pulling away from her and spilling his warm seed on her belly.

She knew he'd done this to protect her from pregnancy, and tears sprang to her eyes at the gesture. Of course, he would, even in this moment, protect her. She wanted to feel his cock pulse with pleasure as he climaxed inside her, but he wasn't ruled by instinct, as she often was. At his heart, he was a protector.

She lay spent and breathless for a long, long time, listening to the rain on the roof and the thunder in the distance. At one point, Nash brought a wet cloth and cleaned her. Then he climbed into bed beside her and pulled her close. She burrowed into him, wishing they could do it all again. He kissed her temple, holding her gently as though he really cared about her.

Pru knew she shouldn't allow that thought to take root, but she was weak and spent and not able to fight her own worst instincts. She couldn't stop herself from imagining what it would be like to lie with him like this every night, to feel his strong arms around her and his heart thudding with desire for her.

Gradually, his grip loosened slightly, and he ran his hand over her body, squeezing the curve of her hip and stroking a breast lightly. "Are you cold?" he murmured.

"How could I be?" she asked. He was like a fire, creating his own heat. After a while, he dozed, and she could not resist rising on one elbow to peer at his face. She couldn't believe she was here with him. She couldn't believe a man so gentle and attentive was at risk for an asylum. He didn't belong in a place like that. He was not mad or dangerous. He'd suffered a trauma. He needed compassion and patience.

Her gaze wandered and finally fell on the table beside the bed. There, gleaming in the lamplight, was his pistol. The handle was dark wood, polished until it gleamed. Pewter, embellished with designs, ornamented the pistol. It really was a work of art—a deadly work of art. Though she had noted he reached into his pocket to touch it less often now, he still kept it with him or nearby. He still needed it.

"What are you looking at?" he asked.

She glanced at him. His eyes were still closed, but he was not asleep as she had thought. "Your pistol," she said. "It's here on the nightstand."

"Useless for the moment. Clopdon keeps taking the powder and balls, and every day I have to make him give them back."

"It's beautiful. Who made it?"

"It's French. The creation of a Monsieur Gribeauval."

"The French make better pistols than the English?" she asked.

"Not necessarily. I also have pistols by Manton, Hawkins, and Twigg—all British gunsmiths. But none fit my hand so well as the Gribeauval."

"I notice you seem to need it less these days."

He didn't answer for a long time. Then he finally said, "I'll always need it."

"We'll see," she said. She snuggled close to him again. "Is that the pistol you used to shoot the Scotsman?"

He let out a surprised laugh. "How long have you known about that?"

"Since almost the beginning. The surgeon says the man you shot was a friend of yours."

Nash's expression grew serious. "He is...well, he was. We were in the war together, so he should have known better." His expression turned dark, and Pru wished she hadn't said anything. She did not want to ruin this closeness between them.

"We don't have to talk about it."

"We should," he said, pushing himself to sit. She pulled the sheets up around her nakedness, even though he couldn't see. She suddenly felt vulnerable. "You should know the dangers of being with me."

"I'm not afraid of you." She tried to take his hand, but he withdrew it.

"You should be. Duncan Murray wasn't afraid of me either. He didn't have any reason to be. But I can't be trusted."

"I don't believe that," she argued. "You're not dangerous."

"Tell that to the hundreds of men I killed in the war. Tell that to the women and children. Yes, Pru, I killed children. I'm dangerous, perhaps more so now because my mind plays tricks on me."

Pru let his words sink in for a long moment. She had known he was a sharpshooter. Of course, he had killed men, other soldiers, during the war. War was kill or be killed. And war was terrifying. Her own parents had fled countries or cities when fighting came too close. Not even a missionary was safe in the midst of a siege or battle.

But a sharpshooter chose his targets. Why would he shoot women? Why would Nash shoot children?

"Do you know why I shot Duncan?"

"No."

"I thought he was the enemy. I thought he was the French attacking."

"I don't understand. You were at home, here at Wentmore, and the war is over."

He shook his head. "It will never be over for me. Sounds or smells can bring it back in an instant. And then I'm in the midst of it again, the scream of horses, the smell of gunpowder, the ground shaking when a cannon fires. And I was expected to stand still, stand steady, and fire. To kill and kill and kill."

Pru took Nash's hand then, and when he tried to pull away, she held on. "They asked you to do something horrible. War is horrible. You did what you had to."

"Not always. I made mistakes, and it's the mistakes that haunt me. I might be able to let go of it if not for those. But I'll never let go of it, and even when I think I have, it can all flood back in an instant. I hear the crack of thunder, and I'm back in a battle. I hear the whiny of a horse, and I'm at my post. That's what happened the day Duncan showed up. I don't know exactly what happened. I heard a pounding, and my mind went back."

She could see him struggling to explain, struggling to put into words how he had felt that day. She gripped his hand tighter.

"It was as though I knew in one part of my mind that I was home. I was safe. But another part of my mind wouldn't accept that. It told me to fight, to shoot at the enemy. I can't even bloody see, but all around I *did* see."

"What do you mean?" she asked. "Your vision returned?"

"No. I think it was a memory. I saw a battlefield, men running, falling when shot, the spray of blood and the clash of bayonets. But it was so clear. It was like it was right in front of me. One part of my mind told me *this is Duncan. He's no threat.* But the other part of me screamed, *fire! Kill him before he kills you!*

"And so I shot him. Thank God I couldn't see and was drunk off my arse. I only shot him in the arm. I would have blown my own head off that day if I'd killed him."

"Nash, no." She clutched his arm tighter.

"The truth is, Pru, I *do* belong in an asylum. No sane man imagines those things. No sane man behaves that way."

"You are sane, Nash. You were just frightened, and fear can make us behave in ways we don't expect or understand."

"There is one thing I understand," he said, his voice carrying a note she did not like. "I'm a danger to you and to the other people around me."

"How can you say that? After what we just shared? After the past few days? You are *not* dangerous."

"Do you think I haven't had good days or good weeks before?" She had been gripping his hand, but now he tightened his own grip almost painfully. "All it takes is one loud noise, one *bang*, and I'm back. If I think I'm in battle, if I think I'm being fired upon, I'm a danger."

He took her shoulders in both hands, holding her so she could see his face fully, not only his profile. "You are not safe with me, Pru. You will never be safe. I may be able to avoid the asylum. I may be able to convince my father not to send me, but that doesn't mean I can live like other men."

"What are you saying?" she asked. But she knew what he was saying, and she didn't want to hear it.

"I can't be with you. I can't be with anyone. I was living here at Wentmore, alone, because that was the only way I could keep from hurting others. Rowden came and upended that, and I know why he did it. But he won't stay. And once he's gone, I'll send Clopdon and the footmen, and Mrs. Brown away again."

"And me," she said quietly.

"I have to."

"You don't."

"But I will." He released her, stood, felt for his discarded dressing gown, and pulled it on. Pru had the distinct feeling she was being dismissed. She didn't like the feeling. She didn't like the silence in the room. She tilted her head, listening, and realized the rain had stopped. The world seemed almost too quiet now after the roar of the thunder and the finality of Nash's words.

"Nash—"

"I don't want to hurt you," he said, his back to her as he fastened his robe. "I shouldn't have given in tonight. I don't regret it, but I should have realized it would make this…" His hand gestured vaguely. "More difficult."

*This*. That's what he called tonight. *This*.

Did the pronoun refer to the way he'd kissed her? The way he'd held her? The way he'd thrust inside her until they were both spent?

All of it? None of it?

She was a *this* and their lovemaking was a *this* and all of it was now difficult for him.

She tried not to feel hurt. She knew he was doing this to protect her. He was a protector, after all. His entire adult life had been spent in service to others. He was the one who stepped out from hiding and fired the shot to cover other men when there was danger. He was the one who had to make the hard decision of who lived and who died.

She couldn't imagine having to make decisions like that, having to muster enough courage to step out from hiding in the midst of danger and expose oneself in order to protect others. And to do it all with a steady hand and clear eyes.

But she did feel hurt. She'd given all of herself—not just tonight and during *this*—but in the last few days and weeks when they had been together. She was the kind of person who always gave all of herself, and she'd been hurt before. But she couldn't remember a time when the pain had felt quite so sharp or so deep.

"I should go back to my chamber." Her voice sounded wooden and flat. Nash's shoulders went rigid, and she knew he heard her pain. But he didn't turn and take her in his arms, as she'd hoped and wanted. He continued to face away from her.

Pru found her shift and pulled it on, twisted her hair into a knot at the nape of her neck, and went to the door. "If the rain holds off, we'll be gone first thing in the morning," she said.

"I think that's for the best," he said.

"I'm sure you do." She took the key, unlocked the door, and opened it. She hesitated, almost looked back at him, then walked away, keeping her head high and her shoulders square.

## *Sixteen*

"Stop walking around like that," Rowden said, looking up from the paper in disgust.

"I can't help how I walk."

"Then go walk somewhere else."

"Go sit somewhere else," Nash said. "This is my bloody house."

Rowden, of course, ignored him. He turned the page and continued reading. But now he read silently. He'd been reading to Nash, but Nash didn't want to hear about life in London, the contrivances of the Prime Minister, or the price of crops. He probably should be listening to the last of those. He had his own crops to sell. He told himself he would go over prices with Forester later.

Today was Sunday and there were no workers hammering and sawing. Nash should have been pleased at the peace and quiet. He should have spent a pleasant morning eating food Mrs. Blimkin had sent and listening to Rowden read the paper.

But nothing was pleasant, nothing was right, without Pru.

It had been five days since he'd last seen her. Scratch that. It had been five days since he'd sent her back to her room without so much as a *good night*. He'd taken her to bed then sent her away like she was a common trollop. He hadn't meant to dismiss her that way. He hadn't meant to dismiss her at all, but in the aftermath of their lovemaking, he'd been gripped by a crippling fear—he could hurt her. He could mistake her for an enemy and shoot her dead. He'd almost killed Duncan over the summer. Nash couldn't trust himself with Pru or with anyone.

He'd tried to talk Rowden into leaving the next day, but Rowden was as immobile as ever. Undoubtedly, that's why Draven had sent him. Rowden had told him to stubble it—but in less complimentary terms—and he'd stayed right where he was.

"If you miss her so much," Rowden said, turning another page of the paper, "why don't you send for her?"

Nash stopped pacing. He'd been pacing for the last half hour, and not only because it helped alleviate his restlessness. He knew it annoyed the hell out of Rowden. Of course, he'd forgotten Rowden could take a punch to the face stoically, so of course he could put up with Nash's petty annoyances. Now Nash was the one irritated.

"Send for whom?" Nash asked.

"Stop playing the idiot."

It seemed a role he was destined to play, though. He shouldn't have sent Pru away as he had. He should have been gentler. He should have taken more time. It wasn't always best to shoot for the head. Sometimes one could fire a warning shot, give a bit of notice.

"I'm not sending for her," Nash said, pacing again. "She's better off without me." He could almost hear Rowden rolling his eyes.

"She probably is, if this is how you treat her after taking her to bed."

"I never said I took her to bed."

Rowden made a sound something like a laugh. "I saw the way the two of you looked at each other that night. A team of horses couldn't have kept you apart."

Nash took a wrong turn and rammed his knee into a piece of furniture. He winced. "I sent her away for her own good. She's not safe here with me."

"You plan to shoot her like you shot Duncan Murray?"

Nash sank onto the chair. "I didn't plan to shoot Murray, and that's exactly the problem."

Nash breathed through the long moment of silence. "You thought you were under attack," Rowden finally said. "That's what Draven believes. It was a mistake and Murray's fault because he probably stormed in here like the lunatic he is. Notice when I arrived, I was a bit more circumspect."

"You're still not safe. My mind could go back there. I could shoot you, and I'm unfortunately and unwillingly sober now. I wouldn't miss."

The paper rustled as though Rowden was either reading it again or setting it aside. "I would prefer you didn't carry your pistol with you at all times, but so long as Clopdon is in possession of the powder and balls, I feel somewhat better."

Nash didn't feel better. Clopdon had found a new hiding place two days ago, and Nash hadn't discovered it yet. He reached into his coat pocket and touched the pistol there. Pru was right that he didn't seem to need the comfort of it as he had before. He still liked to have it close by, but he didn't need it as much.

"You think you will shoot Miss Howard as she climbs into your bed one night? If you did, you'd be an even bigger rattlepate than I thought. And no one is that much of a nodcock, not even you."

Nash sincerely wished he could find his powder and balls. If anyone deserved a hole in his head, it was Rowden.

"I suppose you think you're being noble and protecting her."

"And what would you have me do?" Nash asked. He still didn't fully trust himself to keep Pru safe, but he hadn't expected to miss her this much. Surely, he could see her one more time.

"Send for her—no, better yet. Go to her. It's time you made some effort."

"I made a clean break," Nash said. "I should leave well enough alone."

"If you don't want to see her, fine. Be a nodcock. But the more I think about it, the more I think it would be wise for you to go into Milcroft. Show yourself. We want word to reach your father that you're doing well. I don't know why I didn't think of this before."

"You want me to march into Milcroft and what—go shopping at the general store?"

Rowden stood. "Excellent idea, but you shouldn't march. You're the son of an earl. We'll go in a carriage. Unfortunately, nothing will be open today and most people will be home. It's Sunday. We should go tomorrow."

"I don't want to go into Milcroft." The idea made him shiver with loathing. He didn't want to be exposed to the villagers. Everyone would stare at him. There would be whispering and murmurs behind fluttering fans.

Pru would be there.

"I didn't want to come here," Rowden said. He opened the paper again, or at least Nash assumed that was what the rustling of the pages and the accompanying silence indicated.

Nash went to stand by the window. He couldn't see the view as he once had, but he could feel the sun on his skin. Funny how Pru had made him take notice of little things like the feel of the sun on his face or the breeze in his hair. Funny how, hard as he tried, his thoughts always returned to her. Even now, if he allowed his mind to wander, it would return to that night of the storm and the feel of her trembling with need beneath him. The rake of her nails against his back and the deep-throated moan she gave when he slid into her.

Nash wanted to moan himself. He wanted her back and in his bed. And he also knew that sending her away had been the right decision. For both of them.

He heard a sound like a baby's cry and went completely still. He knew that cry. Once all of Wentmore seemed to echo with it. Once Wentmore had echoed with laughter and voices. It hadn't always been the silent tomb it was now. But the peacocks were gone and so was the joy.

Nash felt very much akin to the lone peacock calling outside, crying for his companions, his mate. Crying for a time that would never come again.

\*\*\*

"How much longer, girl?" Mrs. Northgate asked as Pru stood behind the privacy screen in her boudoir and waited for Sterns, the lady's maid, to do up the last of the buttons on her new dress.

The dress she had sewn—well, mostly sewn. It was ready and Pru was both thrilled to finally be able to try it on and also a little sad that her daily visits with Mrs. Northgate would be at an end.

She wouldn't miss Eliza, Mary, George or their mother. But she had begun to think of Mrs. Northgate as a friend.

"There," said Sterns, taking a step back. She nodded approvingly, and it was the first time she'd ever looked *at* Pru and not *through* her. "You look very well," she said.

"Thank you," Pru said in surprise, forgetting one wasn't supposed to thank servants. Ridiculous rule at any rate.

"Well, step out then," Mrs. Northgate ordered. "Let me see."

Pru moved out from behind the screen and stood in front of Mrs. Northgate, who removed her spectacles so they dangled from her hand, the gold chain glinting in the midday sun. Her face gave nothing away. It was still the handsome, formidable face that had become so familiar to Pru. She should have known the woman would never allow so much as a smile to slip.

Mrs. Northgate made a twirling gesture with one hand, and Pru turned around, slowly and awkwardly.

"Stop," Mrs. Northgate said when Pru's back was to her. Then, "Go ahead."

Pru finished her turn and looked at Mrs. Northgate expectantly.

"Don't look at me. See for yourself," she said, gesturing to the cheval mirror in one corner. Pru moved hesitantly toward it, filling her lungs with air. But when she caught sight of herself, she let the air out in a burst. She was still the same person she had been when she'd come this morning—hair a bit unkempt, freckles dotting her face, slight hollows under her eyes. But she looked...oh, she looked like a lady.

She looked like she had a bosom!

Pru turned from one side to the other, admiring the way the ruffles on the bodice gave the illusion of more and the tapering of the skirts highlighted her small waist.

"Well?" Mrs. Northgate asked, and Pru realized she had been waiting for Pru's verdict. Pru turned to her.

"I love it!" And then even though she knew the older woman would hate it, she threw herself into her arms and hugged her. "Thank you! Thank you! I could never have done this myself."

Mrs. Northgate patted her for a moment, and then to Pru's surprise she put her arms around her and embraced her back. "It was my pleasure," she said quietly. Then she stepped back and flicked her gaze at the maid. "What are you looking at? Don't you have something to do?"

"Yes, ma'am." But Sterns only smiled as she pretended to be busy straightening items on a dressing table.

Pru was looking at herself in the mirror again. "I must admit, I had my doubts about the color, but it does suit me."

"Yes, it does. It even lessens those dark circles under your eyes."

Pru supposed it was too much to hope that Mrs. Northgate hadn't noticed those.

"I haven't been sleeping very well lately."

"Care to tell me why?" she asked.

"No reason," Pru said, turning from side to side, admiring the dress and feeling very vain.

"And has Mr. Pope been sleeping well?" Mrs. Northgate asked.

Pru gave her a sharp look. "I'm sure I don't know."

Mrs. Northgate frowned. "If I were your age, I wouldn't waste a moment of my time being unhappy. No doubt he's as miserable as you. And don't give me that look, Miss Howard. I know you're in love with him, even if you don't. I can't imagine he doesn't love you back. You have a way of making people love you."

Pru stared at Mrs. Northgate. "That's the kindest thing anyone has ever said to me."

"Oh, bother. Do not start weeping. Sterns, give her a handkerchief."

The maid brought a clean one from the drawer and handed it to Pru, who dabbed at her eyes. She had been trying very hard for the last few days not to think about Nash Pope. It seemed to take a great deal of effort to *not* think about him. And the more she told herself not to think about him, the more she was actually thinking about him.

And then she began to think about herself and wonder what was wrong with her that no one ever wanted her. Her parents hadn't wanted her. They'd left her with a stranger with hardly a good-bye. It might be years before they returned. *If* they ever returned. Mr. Higginbotham didn't want her. He'd only taken her in out of Christian charity.

Abubakar hadn't wanted her. One thing she had not told Nash was that when her parents had discovered Pru had been ruined, they'd demanded Abubakar marry her. He'd refused and his father had blamed the entire affair on Pru. As a further sting to her parents, the father had said he would never allow his son to marry a heathen whore. Pru still grimaced when she remembered her parents hurling insults back, accusing Abubakar and his family of being the true heathens.

It was no wonder they'd had to leave Cairo quickly after that.

Pru thought she had learned her lesson after Abubakar. She'd thought she had closed her heart after her parents left.

But she'd obviously learned nothing because here she was, sobbing in Mrs. Northgate's boudoir, over Nash Pope.

He didn't want her either.

She still had Anne, her dear sister Anne. Perhaps she would write and suggest, again, that she come for a long visit. Surely, Anne could use help with little Rose. She knew Anne and Mr. Thomson did not have much money and lived in a modest one-bedroom flat, but Pru didn't eat much. She could sleep on a pallet in the kitchen and stay out of the way.

But Anne hadn't yet answered her last letter, and Pru didn't want to ask to come for a visit in *every* letter she wrote. She didn't want to seem desperate.

Even if she was, now more than ever.

But she couldn't stand here weeping all day. She had to go back to not thinking about Nash and all the other people who didn't want her. Besides, Nash still needed her. She would not allow his father to have him sent to an asylum. She didn't yet know how she would prevent it, but she knew she had to try.

"Ah. I see that pointy chin of yours lifting," Mrs. Northgate said, taking a seat in her highbacked chair. "Stop watering and sit down."

Pru wiped her eyes once more and did as she was bid.

"Did I ever tell you about Mr. Northgate, my husband?"

"No," Pru said, trying not to sniffle.

"He was a curmudgeon of a man, even when I met him at six and twenty. Never a smile out of him, so sober and serious, while I was his opposite."

Pru narrowed her eyes. "You were?"

"Oh, yes. I was always laughing and dancing and flirting. Do not look so shocked. It was a different time. Our skirts were wide and our necklines low. My hair was white with powder then, not age."

Pru refrained from mentioning that she was less shocked at the idea of Mrs. Northgate flirting—though that was inconceivable—than she was at the woman dancing and laughing.

"But we fell in love, despite our differences. It was not at all fashionable to marry for love in those days, so we were fortunate that our parents approved the match. And it was a good match for forty years. I made him laugh a little more and he taught me to cultivate an air of gravitas."

"It sounds as though it was a happy marriage," Pru said.

"Not always. We fought and faced hard times. Our first two babies were delivered stillborn. William was the only child that lived, and he has blessed me with two granddaughters and a grandson to carry on the name." She leaned closer. "He's also saddled us all with that shrew of a wife, but that's what happens when a boy does not listen to his mother. I told him not to marry her, and now he regrets it, of course."

During the past few months, Pru had become used to the way people in the village would gossip. She had always felt so anonymous in London or Rome, but here everyone knew everything about everyone else. Still, Mrs. Northgate's words were a rather shocking revelation. Not because Pru doubted their truth, but because no one of the Northgates' status ever admitted to matrimonial discord. But Mr. Northgate was never at home, and Pru could only assume that was his choice. Of course, if she had to live with Eliza and Mary Northgate and their sharp-tongued mother, she would find somewhere else to spend her time as well. Poor Mrs. Northgate. She was trapped with them all the time.

"I don't tell you this so you'll pity me," Mrs. Northgate said, sitting forward. "I'm not to be pitied. I do just fine, and I have my diversions."

Pru could only suppose she was one of those diversions. Knowing Mrs. Northgate, Pru supposed the lady not only enjoyed having something to do away from her daughter-in-law but was also pleased that her diversion was something that rankled said daughter-in-law.

"We all need diversions, Miss Howard," Mrs. Northgate said. "I imagine Mr. Pope and his peacock are quite the amusement."

Pru sighed. "I have enjoyed spending time with him. He's intelligent and easy to talk to and forthright. But..." She trailed off, fingering the fine material of her russet gown.

"Go on," Mrs. Northgate said. She looked at Sterns and made a shooing motion. "Out."

When the door closed and they were alone, Pru said, "But he won't marry me."

The older woman sat back. "I assume he has not compromised you else I would have heard the tale."

"No," Pru said, not offering any details.

"So he knows you have feelings for him? Does he feel the same?"

"I think so."

"Is it an issue of class? He is the son of an earl, albeit the youngest son, and you are the daughter of...well."

"I don't think that's it." Although the differences in their class probably did not help the matter.

"I see. Do you want my advice? Because I do not want to give advice where it is not wanted."

This was news to Pru who had been on the receiving end of Mrs. Northgate's advice more times than she could number.

"Yes."

"Life is short and when you find happiness, you should embrace it with both hands. Even if that happiness is to be short-lived."

Pru looked at Mrs. Northgate for a long time. "Do you know," she finally said, "I believe we are more alike than anyone could guess."

"I suppose that may be true." Mrs. Northgate stood. "But do not ever tell anyone I said that."

"Grandmama!" A quick tap sounded on the door and before Mrs. Northgate could call out, it opened to admit Miss Mary Northgate standing in the doorway, her blond curls bobbing. "Oh, I beg your pardon," she said to Pru, probably forgetting that she was too good to speak to Pru. She looked rather out of sorts. "Grandmama," she gasped. "I have such news."

"Catch your breath, child, and then out with it."

Miss Mary pushed a hand to her abdomen and tried to gulp in air. Meanwhile Miss Northgate strolled behind her. "Mr. Pope is in the village," she said, smiling triumphantly.

Miss Mary whirled on her, grasped one of the artful tendrils of hair dangling down the side of her sister's neck, and yanked it.

"Ow!"

"I wanted to tell the news!"

"You took too long." Miss Northgate grasped one of Miss Mary's curls and yanked. Pru looked at Mrs. Northgate, who was watching her. Their eyes met and Mrs. Northgate nodded. "Go," she said. Then, "Girls, move aside right away. Miss Howard was just leaving."

The girls stepped aside without ever pausing in their squabbling. Pru rushed past them, Mrs. Northgate's admonishments ringing through the vestibule of the house as she collected her coat and gloves and raced toward the center of town.

## *Seventeen*

Nash supposed the benefit of being mostly blind was that he could not see the good people of Milcroft staring at him. He imagined he could feel their gazes on him, but Rowden said it was only his imagination and no one was paying him any attention.

Nash didn't believe that rot. He could hear the way conversations stalled or petered out as he approached. They'd driven into the village just a quarter hour ago, leaving the carriage at Mr. Langford's.

He and Rowden had visited the bakery and the blacksmith. Nash had said very little, allowing Rowden to engage in the awkward conversations with the villagers. Finally, on the way to the general store, he heard a familiar voice.

"Mr. Pope!"

Nash turned toward the sound of Mrs. Blimkin's voice. "Mrs. Blimkin," he said, bowing in her general direction. "Who let you out of the kitchen?"

"Oh, you're very naughty, you are. Mr. Higginbotham is out and about today. I was on my way home until I heard you were in the village. Is Mrs. Brown at Wentmore all alone?"

"I daresay she isn't alone," Rowden added. "We have our usual contingent of workmen there. When we left, she was in the kitchens muttering something about dinner."

Nash doubted Rowden had been anywhere near the kitchens today, but he didn't contradict the other man.

"She isn't thinking of making something herself, is she?" Mrs. Blimkin asked, sounding alarmed. "I left her with provisions."

"I'm not certain, Mrs. Blimkin. I heard Clopdon ask her if she could make a porridge."

"Oh, that awful man! He should not be allowed anywhere *near* the kitchens."

"If you'd like to accompany us back to Wentmore, you are welcome to join us in the carriage."

Nash couldn't see Mrs. Blimkin's reaction, but he could hear her sharp intake of breath. He was perplexed by it for a moment, until he realized she had probably never ridden in a private carriage before. First, the reference to Clopdon and then the offer of a carriage. Rowden must be quite hungry to be going to such lengths to persuade Mrs. Blimkin to come to Wentmore.

"Well, I would be honored. I need to stop in at the vicarage and gather a few supplies and set something out for dinner."

"We shall come by in a quarter hour for you," Rowden said.

"Oh! Yes. Well."

"Good day, Mrs. Blimkin," Rowden said. Nash echoed the sentiment. With a light touch on Nash's arm, Rowden indicated he would begin to walk again. Nash started after him, trying to keep the little vision he possessed on the shadowy form of his friend. Thank God for Mrs. Blimkin. This torture was almost at an end. All that remained was to call at the store and then collect Mrs. Blimkin from the vicarage.

The vicarage. Where Pru lived.

"You won't believe who is striding toward us right now," Rowden murmured under his breath.

Somehow Nash already knew. The air had shifted just a moment before, and he'd known she was close. It was as though he had conjured her with his thoughts. That was ridiculous, of course. She'd no doubt heard he was in the village and came to…what? Tell him off? She wasn't the sort to pretend to feel anything she didn't truly feel.

"I wish you could see her," Rowden continued. "She's wearing a dress I haven't seen before and she looks…hmm." He made a sound of approval that Nash didn't care for. He wanted to punch his friend for looking at Pru that way, but instead he tried to prepare himself for the lash of her tongue.

Perhaps that was the wrong terminology as it produced a very pleasant image in his mind.

"Mr. Pope and Mr. Payne, how unexpected this is!"

Nash frowned, hearing neither real warmth nor wrath in her voice.

"What brings you into the village?" she asked. Nash realized she was providing him the perfect opportunity to answer the question probably everyone in Milcroft was wondering.

"Well…" Rowden began, but Nash cleared his throat, cutting his friend off. Rowden had been doing all he could to save him from the asylum. It was time Nash saved himself.

"Good day, Miss Howard," he said, giving her a slight bow, which served to remind the curious villagers that he was the son of an earl and a gentleman, not some monster at the castle on a cliff. "I have fond memories of Milcroft from my childhood. I told Mr. Payne I wanted to stop in at some of the shops now that my—er, health has improved."

"I see," she said. They must have several people around them because she wasn't chastising him for the way they'd last parted. "I won't keep you then. Good day." Her step sounded on the stones, and Nash struggled for a way to keep her from walking away.

"Miss Howard," he said, grateful when her steps halted. "We are on our way to the vicarage after this stop to collect Mrs. Blimkin." He didn't know why he said this, other than to keep talking to her. Perhaps to let her know the best way to avoid him…or to see him again?

"The vicar is not at home today," she said. "After the rains the other night"—there was a slight pause that he thought perhaps only he detected—"the field where we had thought to hold the autumn festival is now far too muddy. Mr. Higginbotham went to inspect several other possible settings."

"Autumn festival?" Rowden said, and Nash did not like the tone in his voice. "What is an autumn festival?"

"Oh, but you must come," said a woman's voice. "It is ever so diverting."

"We have food and games and fellowship," another woman added.

Clearly, Rowden had some admirers here in Milcroft. Nash didn't know anything about an autumn festival. It must be something that had begun in recent years.

"Of course, we will come," Rowden said. Nash muttered, "Speak for yourself," under his breath. He was not going two miles within range of an autumn festival. He'd had enough people looking at him for a year.

"In fact," Rowden added. "I think we should host the festival at Wentmore."

Nash jerked in surprise.

"The grounds are extensive enough, and we have enough workmen at the house to…er, tidy them up."

Nash had not seen the grounds, of course, but he imagined they needed more than tidying.

"When is this festival?"

"Saturday," Pru said, her voice catching Nash's attention. She was too far away to touch, which was a good thing as Nash desperately wanted to touch her.

"I'm afraid that's not enough time," Nash said. "I would be happy to host next year."

"Oh, you are being too modest," Rowden said, clapping a hand on Nash's shoulder hard enough to rattle Nash's bones. He gripped Nash tightly, and Nash had to struggle not to flinch. "The grounds will absolutely be ready. Miss

Howard, would you let the vicar know that it would be Mr. Pope's honor to host the autumn festival this year?"

There was a measurable pause. "Of course," she said, her voice full of skepticism. Clearly, she knew Nash was being strong-armed, literally, into hosting. "I will speak with him this evening," she said. "Good day."

"She's walking away," Rowden muttered.

Nash knew this, and he knew he should allow her to go.

"Do something," Rowden muttered. "Or you'll regret it."

"Miss Howard!" Nash called.

"Yes?" she answered, sounding slightly farther away.

"Might we drive you back to the vicarage in the carriage?"

"That's the idea," Rowden said.

"It's not a long walk," she said. "I can manage."

*So much for his idea*, Nash thought.

"Surely you don't want to get dust on your new dress," Rowden said, sounding so completely unlike himself that Nash would have questioned the speaker was his friend if he hadn't been standing beside him. Rowden smacked Nash's shoulder.

"I really must insist," Nash said.

"Very well." Pru didn't sound annoyed, exactly. She sounded confused and wary. Nash couldn't blame her. He was confused himself. Why could he not allow her to walk away?

"We'll have to stop in at the store another day," Rowden said, no doubt for the benefit of their audience. "Come, Miss Howard."

Nash imagined he was taking her arm, but instead he yanked Nash forward and locked her hand on his arm. The feel of her warmth beside him was like coming home to a cozy chamber after being out in the freezing rain. He instantly relaxed, the eyes of the villagers not mattering quite so much. He could manage the whispers and stares with her at his side. He leaned closer to her, catching a hint of her scent, mixed with something new. It must be the fabric of her dress. She hadn't worn it enough for it to soak up her fragrance. Nash could remember burying his nose in her hair that night they'd spent together, wanting to drown every one of his senses in her.

"Why are you doing this?" she hissed, sounding as though she were speaking out of the corner of her mouth.

"Seeing you to the vicarage seems like the gentlemanly thing to do," he said, knowing full well that was not at all what she meant.

*Sweet Rogue of Mine* | 325

"Don't be obtuse."

Nash had always been anything but obtuse, but he felt incredibly dull-witted at the moment. All of his life he had sought to keep hidden, to use surprise to his advantage. As long as he kept his head down and his aim steady, he was safe. But Pru would pull him out into the open. And if he didn't control his feelings for her now, she would paint an enormous target on his chest. Without his only defense, his sight, he was even more exposed and vulnerable.

Nash had always prided himself on making split second decisions—fire or hold fire. Kill or stand down. The few times he had made the wrong decision—when he'd fired at a child or an unarmed woman—he had known, even in the instant he pulled the trigger, that he'd made a mistake. It was as though his mind screamed *no* and his body acted anyway. The experience of losing control of his actions for that instant had been jarring, all the more so because of the regret and guilt he'd felt afterward.

He felt that way now. His mind told him no, but his body acted without him. His hand covered Pru's, and he pulled her slightly closer. "I've missed you," he said. He didn't want to say it. He didn't know why he said it. Yes, he'd missed her, but she didn't need to know that. It didn't change anything to tell her. She wasn't safe with him, and when his father sent him to the asylum, her association with him would only hurt her reputation. She couldn't afford that. She was the daughter of poor missionaries who had foisted her on a vicar. A charity case.

A true gentleman would let her go.

And he would, Nash told himself. He just needed one more minute with her. One more hour. One more day.

One more night.

"You've missed me?" Pru asked, her voice softer than it had been. That was when he heard the hurt in her voice, and the ache that lanced through him, knowing he'd caused her pain, almost left him breathless. He wanted to ease that pain, soothe it away, atone for it.

"Terribly," he said, and it was true. He hadn't let himself feel how much he had ached for her until this moment when she was at his side again. He couldn't allow himself to feel it because the anguish would have been too much. How was he ever to let her go again?

She seemed to make the decision for him, pulling away from him. "Here is the carriage," she said. He could make out the large form of it and was glad to climb inside so as to be somewhat hidden from the curiosity of the village.

The carriage began to move and Pru made a sound of pleasure. "I've only been in a carriage a few times in my life," she said. "Most of those were hackneys. None as lovely as this."

Nash had a vague memory of the coach. It was nothing special, but then he'd grown up as the son of an earl and took carriages for granted, he supposed.

"Now that it is back in good working order, we'll have to make sure to send it for you," Rowden said.

"Thank you."

Nash could hear the rejection in the tone of her voice. There was a *but* coming, and Nash didn't want to hear it.

"But Mr. Pope and I have finished with our lessons in night writing. He knows the chart now and just needs to practice, and he doesn't need me looking over his shoulder."

Nash would have argued he *did* need her looking over his shoulder. And at his side. And in his arms. Instead, he said, "I need you to help with the autumn festival."

"Me? I've never been to the autumn festival. I have no idea what the village expects. Mrs. Blimkin can be of much more service than I."

"We have promised to fetch her from the vicarage," Rowden said. "We need all the assistance we can muster. Ah, here we are."

The coach slowed, and Rowden opened the carriage door before the servants could jump down and do so. He closed it behind him, quite purposefully leaving Nash and Pru alone.

"Excuse me," she said, moving toward the door.

Nash reached out and groped until he managed to grasp her wrist. "Wait."

He could feel her tense, could feel her desire to escape him. But she didn't move, didn't pull away. That must mean she still felt something for him. Didn't it?

"Walk with me," he said on a whim. He was no great walker, but it seemed the only way to be alone with her and to ensure she wouldn't make an excuse and stay behind in the vicarage.

"Nash, I—"

"We have promised Mrs. Blimkin a ride in the carriage. Rowden can escort her, and you and I can walk to Wentmore."

She sighed, and he knew she was thinking of how to refuse.

"It's a perfect day for a walk," he said. "The breeze in your hair. The sun on your shoulders. We might even come across fairies on our way."

She gave a quick laugh. "The fairies won't be out until dusk."

"Oh. You see, I have much to learn." He squeezed her wrist lightly. "Please, Pru."

If she rejected him now, he would not ask again. He was practically begging, and while he did not have much pride left, he had some honor. And he would never force a lady to do something she did not want to do. He would not force her to be with him, if she didn't want him.

"Very well. We will walk there, and by the time we arrive, Mrs. Blimkin will be ready to return. You'll send us back in the carriage?"

"Of course."

The carriage door opened, and Nash released Pru's wrist.

"I have Mrs. Blimkin," Rowden said. "She's bringing half the vicarage kitchen."

"I suppose you will need more room then," Pru said. "It's a lovely day. Mr. Pope and I can walk."

"Oh, but there's plenty of room in the—" Mrs. Blimkin began.

"Go ahead then," Rowden interrupted. "I will have to mind my manners, alone with my favorite cook in the world."

"Oh, you!"

Nash could all but hear the blush in Mrs. Blimkin's cheeks. He climbed out after Pru and stood beside her as the coach departed. "Shall we?" he asked.

"Yes. I must admit, it is a glorious day." She took his arm, and though he knew it was to help guide him, she did it so unobtrusively that it was easy to believe she just wanted to be beside him.

They walked a little way, she telling him about the fields of brown grass and the trees turning colors and forcing him to stop and hold very still when she spotted a fox ahead. He'd walked this path many times in his youth, and he could see it again through her eyes. Nash recognized and remembered the landmarks she pointed out—the big tree perfect for climbing, the post at the crossroads, the farm of this family or that—but he'd never seen it as she did.

To him, it had all looked like land to be crossed on the way to his destination. But to Pru, the path was full of wonders and pleasures and the noticing of every small detail. To her, the journey was as important as the destination.

"When will you tell me about the peacocks?" she asked, jolting him out of his reverie. The picture she'd been painting in his mind of the landscape they traversed suddenly washed away, dripping off the canvas in a mix of colors most days he could barely remember.

"Not the peacocks again," he said. But he knew this time he would not be able to avoid the topic. And perhaps he didn't want to. He'd been thinking about his father and the years before the war more and more lately. It was easier to think about those times now than it had been even a few weeks before.

"My father had them brought here from—I actually don't know where they came from. We had five peahens and five peacocks," he continued. "The earl wanted to show them off at a garden party. Most of the guests had never seen a peacock, and he thought it would impress them."

"Did it?"

"Yes. The peacocks were all anyone could talk about. Until I put on a show."

"Your father asked you to show your skills in shooting. Mrs. Northgate told me," she said, by way of explanation. "She said you were better than any other man there by a long shot—pun not intended."

He smiled. "Yes. My father liked to show me off. He was proud when I went into the army and was distinguished with all sorts of medals and awards."

"Were you?" she asked. "I never knew that. Where are they now?"

"I tossed them in the fire," he said.

Her step faltered, and he halted.

"I understand," she said.

"I doubt that."

"You didn't want honors for doing what you had to do to survive. You didn't want to be distinguished for killing."

That was it, exactly. She'd put his feelings into words in a way he'd never really been able to. "I apologize," he said. "You do understand."

"But your father didn't." She took his arm again and they began to walk, more slowly now.

"I'm like the peacocks to him," Nash said. "I was something to show off and be proud of. He was proud of the peacocks, but he bought them on a whim. He didn't know how to care for them, didn't hire gamekeepers who knew what they were about. The peahens and peacocks died of illness or were caught by foxes and eaten. After a time, we stopped coming to Wentmore because it reminded my father of his failure with the peacocks. And after the war, once I was injured, once I was damaged, he was only too happy to send me away and pretend I'd never existed."

"But you're his son."

Nash shook his head. "All the more important that I make him proud. When I shot Duncan, I embarrassed him.

People were talking about me, about *him.* Like the peacocks at Wentmore, he wants me out of sight and out of mind."

"I think you're forgetting something," she said.

"What's that?"

"There's still a peacock at Wentmore."

He stopped walking, and the meaning of her words struck him. There was still a peacock at Wentmore. Despite all the obstacles, despite all the years of neglect and hardship, the peacock was still alive. Pru had described him as old, feathers bent and gray in the face, but he was still there, still fighting after all these years.

"No matter what happens between us," she said. "I will find a way to keep you out of the asylum."

"I don't deserve you," he said.

"No, you don't."

"And I shouldn't want you," he said. "But, God, I've thought of nothing but kissing you these last days. I can't stop remembering the feel of your skin under my fingertips, the scent of you, the taste of you."

"Are you trying to seduce me?" she asked, her voice low and husky.

"Is it working?"

"Yes." She moved closer, and he swept off his hat and pulled her into his arms, kissing her in the middle of the road to Wentmore.

## *Eighteen*

Being in his arms again was like coming home—or at least what she imagined that would be since she'd never really had a real home to come back to. But his lips, his hands on her waist, his tongue teasing her until she was breathless, those were her home, her sanctuary, her refuge.

She'd tried to remember the pain she'd felt earlier. He had sent her away and made her feel unwanted, but try as she might, she couldn't manage to summon those feelings again. Not when he was holding her tight and kissing her like he might die without the taste of her.

Her mother always said trouble followed her like a hungry puppy, but Pru knew trouble stuck around because she fed that puppy. She couldn't seem to help it. She knew feeding him was a bad idea and yet, in the moment, she just couldn't resist. How could she resist a puppy?

And how could she resist Nash Pope and his skillful lips and tender touch? If he didn't care about her, would he treat her so gently? Behave as though she were precious and cherished?

He pulled away. "I apologize."

"Don't apologize," she said, breathless. "I liked it."

He raked a hand through his hair. "I'm trying to be a gentleman and not accost you in the middle of the road."

"Then we'll move out of the road."

She took his hand and pulled him off the road toward a grove of trees that differentiated one large farm from another. Lifting her skirts, she traipsed through the tall grass between the fields, liking the way the yellow stalks swept softly against her skin.

Once in the cool shade of the trees, she moved to a small clearing where the sun cast a patch of warmth. She could not see the road and thus knew she couldn't be seen. It didn't mean they wouldn't be discovered by someone surveying the fields or hunting in the grass, but she was willing to take that chance because she wanted to be with Nash again. Being with him wasn't safe, but it made her feel alive. And she rarely took the safe path if a more exciting one lay ahead.

Nash turned toward her. "Where are we?"

"A clearing between the Watson and Stone farms."

He nodded. "Are we surrounded by grand old oak trees?"

"You know it?"

He nodded. "My brothers and I used to come this way sometimes if we were out when we shouldn't be and didn't want to be seen on the road and have our misdeeds reported to my father."

"And did you ever bring a girl here and kiss her?" Pru asked, moving into his arms.

"No. I never kissed a girl or a woman at Wentmore or Milcroft until you."

"Then this can be our place," she said. He nodded and unfastened his coat and pulled it off.

"Put this on the ground so we have somewhere to sit."

She arranged the coat on the soft grass and pulled him down beside her on it. "What should we call it? This place?"

He leaned in, finding her mouth and kissing her. "Does it have to have a name?"

"It's more romantic that way."

His mouth drifted to her neck, and she shivered. His lips left a trail of heat in their wake. "Far be it from me to stand in the way of romance." His breath on her skin was warm, and she closed her eyes and let herself do nothing but feel the brush of his lips, so warm in comparison to the weak sun of this autumn day.

He pulled her down, coming down beside her and propping his head on an elbow. She knew he had a little vision in his right eye, and the way he looked at her felt as though he could really see her. Perhaps he could, or perhaps he was just trying very, very hard.

She brushed the hair back from his face, and he barely flinched when his left eye was revealed briefly.

"What do you think of Cupid's Clearing?" she asked, his face in her hands as she marveled at his straight nose and the arch of his brows, marred on the left by a scar that somehow made him look even more handsome because he wasn't perfect.

"I think it's trite."

She laughed. "Well, you try then."

"What color is the grass?" he asked. "And the oaks?"

She forced her gaze from his features and looked about. "The trees are all shades of autumn colors—brown and red, some yellow and orange, a few green leaves hanging on yet. The grass is golden, almost the color of wheat. You can feel how soft it is, as though it died only recently and hasn't dried out and turned brittle and tough yet."

He didn't speak for a long moment. "You're so beautiful," he said, finally. "The way you see the world. The way you see me."

"That's because you show me the real you," she said. "Everyone else only sees gruff and angry Nash Pope."

He grinned. "Is that what I sound like? That low, growly voice?"

"Perhaps. Sometimes."

His mouth found her lips again, and she wrapped her arms about him, closing her eyes and letting her skin revel in his touch. When he'd grinned down at her, she'd felt a sudden twist in her heart. And she'd almost said exactly what she was feeling. It had taken a swift bite to the inside of her cheek to reign in the impulse to tell him she loved him.

She hadn't even realized she did until that moment. And as soon as she did, she wanted to say the words, but some shred of sense was left in her somewhere and she knew he was not ready to hear them. Perhaps he never would be.

Her hands went to work untying his neckcloth and then unfastening the buttons of his collar. She returned his kisses then, teasing the skin of his neck with her lips and tongue until he was breathing heavily. She unfastened his waistcoat and pulled the tail of his shirt from his trousers, sliding her hands under his shirt to feel the warmth of his bare skin.

It was too chilly on this autumn day, even in the sun, to undress, but she wanted to touch as much of him as she could. His hands slid over the bodice of her dress then down to her waist and over the hot place between her legs. He gathered her skirt and tugged it up until she felt the cool air on her calves. She hadn't worn her drawers as she'd known she was to try on her new dress today, and Mrs. Northgate would have lectured her on drawers. And so Nash's warm hand soon made an erotic contrast to the breeze as he slid up her leg and toward her core.

"Touch me," she whispered. His lips found hers and his hand brushed over the damp curls of her sex. He made a sound of approval as he stroked her, his fingers finding the small bud that gave her the most pleasure easily and then teasing it until she was writhing and fisting her hands in his shirt.

"Nash, I want you inside me," she ordered, not caring that a lady would never say such a thing.

"Yes," he said. "But first let me give you—"

"Now," she said, reaching for the fall of his breeches. She opened it, and his erection was warm and hard in her hands. He made a slight groan as she slid her hand up and down him, moving their bodies closer together. When he moved inside her, she couldn't stop the feral moan from rising in her throat. The way he filled her, stretched her, stroked her was like no other feeling in the world.

"I'll go slowly," he said between clenched teeth.

"Yes," she agreed as he moved inside her, so very slowly that she felt she might go mad. At the same time, she enjoyed the torture, the slow build to climax, the rushing of blood in her ears, and the way everything in the world dimmed but the scent of him and the feel of him and the taste of his lips as he kissed her.

"Pru," he said, his voice gruff as she tensed around him, the spiral of pleasure rising and rising now. "*Pru.*"

She liked the way he said her name, liked that even though he couldn't meet her eyes, couldn't look at her, he was with her. He was thinking only of her.

She arched back as the climax reached its peak, thrusting her hips hard against him and crying out as he plunged deeper inside her. He cried out too, pulling out as she reached the last throes of pleasure to spill his seed on the grass beside them. Then he was back beside her, kissing her, holding her, whispering that he didn't know how he'd managed without her.

She held him close, her heart pounding from pleasure and also that new, unfamiliar emotion she knew must be love. Her heart squeezed painfully at the fullness she felt. She wanted them to stay like this forever. In this enchanted clearing, in this world that was only the two of them.

And that's when she heard the crack of a stick.

***

Nash raised his head at the sound. Pru had heard it too. Her body tensed suddenly. Nash looked about, forgetting in the moment that he couldn't see. Cursing under his breath, he stilled and listened. There were no other sounds of intrusion—no leaves rustling, no murmur of voices or the sound of horses' hooves. Beneath him, Pru moved to the side and rose up.

"Do you see anything?" he asked.

"No," she said after a moment. "Perhaps we imagined it."

"Unlikely that we both imagined the same sound." He rose, tucking his shirt in and closing his trousers. He moved carefully about the clearing, listening for any telltale sounds, thinking he might flush out a fox or rabbit. But they were too small to have made such a sound. It had to be something larger, like a deer.

Pru moved to his side, straightening her skirts as she used her eyes while he listened closely. "It must have been a deer," she said, coming to the same conclusion he had.

"Yes." But if that was all it had been, why were his fingers tingling for a trigger? Why did his hand reach for the pocket of his coat, where his pistol usually rested? Pru took his hand in her warm one.

"You probably startled the poor creature," she said.

"Me?" He tossed her a scowl, which caused her to laugh. "You were the one entreating God—or perhaps you were referring to me when you called out, *oh God*!"

She smacked him. "I have no recollection of that."

He pulled her into an embrace. "Then I should remind you."

"You should get dressed," she said. "We have already spent far too long on this walk. Mr. Payne and Mrs. Blimkin will wonder where we are.

Nash wished he didn't have to hurry away from her. He wished he could spend all day, undressing her, kissing her, laughing with her. It had been years since he'd felt so happy and carefree as he did in her arms.

But she wasn't his, and he couldn't make a claim on her even if he wanted to—there was still the likelihood of the asylum in his future.

And he was still blind. But that didn't seem as much an obstacle any longer. He didn't feel quite so useless and inept. He'd thought his life was over when he'd lost his sight, but now he was beginning to think he still had a lot to live for. And though he couldn't see, he wasn't helpless or useless. He was, apparently, hosting the village autumn festival.

Nash squeezed Pru harder. "You have to help me with the autumn festival," he said.

"As I told you before, I've never been to the festival. I have no idea what's expected."

"But you know people who do—Mrs. Blinkin and Mrs. Brown. The vicar and the shrew who makes you sew."

"Mrs. Northgate is not a shrew—well, not the dowager Mrs. Northgate, at any rate. And I asked her to help me make this dress."

"Regardless, you can ask for their assistance."

"I could, but you are hosting the festival, not I. I'm not...I have no official connection to Wentmore."

"Then be discreet."

She gave a small laugh. "I've not been terribly successful with discretion in the past. But I'll do my best. Does that mean..." She hesitated. "You said before—"

He lowered his head to her shoulder. "I know what I said, and I didn't mean to hurt you, though I know I did. I wanted to keep you safe."

"I *am* safe with you."

She wasn't, but he didn't want to argue with her now. Soon enough his fate would be sealed. If he managed to escape the asylum, he could end this—whatever this was—then. He could part with her before either of them were hurt, emotionally or physically. Because Nash knew it was only a matter of time before he again made a mistake like he had this summer with Duncan. Only this time he feared Pru would be the one to take the pistol ball, and he couldn't live with himself if he ever hurt her.

***

With two days before the festival, Pru was busier than she had ever been in her life. She had spent the better part of the week at Wentmore, making certain the estate was ready for the upcoming festivities. Mr. Payne had the workmen and the landscaping well in hand, so Pru spent a great deal of time in the kitchens with Mrs. Brown and Mrs. Blimkin, planning the menu and the activities. Certain games, like bobbing for apples, were tradition, as were certain dishes. Mrs. Blimkin assured everyone the villagers would bake pies and cakes and bring their best savory dishes to share. But being that the event was to be held at Wentmore, where few had visited in over a decade, the autumn festival would be attended by even more people than usual. Mrs. Blimkin insisted Wentmore provide a dozen or more dishes to ensure no one left hungry.

"Where is that wretched Clopdon?" Mrs. Blimkin asked after surveying the newly repaired kitchens to be certain all was ready for the real work—the cooking that would begin tomorrow. "I sent him to inventory the tablecloths an hour ago."

Pru's eyes had glazed over at an argument about tarts versus cobblers, but now she jumped to her feet. "Shall I go look for him and ascertain his progress?"

"Oh, would you, dear?" Mrs. Brown asked. "My old feet would thank you to save me another trip up the stairs today."

"Of course! I'll go right now." She turned and practically ran for the stairs. She had no real expectation of finding the valet. He had made it clear he was not a butler and loath to do any sort of fetching and carrying or, for that matter, supervising of the footmen. His one task, he claimed, was to ensure Mr. Pope looked his best, and Pru could not argue that he was accomplishing that admirably.

She had yet to catch more than a glimpse of Nash today, and she'd been waiting for the chance to sneak away and spend a few private moments—or perhaps more than a few—with him. Lately they'd been meeting in the butler's pantry. It was right off the stairs leading down to the kitchens, so a bit of a risk but, as there was no butler, safer than many other areas of the house. Pru would slip into the room, and Nash would grab her about the waist and kiss her until they were both breathless.

Now she practically ran up the stairs and dashed into the butler's pantry but found it empty. Frowning, she went into the dining room, but it was empty as well. She moved into the foyer and spotted Clopdon coming down the stairs, his arms full of linen. He gave her a warning look. "If you have come on behalf of that termagant to ask me to do some menial task—"

"I haven't," Pru said quickly. Perhaps she could count the tablecloths herself... "I was looking for Mr. Pope. Is he in his chamber?"

"He is not. I caught him earlier and forced him to submit to the tortures of my measuring tape. God forbid we have a coat that fits him properly on Saturday."

"I have no doubt he will look very well at the festival."

"No thanks to Mr. Payne who seems to think it acceptable to agree to host large events without even a week's notice."

"Well, if anyone is up to the task, Clopdon, it's you."

"Flattery is always appreciated, Miss Howard. Now I must scuttle away before that harridan finds me and asks me to count silver or some such nonsense."

"Of course." Pru watched him walk away, still wondering where Nash might be. She could try the parlor.

She started that way when the front door opened, and Nash himself, followed by the vicar, entered.

Pru's smile at seeing Nash turned to a look of surprise at spotting Mr. Higginbotham. "Ah, there you are, Miss Howard," the vicar said. Nash paused and looked about him until he found her. Pru's entire body warmed when his gaze touched her. Even though he'd told her he could only see vague shapes and outlines, she knew he was more than familiar with her shape.

"Yes, I'm here. Good day, Mr. Pope. Mr. Higginbotham. I didn't expect to see you, sir."

"Well, my housekeeper seems to have taken up residence here, so it is here I must come if I wish a decent meal."

Pru knew Mrs. Blimkin made sure to leave meals for the vicar every morning and evening, so this was a flimsy excuse. No doubt, the vicar was as curious as everyone else in the village about Wentmore and its master.

"If I'd known you were here," Pru said, "I would have taken you to Mrs. Blimkin immediately. She's in the kitchen with Mrs. Brown."

"Oh, that's quite alright," the vicar said with a wave of his hand. "I also came to tell Mr. Pope that Mr. Smith is improving and to thank him for his generosity toward that family."

Pru raised her eyebrows. She knew nothing about the Smiths, but she was not surprised that Nash had done something generous.

"And then Mr. Pope offered to show me about the grounds and the location for our festival on Saturday," the vicar said. "I must say, it is quite a pleasing prospect."

"Yes, it is," Pru agreed. Now that the hedges had been trimmed, the trees pruned, the lawns tended, and the ivy on the house tidied, she hardly recognized the place herself. It looked so different from the wild place where she and Nash had sat on the grass and spoken of fairy gatherings. The fairies would have to find other haunts, though, as Wentmore had once again been tamed.

"Shall I show you to the kitchens, sir?" Nash asked the vicar.

"I can find them myself, if you don't mind me wandering about a bit."

"Not at all," Nash said, and the vicar meandered away.

When he was out of hearing range, Pru moved toward Nash. "May I speak to you in the parlor, Mr. Pope?"

His brows rose. "The parlor? Not the butler's pantry?"

She smiled. Wicked man, and she did love him for it. "I wouldn't want to interfere with the inventory of the tablecloths," she said, taking his hand. He leaned the walking stick he used outside beside the door and allowed her to lead him into the parlor. Then he closed the door and pushed her up against it, kissing her hard and fast. Pru kissed him back, wrapping her arms about him and sliding her fingers through his hair. It had been cut again, no doubt by Clopdon, but as Nash would not consent to have it shorn enough to show his wounded eye, the top was still somewhat long.

She pulled back. "You didn't even give me a chance to make sure we are alone."

"Are we?" he asked.

She peered over his shoulder and looked about the chamber. "Yes."

"Good." He kissed her again, his hands running up her sides and along her arms until he captured them and held her wrists. He secured them against the door and held her there, his captive. He had gained back some of the weight he had lost and no longer looked pale and gaunt. He was now quite a formidable form, and she liked the feel of him pressed against her. He was so warm, so alive, strong but gentle.

"You have me," she murmured as he moved his mouth to kiss her neck. "Now what will you do?"

"I've been hoping for more rain," he said.

"Never say so! The festival will be ruined."

"But you might be forced to stay the night again." He kissed her earlobe and she shivered. "I want you in my bed," he whispered.

She wanted that too. She wanted to undress him slowly and touch every inch of him, kiss every part of him, then push him down, clamp her legs about his hips, and take him slowly inside her.

"I don't know what you're thinking, but your pulse just kicked," he said.

"Nothing I should admit to anyone, lest I go to hell."

"We'll go together." He kissed her again, wedging a knee between her legs and pressing against her core until she wanted to roll her hips to increase the friction.

"Hello!" a too-familiar voice called from the foyer. Pru jolted and pushed Nash away. He released her immediately.

"Who is it?"

"I say hello there!"

"I think it's Mrs. Northgate," Pru said. "I'd better go see."

"I need a butler," Nash muttered. Pru grinned at him.

"And here I thought you didn't like servants."

He moved aside, and she opened the parlor door and blinked in surprise as indeed Mrs. Northgate was standing in the foyer of Wentmore, looking up at the large chandelier with an assessing eye.

"Mrs. Northgate!" Pru said, genuinely pleased to see her friend.

"I might have known I'd find you here," Mrs. Northgate said. She wore a lavender dress today, quite elegant in style. Her coil of silver hair was lower than usual, being that she'd had to fit it under a hat, but with the plumes of the hat, the woman was over six feet tall.

"I've been helping Mrs. Blimkin and Mrs. Brown with preparations for the festival," Pru said.

"I'm sure you have." Mrs. Northgate looked past Pru, and she realized Nash had come out of the parlor to stand behind her. His hair was still mussed from her hands running through it.

"Welcome, Mrs. Northgate," he said. "I've heard a great deal about you, and though I cannot see Miss Howard's new dress myself, I hear it is quite fetching."

"It is, if I do say so myself. I must commend you, Mr. Pope, on the state of the house. I was given to understand it was in ruins, but it looks very much the way it did the last time I was here. Perhaps a few improvements here and there."

"Thank you." He gave a formal bow. "If you'll excuse me."

Pru watched him start up the stairs and wished she could follow him to his bedchamber. Instead, she turned a smile on Mrs. Northgate. "Would you like me to show you around a bit?"

"Certainly, since you are so much at home here."

Pru nodded and gestured for Mrs. Northgate to follow her. There were still some rooms not ready for public viewing, but she could steer her friend away from those. The truth was, she did feel at home at Wentmore, but her time here was coming to an end. She and Nash had made every excuse they could think of to be together these past weeks. But the festival would be over soon and so would their time together.

## Nineteen

Nash waited until he heard the Northgate carriage depart before he made his way downstairs. Mrs. Northgate had taken the vicar and Mrs. Blimkin in the carriage with her, and Nash feared Pru had gone as well.

Except the house had a different feeling when she was about, and he could still sense her presence. The Cloud of despair that always seemed to hover on the horizon was banished when she was near. He couldn't sense it at all right now, which meant she was here...somewhere. The front door closed, and he made out her form coming toward him.

"I was afraid you'd gone," he said.

"I made an excuse to stay a bit longer."

He raised a brow. "Without your chaperone?"

"The vicar didn't even seem to realize he was leaving me without one. He was so anxious to have a quarter hour with Mrs. Northgate in order to convert her."

"And Rowden?"

"He sent the workmen home and went riding with your land steward. Clopdon was supervising the laundress washing your shirts. I believe Mrs. Brown went to lie down as Mrs. Blimkin wore her out. The footmen are here somewhere."

"Probably smoking in the yard while they have the chance. I really do need a butler."

"But you don't have a butler," she said. "And you know what that means?"

"Tell me."

"It means there is no one to see me run into your bedchamber. I will meet you there."

And before he could grab her, she'd run past him and up the stairs.

With a smile, Nash followed her, his pulse pounding as he imagined what he would do to her when he had her behind closed doors. They didn't have long. Dinner was in an hour or so, and he didn't want to waste any time.

Nash reached his bedchamber and pushed the door open. "Pru?" he said.

"I'm on the bed. Naked."

That revelation jolted his body, making his cock go hard instantly. He imagined her lithe body sprawled on the bed as she lay on her side with one hand propping up her chin. His hands ached to run a path from her shoulder, down to the dip in her waist, and over the curve of her hip. "How did you manage that so quickly?" He loosened his neckcloth and tugged off his coat.

"When I was young, we never had enough coal to use for anything but cooking. Anne and I learned to undress, wash, and scurry under the bedclothes very quickly else we'd freeze. She is actually even faster than I."

"A talent I'm sure her husband appreciates."

"I can see you appreciate it too. Come here and let me help with that waistcoat."

He moved toward the bed and she grabbed his neckcloth and pulled him in for a kiss. He reached for her and felt bare skin, warm and soft. With a small groan, he ran his hands up and down her back, finally gently squeezing her bottom. She was naked, as she'd claimed, and he wanted desperately to join her.

She made quick work of his waistcoat then helped with his cuffs, tugging the shirt over his head even as he tried to remove shoes and strip off his trousers. They knocked heads in their haste, and he moved back. "Let me finish."

"May I watch?" she asked. He liked that she asked him. He couldn't see her watching, but he liked that she let him know she wanted to.

"If you like."

"I do." Her voice dropped slightly as he removed his trousers. "You're all muscle and sinew and leashed strength."

He paused. "Leashed strength?"

"Too flowery?"

"It sounds as though you've been reading Gothic novels." He tossed the trousers aside and climbed into bed, just as naked as she.

"And how would you know how they sound if you hadn't read one yourself?" she teased as she pulled him into her warm embrace.

"You caught me," he said against her lips.

"Yes, I did." She kissed him long and deep, her hands exploring him as her tongue teased his. He couldn't get enough of the feel of her under him. She was slim but strong and solid. She wouldn't break easily, and that made him want to treat her all the more gently.

He kissed her jaw, her neck, her breasts all while his hands relearned the shape of her. When his fingers found the soft curls between her legs, she was already wet for him. He wanted to slide inside her and bury himself deep. But just as he nudged her legs open, she moved over him, pushing him back and throwing one leg over him until the heat of her sex met with his waiting cock.

She didn't take him inside her yet, and Nash could hardly breathe waiting for her. Instead, she slid her hands over his chest, up his arms, and back down again. Then she moved, slowly, to his face and slid the hair away from his damaged eye.

"Pru," he said, trying to shake it back into place.

"Don't," she said. "I want to see your face when I do this." She moved her hips and the friction made him catch his breath.

"If you insist," he grit out as she took his head inside her tight warmth. She leaned forward and locked her hands with his, pinning him to the bed as she took more of him, so slowly that he felt dizzy with need.

And then she moved her hips and he swore.

"Using the old Anglo-Saxon word?" she teased. "You have barbarian ancestors."

"And you clearly have ties to Druids. You've bewitched me." He clenched her hands as she moved. *"God, yes."*

"I can see exactly what you like," she said, her own voice tinged with pleasure now. "I want to see your face when you climax."

He stilled for a moment then looked up at her, wishing he could see more than the vague shape of her. "What does it look like?" he asked. "My left eye? I've never seen it."

She stilled, and for a moment he feared she would tell him something ridiculous, like *you're beautiful*. But he wanted the truth. This was the only time he'd ever asked this question, and he wanted to know how badly he was scarred.

"You have dark brows," she said finally. "They're part of the reason your scowl is so lethal, but on your left side the brow is bisected by a scar, a thin line that runs almost through the center of the brow."

He'd felt that raised ridge of skin and knew what she said was true. "Go on." He hadn't meant for her to go on riding him, but she moved her hips then, slowly and gently.

"The scar descends over your eyelid." Her voice was a bit strained now as she slid against him. "And down just beneath your eye. The skin there is pink and still a bit raw, though I imagine given a few more years the scar will whiten and fade." She swallowed. "Nash, yes. Like that with your hips."

For a moment they were both lost in the sensations of their bodies coming together, but he wanted to hear more.

"Go on," he said breathlessly.

She paused and caught her breath. "Ah, it's hard to think. Ah...I can see where the—was it shrapnel?"

"We think so. That or a piece of brick dislodged by a pistol ball and turned into a projectile."

"*Yes.*" She rolled her hips and he could feel her body beginning to tense, knew she was getting close to climax.

"Go on," he said.

"The shrapnel or brick flew at your eye, and where it struck is white and cloudy. You have such beautiful blue eyes, but part of your left is scarred. But it doesn't look much different than someone with a cataract. A cataract covers more of the eye, though, whereas this is just a thin slice."

He gripped her hands hard. "And it doesn't disgust you to look at it?"

"*No,*" she said, gripping his hands back. "Even if it looked ten times worse, nothing about you could disgust me, but believe me when I say, this is not much more than a small scar. You're a very handsome man, with or without it."

His throat felt tight at her words. She wasn't simply saying them to be kind. He knew she meant them. He knew she told him the truth. For the last several years, he'd imagined the worst. He'd imagined himself looking like some sort of monster. But she made him feel almost normal again, like the wound he had made so large and grotesque was little more than a scratch. He felt lighter and freer than he had in years.

"Are we done talking now?" she asked, rolling her hips.

Oh, they were finished. He didn't think he could have said another intelligible word even if his life depended on it. Her movements quickened, her body taking him deeper, her grip on his hands tightening even as he felt the muscles of her sex constrict around him. He wished he could see her face, but he could hear the rasp and catch of her breath and her soft moans. He could feel the way she slid over him, bringing him pleasure even as she took her own. He could smell the scent of her—a mixture of pine and Pru and her arousal.

And then she took his mouth, and he could taste her, taste the need on her lips. He caught her gasp as she tipped over the edge. Her inner muscles clenched hard around him, and he had to grit his teeth to keep from following her over the edge. Instead, he lifted his hips, driving deeper into her until she was crying out with pleasure and begging him for *more* and *more* and *yes, yes*.

And then her body went slack, and he rolled her over, thrust once more, causing her to moan in pleasure, before he withdrew and spilled his seed on the bed clothes. Then he collapsed on top of her, his mouth against her shoulder, both of their bodies heaving and gasping for breath.

Somewhere in the house, a door slammed. Nash stiffened, the vague image of a battlefield rising in the back of his mind. "I'm sure it's just Mr. Payne returning," she said, her voice thick. Her hand touched his back, rubbing it soothingly as though she knew the images unexpected noised conjured in his mind. "I should dress," she said.

He didn't want her to dress. He wanted her to stay right where she was, warm and naked and underneath him.

He heard the front door open and close again and the sound of voices, and Nash sat, alert and concerned now. Pru slid off the bed, and he could hear her rustling beside it, probably pulling on her shift and stockings. "Mr. Payne probably has Mr. Forester with him," she said. "Nash. Nash." She waited until he turned his head in her direction. "Remember where you are. This isn't France. You are home at Wentmore."

Yes, he needed to remember that. And yet, he couldn't stop himself from opening the drawer of the table near the bed and removing his pistol. The weight of it felt safe in his hands. He could breathe again with the familiar walnut gunstock warming in his palm.

"Where the devil is everyone?" a man's voice called. Nash tightened his grip on the pistol. Of course, the enemy wouldn't announce himself that way, but that wasn't Rowden's voice. Someone was in the house, *his* house.

"Get behind me, Pru," he said.

"Nash, I don't think—"

"Get behind me! I don't want to hurt you."

He climbed out of bed and wrapped the sheet around his waist, never once lowering the pistol. Pru didn't argue with him. He felt her move behind him and knew she was safe. She shouldn't be here. He knew she wouldn't be safe with him. If she were back at the vicarage, she would be far safer than here with him.

"Well, this is a fine welcome," the voice said.

"Nash, it's not an enemy. It sounds like a gentleman."

The voice did sound familiar, but Nash could hardly hear it. In his mind, he heard the boom of cannons firing, the shout of voices speaking French, and the clink of a hammer pulled back. That was the hammer of his pistol. That had been real, not imagined.

The sound of someone tapping on his door was real as well. As was the clink of the latch being lifted and the door creaking open.

"Good God!" said the man. Nash saw the shape raise his hands. For a moment, he thought he should fire. The intruder might have a pistol, but Pru's hand was on his arm, her fingers digging in deep. "Now you think to shoot me?"

That voice. Nash shook his head, trying to place it. But he was in the middle of a battle. And there was a child running toward him.

"My lord," Pru said, her voice sounding far away as well. "I am sorry to be so forward, but you are Lord Beaufort?"

Nash tried to see the child through the smoke. Did he have a weapon? Something glinted in his hand. A knife?

"I am. Who are you? More importantly, can you persuade my son to lower that pistol?"

*My son. Beaufort. His father.*

On the battlefield, Nash had to make a decision. He pulled the trigger, and the boy's small body flew back.

"I will, my lord, but you needn't worry. He has no pistol balls or powder."

The sound of a throat being cleared came from outside the door, presumably behind the earl.

Now Nash had to make another decision—an action that might haunt him for the rest of his life.

"Actually," said Clopdon, "that's not quite true. I'm afraid Mr. Pope found my hiding place. We must assume the pistol is primed and ready to fire."

\*\*\*

Pru felt almost dizzy as the valet's words washed over her. The scene in the chamber was nothing short of a nightmare. The earl stood in the open door, hands held up in a show of surrender. She had known he was the earl not only because his voice and accent had declared him one of the uppermost classes, but because Nash bore a resemblance to his father that was impossible to deny. They both had dark hair, though Nash's was longer and unruly, and they both had blue eyes. Again, Nash's were bluer and more vivid, but they crinkled in much the same way as the earl's. Their mouths were the same as well—that same scowl that pressed their lips into a thin line.

Behind the earl stood Clopdon, his arms empty, seeming to have stepped out of thin air. Pru wasn't fooled. The valet had been nearby in case his master needed anything. He'd probably heard the sounds coming from the bedchamber and withdrew to wait until she departed. Or perhaps the valet had discovered his hiding place had been pilfered and Nash's pistol was once again lethal.

Nash's pistol. The same one pointed at the Earl of Beaufort. Pru closed her eyes and prayed. It had been years since she'd prayed, for all that she was constantly in church, but she prayed now. *Please don't let him fire.*

"Nash," she said quietly, stroking his bare arm. She'd managed to don her shift and a petticoat, but she was still only half-dressed. It was not the way she'd imagined meeting the powerful lord. "It's your father. Lower the pistol now."

Nash didn't react to her words. He didn't move, hardly seemed to breathe. She had a glimpse of what he must have looked like as a sharpshooter during the war—utterly calm and utterly deadly.

"Nash," Pru said again. "Listen to me."

"He's entirely mad," the earl said. "He'll kill us all."

"He's not mad," Pru argued. Did the earl think saying such things would help the situation? "You arrived unexpectedly and surprised us. Nash doesn't do well with surprises."

"I should say not," the earl said.

"Nash," Pru ran her hand down Nash's arm. It seemed impossible, but it was tenser and tighter than even a moment ago.

"Might I try, Miss Howard?" Clopdon asked.

"By all means," the earl said. "Step into the line of fire."

"Sir," Clopdon said, speaking to Nash. "Lower the pistol. It's time to dress for dinner." He walked into the bedchamber as though there was no danger. "I see we shall have to start all over," the valet said, gathering clothing from the floor. "So we'd best begin or Mr. Payne will be cross. You know he is rather unpleasant when he is hungry."

Nash's gaze flicked to Clopdon, and Pru began to feel a glimmer of hope. The valet moved into the dressing room and returned with a silk dressing gown. He crossed to Nash and held the gown out. "I do believe we have progressed beyond the Roman habit of wearing bedsheets about all day. Put this on." He shook the dressing gown impatiently, and Pru saw a muscle tighten in Nash's jaw. He was probably more annoyed than angry at the valet, but she couldn't deny Clopdon was very effective. She would have done as he bid her.

"Come now, sir," Clopdon said. Then he looked at Pru, his eyes meeting hers with a seriousness belied by his tone. "Miss Howard, do take the earl downstairs and offer him some refreshment. Mr. Pope will join his father in a moment."

Pru swallowed. The valet was asking her to step into the line of fire. He knew what he asked of her. His expression was serious and also questioning. She could say no. She could refuse and no one would blame her.

But if she appeared afraid of Nash now, she would most certainly doom him to an asylum—if he hadn't already doomed himself. Worse, when this was over, he would hate himself for causing her fear.

She couldn't allow that. Moreover, she was not afraid. Nash wouldn't shoot her. She knew it as well as she knew her own name. He might be back in the midst of a battle in France, but he would never shoot her.

"Certainly, Clopdon." Pru moved cautiously to the other side of the bed and gathered her dress and shoes. She left her stays and stockings. She'd worry about those later. Then, taking a deep breath, she moved toward the earl, putting her body between the pistol and Nash's father.

"Shall we, my lord?" Pru asked gesturing to the door as though she didn't have a pistol pointed at her back. She reached the earl, who stared at her as though she were an as-yet-to-be-discovered species of bird. Keeping her body between the earl and Nash, she ushered the earl out of the room then closed the bedchamber door behind her.

Her legs felt wobbly, and she wanted to collapse right there, but she bit the inside of her cheek and maintained her composure.

"My God," the earl breathed, clutching his chest. "He wants to kill me."

"No, he doesn't," Pru said. "Let's go downstairs to the parlor."

"I could use a drink," he said. Pru didn't bother to tell him that he wouldn't find anything stronger than tea at Wentmore. Instead, she showed him into the parlor then made her way to the butler's pantry to dress. She passed the footmen en route and found Mrs. Brown in the butler's pantry.

"Oh, Miss Howard! I heard Mr. Pope pointed a pistol at the earl. What happened to you?" she asked, eyeing Pru's dishevelment.

Pru merely held out her dress. "Would you help me? My hands are a bit shaky."

"Of course, dear."

While Mrs. Brown helped her don her ugly pea-green dress—why was she always wearing this gown when she met important and fashionable people?—Pru tried not to think about the fact that the entire household knew she'd been alone and undressed with Nash. And while she didn't have much to show off, she was nonetheless chagrined to have been seen by half the household in her underwear.

"There you are, dear," Mrs. Brown said.

"Thank you. I believe it might help if we had tea in the parlor," she told Mrs. Brown. "The earl mentioned wanting something to drink, so if you have a splash of brandy you can add to his cup—"

"I have just the thing. Don't you worry."

Pru wanted to hug the other woman, and so she did. Mrs. Brown hugged her back, and for a moment Pru just closed her eyes and allowed herself to be surrounded by the scents of flour and dough. Tears pricked at her eyes as she remembered the times when her own mother had held her.

It seemed years ago now. She supposed it had been.

The front door banged open, and she heard Mr. Payne call out for Nash. Pru withdrew. "I had better go." She wiped her eyes and hurried through the dining room and into the foyer.

Mr. Payne turned to face her just as the parlor door opened and the earl stepped out. "There you are!" he said, his tone accusing.

Mr. Payne looked at the earl and then at Pru, clearly hoping for an explanation. "My lord, I thought you would write before traveling to Wentmore."

"Why? So you could make everything look rosy? Now I see what the real situation is."

Mr. Payne looked…well, pained. "Miss Howard, what happened?"

"I'll tell you what happened," the earl said. "My son almost shot me."

Payne kept his gaze on Pru. She didn't want to contradict the earl, but she didn't want to agree with him either. "Might we speak alone for a moment, sir?" she asked Mr. Payne. Then she turned to the earl. "Mrs. Brown is bringing tea, my lord. She will be just a moment."

Instead of retreating to the library or the dining room, Mr. Payne went back out the front door and closed it behind Pru. "What the devil happened?" he asked.

Pru swallowed, keeping her tears in check. How had this day gone so wrong? Everything had been going so well and now...

"The earl arrived suddenly and without warning. I think the loud noise and the shock of it triggered some sort of protective response in Mr. Pope."

Payne nodded. "He can be jumpy on the best of days. Where is he now?"

"In his bedchamber. Clopdon is helping him dress."

Payne's eyes narrowed. "Why wasn't he dressed?"

Pru didn't answer, and Payne swore. "Bloody hell, what a fiasco. I was hoping to keep this quiet until he asked you to marry him, but now I suppose everyone will find out."

"What did you say?" Pru all but shrieked, reaching out to grasp the door frame so as not to fall over.

"You heard me. Did you think Nash would just…er—bed you and then put you aside? He's not that sort. He might not know it yet, but he'll ask you to marry him."

*He might not know it yet…*

"You mean, you'll force him to ask me."

Payne laughed. "I don't know if you've noticed, but no one forces Pope to do anything. He wants to marry you. He either hasn't realized it yet or has some asinine reason for waiting to ask. Probably something to do with honor."

"He's afraid I won't be safe with him," Pru said quietly.

"Yes, something like that. I'm sure the events of this evening will do nothing to reassure him."

"The earl will surely send him to an asylum now," Pru said.

"Let me worry about that. You had better go home. It will be dark soon, and the vicar will begin to worry."

"But I can't leave him," Pru said. "He needs me."

Payne gave her a sympathetic look. "I'd rather you stayed as well, but the earl just found you in bed with his son. He isn't likely to think of you as more than a…well, he isn't likely to think very highly of you at the moment. I'll deal with him and with Nash. Do you need a horse or cart to take you back? I can see if we have a groom to ready a vehicle."

"No," Pru said. "Go back in and help Nash. I don't mind the walk. In fact, I can use a walk to clear my head now."

Payne nodded. "Come back tomorrow. I'll have everything in hand by then."

Pru nodded and watched Mr. Payne go back inside. She stood outside, as usual. She was always on the outside, so it was a familiar feeling even if she understood the need for it tonight. She'd return in the morning, and all she could do was hope that Nash wouldn't be taken away in the middle of the night.

# *Twenty*

Nash paused outside the parlor. His throat felt tight—partly because Clopdon had tied his cravat within an inch of its life and partly because he could hear his father railing behind the parlor door.

"My lord, this is not a time to make hasty decisions." That was the low, calm voice of Rowden.

"Hasty! My son pointed a pistol at my head. I think the time to drag one's feet has long since passed." That was the angry bark of his father.

"Sir," Clopdon said from behind him. "You must go inside now. They are waiting for you."

Nash turned back to the door.

"My lord, what happened was unfortunate—"

"Unfortunate! Mr. Payne, I have given you plenty of time to take control of the situation. What is unfortunate is that my son cannot be controlled. He is a danger to others and himself. He *must* be taken away."

Nash held out a hand toward Clopdon, who he could feel still standing behind him.

"Sir?" Clopdon said, pretending he didn't know what Nash wanted.

Nash snapped his fingers and finally Clopdon placed his pistol in his hands. The weight of it was instantly reassuring, even though Nash knew the valet had emptied it of balls and powder. Nash put the pistol in his pocket and pushed the door open.

As soon as he entered, all conversation ceased. Nash wished he could see the faces of the two men in the room. He imagined Rowden looked exhausted and annoyed. Nash wasn't certain what his father looked like. Was he scared? Determined? Angry? He wasn't proud. It had been a long time since his father had been proud of him. The clearest memory of that pride was back in the time when the peacocks had arrived. Nash was certain there had been moments after that, but none so vivid and unassailable.

"My lord," Nash said with a slight bow toward the shape of his father—a short, stocky man who was more muscle than fat. Nash remembered him having dark hair like his own, only with some gray at the temples. It was probably grayer now and the lines around his blue eyes probably deeper. "I regret I was indisposed earlier."

"Is that what we're calling it?" his father said, dispensing with any pleasantries. "I walked in on you with a whore in your bed and you pointed a pistol at me."

Nash clenched his fists. "She is not a whore."

Silence dropped on the room, and for a moment Nash thought he could hear his own heart beating.

"That is the point you wish to discuss?" his father said, tone calmer. "Whether or not the woman in your bed is a wh—"

"She is not," Nash interjected. "Miss Howard is the daughter of missionaries and under the care of the vicar of Milcroft."

More silence. "Well, it seems not only are you shooting your friends, you are debauching the upstanding maidens of the village. I never took you for a rake, Nash."

"I'm not a rake, my lord," he answered. "I...care for her." He'd almost said *love,* but he couldn't quite make the word come out, and especially not now when his father was intent on locking him away for the rest of his life. There was no time to think about his feelings, about what he might lose if his father had his way.

"So you've found a village girl to entertain you. Wonderful. I thought you wanted to come to Wentmore to lick your wounds."

"And I thought you were never speaking to me again!" Nash exploded. Unbidden, his hand went to his pocket. He needed to touch the pistol to keep his temper in check.

"That was because the last time we met you pointed a pistol at me!" his father yelled. "But that was before you burned down my country estate, fired at my solicitor, shot your friend, and debauched the vicar's ward!"

"It seems to me," Rowden said, voice calm and controlled, "that we have much to discuss and these accusations—on both sides—will only get in the way. If I might, Lord Beaufort, I would point out several items you might have missed upon your arrival."

His father grunted.

"First of all, the kitchens have been repaired. They have also been updated and I do believe we have a delicious meal waiting for us if we ever stop screaming at each other."

"I'd wager that is more due to your efforts than my son's," the earl said.

"I engaged the laborers, but Nash has been here every day to oversee the repairs."

Nash wouldn't have called what he did overseeing the repairs—especially since he couldn't see—but he had been here and he supposed in the last days of the work, when issues had arisen, he had attended to them and resolved them. Funny how he hadn't thought of that as progress. But the truth was, when the work had begun, he'd hidden in his room, hands over his ears. By the time it ended, he was moving about the house and handling any problems that arose.

"Second of all," Rowden continued, "you will notice Nash and I have hired not only a valet but two footmen, a number of grooms, and he will soon be hiring a butler and cook."

Nash wasn't so certain about that, though he supposed Clopdon would hound him about the butler and unless Mrs. Blimkin was to continue coming several times a week, he would need a cook. Mrs. Brown was a competent enough housekeeper.

"Thirdly, I am actually glad you are here as you are in time to partake in the festivities on Saturday."

"What festivities?" the earl asked.

"The autumn festival," Nash said. "I have offered to host it this year. That is why we had landscapers and workmen about. They're readying the grounds."

"That is also why Miss Howard was at the house," Rowden said. "She was helping with the arrangements for the celebration. She was initially engaged as a tutor for your son."

"A tutor?" the earl said.

"Yes," Nash added. "She studied under Monsieur Barbier, the French scientist who invented a type of writing called *Ecriture Nocturne*. It was invented as a sort of code for the military, but it is being used as a way for the blind to read and write."

"You can read and write?" the earl asked, sounding more intrigued than disbelieving.

"Of a fashion," Nash said. "I'd be happy to show you later. It is basically a system of raised dots that correspond to letters. I can feel the raised marks and can put the letters together into words and thus sentences."

"I see."

Nash's breathing had slowed. He was doing well. He knew he was doing well. Rowden had stepped in and allowed him to gain control of himself. The stakes were still high—his very life hung in the balance—but Nash had lived with stakes like that before and maintained his composure. He had to do it again.

"I will admit," the earl said, "that the house looks better than I expected, though I only made a cursory appraisal, and my son looks healthy and sober. That is an improvement. But there's still the matter of the pistol pointed at my head."

Nash stiffened.

"Even now he has it in his pocket," the earl said. "I can see him touching it as though it were some sort of talisman. You must admit he is still a danger to others and quite possibly himself."

"My lord," Nash said, reigning in his anger. "I am standing right here. If you want to say something to me, say it."

"Very well. I think you need help. Help neither I nor Mr. Payne can give you. Help only a doctor can provide."

"Is that what they are doing in asylums now?" Nash asked, voice carefully light. "Providing help? I thought that was where wealthy families sent their black sheeps to avoid further embarrassment."

"Is that what you think of me?" the earl said. "That I want to send you away because you've embarrassed me?"

"Haven't I?"

"Yes, but—"

"So you're willing to lock me up for the rest of my life so you can walk among your wealthy friends without having to explain a blind son—a cripple."

"I don't see you that way. You're still the same to me."

"Then you don't see me, because I am not the same. I'm blind, and yes, I'm haunted by the things I saw and the things I did. All the more reason for you *not* to come storming into this house and my room without any warning. I regret how I reacted, but I was..." How to explain how he'd felt? How to explain the world he was transported to when the sound of a loud bang or a sudden shock jolted him? "I was not myself. I don't know how to explain it. But I go back to the war. Back to a time when the enemy is firing, and I can't see how I will ever get out alive. Back to the smoke burning my eyes and the smell of blood and offal and there's only one weapon I have against the death all around me." Nash pulled his pistol out of his pocket, pointing it at the floor.

His father took a breath, and in the ensuing silence Nash heard the clock on the mantel ticking.

"I had no idea," the earl said, finally. "That sounds like a hellscape, and I do apologize for causing you to remember such a time."

Nash took a step back. The words were such a surprise to him that he wasn't sure he hadn't imagined them. Was his father actually trying to understand? Nash hadn't thought anyone would ever understand, least of all his father. For a moment, he had the urge to go to his father, embrace him as he had when he'd been a boy. Pru would have told him to go and hug him tightly, but Nash held back because he did not know if his father would accept an embrace. And he did not yet trust his father. The threat of the asylum still hung between them.

"But this revelation of your mental state only underscores the need for help."

And there it was. They were back to the asylum.

"Nash does need help," Rowden said. "And he has received help. I am here. Miss Howard is here. Clopdon and Mrs. Brown are here—all offering help each day. He is making improvements, but it's not something that will happen overnight. I asked for time, my lord, and I need more of it. Your son needs more time. I think he's shown incredible progress already."

"I'll consider it," the earl said, and Nash wanted to punch him. "In the meantime, I won't feel safe under this roof if he has that pistol."

"All the rifles and other pistols have been removed from the house," Rowden said. "And Clopdon has disarmed that one. You're quite safe."

"And yet it was armed earlier—primed and ready," the earl said.

Nash swallowed. "I admit I found Clopdon's hiding place for the ball and powder. I feel safer when the pistol is loaded."

"And I feel threatened. If I'm to give you more time, if I'm to stay through the festival and see if things really have improved, then I'll need that pistol," the earl said.

Nash's fingers closed on the pistol's stock, and he shook his head. "No."

"Then I suppose my decision is made," the earl said. "I'll take my staff and decamp to a tavern—"

"My lord," Rowden said. "Give us a moment alone. Clopdon!"

The door opened and Clopdon said, "Yes, sir?"

"Would you take the earl into the dining room?"

"Yes, sir." For once the valet didn't complain that he was being asked to do the work of a butler. "This way, my lord."

"I want the pistol," the earl said.

The door closed and Nash said, "No."

"Listen to me, Nash."

"No."

Rowden crossed the room and put a hand on Nash's shoulder. "It's wood and metal. Nothing else. You don't need it."

He did need it. It was his only defense against the memories and the fear. The pistol and Pru, but Pru wasn't here.

"Nash, do you remember that church in Portugal?"

Nash's swirling thoughts slowed, and he shook his head.

"Yes, you do. Three or four of us were hidden in the crypt. We were packed together so tightly I couldn't scratch my nose without scratching yours as well. You were there and Aidan. He was the one who got us into the crypt. And Colin—he was dressed as a priest."

Nash couldn't help but smile. It was coming back to him now. The four of them had been sent to ascertain if any weapons were being stored at a local church in some city in Portugal whose name he didn't remember any longer. Colin had dressed as a priest and gained admittance. The other three hid until after dark, when Aidan broke into the church. Once inside, they met up with Colin and crept into the crypt. Rowden was there to provide muscle should they need it. Nash had been there to evaluate any weapons they found.

Colin held a lamp while Aidan used his pickpocket skills to open everything from toolboxes to sarcophagi. Nash saw more bones than he liked and no weapons.

"I remember. There weren't any weapons, and we realized Rafe had been given false information, the French probably hoping he'd pass it along and they could ambush us."

"Which they did," Rowden said.

Nash remembered the feeling of cold dread that formed like a pit of ice in his belly when he'd heard the voices of the French soldiers they'd been fighting all over Portugal. He remembered the panic as the four of them scrambled to find hiding places as the booted feet seemed to come inexorably closer. Nash and Rowden had been closest to the door, and Nash regretted the position almost immediately. He and Rowden were clustered so tightly together he couldn't easily load his pistol. When he'd been trying to do so, Rowden had knocked his arm and he'd dropped his powder bag.

And then it had been too late because the soldiers were searching the crypt and Nash was weaponless and helpless. It was the first time he'd ever really been afraid. He thought he'd known fear before then, but it was nothing compared to the feeling he'd had then. He realized this must be what the other men felt all the time. They had to run at the enemy with nothing but a sidearm and their brute strength, while he stood back in the shadows and provided cover.

Nash had closed his eyes and tried to keep down the bile rising in his throat. And then there seemed to be some sort of unspoken signal because Rowden struck one soldier passing by at the same time Colin or Aidan struck another on the other side of the crypt. The soldiers couldn't shoot. They didn't know where the attack came from and whether they'd hit one of their own or the enemy. There had been six soldiers, and before Nash knew what happened, there were only three.

"Follow me," Rowden said. "I'll get us out of here."

Nash had been shocked when the other man, who he'd only known for a few weeks, tackled a soldier and struck him then motioned impatiently for Nash to make for the crypt door. Nash finally ran, his back tingling all the while, almost as though he was waiting for the pistol ball to strike him. He even heard the cock of a hammer, but when he'd braced for the impact, none came. A quick look back showed him Rowden with one hand on the rifle and the other on the soldier's throat.

There had been more soldiers upstairs, but Rowden had emerged from the crypt with the French soldier's rifle, tossed it to Nash, and that had been the end of the soldiers.

Later that night, what felt like years later but must have only been hours, the four of them slept out under a canopy of stars with a low fire burning between them. Aidan had taken first watch and Nash, Rowden, and Colin were trying to sleep. Colin had long since stopped moving, but Nash couldn't seem to get comfortable. Finally, he stilled and then he heard Rowden's voice carry over the crack and hiss of the fire.

"Why didn't you go when I told you?" Rowden asked. "I said *follow me*, and you were still in the same spot when I looked back."

Nash raised himself on an elbow. He didn't want to admit he'd been afraid, so instead he said, "I didn't know the plan."

Rowden had rolled over on his stomach and stared hard at Nash, the orange from the fire making patterns on his face, his jaw dark with hair from days of not shaving. Nash, Colin, and Aidan had only patches of hair, but Rowden had seemed to grow a full beard in less than a week.

"I told you to follow me. That was the plan."

"I could have been shot in the back," Nash said, forgetting he was pretending not to show fear.

"You let me worry about your back. You worry about mine all the time. We all have a date to dance with the devil. Yours wasn't today."

Nash had been able to sleep after that. There hadn't ever been another time he'd needed to rely on Rowden as much as in the crypt, but even if he hadn't thought of the incident for years now, he'd never forgotten the feeling of brotherhood with Rowden.

"I told you that night that I would watch your back," Rowden said, bringing Nash back to the parlor and

Wentmore. "I'd protect you, just like you protected me from a roof or a balcony."

"I remember," Nash said.

"That didn't change because we're back in England. I'm here."

Nash didn't speak. Rowden didn't need to say the rest. He was here for Nash, still protecting him, still there for him in his time of need.

"Give me the pistol, Nash. I'll watch your back just like I did in Portugal."

Nash took a long breath. Strangely enough, it seemed he needed the pistol more now than he ever had in that crypt, surrounded by soldiers. But he'd had to take a leap of faith then and he had little choice now.

His belly roiled and sweat broke out on his forehead, but he swallowed his fear and held the pistol out.

Rowden took it, and inside his head, Nash could feel a scream building. But then Rowden was beside him, his arm across his shoulders. "Let's go to dinner. You'll sit there and make polite conversation and behave like you're at a goddamn dinner party."

"My pistol."

"I'll keep it. I won't give it to your father. When he's gone and this is over, I'll give it back to you."

Nash didn't like it, but he didn't have any other choice. He took a breath and opened the parlor door, unarmed and ready for the real battle.

## Twenty-One

Pru wasn't watching where she was walking on the way home. Her mind was too full of all that had happened that day. Nash's face had looked so cold, so utterly devoid of any emotion as he'd stared at his father, his pistol pointed at the earl's head. His hand had been as still as a statue. She imagined his resolve was as solid as well. He could have killed the man, and she knew that would have killed Nash too. Because he hadn't seen his father in that moment. She had no doubt he'd seen a French soldier, the enemy.

She almost turned around and went back to Wentmore twice. She was terrified that the earl would send his son to an asylum tonight, and she'd never see Nash again. But Mr. Payne wouldn't let that happen. Payne was big and strong and soft-spoken, and she doubted even an earl would cross him. Why had the man chosen to arrive today? Everything had been going so well. Nash had taken her to bed, and she'd been ready to tell him that she loved him. It seemed a foolish thing to do. She didn't think he loved her back, and she didn't think telling him would change anything. She understood now why he didn't think she was safe with him.

But she wanted to tell him nonetheless.

"You really should watch where you walk," a voice said.

Pru jumped and let out a little scream. She'd taken a shortcut back to the village, traipsing through the farms and woods rather than staying on the road, which would have taken longer but now she saw would have also been infinitely smarter.

She whirled around and there, leaning against the fence she'd just climbed, was George Northgate. "You didn't even see me just now," Northgate said.

"Mr. Northgate," Pru said, trying to catch her breath. "I admit, I didn't see you."

"I doubt you would have climbed over that fence and shown me half your calf if you had. Did you lose your stockings somewhere?"

Pru thought of her stockings, probably still on the floor of Nash's bedchamber. No, Clopdon would have picked them up by now. She'd probably have them returned, cleaned and mended, tomorrow.

"A gentleman would not have looked at my legs," she said, sounding prim and prudish to her ears. She didn't usually say such things, but she suddenly felt a sense of violation. He should have made his presence known.

"As though you're a lady." Northgate sneered at her. She hadn't seen him like this before. Granted, she didn't know him well, and what she knew she didn't like, but she felt uneasy. "You may not be much to look at," he said, "with those spots on your face and that flat chest, but I'll admit your legs aren't half bad."

"The vicar is waiting for me," Pru said, starting away. She'd known men like George Northgate before. They were bullies who thought they could treat others like rubbish just because someone didn't have as much money or their family name. The best course of action was to ignore them. Pru started away, but a moment later, Northgate was in front of her, running to slide right in front of her so she had to take a step back to avoid smashing into him.

"What's your hurry? I thought we could talk for a few minutes."

"No, thank you." Pru tried to move around him, but he stepped in front of her.

"Don't you like me, Miss Howard? Or do you only tumble blind madmen in the clearing off the road?"

Pru tried to prevent her face from showing any emotion, but she knew she'd failed when he gave her a satisfied smile.

Her heart was pounding now, the sound loud in her ears. Northgate had seen them. He'd seen her with Nash. She remembered the sound of the snapped branch, and she wished she'd looked harder or at least investigated. She didn't want to face Northgate alone.

"I'm expected for dinner," she said. "Move out of the way."

"What? No sweet words for me? If you want me to move, you have to ask nicely."

Pru swallowed. She was in trouble. She knew it, and Northgate knew she had few options. Yes, she was expected at dinner, but no one would come looking for her. Not yet. Not for hours. She often stayed late at Wentmore, and Mrs. Blimkin and the vicar wouldn't worry about her for at least another hour or more.

"Please let me pass," Pru said, making her voice as sweet as possible.

"That was nicely done," he said. "But I think you can do better. Give me a compliment."

Pru swallowed her distaste. This would not work. The more she appeased him, the more he would want. She would have to try another way. "Please, Mr. Northgate," she began.

"You are so handsome and intelligent and—what is that?" She gasped and pointed, and Northgate turned sharply to look behind him.

Pru took the chance and used both hands to push him as hard as she could. He'd already been in motion, and the momentum carried him forward, and he stumbled and fell. Pru didn't wait to see what would happen when he stood again. She lifted her skirts and ran.

She was a fast runner. The skirts slowed her down, but only a little. She'd always been fast, though her mother had told her running was not ladylike. When her mother was busy or not about, Pru had challenged other children in places like Rome and Constantinople to foot races. And she almost always won.

So it surprised her when she heard Northgate behind her. He was chasing her, and she didn't dare waste a moment by looking back. He didn't sound too close, but she hadn't expected him to chase her.

"You stupid bitch!" he called after her, words broken by ragged breaths. Thank God he sounded winded. He wouldn't be able to sustain his pace for much longer. "You will be sorry. I'll tell everyone what I saw."

His voice was fading, but his threats were clear enough.

"You'll apologize to me. You'll get on your knees before me or I'll make sure that sightless monster is taken away within the hour. I can do it."

His voice was far away now, but Pru didn't slow. She had met men and women like him before. He was the sort of person who her mother said needed to look hard at the tenth commandment—Thou shall not covet thy neighbor's house. There was something in there about a neighbor's wife and oxen as well. George Northgate couldn't stand for anyone to have something he did not. He didn't want Pru, but he didn't want Nash to have something he didn't. He would carry out his threat. People like him always took perverse pleasure in the suffering of others.

The only way to forestall him—and it was a temporary solution—was to do as he asked. She'd have to apologize. He'd said he wanted her on her knees, and she had no illusions what else he'd want when she was on her knees before him. Even if she could stifle her pride and give him what he asked for, she couldn't be his whore. She had to find another way to save Nash from the asylum.

***

Mr. Higginbotham offered to drive Pru to Wentmore the next day. He had a small gig he used once a month to visit the farms the farthest from Milcroft or on the occasion when he was asked to preach at a neighboring congregation because their clergyman was indisposed. The horse who pulled the gig was quite plump, spending most of his time grazing and eating apples Pru fed him, and seemed in no hurry to make the three-mile trek to Wentmore. Pru thought she could have walked the distance faster, but that was probably because she was anxious about what she would find at Wentmore.

She was anxious too at whether or not the earl would tell the vicar that he'd found her in Nash's bedchamber. She'd considered telling Mr. Higginbotham the night before, but she hadn't been able to do it. He had been so complimentary of Nash at dinner. He'd gone on and on about the preparations for the festival and how gracious Mr. Pope had been that Pru hadn't wanted to tarnish the vicar's good opinion—of Nash or herself. Nash needed all the support he could muster at the moment. He definitely did not need an angry clergyman descending on his home.

If he was still at home.

She hadn't been able to sleep all night, worrying that Nash had been taken to the asylum under the cover of darkness.

But once the great house came into view and she spotted the maid sweeping the front stoop and a groom smoothing the gravel on the drive, she dared to hope.

"What a pleasant prospect," Mr. Higginbotham said. "The earl must be very pleased with the work his son has done on the place."

"I'm certain he is." She hoped he was. She'd mentioned the earl's arrival at dinner last night. Being that the earl provided a living to the vicar, the two men were acquainted, but Mr. Higginbotham had not seemed to know any more than Pru herself that the earl had planned to arrive that day.

The groom stopped his work on the drive and took the horse's reins. "I wrote to Lord Beaufort many times to comfort him concerning Mr. Pope. I told him if we trusted in the Lord and prayed without ceasing, his youngest son would come to see the light—er, figuratively, of course."

Pru took the vicar's hand and descended from the gig, keeping her smile pasted on her face. She rather thought Mr. Higginbotham had written to the earl to report on Nash and the poor state of the house. It was more the arrival of Mr. Payne than anything the vicar had done that helped Nash, but being that she was in a precarious position herself at the moment, it seemed wise to hold her tongue.

A footman met them at the door. Pru didn't recognize him and realized he must be part of the earl's household. He showed them into the drawing room, which was a chamber Pru had only entered a time or two, and though she could see some of the furnishings needed reupholstering and the draperies were a bit faded, the room was clean and airy. The earl's servants must have stayed up all night readying it for the earl, who was seated near a window, but stood as they entered.

"Mr. Higginbotham," the earl said. His gaze moved to Pru and lingered for just a moment. "And Miss Howard. How good to see you again." She had worn her new dress today, though that meant she would have to wear it two days in a row as she wanted to wear her best dress to the festival tomorrow. Pru held her breath that the earl would not mention the state of *un*dress he had found her in yesterday.

She glanced about the room, but it seemed the earl was alone. Did that mean he'd sent Nash away? Where was Mr. Payne? If only she could catch his eye, she might know something.

"My lord," she said with a tight smile. "I hope you passed a restful evening."

"Very much so. I have forgotten how quiet the country is. Very conducive to rest. Please, both of you, take a seat."

They sat and Mr. Higginbotham began to rhapsodize on the virtues of the country. Pru looked about, still hoping for some sign of Nash. The quarter hour dragged into a half hour and finally the earl suggested they walk to the back of the estate where the tent that would house the baked goods to be judged this year had finally been erected. Pru practically jumped out of her chair and then had to force herself to walk slowly and demurely behind the two men.

Finally, they emerged into the crisp, sunny afternoon, and Pru shaded her eyes to catch a glimpse of not only the tent for the baked goods but also a small stage and several booths in the final stages of construction.

"Quite the undertaking," Mr. Higginbotham said.

"Yes," the earl agreed. "I'm given to understand your Miss Howard played a pivotal role in managing all of this."

Pru nodded at the compliment, but her heart was beating too fast for her to form a polite response. She'd spotted Nash. He was turned away from her, looking toward the informal gardens. From the way he stood, she could tell he was uneasy. She wanted to go to him, comfort him, ask him if the sounds of the laborers were troubling him, maybe walk with him in the informal gardens. Perhaps steal a kiss...

"Miss Howard, would you walk with me?" the earl asked her. Pru looked at him, startled at hearing her name.

"Of course. I wanted to show Mr. Higginbotham the area where I thought the children's games could take place."

"Perhaps you can show him later. I would speak with you alone."

Pru looked at the vicar and he cleared his throat. "Excuse me. I will say good day to Mr. Pope."

Pru watched him walk toward Nash and wished she could take his place.

The earl offered his arm, and Pru took it. Now was the time he would chastise her. She supposed she should be grateful he hadn't done it in front of the vicar.

"Which way to the games area?" the earl asked.

"That way," she said. They walked in silence for a few moments and when they were away from the main house and within sight of the lawns, Pru took a breath.

"I thought we could section off different areas for foot races and…" She was so nervous she couldn't even think of any of the other games. This was ridiculous. She released the earl's arm and turned to face him. "I'm not sorry," she said. "I know you probably think I'm some sort of lightskirt and feel obligated to tell the vicar the situation in which we met yesterday."

The earl raised his brows, his blue eyes grave.

"But I cannot apologize for it or regret it. I cannot bring myself to regret a single moment I have spent with your son. And if that means my reputation is ruined, well, there are worse trials."

"Miss Howard," the earl began.

She shook her head. "I'm not done."

The earl's brows shot up higher.

"I simply ask that you don't accuse Nash of ruining me. He did not ruin me. I seduced him."

The earl's lips pressed together. "I see."

"He's a very good man, and I know he pointed that pistol at you yesterday, but he didn't realize it was you. I have never been in a war, so I cannot imagine what it must be like. Have you ever been in a war, my lord?"

"No."

"Then you cannot understand either. Nash isn't dangerous. He just needs time to recover. And he really is recovering. He is so much better than he was—"

"Miss Howard."

"And I think given time—"

"Miss Howard."

"Sir, I am trying to talk you out of sending him to the asylum."

"I realize that, Miss Howard. And your feelings for my son do you credit. He is a good man. He always has been."

Pru stared at the earl. "Have you told him you think so? You can't imagine how much that would mean to him."

"We have not been on good terms for some time." The earl looked past Pru, toward the lawns.

"All the more reason to make amends now."

Beaufort's gaze flicked back to her. "Miss Howard, you are very forthright for a young person."

"I know. I keep telling my mouth to shut up, but it keeps ignoring me. Oh!" She grasped the earl's hand and squeezed it.

"Miss Howard, this is quite—"

"Shh!"

"Miss Howard," he hissed.

"Look." Slowly, she raised her free hand and pointed into the hedges bordering the far end of the lawn. "Do you see him?"

"Do I see who? Really, you should release my hand."

Pru released him and placed her hand on his arm. "The peacock," she said. "He's just right there."

She felt his arm stiffen under her hand and then his shoulders dropped, and he let out a small chuckle.

"I'll be damned."

Pru glanced at the earl. He was smiling broadly, his eyes dancing with merriment as he watched the peacock strut in front of the hedges.

"I'd quite forgotten about those birds. How can he still be alive? I brought them here years ago."

Pru told him what she'd learned about the peacock lifespan in Constantinople. "Mrs. Northgate told me the day of the garden party you asked Nash to give a sharpshooter demonstration."

The earl's smile faded slightly. "Yes, I did."

"She said he was only about ten and was better than all the men of the village."

"Quite true. He was always a natural with a firearm. I'm quite a good shot myself, so he comes by it honestly."

"My lord, you were proud of Nash that day," Pru said. "Do you not think you could be proud of him again?"

The earl let out a sigh. "Miss Howard, you are speaking of things you know nothing about. Much has happened in the years between, and Nash is not the same man he was when he left for the war."

"But he's still your son. And he still needs your love."

"Miss Howard, these matters do not concern you."

"I know." She spread her hands wide. "I told myself a dozen times to keep my thoughts to myself, but how can I when all the signs tell me to speak out?"

"What signs?"

"The peacock!" Didn't the earl see that as a sign? What were the chances that the elusive peacock would be here, in this exact place, just as the two of them happened to come to stand here? "I can't stay silent when the peacock is there."

The look on his face indicated perhaps he thought *she* should go to an asylum. "I don't follow you, Miss Howard. What has the bird to do with whether or not you mind your own business?"

Really. She could see the family resemblance more than ever. Neither Nash nor his father seemed to have any imagination. "My lord," she said, summoning all her patience. "The peacock is part of your past—a symbol of the love and pride you once had for your son. To see one now is a clear sign that Nash needs that love and pride from you again."

"Or it might just be that the bird has managed to survive all these years."

As she'd thought—no imagination.

"Have you not been back to Wentmore in the last twenty years?" she asked, trying logic, though it pained her.

"I have."

"And have you ever seen the peacock? Your son led me to believe everyone thought the peacocks dead—succumbed to the elements or eaten by foxes."

"I have not seen this peacock until today. What of it?"

Pru moved to stand directly in front of the earl. "It is a *sign*. Give him a chance, my lord. Please."

A movement behind him caught her attention, and she craned her neck to see the vicar and Nash making their way toward them. "Here he comes, my lord. This is your opportunity."

## Twenty-Two

Nash did not like his empty pocket. He continued to reach for it, touch it, even though he knew it was empty. He tried not to panic. He reminded himself Rowden had his pistol. Rowden had his back.

The vicar arrived and came to speak to Nash, and Nash nodded and smiled. But he had no idea what the man said. Nash could only think about the pistol. And then he realized if the vicar was here, Pru might be here.

"Is Miss Howard with you?" Nash asked, interrupting some monologue on God creating Eden.

"Eh? Oh, yes. She is showing Lord Beaufort the lawns set aside for the games."

She was with his father? Alone?

"Speaking of Eden," Nash said. "You should see that view as well. Come." Without waiting for Mr. Higginbotham, Nash started in the direction of the east lawn. He brushed his walking stick before him periodically to make certain he would not crash into any unexpected objects, but for the most part, he knew the way well now.

"Mr. Pope!" Pru said as he neared and just the sound of her voice calmed him. He wanted to reach out and take her in his arms, but he had enough sense to give her a formal bow.

"Miss Howard, thank you for coming to assist with the final preparations. We can certainly use your support." He hoped she understood what he was really saying.

"I wouldn't dream of staying away," she said, and her voice was warm. "But now I think your father wishes to speak with you. Mr. Higginbotham, might I request your counsel on that area over there? I thought we might set up skittles."

"Skittles? Where?"

"Come. I'll show you."

He heard the swish of her skirts as she moved away, and Nash wished he could go with her. Standing before his father now, he felt like the little boy he'd been twenty years ago. It might have helped to be able to see the man, reassure himself he was taller than the earl now, but the brightness of the sun made even seeing shapes impossible at the moment.

"You're looking well this morning."

Nash swallowed and tried not to touch his empty pocket. Funny how he'd forgotten about it when he'd known Pru was here and when he'd been in her presence.

"I feel like hell," Nash said, surprising himself with his honesty. "I didn't sleep all night, wondering if my door would be knocked down by a drove of doctors paid to take me away."

"Come now, Nash. Is that what you think I would do? I'm not a monster."

"No, you're not. You'd drive me yourself and tell yourself you were doing the best thing for everyone."

The earl sighed. "Can you blame me? When you came home from the war, your mother and I didn't even recognize you. You looked the same, but it was as though a stranger had taken over your body. You would not come out from under your bed for three days, Nash. You shot a hole in the ceiling of the music room, scaring your sister half to death."

Nash had a vague recollection of being in the town house, but he did not remember these specifics.

"And you drank like a fish. You stumbled into your mother's annual charity ball drunk and belligerent."

Nash did remember that incident. The noise of the orchestra and the people had grated on his nerves. He'd just wanted it to stop.

"I remember. That was when you sent me away."

"We thought the country air might help revive you."

"You told me you would never speak to me again."

There was a long silence. "I think you also said some things that day you might now regret."

Nash couldn't remember what he'd said that day. He doubted it was anything he wanted to remember. The point that stuck with him was that his father regretted saying he wouldn't ever speak to him again. "You have regrets?" he asked, hating that he needed the answer to be affirmative so badly.

"I do. I shouldn't have sent you away alone. And when I heard about the fire—"

"You mean when the vicar reported me."

"Yes. And that you had shot Lieutenant Murray, I should have come. But quite honestly, Nash, I didn't think my presence here would help."

Nash nodded. "Probably not." He could admit it now—he'd been out of control. He still didn't feel he had a good grip on his control. Not unless he was with Pru.

"I thought about sending that giant friend of yours. The one with the pale blond hair and the pugilism studio."

"Mostyn. His wife is expecting."

"Yes, and I thought you might need someone you could talk to. Colonel Draven suggested Mr. Payne. I think that was the right decision."

Nash let it sink in for a moment that his father had consulted Colonel Draven about him. He'd wanted to help.

"Rowden is the one responsible for all of this." Nash gestured vaguely toward the house and grounds, which he imagined looked a good deal better than it had a few weeks ago.

"And you are doing better too."

"I pointed a pistol at you," Nash reminded him. "Again, apparently."

"Yes, but you also had a woman in your bed. I took that as a good sign."

"About that—" Nash began.

"If you are about to tell me she is not a lightskirt, you needn't. She has already informed me of that."

Nash couldn't help but laugh. "Of course, she has."

"She also told me the peacock wandering about the lawn was a sign…from God, I suppose. I have a feeling she might have done more to restore you to yourself than Wentmore or Mr. Payne."

"She has helped me see the world again," Nash said. "Though her view of it is quite different from what mine was when I had my sight."

"I imagine. She is what your mother would call unconventional."

"And what do you say?" Nash asked, surprised that he really did care.

"I call her odd. But I like her."

"So do I," Nash said. "I like her very much."

Nash clasped his hands behind his back because he wanted to touch his empty coat pocket again.

"Are you thinking of marriage?" his father asked after a long moment.

Nash shook his head. "How can I when I might be sent to the asylum at any moment?" And when he might wake up and think he was in the middle of a battle and shoot her.

"And you might not. I have not decided yet, Nash. I am trying to give you every opportunity."

"Like a dog you are training who has not yet mastered all his tricks? I won't roll over when you whistle. If you're to send me, then do it already. I'd rather be gone than live in this hell of indecision." Nash walked away, ignoring his father's calls for him to return and discuss the matter further.

He went inside and made his way into the parlor, where he sat and tried to tamp down his fears. When Rowden had arrived and told Nash of the earl's plan, Nash had formed his own plan. If he was to be sent to an asylum, he would simply shoot himself in the head before he could be taken away.

But now he wasn't certain he could go through with it. He didn't want to die if there was still a chance he might be able to talk to Pru again, touch her, kiss her. Because when he was with Pru—when he even thought about Pru—he forgot his pain. He often had no idea what to say to her, what to do with her, how to react to her more outlandish statements. He wanted to pull her close and at the same time, push her away.

She scared him because he wanted her too much. She was a constant reminder that at one time he'd thought he had everything he ever wanted in life, and he'd lost it all.

He thought he had mourned those losses, but this past day and the very real prospect of losing Pru made him realize how devastating true loss might feel. The idea of living without her—truly losing her—terrified him because he could see the black void of nothingness that would be the rest of his life without her ray of sunlight piercing the dark hole in his soul.

"There you are," Pru said, and for a moment Nash wondered if he was imagining her. But then she was beside him, her hand on his, kneeling next to his chair. "I saw you speaking with your father. Did he tell you?"

Nash gripped her hand tightly. "He's still deciding."

"Still...oh, you mean about the asylum. Idiot. I won't let him send you to an asylum." But something in her voice sounded unsure. "So then he didn't tell you how much he loves you?"

Nash gave a short laugh. "No."

"Or that he's proud of you?"

"No." Sometimes he felt quite dizzy speaking to her. She said the most unexpected things. "Did he say that to you?" Nash asked.

"Not exactly, but I thought for sure the peacock would sway him."

"Why would the peacock—" Oh, why waste the time he had with her trying to parse out what he would not understand anyway? "Pru." He took her hands. "I apologize for yesterday. I shouldn't have put you in that position."

"If I recall, I was the one who chose the position."

"You know what I mean."

"I do, and I don't want your apologies. I only have a moment before Mrs. Blimkin or the vicar finds me, and then I shall be put to work again. And that means I only have a moment to tell you."

Nash braced himself. She was leaving him. She'd finally had an invitation to stay with her sister. Or she couldn't risk being caught with him again. She wanted to end things. The black void opened, and Nash stared into the swirling abyss.

"Tell me then," he said, his voice flat.

He heard her take a shaky breath and realized it must be worse than he thought. She was never scared to say her mind.

"Go on," he demanded. He wanted the bandage ripped off. The pain would be so great, he might welcome the nothingness of the void.

"Fine. I wanted to tell you that—"

"Miss Howard!" came a distant voice. It was Mrs. Blimkin.

"Coming! Nash, I wanted to tell you that I—" She swallowed again.

"Say it." His voice was harsh, and her hand in his flexed.

"I love you," she said, the words sounding like bells tumbling out of a box. "I love you, Nash Pope. That's all I wanted to say."

"Miss Howard! There you are. Oh, am I interrupting?"

Nash sat perfectly still. He didn't move, didn't react when Pru released his hand and stood.

"Not at all, Mrs. Blimkin. Do you need help?"

"I do."

Their voices faded as they moved away, and Nash looked down again. But the abyss was gone. The maw had closed. Pru loved him.

It was a fact. It was a truth. She had said it, her voice low and full of emotion. She loved him—despite his blindness, despite his weakness and terror yesterday, despite the very real possibility that he would soon be residing in an asylum.

Pru loved him.

Heavy footsteps sounded and the door creaked. "Are you well?" Rowden asked, his voice coming from the doorway. "You look as though you were just punched in the breadbasket."

Nash nodded. "I feel like I've been punched." He turned to look at the shape that was Rowden. "Pru loves me."

Rowden blew out a quick breath. "Did you just realize that? I suppose you can't see the way she looks at you. She's been taken with you from the start."

"What do I—what am I supposed to do about it?"

*Sweet Rogue of Mine* | 417

"Do about it? How the hell do I know? Love her back, I guess." Rowden walked away, and Nash shook his head.

If only it were so simple.

\*\*\*

Pru had kept busy the rest of Friday, and Saturday morning she'd arrived at Wentmore just as the sun came up. There was much to do and only a few hours before the festival would begin.

"Slow down, dear," Mrs. Brown said when Pru dropped a basket of folded tablecloths on her way outside. "You needn't hurry. Sit a while, if you like. With all the servants the earl brought, we'll be done in no time."

But Pru needed to be busy. If she paused to think she would remember Nash's expression when she'd told him she loved him. He'd looked as though he'd been struck by lightning. He clearly hadn't expected her to say such a thing. He clearly didn't love her back; else he wouldn't have looked so shocked.

Pru didn't regret saying the words. She rarely regretted anything, and why should she regret telling the man she loved how she felt. She might have waited for another chance to be alone with him, one where they might not be interrupted, but she didn't have the luxury of time. If the earl did send Nash to an asylum, Pru wanted him to know how she felt. She wanted him to know she would never abandon him.

"I'm fine, Mrs. Brown," Pru said, gathering the tablecloths and making her way outside to begin covering the tables. The sky was cloudy this morning, promising rain later in the day. Pru hoped it held off until late afternoon. The bite in the air also hinted at the coming winter. Pru did not relish the thought of long weeks and months inside the vicarage with nothing but sermons to read. Wentmore was too far of a walk to attempt in inclement weather. Mrs. Northgate was close enough, but if she went there, she risked seeing Mrs. Northgate's grandson.

Pru sighed as she began shaking out tablecloths and laying them over tables. She still didn't know what to do about George Northgate. Certainly, he wouldn't accost her at the festival. There would be too many other people around. But he would look for an opportunity soon afterward. Who could she speak to about him? Mrs. Northgate was the first person that came to mind, but George was her own grandson. Of course, she would take his side. Perhaps if Pru phrased it as a hypothetical...

The hair on the back of her neck tingled, and she looked about, knowing Nash must be near. She spotted him, having just emerged from the house. He was a vision, and she had to take a bracing breath at the sight of him. Clopdon had outdone himself. Nash was dressed in dark breeches and coat with a waistcoat the color of...Pru looked down at her new dress. It was almost the same russet color as her dress. She'd never seen the waistcoat before, which meant it might be new. She suddenly felt a rush of affection for Clopdon. The dear man.

Nash was standing outside the house, like a feudal baron surveying his domain. She realized it wasn't the waistcoat that took her breath away as much as the way the sun streamed over him, making his dark hair look almost fiery and highlighting the curves and planes of his face. She wanted to go to him and kiss him, but she controlled her impulse and shook out another tablecloth. Good thing as the earl emerged from the house to stand next to his son a moment later. The two spoke briefly, and Pru's quick glances at them were enough to have her worried.

The earl still seemed stern and, when he looked at Nash, his gaze was assessing. He was still deciding whether or not to send Nash away. He was still waiting for Nash to do something that would seal his fate. Pru snapped a tablecloth so hard that the sound echoed. She didn't care. The earl obviously hadn't listened to a word she said yesterday, and she had to take out her anger somehow.

Pru had hoped to have a moment alone with Nash—he might tell her he loved her back. She almost laughed at the thought. More likely, so he might tell her she was an idiot and why couldn't they just have a bit of fun and not be so serious? That's what Abubakar had said when she'd asked how he felt about her. She hadn't loved him, but she'd desperately wanted to be in love. With Abubakar, she'd known there was nothing but lust between them. She'd felt more for Nash from the beginning, though.

But there was no opportunity to speak to Nash alone before the first guests for the festival—the vicar and Mrs. Northgate—arrived. They arrived together, which puzzled Pru as she hadn't thought the two had much affinity for each other. Pru went to greet her guardian and her friend then took Mrs. Northgate aside on the pretext of showing her the table where she could put the apple tart she had brought.

"I thought you did not care for the vicar," Pru said.

Mrs. Northgate gave her a sharp look. "Well, good day to you too."

"Oh, I'm sorry. Good day. How are you? The weather looks like rain, does it not? I thought you did not care for the vicar."

Mrs. Northgate laughed. "I don't care for religion, and I don't care to be chided for not attending church. The other day when Mr. Higginbotham drove me home, I told him we would be good friends if only he never mentioned the subject again. He declined, of course. He has a moral duty or some such rot. Oh, my! Yes, this looks very well, Miss Howard."

Pru smiled at the way Mrs. Northgate nodded in approval at the tables draped in white and festooned with ribbons and colorful bunches of leaves. The tent for the baked goods being entered in the contest was decorated in a manner similar to the tables. It was located south of the tables and the stage where announcements could be made and where Dr. Langford had promised to play his violin.

"You were speaking of the vicar's rotten moral duty," Pru said a moment later.

"Horrid girl. That was not what I said. But he did go on and on about it, so I told him that whenever we met he could have five minutes exactly to preach and convert me. I have a small watch you see." She withdrew the pretty gold piece from her reticule. "I would time him and at the end of five minutes, he must shut up. And it's worked remarkably well. I can almost tolerate the man now." Mrs. Northgate set her tart on the table.

"How...lovely," Pru said. "But you did not want to come with your family?"

"Oh, those girls will take hours to dress their hair and change their clothes. I'm an old woman. If I wait for them, I will be dead."

"Don't say that!"

"You're still young. When you reach my age, death is not so frightening. But look what we have here. My, but he is the vision of his father when his father was younger. The earl was the only man for whom I would have ever thrown my Mr. Northgate over."

"Mrs. Northgate!"

She cackled. "Oh, he never gave me so much as a second glance. I was pretty enough, but he was only attracted to money. The countess came with a large dowry and an excellent pedigree, so I suppose he got what he wanted." She patted Pru's hand. "And so did I."

"Do you miss him very much?" Pru asked. "Mr. Northgate, I mean."

"Every day." She gave Pru a meaningful look. "When you're young, it seems like you have all the time in the world. But it will be gone before you know it. Don't waste a single moment."

"I won't," Pru said.

Mrs. Northgate laughed. "I do believe you!"

The guests continued to arrive, and Nash and his father greeted them all. Pru kept busy helping in the competition tent. All of the entries had to be catalogued and assigned a number. Mrs. Blimkin was in and out, complaining that she was fair starving because she was one of the judges and did not want to eat before the contest began. She claimed it was to preserve her palate, but Pru rather thought it was because she wanted to have room to eat more.

Once the competition began, Pru slipped out and started for the east lawn to watch the children's games. She could hear the children's laughs and shouts and squeals of delight. Nothing gave her more pleasure than watching children play. But she'd barely taken two steps before a hand caught her arm. She turned, expecting the vicar—or truth be told, wishing it were Nash—but she instantly recoiled.

It was George Northgate.

"Good afternoon, Miss Howard," he said, smiling pleasantly.

"You'll have to excuse me, Mr. Northgate," she said, trying to pull her arm away. But his grip held, and even as he smiled, he forcibly escorted her toward the back of the tent, which was bordered by the informal gardens and well hidden from view. Pru struggled but his grip was unbreakable. She thought of screaming but then how would she explain?

Northgate, with his back up against a wall, would reveal everything. The vicar would be required to take some action, perhaps to send her away. She couldn't leave Nash now. Not in his greatest moment of need.

Northgate shoved Pru to her knees and held her in place with a hand in her hair. She winced at the pain of his tight grip and recoiled as he tried to push her toward the fall of his breeches.

"Good afternoon, slut. I'm here for my apology."

Pru knew she should just give one and hope that would suffice for now. Perhaps if she apologized, he would allow her to go. She had no illusions he would not seek her out again, but she would be more careful in the future.

"I'm waiting."

Pru tried to form the words, but she just couldn't do it. She would rather face every kind of indignity before apologizing to this man. As her father had always said, she had an allergy to authority, and she simply could not give in.

Pru shook her head stubbornly. "Go shove a stick up your arse," she ground out, trying to keep her voice from rising at the increasing pain in her scalp.

"Foul-mouthed bitch," he said, reaching for the placket of his breeches. "I'll give you something to do with that mouth."

His hand on her hair tightened as he pulled her closer. It felt as though he was pulling half her scalp off. Her nerves screamed and she could barely focus on anything but the pain. She closed her eyes and tried to think of something happy—the peacock's splayed tailfeathers, her young niece's smile, Nash's gentle touch.

And then the world went black.

## Twenty-Three

Nash had finally managed to escape the reception line. He'd hoped Pru would appear at his side as soon as he stepped away, but he wandered about the grounds for a good while without finding her. He would have asked where she was, but he'd walked about for at least a quarter hour without a single person speaking to him. He could hardly blame the villagers. They were probably afraid of him. Perhaps they thought he would shoot them.

Nash touched his empty coat pocket. He would have felt better with his pistol in his pocket. Rowden still had it in his possession, and that meant Nash needed to find Pru. She would calm his nerves. Everything would be well with Pru at his side.

"Oh, Mr. Pope," said a familiar voice. Nash paused and turned to face the speaker.

"Mrs. Brown?"

"Yes."

Oh, thank God. Finally, someone he knew.

"Are you looking for Mr. Payne?" she asked.

"No." He could guess where Rowden was. Somewhere there was a group of men who liked a little sport. Rowden could needle the most obnoxious among them, stir up a fight, and make a few pounds from the betting when he knocked the man on his arse. "Actually, I had a question for Miss Howard," he said.

"Oh, is it something I can answer?" Mrs. Brown asked.

Nash sighed. "No."

"I see. I saw her in the tent earlier. I believe she was helping with the baked goods competition."

"Thank you, Mrs. Brown. The tent is…" He tried to orient himself, which wasn't easy with all the changes to the lawn of late. "This way?" he asked.

"Yes, sir. Straight ahead."

He started away then turned back.

"Was there something else, Mr. Pope?"

"Yes," he said. "I owe you my thanks."

"Not at all, sir."

Nash clenched his jaw. "Let me get this out, Mrs. Brown."

"Of course, sir."

"Thank you for staying here through…everything. I realize I behaved abominably."

"Not at all, sir."

"Mrs. Brown." He drew her name out.

"Oh, very well. You were perfectly horrid."

"Thank you for not abandoning me. You kept me alive."

"Nonsense. I practically poisoned you with my cooking."

Nash laughed. "I would beg you never to cook again, but at least your broths and soups kept me from completely pickling my innards with gin. Thank you."

"No thanks necessary, sir." She paused for a moment. "But I appreciate hearing it nonetheless."

"Good, and I would appreciate it if you would go and enjoy yourself. I'm giving you the rest of the day off. Tomorrow as well."

"Oh! That's not necessary. And there's so much to do here after the festival."

"You won't do any of it. Go see your family. Sleep late tomorrow morning. I don't want you lifting a finger here, Mrs. Brown. Is that understood?"

"Yes, sir."

He could hear the emotion in her voice, and he let out a huff. Why was she crying when he'd given her a day and a half off? "Good day, Mrs. Brown."

"Good day. He always was a good boy," she said as he walked away. Nash hoped to earn that praise again someday.

He knew when he neared the tent as he could hear the voice of Milcroft's mayor. He was making a last call for all sweet dishes to be entered. The judges would begin tasting in just a moment. Nash hesitated at the entrance. He needed a moment before he went inside. He would take a few minutes to breathe just behind the tent. No one would see him there. But as he made his way toward the back, he heard the sounds of a scuffle and then Pru's sweet voice enjoining someone to...shove a stick up his bum?

Nash didn't hesitate. One hand on the side of the tent to guide him, he rounded the corner. With the informal gardens on one side, the light was dimmer here, and Nash could see two shapes. One seemed to be kneeling and the other standing over the first. As soon as Nash appeared, they broke apart. The figure he would recognize anywhere as Pru fell backward with a cry and the man who had been holding her stepped away.

"What's happening here? Miss Howard?"

She didn't answer, and Nash stepped forward, reaching out and catching the man by the neck. He hadn't even tried to avoid Nash, obviously thinking he couldn't see well enough to be a threat. But Nash didn't need his eyes. He squeezed tightly and pushed the other man against the back of the tent. "I asked you a question."

"We were just having a bit of fun," the other man said.

Nash's breath whooshed out of him for a moment. Pru and this man? She'd been on her knees. Nash shook his head. "I should kill you for touching her." He began to squeeze.

"Nash."

He turned his head slightly as Pru's voice penetrated the red haze beginning to descend.

"Let him go. I'm fine."

"I'll let him go after I kill him."

"No." She was beside him, her hand on his arm. At her touch, much of his rage leaked away. The red haze began to dissipate, and a calm blue replaced it. "If you hurt him, he'll use it against you. He'd like nothing better than to see you sent away. Let him go."

Nash opened his hand and released the man, who crumpled, gasping for breath.

"You're not hurt?" Nash asked, pulling her close. The feel of her in his arms was exactly what he needed. The world felt right again.

"No."

"Who?" he asked, gesturing to the man.

"George Northgate. He saw us in the field that day and thought...well..."

She didn't need to finish. Nash knew exactly what the man had thought. And he wanted to kill him all over again. Pru gripped his arm tightly, though, and steered him away. "Let's go. We can leave him here in the dirt."

"Walk away," Northgate called as they turned their backs on him. "I'll tell everyone you threatened to kill me. You'll be on your way to the mad house before nightfall."

"Come on," Pru urged. Nash went with her. As much as he would have liked to kill the man, that was a sure way to be sent to the asylum. But they had gone no more than three feet before a man yelled, "No! Mr. Pope, please! Don't shoot!"

Nash paused, confused.

And then a shot rang out.

\*\*\*

They were just emerging from behind the tent when the shot startled Pru enough that she jumped. She was already shaking with rage and shock at what Northgate had tried to do to her, and it took little to upset her. But it was not only Pru who was surprised. The shot startled the rest of the assemblage as well, judging by the silence that descended and the immediate halt to all movement. Pru glanced at Nash. He seemed confused, but she knew exactly what had happened. And she knew in that moment she had failed Nash. George Northgate would have the last word, just as she'd feared.

"Nash." Pru gripped his arm. "Stay calm." The words were as much for her as for him. Her legs felt like jelly and her head still screamed in pain. She imagined her hair looked a fright, but fortunately her hair always looked a fright and people probably wouldn't find its current state remarkable.

"What happened?" Nash asked

"What the devil was that?" The earl emerged from the crowd of people near the house and started for them, the vicar on his heels. "Was that a pistol shot?" he yelled.

"I'll stay by your side," Pru told Nash. "As long as I can. No matter what happens, Mr. Payne and I will find a way to come for you. Remember I love you."

"Why are you telling me good-bye?" he asked.

He would understand soon enough, she thought as his father reached them, still cursing and shouting. "What the hell was that?" he demanded.

A crowd had formed, and Pru searched it for help. There was Mrs. Northgate, looking concerned and sympathetic. Where was Mr. Payne? She needed him. Nash needed him.

"Mr. Northgate," Pru began.

But then George Northgate stumbled out from behind the tent. "He shot at me," Northgate said. "He threatened to kill me."

Pru could have cheerfully murdered George Northgate. She wanted to scream that he was a liar, but for once, she checked her impulses.

The earl looked at Northgate and then at Nash and back at Northgate. "Who shot at you, sir?"

"Mr. Pope," Northgate said. "I was speaking with Miss Howard, and he mistook my intentions. He pulled out his pistol and fired at me."

The earl's face hardened as he looked at his son. "Is this true, Nash?"

"No." Nash didn't even hesitate. He didn't elaborate either.

"Do you want to explain?" the earl asked.

Nash shrugged. "He's lying. If I'd shot at him, I would have hit him."

The crowd gasped, and Pru closed her eyes. That defense, if it could be called that, could not have helped him.

"I see."

"He came within an inch of hitting me," Northgate said. "I felt the heat from the pistol ball as it flew by my face. That man isn't safe. He needs to be locked up."

The crowd began to murmur, and Pru tightened her grip on Nash's arm. All she had wanted was to bury her head in his chest and feel safe after Northgate's attack. But it seemed she would never get that chance now. Nash evinced no reaction to Northgate's accusation. It was as though he heard nothing and blocked all of the unpleasantness. He appeared completely unconcerned.

"If this is true," the earl said, raising his voice to be heard above the crowd, "he should be locked away. For his safety and yours."

The people in the crowd nodded and muttered agreement. It seemed the entire village was there now. Even the children had left their games to see what the commotion was about.

"That isn't what happened," Pru said, feeling all the eyes of the village turn to her. "There was a pistol shot, but Mr. Pope didn't fire it."

"Then who did?" someone in the crowd yelled.

"We all know he carries a pistol in his pocket," someone else said.

And then the entire village was yelling and talking over each other, and Pru knew it was hopeless. The earl would have to send Nash away just to prevent a riot. She drew her attention back to Nash and twined her fingers with his. She'd stand beside him as long as he could. He stood straight, head up, but his hand gripped hers back.

*\*\*\**

It was over. Nash knew when a battle was won or, in this case, lost. Pru thought she could save him, and if anyone could, it was she. But Nash didn't think anyone or anything could save him now. And it was his own fault. If he hadn't allowed himself to sink into despair. If he hadn't carried that pistol around all the time. If he hadn't shot at the solicitor and Duncan Murray...

He would lose her now. He would lose Pru and he hadn't even told her that he loved her. He hadn't even told her how much she meant to him. How she had helped him when he needed it most.

"What is this about?" The voice rose above the rest, cutting clearly through the noise. It was the voice of a man used to speaking to rowdy crowds. It was Rowden Payne. "No, don't all speak at once. My lord, what has happened?"

The earl cleared his throat. "Apparently, my son shot at this man in what appears to be a lover's quarrel."

The crowd murmured again, and Rowden seemed to wait for them to quiet before speaking again. "Is that true, sir?"

Northgate—cowardly bastard—moved forward. "It's true, sir. He almost killed me."

"I see." Rowden's voice was slow and deliberate. "This is very serious."

"Lock him away!" someone called.

"Good idea," Rowden said, making his voice heard above the crowd. He'd commanded the attention of far more belligerent crowds from a pugilism ring in London's underbelly. Nash knew this gathering was nothing to him. "You there—take this gentleman away."

Nash waited for rough arms to seize him, but instead he heard more murmuring. No one moved.

"What are you about?" Northgate said. "*He* tried to kill *me!*"

"Is that so?" Rowden drawled. "With what weapon?"

Nash didn't allow himself to smile yet. After all, Rowden would not appreciate it if he ruined his moment.

"A pistol," Northgate said, sounding as though he were speaking to a child. "The one he always carries with him. Same one he shot the Scot with, I imagine."

"This one?" Rowden said.

Beside him, Pru gasped, and Nash could imagine Rowden drawing Nash's pistol out of his own pocket.

"Not that one! He has a pistol!" Northgate said, but he sounded uncertain now. He sounded as though he knew he had just taken a wrong step.

"Mr. Pope," Rowden said. "Would you empty your pockets, please."

"Of course," Nash said. He reached into his outer coat pockets and turned them inside out. Then he made a show of removing his coat and emptying the inner pockets and the pockets of his waistcoat. In the end, he had nothing to show for it except a few pieces of lint and a couple of coins.

"He threw the pistol into the garden!" Northgate said, sounding panicked. "He gave it to her." He must have pointed at Pru because Nash heard people murmuring her name. But it must have been obvious she wasn't hiding a pistol in her dress because the next voice Nash heard was that of his father.

"I'd like for you to empty your pockets, Mr. Northgate."

"I will *not*," Northgate said. He sounded very much like he was cornered now.

"I'm afraid that was not a request," the earl said. "Empty your pockets, sir."

"No."

"Clopdon," the earl said, his tone one of weariness.

"Yes, sir."

Pru's hand on his tightened. She leaned closer. "Clopdon has gestured to two footmen to take hold of Mr. Northgate, and they're searching his pockets."

Nash could have guessed as much from the sounds of a scuffle he heard. Then Northgate swore and said, "What does it matter if I have a pistol? That doesn't prove anything."

"Let me see it," the earl ordered. "Bring it to me."

The crowd gathered around them seemed to collectively hold their breath. Nash wished them all gone. He wished the entire day over. He wanted to pull Pru close, breathe in her scent and kiss her until they were both dizzy with need. For the first time in weeks, Nash wasn't afraid he would be violently snatched from his bed and driven to an asylum this night. He had a reprieve and, whether it was for one day or more, he knew he wanted to spend it with Pru.

"It's been recently fired," his father said. "The stock is still warm and there's powder at the muzzle."

"I fired in self-defense!" Northgate shouted, which was clearly a last desperate grasp at a defense. Everyone had heard only one shot.

"George, do shut up now."

Nash didn't recognize the voice, and he waited for Pru to name the speaker, but he had to nudge her to remind her.

"It's Mrs. Northgate," she said, her voice full of wonder. "The dowager."

"I want to apologize for my grandson," Mrs. Northgate said. "He is, unfortunately, too much like his mother."

The crowd chuckled quietly, and Nash assumed the younger Mrs. Northgate was not well-liked.

"I will take him home now, if that is acceptable, my lord. Or do you wish to summon the magistrate?"

"Grandmama!" Northgate shouted.

"I told you to shut up. I will, of course, give a statement," Mrs. Northgate said. "But if you allow me to take him home, I think a nice long trip to the Continent is in his future."

"Take him," the earl said. "I do not wish to see him again."

"Yes, my lord."

The crowd shifted and there was some jostling as, presumably, the footmen led Northgate away. Pru squeezed Nash's hand. "I am going after them."

"No," Nash said. He didn't want Pru anywhere near George Northgate.

"I want to speak to Mrs. Northgate," she said. "I'll be back shortly."

And then she was gone, and Nash stood awkwardly in the center of a ring of people he did not know. He took a deep breath, tried to stand still and not fidget. Finally, a voice he did not recognize said, "Well done, Mr. Pope."

Next came a female voice. "We always knew you weren't dicked in the nob."

"Er—thank you," Nash said, realizing the villagers about him were speaking to him.

"This will be a festival we won't soon forget," another said.

"Lot more exciting than last year's," another man said.

"Excuse me," came a voice Nash knew well. He braced for whatever his father would do next. But the earl put his arm about Nash's shoulder and led him away, up toward the house. Nash stiffened at the unfamiliar feel of his father's affection. It had been years since his father had draped a casual arm about him and walked with him.

When they were away from the crowd, the earl patted Nash's back and said, "Well, that was certainly exciting."

"I don't know if *exciting* is the word I would use for it."

"Lies, deceit, treachery—I feel almost as though I am back in London."

"And when will you be returning?" Nash asked.

He'd expected a flash of anger from his father, but the earl slapped him on the back affectionately and laughed. "In a day or two. I came here for answers, and I suppose now I have them."

"Do you?" Nash asked, turning to look at his father. He wished he could see more than the shadowy outline, but he would have to guess at his father's expression.

"You are clearly not mad and you don't belong in an asylum. Is that what you wanted to hear?"

Nash felt as though an enormous weight had been lifted from his shoulders. He slumped and let out a breath.

"I can see you are relieved," the earl said. "I am sorry I ever caused you so much anxiety. You know if I sent you away, it would have been for your own good."

"I know you would have believed that," Nash said.

The two stood a long moment, side by side.

"The country has been good for you," the earl said. "But your mother would like to see you soon. You will come for a visit, won't you? Perhaps at Christmas."

"Perhaps," Nash said. He wasn't quite sure he was ready for the noise and commotion of his siblings and their families all around him. But one day. He could see himself enjoying such a gathering one day. He could see himself with his own family one day. And there was only one woman he wanted to share that future with him.

"My lord?"

"Oh, no. You only speak to me so formally when you want something, and I already know what it is."

"I don't think you do."

"You want my blessing to marry Miss Howard."

Nash stiffened. "I—yes. I don't know if she'll have me, but I will do my best to persuade her."

"She doesn't strike me as a fool, and she would be a fool to turn down an offer from the son of an earl. She's not likely to have any others. I had my man investigate her after I found you two *in flagrante delicto.*"

Nash blew out a breath. "Of course, you did."

"She has no connections and no money. Her sister is quite poor and living in Chelsea. Her parents are reportedly missionaries gone to the Far East. We may never see them again. And there was some business in Cairo…"

"I know all about it."

"And you still want her?"

"Yes."

"Then marry her. Wentmore is unentailed. I'll gift it to you as a wedding present."

Nash started. "You will?"

"Why not? The place looks better than it has in years. You've done well here, son. Now, go enjoy the day."

His father walked away, and Nash laughed to himself. He would enjoy the day, but first he had one more task to attend to.

## Twenty-Four

"Mrs. Northgate!" Pru called as she ran after the woman. She walked remarkably quickly for a woman of advanced years. The dowager paused and looked back at her. As Pru approached, Mrs. Northgate nodded.

"That dress looks quite well on you, if I do say so myself."

Pru looked down at her russet dress and brushed some leaves from the skirt. "Thank you. It wouldn't look half so well if you hadn't helped me with it."

"I daresay it wouldn't."

Behind them the footmen shoved George Northgate toward the wagon he had driven to the festival. Mrs. Northgate seemed oblivious to the commotion. Pru moved to the side, partly hidden from Mr. Northgate's view by some shrubbery. She didn't want his gaze on her. Now that the immediate danger of Nash being taken away had passed, she'd started trembling again. She closed her eyes and tried to erase the feel of Northgate's hand fisted in her hair and the smell of his sweat as he dragged her head closer and closer. If Nash had arrived only a few moments later…Pru did not want to think of it. She stepped back again, into the shadows, and Mrs. Northgate followed.

"I am sorry to have to depart early. I imagine my daughter-in-law and granddaughters will not be attending either. I also imagine no one will miss them."

Pru reached out impulsively and grasped Mrs. Northgate's hand. "You aren't angry with me, are you? I feel as though this is all my fault." Pru couldn't say why she blamed herself. She just couldn't stop thinking that if only she'd left the tent a few minutes later. If only she'd fought harder. If only she and Nash hadn't made love in the field that day—no. She would not regret that.

"*Your* fault? This is not your fault. George is the one at fault, and if anyone is to blame it's his fool of a mother who indulged him far too much and his fool of a father who took no interest at all. The boy has always had a mean streak, and he was never once punished for pulling his sisters' hair or tripping the servants. I am only too happy to do what I have wanted to for years."

"Send him to the Continent?"

She nodded. "It will do him good to have to stand on his own feet and make his own way for a few years. Perhaps when he returns, he will have gained some maturity."

Pru nodded. Her own travels had certainly opened her eyes to the world beyond England's shores. She could only imagine that a man like George Northgate, who had lived his entire life in a small village, would mature if given a chance to see more of the world and make his own way in it.

"I suppose after this I won't see you again," Pru said. "I can't imagine being welcomed into your home."

Mrs. Northgate smiled. "I would welcome you, but I agree it's probably not wise. Perhaps I can come and visit you."

Pru gasped and then hugged Mrs. Northgate. "Would you?"

"Of course. I have many topics of interest to discuss with that ridiculous vicar of yours. He becomes quite vexed when I point out his lack of rational thought on several points of philosophy. I will call on you in a few days."

"Until then," Pru said, stepping away, quite aware that all of her affection made Mrs. Northgate uncomfortable. But then the woman did something Pru wasn't expecting. She pulled Pru into a warm embrace. Pru stood still for a moment, a little shocked, and then wrapped her arms around Mrs. Northgate. Pru had wanted a hug desperately, and now she wanted to stay like this forever.

"I will see you soon, dear girl," Mrs. Northgate said. She pulled back and smiled down at Pru. "Thank you for knocking on my door that day. I didn't realize how much I needed a friend." Then she released Pru and started for the wagon, where her grandson sat staring sullenly straight ahead. Pru would have liked to watch them go—watch what she hoped was the last she'd ever see of George Northgate—but she had left Nash alone and wanted to return to him as quickly as possible. She had a thousand questions for him—chiefly, when he had given his pistol to Mr. Payne. And secondly, though much more important in her mind, when he could sneak away so she could steal a kiss.

\*\*\*

"Well, this gathering has proved more entertaining than I thought," Rowden said after the earl had moved away. Nash folded his arms across his chest.

"I could have used less excitement."

"Oh, this gives them something to talk about for the next few months. What is that line in *Henry V*? 'And gentlemen in England now-a-bed shall think themselves accursed they were not here.'"

Nash frowned. "I didn't think you were one for Shakespeare."

"You don't know everything about me."

"I know you said you would guard my back. And you did."

"I did, and I will. Though I daresay you don't need me anymore. I believe I will start making plans to return to London."

"Alone at last," Nash said, though he felt a pang of sadness at not seeing Rowden every day. He held his hand out. "And I think it time you gave me my pistol back."

Rowden laughed. "I'm not feeling that sentimental, my friend. I'll just hold on to it a while longer. Ah, Miss Howard."

Nash stilled, waiting for the sound of her voice and the warmth of her presence to wash over him.

"Mr. Payne."

Nash reached for her as soon as he heard the sound of her voice. But there was no need as she anticipated him and was already at his side. He wouldn't let her walk away again. He was determined to keep her safe and close for the remainder of the day. He might have liked to keep her that way forever, but she would have fought any sort of cage or restraint. She had to be free, and he had to trust she would always come back to him. "Is he gone?" Nash asked. He didn't want to say the man's name, and fortunately he needn't.

"Yes. His grandmother has taken him home and will send him away as quickly as possible. I can't say I will be sorry to see him go. But I don't want to speak of him. Mr. Payne, exactly how long have you had that pistol? And Nash, what possessed you to give it to him?"

"That's a story for another time," Rowden said. "But I will tell you what Nash knows very well. I protect my friends. I think we are alike in that regard, are we not, Miss Howard?"

"We are."

"Excuse me, then. I can see Nash is trying to work out how to get you alone. I'll oblige him by walking away and pointing out that the house is all but empty at the moment."

Nash could hear the smile in Rowden's voice and then his footsteps retreated.

Nash clasped Pru's hand and pulled her into the house behind them before anyone else could delay or interrupt them. He moved so quickly that she was laughing and breathless by the time he reached their favorite destination—the butler's pantry. Nash could hear a few pots and pans being moved about in the kitchen below, but there was no need for anyone to come up this way as any food being prepared would be taken outside.

Which meant he had Pru all to himself for the moment. He didn't hesitate to pull her into his arms, and then he was shocked when she began to sob. "He hurt you," Nash said, his arms tightening around her. "I'll kill him."

"He pulled my hair," she said. "Nothing more. I'm fine, just...oh, I don't know why I'm weeping. Just hold me."

Nash obliged, holding her tightly and patting her back. He had never heard her cry before, and he did not ever want to hear it again. The sound tore at his heart, and he felt helpless to stop her pain. Gradually, she sniffed, and he handed her a handkerchief. She blew her nose loudly and tried to hand it back to him.

"Keep it," he said. "In case you start watering again."

"I won't," she said. "I feel better now. I needed to get all of that out."

"And I have something I need to get out." He stepped back and went down on one knee. He heard Pru gasp.

"What are you doing?"

"Asking you to marry me," he said.

"But I wanted to ask *you* to marry me. I had a speech planned and everything. I wanted to convince you it would be safe to marry me. I know you'd never hurt me."

"Pru," Nash said, "we can ask each other. Come here." He pulled her to her knees before him. "But I don't need convincing. When I'm with you, my world quiets. I feel—more myself. I still don't trust myself completely. There are times when I might sink back into melancholy."

"And I will be there to pull you right back out."

"It might not be so easy."

"I'm not one to shrink from a challenge."

He laughed. "That's true enough. I should speak to the vicar then. I've already secured my father's blessing."

She grasped his hands tightly. "Your father agreed?"

"Yes. You thought we would have to run away together?"

"It would have been more romantic."

"There's nothing romantic about a long journey on a rough road, and Scotland is cold and miserable this time of year. I'd rather marry here than like a fugitive in Gretna Green." He tugged her close and kissed her. "I'd marry you today if I could. I don't want to wait another minute to have the privilege of doing this whenever you'll allow it." He kissed her, marveling that her lips were so sweet. Though he had kissed her many times now, the press of her mouth against his was still something of a surprise.

"Nash," she said, pulling away.

He sighed. "Can we not discuss details later?" He tried to kiss her again, but she put a hand on his chest. "What is it?"

"I haven't said yes yet."

Nash froze. That was true. She hadn't said yes yet. He'd assumed she wanted to marry him, but what if he was wrong? What if she objected to marriage?

He'd convince her. Or he'd live in sin with her like one of those debauched poets all of Society loved to whisper about. But—no. She had said she wanted to ask him to marry her. So perhaps the problem was that he was a complete idiot. "I forgot to ask you," he said. "I never said the question."

"That's—" She broke off. "No, go ahead and ask."

Nash cleared his throat. "Prudence Howard, will you consent to be my wife?"

"Maybe."

"Maybe?" Nash roared. "Explain."

"I will." She was laughing. He could hear it, and it took the edge off his temper. He stood, running a hand through his hair, knowing to do so would reveal his damaged eye, but he was alone with Pru. He trusted her—as frustrating as she was some days.

"Nash, I don't need you to ask me to marry me. I need you to tell me you love me."

Nash froze, hand on top of his head. He hadn't considered he'd need to say anything like that. He did love her, of course, but to say the words seemed...well, he wasn't certain how to even begin. He'd never said anything like that before. "I don't know how to begin," he said, thinking voicing his problem might fill the silence.

"Start by telling me when you first fell in love with me. Was it the first time we kissed? Perhaps when we sat on the front lawn and laughed together."

Nash frowned at her. "You seem quite confident I *do* love you. Are you certain you need to hear this?"

"Quite."

"Very well." He thought for a moment as he hadn't tried to pinpoint exactly when he had fallen in love with her. It seemed he was in love with her before he knew he felt anything at all. "I believe it was when I heard you singing that bawdy tune on your way through the informal gardens," he said.

"No! You didn't even know me then."

Nash held out his hand, and she took it.

"I knew I had to love any woman singing a song like that so confidently and loudly."

"Be serious."

"Pru, I am serious. I loved you from the first moment I met you." He hadn't thought words like those would be so easy to say. He didn't even feel like an idiot saying them. He wanted to say it all over again. "I love you. Prudence Howard, I love you."

She went into his arms, resting her head on his chest. "And I love you, Nash Pope." She kissed him and after a while, quite a long while, he drew back.

"You didn't tell me when you fell in love with me."

"I think it was a gradual thing," she said. "I can't pinpoint a day."

Nash blew out a breath. "If I'd known I could give that as an answer—"

"But I think it began," she interrupted, "the day we first saw the peacock."

"You and the peacock. I half think you're marrying me for that bird."

"I *am* marrying you for that bird. He's magnificent."

"I might have known."

She hit him lightly. "It wasn't the bird that started it, though. It was the feeling I had when I was with you. I wanted to feel it again, to be in your presence again. I think I came up with the idea to teach you night writing just to have an excuse to be with you."

"I'm shocked."

"You should be," she said, running a hand through his hair and kissing him. "You have no idea the feminine wiles I might use on you."

Nash pulled her close. "I am eager to find out."

# *Epilogue*

She was married with flowers in her hair. Mrs. Northgate said she looked like a perfect heathen, and it was the loveliest compliment Pru had ever received. She'd worn a green dress she'd made herself—well, she'd had a bit of help from Mrs. Blimkin and Mrs. Northgate—staying up late too many nights sewing small flowers on the hem. She'd described the dress to Nash in excruciating detail and he'd pretended to listen. He was much more interested in stealing kisses, and she hadn't minded at all since it had been a long winter. Their spring wedding couldn't come soon enough.

And now she was a married woman, Pru thought as she looked out the window of Nash's bedchamber. It had been refurbished with new pieces, her favorite of which was the tall four poster bed. And not just because Nash was lying on said bed telling her to join him.

"In a moment," she said with a smile and peered outside again.

Afternoon was fading, casting a soft glow on the well-manicured lawns as well as the riot of flowers she'd planted. She'd felt guilty at the expense as Nash couldn't see them to enjoy them, but he said he could smell them, and the scent reminded him of her.

The lawns were empty now, but this morning they had been full of guests at the wedding breakfast. It had been a perfect spring day.

Nash came up behind her and wrapped his arms about her. "What are you looking at?" he asked.

"Just remembering," she said.

"We only escaped the last guests twenty minutes ago," Nash pointed out.

She poked an elbow into his abdomen. "That last guest was my sister and Rose. We didn't need to *escape* them."

"Rose wasn't climbing all over *you*," Nash objected.

"You made the mistake of turning her upside down," Pru pointed out. "She'll want you to do it over and again until your arms ache."

"Now you tell me." He held her for a long moment as the spring breeze ruffled her hair. "I like your sister. Did you miss your parents?"

"No. Anne was the only one I wanted here, and Mrs. Northgate." She'd written to her parents and told them she was marrying, but she hadn't received a letter back. She half wondered if she would ever see them again.

"Am I mistaken or did Mr. Higginbotham tear up at the church?" Nash asked. "His voice sounded choked."

"He did tear up," Pru said with a laugh. "I'm sure they were tears of happiness."

In truth, the vicar had been difficult to persuade to give his blessing to the marriage. Finally, Pru had threatened to run away and elope, and he'd agreed.

"I'm sure," Nash said, sounding unconvinced.

"I am glad so many of your friends could come," Pru said. "I expected Mr. Payne, but it was lovely to meet Colonel Draven and Mrs. Draven, and Mr. Fortescue said he bore you no ill will for trying to kill him last summer."

"If I'd known he was going to give speeches, I would have killed him," Nash grumbled, but she knew he had been touched, in his way, that Colonel Draven and several other men from his troop, including Mr. Payne, Mr. Fortescue, and Mr. FitzRoy, had attended with their wives.

"Now," Nash said, turning her around and bending to kiss her neck. "I suggest we make good use of the time we have alone. Mrs. Blimkin assured me she has outdone herself with dinner, and I don't want to insult her by being late."

Pru smiled as Nash slipped one sleeve off her shoulder and moved his mouth to kiss her there. In just a few months, he looked even more handsome than she could imagine. The hollow look in his face was gone and he was no longer painfully thin. He had regained the weight he'd lost and was healthy and strong. Her gaze darted to his bedside table that held a beautifully carved walnut case. She had given it to him a few weeks ago as an early wedding present. She'd written to Mr. Payne and asked him to have one custom made to fit the Gribeauval pistol. Payne had sent it, along with the pistol, and now both resided on the table. As far as Pru knew, Nash hadn't taken the pistol out of its velvet lining.

She hoped he would never again feel the need to.

His hands were making quick work of her dress, loosening the ties at the back, and she turned to pull the curtains closed so they wouldn't be observed, and gasped.

Nash lifted his head from her breast. "What is it?"

"The peacock," she said. "He's on the lawns, and he has his feathers displayed. Oh, it's the best wedding present yet."

Nash let out a breath. "You scattered enough seeds about to attract him. I don't know why you should be surprised."

"Just because I hoped he would come, doesn't mean I thought he would. Oh, Nash. He's so beautiful."

"You're beautiful," Nash said, dragging a hand down her body. "Come join me in our new bed once you've had your fill of the peacock."

He left her to undress, and she watched the peacock strut for several minutes before the glimpses of her own husband's lovely form drew her attention away. With a smile, she pulled the curtains closed and went to him, shrugging her loose dress off as she did. He was on the bed, gloriously naked, and he held out his arms to her. She went willingly into his embrace, her heart pounding with anticipation. Not just anticipation for the pleasure she knew was coming, but anticipation of tomorrow and the day after and all the days to come.

"Tell me you love me," she murmured as he touched her, stroked her, kissed her.

"You know I do," he said, levering himself up so he was looking down at her. She didn't know what he could see, but she saw the expression of love so clearly on his face that it almost made her heart hurt.

"Say it anyway," she whispered.

"I love you, Prudence Howard Pope."

"I love you, too."

And she did. She really, really did.

# *A Note on Night Writing and Charles Barbier*

If you're anything like me, you read historical romance because you enjoy history and learning something new about the past. I don't get every detail in my novels correct, but I'm never intentionally inaccurate. With this in mind, I wanted to make a few points about *Ecriture Nocturne*.

*Ecriture Nocturne*, or night writing, was invented by Charles Barbier. He served in the French army in the 18th century and saw the need for a form of nighttime communication in the military. As I describe in the novel, night writing used a two-digit code to represent letters and sounds. Barbier's "key" was a 6x6 square with each letter or sound represented by two numbers. The key was not simply all the letters of the alphabet. Some letters were represented, but the user would have to code the sentence into a more phonemic form and produce that as the message.

I simplified this by having Pru modify Barbier's system for use in English, and, not wanting to create my own form of night writing, didn't go into too many specifics of how she accomplished this. Knowing Pru, she came up with a clever modification.

Louis Braille did much the same thing when he used Barbier's method as a starting point for Braille. The French government wasn't all that interested in adopting night writing for the military, and Barbier presented it to the Royal Institution for Blind Youth in Paris in 1821. Braille learned the Barbier method and reduced the number of dot positions from 12 in 2 columns to 6 in 2 columns.

Barbier designed night writing in 1815, which makes it unlikely that my fictional Pru and her family would have been in Paris after he'd developed it as this novel is set in late 1817. So I have taken some liberty with the date when night writing was invented. It also seems unlikely that Pru and her missionary parents would have reason to know Charles Barbier, but Pru could probably make friends with a rock, so I hope you'll allow it.

## About Shana Galen

Shana Galen is three-time Rita award nominee and the bestselling author of passionate Regency romps. Kirkus said of her books: "The road to happily-ever-after is intense, conflicted, suspenseful and fun." *RT Bookreviews* described her writing as "lighthearted yet poignant, humorous yet touching." She taught English at the middle and high school level for eleven years. Most of those years were spent working in Houston's inner city. Now she writes full time, surrounded by three cats and one spoiled dog. She's happily married and has a daughter who is most definitely a romance heroine in the making.

*Wondering about that incident with the Scot everyone in Milcroft loves to gossip about? Keep reading for an excerpt from The Highlander's Excellent Adventure, on sale now!*

About a quarter hour into the journey, Ines realized it was more difficult than she'd anticipated to pretend she did not understand English. Miss Wellesley or one of the gentlemen often said something she was tempted to comment about. More than once, Miss Wellesley gave her a pointed look when Ines was paying too much attention to the conversation. She knew how one behaved when one did not know the language. She hadn't known Spanish when her sister had first taken her to Barcelona. When one didn't understand what was being said all around, it was easy to ignore the conversation and focus on one's surroundings. But now she was having difficulty ignoring what was said. One method that seemed to work was to watch Mr. Murray speak and notice how his lips moved or his amber-colored eyes crinkled when he laughed.

But she'd obviously stared at him too long because he gave her a questioning look, and she was forced to go back to staring out the window again. Though Ines had been disappointed the Scotsman hadn't tried to take advantage of her the night before, she realized it was probably for the best. Benedict would kill Murray if he ever found out, and Ines didn't want that blood on her hands. But Draven would probably only lecture Murray if he *kissed* Ines. Surely, she was worth a lecture.

The Scotsman caught her looking at him again, but this time he nodded out the window. "If ye look before we start down this rise, ye can see Wentmore below."

Ines waited until Mr. Fortescue and Miss Wellesley looked out the window, then followed their example. She winced a bit at what she saw. Wentmore had probably once been a lovely manor house. It was still lovely, though the stone of the front face was three-fourths obscured by the overgrown ivy that seemed to have wrapped itself around the house in a choking embrace. The front lawns were also poorly maintained. The grass was yellow, and the hedges and topiary were overgrown. Along one side, she caught a dark stain on the stone. She almost forgot herself and asked about it, but Miss Wellesley asked first. "What is that mark on the side of the stone? It looks like a burn."

"I think you're right," Fortescue said. "There might have been a fire." He looked at Murray. "I hope we can go inside to see how bad the damage is and if Nash needs assistance."

Murray snorted. "He wouldnae take it even if we offered."

"Then maybe we don't give him the chance to refuse. I have a plan."

Murray sighed. "Of course, ye do."

He spoke low so only Murray could hear. Ines exchanged a look with Miss Wellesley, who seemed annoyed to be left out of the conversation. A few moments later, the coach slowed, and Mr. Fortescue opened the door and jumped out. No one emerged from the house to greet them and after Murray exited the coach, the coachman called down, "Are you sure this is where you wanted to go?"

"This is Wentmore," Murray said. Then he looked back at the women. "Stay here while we go inside and do a wee bit of reconnaissance." He started away.

Emmeline turned to Ines. "This looks worse than I imagined."

"It doesn't appear anyone lives here," Ines murmured.

"Or if someone does, he does not welcome visitors."

Just then a crash echoed from inside the house, and the women exchanged worried looks. The crash was followed by the sound of raised male voices. Then the door banged open and Murray flew out. When he turned to look at the coach, blood ran down the side of his cheek.

"*Caramba*!" Ines said. She jumped out of the coach, but Murray had already gained his feet and was running back into the house. The door closed behind him. Miss Wellesley joined Ines on the weed-filled drive, and they listened to more shouts and then the sound of a rifle or pistol firing.

"I've had enough of this," the coachman said. He jumped from the box, untied the trunk and various boxes strapped to the back of the coach, and dumped them on the ground.

"You can't leave us here," Emmeline argued.

"Oh, yes, I can. I agreed to drive the man to Scotland. I didn't agree to this." He jumped back on the box, called to the horses, and drove away before the women could say another word.

Ines watched the coach disappear around a bend in the road. "I don't know whether to be terrified or thrilled."

"I feel a bit of both. Should we go inside and tell them?"

Another crash made both women jump. "Perhaps not quite yet," Ines said.

The door burst open again, and this time Murray fell out. He clutched his arm, blood seeping through his hand. Ines gasped, and he held up the bloody hand. "Dinnae fash, lass. It's a scratch." Then he winced and sank to his knees. Ines ran to him and put her arm around him to steady him.

"Is it your arm?" she asked, though she already knew. Her head was spinning and panic seeped in.

"Aye."

"What happened?"

"The bastard shot me."

Ines gasped then stared at him in stunned silence. Emmeline was not so passive. She looked at Ines and Murray then seemed to make a decision. She straightened her shoulders and stomped past them. "This has gone on long enough."

"Dinnae go in there, lass!" Murray called. But she ignored him and opened the door then closed it after her. Murray looked at Ines, who suddenly realized she had no idea what to do next. She'd never seen a pistol ball wound before. She had no idea how to treat it or help Murray. She just knew she could not allow him to die. He stared down at her for another moment, and she became increasingly aware of the warmth of his body and that her arms were wrapped around it. She should let go, but she needed to steady him. Or perhaps she needed him to steady her.

"Did that scratch on my heid damage my brain, or did ye speak tae me in English?"

Ines opened her mouth, but it was too late. As Catarina always said, Ines's face was an open book, and Murray had read the writing there.

"So ye *do* speak English."

"I—" But what excuse could she give?

He held up a finger, cutting off her stuttering reply. "We'll talk aboot it later. Right now, I need tae fall over." And he did, taking her with him.

He landed on top of her, pinning her to the drive. It had once been a gravel drive, but she was thankful for the overgrown weeds to cushion her. Still, she could feel jagged pieces of gravel cutting into her back.

And yet, Ines didn't mind the weight of him. He was warm and solid, and he smelled woodsy and clean. There was no trace of the scent of cologne so many men in London wore. Mr. Podmore had favored a strong fragrance with a cloying sweet scent, and it had made Ines want to gag when she was in a closed room with him for too long. Conversely, now she had to resist the urge to bury her nose in Mr. Murray's chest. Except she really couldn't breathe with his weight pressing into her. She gave him a push, then a harder one, and she managed to free her torso from beneath him. Then after much tugging of her dress and her body, she freed her legs and finally her feet. She had to pause to catch her breath.

One look down told her this was a mistake. Her dress was soaked with blood, the material was dusty and dirty, and she could see pieces of her hair fluttering over her forehead. She blew them out of her eyes. The blood was not a good sign. She could see the crimson coloring the drive beneath Murray. She was no nurse, but she knew the bleeding must be stopped.

Ines pushed the Scot's good arm, trying to heave him onto his back. But he was heavy and large, and he didn't move. She adjusted her position, and with a grunt, pushed again. She raised his body just enough that she could wedge her shoulder underneath and push him higher and then onto his back. Panting heavily and wiping perspiration from her brow, Ines decided she would never manage to free him of his coat on her own. Instead, she took a breath then lifted the hem of her dress and ripped a good portion of her petticoat. She quickly bound the Scot's wound over his sleeve and tied another piece tightly around the arm of his coat to staunch the bleeding. Once inside—if they were ever allowed inside—they could remove his coat and clean the wound and see it clearly. She had no medical experience, but surely a surgeon must live nearby.

Resisting the urge to fall back and close her eyes for a moment, she instead looked up at the house, listening. All was finally quiet. That was either a good sign or a very ominous one. Ines ripped another section of petticoat and wiped Murray's face. The wound on his temple looked as though it came from a sharp object. She dabbed at it, determined it was not serious, then tried to clean the blood from his cheek. She had almost removed it all when his hand came up and caught her wrist. She screeched in surprise, and he shushed her.

"Dinnae fash, lass."

"I will fash!" Whatever that meant. "You scared me." And not just by grasping her when she'd thought him unconscious. All that lost blood terrified her. What if he died? He'd used his good arm to take hold of her wrist, and it comforted her that he was still so strong. No one this strong would die, *não*? He would live, *sim*?

"Help me up, lass," he said. "I have tae go back in."

The man was certifiably mad. What was it the English said? Daft? He was daft. "You need to lie down," she said. "You are bleeding, *senhor*."

"I told ye, it's a trifle."

"It is more than trifle if you fall over. Now stay here and be still until Mr. Fortescue and Miss Wellesley come out. They will either have tamed your so-called friend or you will need your strength to run." She could imagine the wild Mr. Pope bursting through the door any moment and firing at her with his rifle.

Murray let out a surprised laugh. "I willnae run. Nash needs a wee dose of convincing. That's all."

"From the sound of it, he needs a whole barrel of convincing." She cocked her head again. "Things have gone silent since Miss Wellesley went inside. I cannot decide if they are all dead or listening to reason."

He didn't respond, and she looked down at him to find his amber eyes were on her. "Why did ye pretend ye couldnae speak English?"

She should have been prepared for the question. She'd known from the beginning she'd have to answer it at some point. It was just that the shock of seeing him with blood streaming down his face had made her forget her ruse. She'd forgotten, too, how nervous he made her. All of a sudden, her belly began to flutter, and she felt her cheeks grow warm.

His brows came together in concern. "I'm not angry with ye, lass. I'm after an explanation."

That was a relief. Not that she would have been afraid if he'd been angry, but it was already difficult enough to speak to him. "I did not want—"

"Speak up, lass. A moment ago, ye were yelling in my ear."

She took a breath and spoke louder. "I did not want you to take me home."

"Why nae? Where's home?"

But she was saved from answering when the door opened again. Ines and Murray both ducked, but it was only Emmeline.

"Mr. Fortescue and I have the matter in hand now. I think you had both better come in. In—I mean, Beatriz, let me help you with him."

Ines was trying to help Murray to his feet. He swayed once but caught himself. He cut her a glance. "Why do I have the suspicion yer name is nae Beatriz?"

"We can discuss it inside," Emmeline said, taking his good arm and lending support. Ines ducked her head carefully under his bad arm and the three of them hobbled toward the house.

As far as Ines was concerned, she would put that conversation off as long as possible. Except she knew it wouldn't be possible much longer. She'd been seen at the inn in that little village and surely Draven was out looking for her by now. If he didn't know she was with Murray, he would know soon, and he'd find her too. Then it would be back to London and Mr. Podmore or some other awful suitor. She'd have to bid her brief taste of freedom goodbye.

She stepped into the house, turning so Mr. Murray could squeeze in after her, and then stared at the wreck around her in horror. The paper curled off the walls, the rug was torn, and the furniture was smashed into pieces. When Emmeline finally moved in through the door, Ines caught her eye. "Are you certain this is safe?" Ines gave the cracked ceiling a worrying look.

"Safe?" Emmeline shook her head. "Most certainly not, but I'll try to keep you alive until dinner."

Made in the USA
Coppell, TX
13 May 2021